T0278633

THE KING'S CHOSEN

LOST SOULS

THE KING'S CHOSEN

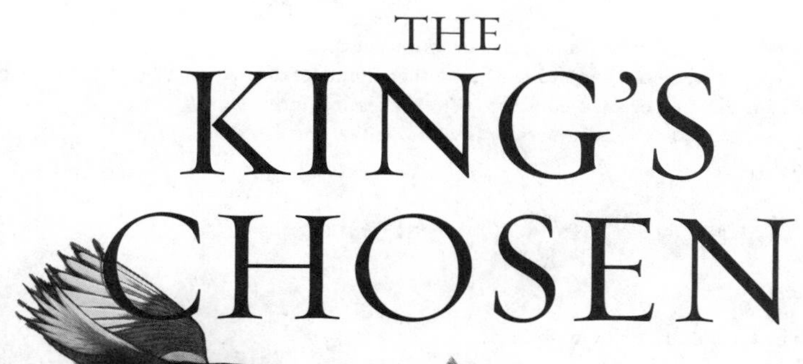

LOST SOULS

BOOK 3

L. WAITHMAN

GREENLEAF
BOOK GROUP PRESS

This book is a work of fiction. Names, characters, businesses, organizations, places, events, and incidents are either a product of the author's imagination or are used fictitiously. Any resemblance to actual persons, living or dead, events, or locales is entirely coincidental.

Published by Greenleaf Book Group Press
Austin, Texas
www.gbgpress.com

Distributed by Greenleaf Book Group

For ordering information or special discounts for bulk purchases, please contact Greenleaf Book Group at PO Box 91869, Austin, TX 78709, 512.891.6100.

Design and composition by Greenleaf Book Group and Mimi Bark
Cover design by Greenleaf Book Group and Mimi Bark
Cover illustration by Carrie-Sue Kay
Map design by Carrie-Sue Kay

Publisher's Cataloging-in-Publication data is available.

Print ISBN: 979-8-88645-142-9

eBook ISBN: 979-8-88645-143-6

To offset the number of trees consumed in the printing of our books, Greenleaf donates a portion of the proceeds from each printing to the Arbor Day Foundation. Greenleaf Book Group has replaced over 50,000 trees since 2007.

Printed in the United States of America on acid-free paper

24 25 26 27 28 29 30 31 10 9 8 7 6 5 4 3 2 1

First Edition

To Ava, my editor and friend,
for encouraging me to continue the story.

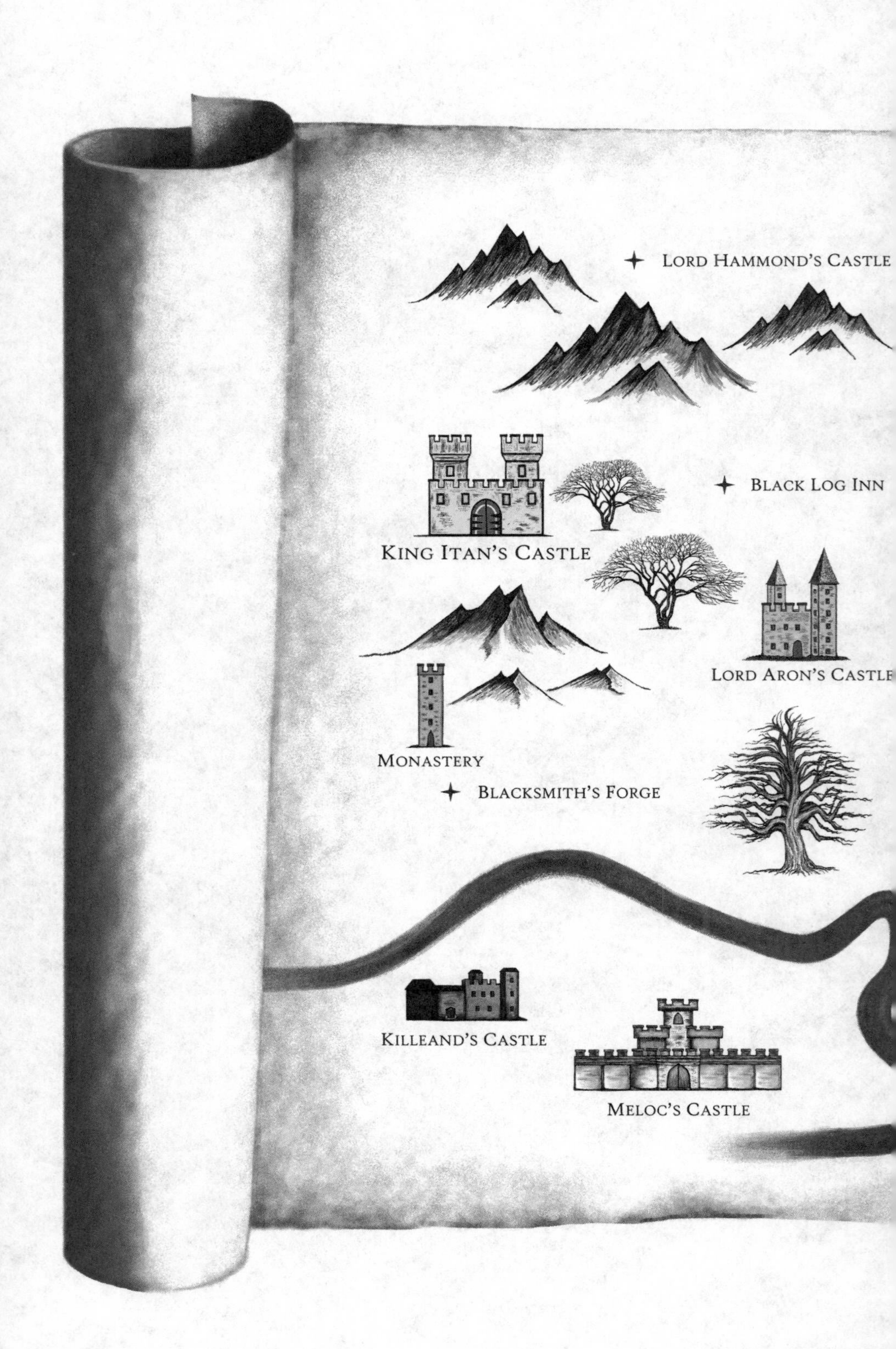

Lord Hammond's Castle
Black Log Inn
King Itan's Castle
Lord Aron's Castle
Monastery
Blacksmith's Forge
Killeand's Castle
Meloc's Castle

Boran's Castle
Ulmer
Hunters' Village
Ruin

CHAPTER 1

Having left his three friends behind on the rim of a cliff, Lucas rode slowly down the mountain towards the massive stone castle belonging to Boran.

Even though Itan's castle had seemed large to Lucas, with its double guard towers, outer bailey, and inner training fields, Boran's castle appeared much larger, with several round stone towers and extra floors. The walls surrounding the castle were also taller, and extended out to touch the mountains on either side, thereby preventing any passage to the part of the valley that lay beyond. He could tell the walls were a later addition because the stone looked less worn, and cleaner.

Davis, ever wary of hidden danger, had expressed his concerns about Lucas going in alone when they had stood on the rim together to view the castle in the distance, but Lucas feared Boran would not hesitate to kill the chosen, since it was only Lucas he wanted. Lucas would be able to stay in contact with Davis telepathically, and if Lucas made it into Boran's castle, word would be sent to King Itan to report on his progress and wait for further instructions.

It seemed like the best plan they could come up with.

He let his horse find his own footing on the rocky ground and continued to ride towards the castle after he reached the valley floor.

He knew they had seen him coming when more guards appeared on the walls to observe his casual approach, but he received no calls from the guards to stay away.

When he was close enough to the gates, he halted.

"I am here to see King Boran," he shouted upwards to the guards on the tower. There was a moment of silence before one of them called down. "The king does not hold audience with unknown persons."

"He knows who I am," replied Lucas. "Tell him Baelan is here—or Lucas, as the people call me."

He could see guards whispering to each other, and one of them left to deliver the message. It was quite a while before the guard returned. More soldiers had gathered in the bailey. Lucas was leaning back in the saddle with the reins loose on his horse's neck when the call came from above.

"Dismount," a guard told him, "and have your arms raised when we open the gates. Make no sudden movements."

An archer had appeared on the wall, with a bow directed at him. Lucas followed the directions he was given.

As soon as the gate opened, several soldiers and a tall, lean officer with dark, short-cropped hair came out to surround him. Two soldiers stepped forward to take Lucas's sword from him. They then tied his hands behind his back. The officer stared Lucas hard in the eye as he searched him for other weapons. The man, clean-shaven yet rugged looking, was confident and efficient, and Lucas could sense he was someone highly respected. Something about him seemed familiar.

Lucas was escorted through the gates of Boran's castle. Armed guards and soldiers stood at attention in the center of the bailey, and from the doorways of surrounding buildings, men and boys in civilian clothing stared at him. A group of women wearing white aprons stood huddled in front of what looked like the entrance to a kitchen. Two soldiers held him firmly by the arms when they stopped in the center of the bailey. In an effort to quell his own nerves, Lucas had not given much thought as to how he would be received, and was beginning to feel he should have. When the gates closed behind him and the officer stepped off to the side as if to wait for someone, Lucas could sense Davis's anxiety. As the crowd stood silently in a circle around him and the sun was beating down on his skin, a magpie flew high above the castle walls. He took a deep breath and dropped his head.

He knew his death had been ordered.

A short, stocky man emerged from the castle, accompanied by an entourage of well-dressed men and a single priest. Lucas recognized him to be the king. He had a full beard and deep dark eyes that demanded respect from the soldiers, who dispersed to let him through. He wore a fur cloak of black bear over tailored clothes in vibrant colors of blue, purple, and yellow. Lucas could feel the tension amongst the soldiers when King Boran stopped at the edge of the circle. And behind the king were two people he had hoped never to see again.

Finton and Eli.

When he heard Boran speak, he took his eyes off them.

"And so, we finally meet," Boran spoke with a booming voice. "Yet I expected a stealthy warrior, not a fool who would walk directly into the lair of the man who has hunted him for all his life."

"I do not see myself as a fool," Lucas replied, "but I can understand *they* may have informed you differently."

Boran looked over his shoulder to Finton and Eli, both of whom were trying their best to look indifferent. "Fool or no fool," he said, returning his gaze to Lucas, "coming here was a mistake. It has come to my attention that you were involved in the disappearance of a hundred of my soldiers in the forests east of the river. I am not a merciful king and I do not waste my time on trials when there can be only one outcome." Without waiting for a reply, he gave the officer the signal to proceed. Lucas was pushed down onto his knees, and he felt the cold steel of the officer's sword on the back of his neck.

He knew he should be quivering with fear, but he wasn't. He lowered his head and waited for the sword to end his life. The crowd was still and silent.

"One moment!" Boran shouted, just before the blade came down.

The officer froze with the sword still in the air, and everyone stared at their king.

"You show no fear," continued Boran. "And are not pleading for your life. Do you not value it?"

Lucas knew his life would depend on the answer he was going to give—referring to the prophecy would likely be his best bet. He raised his head and looked Boran directly in the eye. A slight breeze ruffled the king's hair, and he was frowning.

"My life, sire," Lucas said, "was given to me by the gods in the night of the brightest star. I was sent to protect the true king. If my life is to be taken here today, then they have already made their decision, and my death will be your death."

Lucas lowered his head. It took every fiber in his body to continue to come across confident and serene—he was playing a dangerous game with a dangerous man. The officer took a step closer and waited for the order.

"Who is to say that your death is to be my death?" asked Boran.

"Did your father not die just after my father was killed?" asked Lucas. He had relied on the fact that Boran was a believer of the prophecy and held stock in the curse. Could he have had that part wrong? If so, his life truly was in danger.

"My father was a sickly old man who was already sensing his death when he gave the order to track down the infant boy claimed by the people as a gift from the gods," said Boran. "Who's to say he died of a curse that may or may not exist? Many of the deaths following

Toroun's execution can easily be classed as coincidences. I have no reason to believe the curse holds any weight. You are saying these things in a ploy to save your life, for which, I grant, makes you no fool, and shows you to be cleverer than I thought."

"I do not ask you to spare my life," replied Lucas, without looking up. "But if you want to save your own and want to know if my words speak the truth, then why not ask him," he said, nodding towards Eli—he had remembered something Davis had told him that could put just enough doubt in Boran's mind.

Eli instinctively touched the light scar on his neck and took a step back when all eyes were directed at him. The piercing eyes of his father and those of King Boran were upon him, and he could not find the words to respond.

"Eli!" scolded Finton. "Say something."

"I will tell you what happened," continued Lucas, when he knew Eli would not speak. "A week after my arrival to his castle, King Itan paired Eli and me in a fight to determine if I was a chosen one, but not before I was starved and dehydrated. In the end, I had him pinned, with my sword at his neck. It left a small cut. Since it was not to be a fight to the death, I threw away my sword, so I would not harm him further, but that is when he took revenge for his defeat. If King Itan had not stopped him, I am sure he would have killed me, but his actions still caused me to lose grip on my life. That small cut on his neck started to open up as I died and would have continued to open if it had not been for the king's physician bringing me back to this world."

"That is such a lie," echoed Finton's voice. "I was there, and that *cut* was just a scratch and remained so after the fight. Do not let his words sway you, sire. He is nothing more than a common soldier who happens to be good with the sword. He's mortal like the rest of us. Do not fall for his claim to be Baelan, as King Itan did."

King Boran turned to Finton. "You told me Itan never believed in the prophecy. You told me that he thought Lucas was an elite born, not a chosen one—that it was Killeand who suspected him of being Baelan."

Finton gave a respectful bow. "I apologize for my careless words, which may have been misleading. Nevertheless, sire, it does not take away from the fact that he is lying about my son."

Boran was about to speak, but a movement in the crowd made him turn to a man wearing a grey tunic who had leaned closer to his neighbor. "What did you just say?" the king asked.

The man slowly righted himself and stared at Boran. "Me?" he asked, pointing at himself.

"Yes," answered Boran. "You were looking at the boy, then spoke to the man next to you in a whisper. I want to know what was said."

The man shook his head as if denying the fact, but then seemed to change his mind when Boran approached him. "I told my comrade that the boy's not lying, sire."

"And who are you?" asked Boran.

"My name is Winslow, sire," he answered, glancing over at Finton fearfully. "I worked for King Itan before becoming one of Finton's men."

"You say Lucas is speaking the truth?"

"I think he might be, sire."

"Well, he either is, or he is not," snapped Boran.

"He speaks the truth about the fight," answered Winslow reluctantly. "I was there and saw what happened. He is also speaking the truth about having died. I was in the room where they took him afterward, and I have seen enough dead people to know when they leave this life."

"And what about him—if you don't mind—seemed especially . . . lifeless?" Boran asked.

"His face was pale, sire. His pulse had left him and he lay limp. He was no longer with us, that much I can tell you for sure. The king's physician came in shortly after he took his last breath and asked me to tilt his head back, so he could use the bellows to bring him back."

"But what about Eli's neck? Is he speaking the truth about that?"

Before Winslow could answer, Finton spoke up. "There is no way he could know anything about that, as he's just admitted to being inside the room and nowhere near Eli!"

Boran ignored Finton and impatiently waved his hand at Winslow. "Continue," he said. "I am eager to hear what else you have to say."

"It's true that I was not there when his neck opened up, but . . . Lucas's story explains what I saw when I came out of the room sometime later," he continued. "Eli was waiting to be seen by the physician. He had a scarf around his neck, soaked with blood. I wondered where that blood had come from. Hearing Lucas tell us about the cut makes me believe he is telling the truth, sire."

Boran remained motionless for a moment, before turning to his priest. "Eneas?" he asked.

Lucas looked at the priest, whose piercing blue eyes he had felt on him the entire time others had spoken. He was a thin man, with very short grey hair. He wore a long black robe with gold trim, and a cape hung over his shoulders.

Eneas finally took his eyes off Lucas and turned to his king. "I believe that the decision may need further consideration, sire," he answered. "Killing the boy may not be in your best interest at this time."

"Very well," said Boran. He gave the officer the sign to stand down. "Take him away."

On the rim above the valley floor, Davis stood watching. His sister and Warrick stood a few paces away, and all three took their eyes off the castle when a noise came from behind. Davis turned around to see Orson—the broad-shouldered hunter leader whose dark curly hair and full beard made it hard to detect any facial expression—step out of the forest's shadows with two of his men. Davis knew that the only reason he had been able to hear them was that Orson wanted him to know he was there. Hunters had a way of moving around unheard. Their entire existence depended on it. Seeing Orson here meant that Dastan had been successful in contacting them and informing them of Lucas's plan. Like the mountain people, they needed to know what King Boran was up to.

"Did he make it in?" asked Orson, stepping closer.

"He did, and he's alive for now," answered Davis. He walked towards Orson and extended his hand to greet him—something he would not have dreamt of doing a few months ago. Even after meeting them, it had taken Davis a long time to trust the hunters and to accept that they had a common goal.

"Boran is smart," said Orson, extending his own hand, and greeting Zera and Warrick the same way as they stepped up from their posts. "Once he knows Lucas's capabilities, he will want to use that to his advantage."

Davis glanced over his shoulder to the castle in the distance. He had been anxious when the gates had opened, and he stopped sensing Lucas after he had disappeared inside.

"Dastan said you would need our help once Lucas made it inside?" asked Orson.

"Yes," answered Davis, turning back to face him. "Lucas wants word sent back to King Itan to inform him of where we are." He took the note from a pouch on his belt and handed it to the hunter. Lucas had written it before he left, but moments after the castle gates had closed and before contact was lost, Lucas had instructed him to add a few words. "He hoped you would be willing to send one of your men to deliver this."

"Hmm," grunted Orson, taking the folded piece of parchment. Orson then gestured to Zera and Warrick. "I was told I was to help one of you across the river?"

"That was the original plan," answered Davis, following his gaze to his sister and Warrick. "But Lucas changed his mind once he laid eyes on the castle and now wants all three of us to stay near."

Orson nodded and, without any further words, disappeared back into the forest.

"Do you think he will get the note delivered?" asked Zera as they walked to where their horses waited in a forest gully. "King Itan doesn't know yet that the hunters are on his side and may not bother with questions when a hunter presents himself on his doorstep. You can hardly mistake a hunter by their substantial size and muscular build."

"Or their fur clothing," added Warrick.

"Lucas trusts Orson," answered Davis. "But we can only hope that he does deliver the message." He mounted his horse and rode out of the gully. Zera and Warrick were right behind him when he followed a narrow path down the mountain toward the town. Once there, they would wait for Dastan's arrival. Through the trees, he could already see the water from the lake and the fishing boats docked in the small harbor.

CHAPTER 2

Lucas tried to withdraw into the shadows of the prison cell he had been locked inside of. There were several cells next to each other, all facing a courtyard, and each cell was much like the hole at King Itan's castle, but they were bigger, with the ability to hold several prisoners. The iron bars stretched the length of the cell, and guards stayed close, observing his every move. He knew he'd had a close call. He had not been harmed, but with Finton and Eli present, that could still change. Lucas had connected with Davis as soon as he had seen the father and son at King Boran's side. He had given Davis the words that needed to be added to the message—King Itan had to know they were here.

He was left alone for less than an hour before a guard approached, unlocking the door and stepping aside to let two soldiers in. They grabbed him by his arms and took him just outside of the cell, where they held him until King Boran approached, followed by Finton, who walked directly up to Lucas and pulled on the collar of his shirt to expose his left shoulder.

"There! There it is," Finton said with glee as he pointed to the king's mark. "I told you he has already sworn his allegiance. He is fiercely loyal to Itan, always has been, and was treated differently because of it. He has orders to kill you, no doubt."

Lucas tried to pull away from the guards but they held him firmly. "You are a coward, Finton," he said, as flatly as he could. "From the moment we first met, you have tried to convince everyone to kill me, including your son, but you didn't have the guts to do it yourself when you had the chance. You can say anything you want, but we both know the truth about why Itan felt the need to mark me, and it had nothing to do with him wanting my loyalty."

"Why then?" asked Boran. "Finton, do you wish to elaborate?"

When Finton did not reply, Lucas continued.

"To save his own life," answered Lucas. "I had started a fight with Eli and was accused of causing a riot. Death would have been the only punishment if I had been proclaimed guilty. Itan did not want a trial because he would have no choice but to order my death." Lucas knew he was taking a huge risk by making assumptions about why Itan gave him the mark when he didn't know the real reason. "He must have known that, by doing so," he went on, "it would cause his death. He had no option but to change my ranking, so no trial would ever take place, and I did not die at his hands."

Boran watched Finton closely as he listened. He no doubt noticed Finton's stiff posture and clenched jaw.

Boran stepped forward and pulled Lucas's shirt back to reveal more of the scars visible on his back. "What is this?" he asked, turning to Finton. "Your doing, or Itan's?"

"Mine," answered Finton with his chin held high. "Like I said, Itan always treated him like he was above the rest. Someone had to put the boy in his place."

"Do you not know that flogging a soldier who has stepped out of line only begs for more trouble?" asked Boran. "They have either outlived their use, and you kill them, or you remove them. Releasing a tortured soldier back amongst your troops is like placing a rotten apple in a basket of healthy ones."

"Well," said Finton. "In this case . . ." He stopped when Boran raised his hand.

"Don't contradict what I believe in," said Boran sharply. "You do well to remember you are here because Killeand trusted you. I still think you too readily turned against your king when offered land and riches on my behalf."

Finton remained silent. He dropped his shoulders and gave a quick bow while taking a step back.

Lucas stood still and didn't move a muscle. He could feel Boran's hold over Finton and his power as a king. Never had Finton backed down from a disagreement with Itan.

"Leave us," said Boran and waited for Itan's former general to do so. He then put Lucas's shirt back over his shoulder and addressed the guards. "Bring him to the castle in one hour."

With two guards by his side, two more in front, and two behind him, and his hands tied behind his back, Lucas was taken inside the castle. But unlike before, no one restrained him as he walked, and he was free to look up and turn from side to side to marvel at the size of the hallway they had just entered. The ceiling was higher than two stories and the hall wide enough to have four columns of soldiers walk down it. The floor was laid with polished black and white marble tiles that made the sound of their steps echo off the bare white walls. At King Itan's castle, there had been paintings and weapons on the walls, but here there were only white statues of past kings and queens—noble relics who kept their eyes fixed on the space in front of them.

The hallway continued when they turned a corner and went on much further, but the guards stopped at a door halfway down. Lucas expected to enter the Great Hall but was instead surprised to see a mid-sized room lavishly furnished with comfortable chairs and benches. Four of the guards never stepped into the room, and the two by his side immediately left after they brought him a few steps in. They closed the door behind them on their way out.

"Tell me if I am making a mistake by having them leave us alone," King Boran said. He was sitting in a large chair off to his left. It was cut from marble and inlaid with precious stones that complimented the plush purple cushions.

Lucas, his wrists still bound behind his back, shrugged his shoulders. "I don't think I can be much of a threat this way," he responded.

"Hmm," said King Boran, eyeing him from head to toe. He then rose and walked over to a table where he poured himself a drink and stood with his back towards him like he was in deep thought. He took several sips from the chalice while staring out through the large window in front of him. "What made you come here?" he eventually asked, without turning around.

"King Itan sent me," Lucas answered.

Boran froze for a moment, but then nodded his head as if he already knew. "Do you think he sent you hoping I would kill you?"

"He told me he wants to know if you are planning an invasion," answered Lucas. "But yes, that thought crossed my mind."

"And you still came?"

"Yes."

"Why?"

"Because the time is near."

"The gods have chosen?"

"No, they have not."

"Then, there is to be a final battle?"

"There will be one, yes."

King Boran spun around and returned to his chair, setting the chalice before him as he sat. "Killeand admired and respected your fighting skills," he said, changing the subject. "He never mentioned you were so confident with your words, so . . . upfront and honest."

Lucas sighed as he thought back to the time he first met Killeand, right after his return from the monastery. "When he met me," Lucas said, "I didn't know who I was. I knew I was different, but I didn't know why. I was in a dark place." He watched Boran's reaction to see if he knew what he was referring to, but if he did, he pretended not to.

"When did you find out you were the one who was named Baelan?"

"Sometime after King Itan gave me the mark."

Boran frowned. "Would you have accepted the mark if you knew who you were then?"

Lucas nodded. "Probably."

"Why?"

"I was not born to serve a king, so therefore the mark will not change anything, but it did give me my freedom and the ability to grow into who I am today. For that reason alone, yes, I would accept it again."

"I don't know if I am to thank Itan for that or not," said Boran. "As Itan's former general, Finton seemed to be rather taken aback by the way you were speaking to him. He believes you are extremely dangerous and is still insisting I should have you killed—even offered to give the order himself."

"But he will not do it himself?"

A smile came over Boran's face. "No, most likely not," he responded. "He could, however, make you fight twenty of my best warriors and see how you do? If you were to then die of injuries, we could say it was just an unfortunate accident?"

"If you want to see me fight, then all you have to do is ask."

Boran eyed him with even greater interest than before and then called his guards back in. Lucas found himself being led out of the room without another word spoken. He assumed they would return him to the cell outside, but instead, they took him further into the castle and showed him to a room on an upper floor, where they untied his hands and left him. The door closed behind him, and he heard a latch slide across it on the outside. Lucas waited until the sound of footsteps receded and all was quiet before looking around.

There were no windows in the room, but it didn't feel like a prison cell either. Candles in sconces on the wall were lit and gave off enough light for him to see that the room was clean and comfortable. There was a table with a plate full of fresh bread, cheese and fruit and a chair for him to sit on. In the wall on his right was a fireplace and opposite was a bed, one of the nicest ones he had ever seen, with four posts on the corners, drapes on each side, and a blue velvet canopy overhead.

"How very strange," Lucas murmured.

He then went to sit on the mattress. He bounced a little to feel that it was filled with goose feathers and swung his legs over to lie down. He folded his arms underneath his head and closed his eyes, focusing his mind on the hallway outside his room—it was empty, except for the two guards posted next to his door.

After eating the food, he situated himself on the bed again to let his mind wander as far as it could go. His chamber was in a remote part of the castle, and not much seemed to be happening that was of any interest.

He allowed himself to sleep properly that night and only woke when he heard the latch slide back across the door. Lucas sat up and observed as a servant girl entered, her skin as pale as the marble statues he had seen in the hallways. She couldn't have been much older than himself. She was wearing a long brown dress reaching down to her ankles, and carrying a plate of food. Her red hair was braided and pinned on the back of her head to form a circle. She kept her head down, avoiding eye contact as she made her way to the table and replaced the empty plate with the new one. The guards outside the door watched Lucas closely, and he remained seated on the bed in a relaxed position to assure them he posed no threat. After the girl left, he walked over to the table and sat down.

As hours passed, he was beginning to get bored, but then his door opened again, and two male servants entered this time. One was holding a bowl of hot water and a cloth that he placed on the table, and the other servant had a stack of clothes.

"You are to wash and change," said the servant handing him the clothes. "The king has requested your presence at dinner tonight."

"For what purpose?" asked Lucas.

"I don't know, sir," answered the servant. "But you best hurry. The king doesn't take kindly to those who leave him waiting."

Lucas watched the servants scurry from the room and stared at the door after it closed. Then, reluctantly, he washed and changed into the new clothes, a richly embellished blue tunic and matching trousers, and high brown leather boots. They were made to fit him, and their exquisite quality seemed to represent Boran's desire to show off his wealth.

When he was escorted into the Hall that night, he quickly observed that everyone at the king's table was dressed in their finest. There was a man at the door inspecting everyone before allowing them to enter, and he stopped Lucas.

"Straighten your tunic," said the man harshly. "Then you may go through. You are adequately dressed otherwise."

"What if I wasn't?" asked Lucas, adjusting his belt and tugging at his tunic.

"Then I would send you back to get changed," answered the man absently, as he was already examining the person behind Lucas.

Lucas looked around when he entered the Hall, which was no less impressive than the rest of the castle. It was centrally located and sunken a few feet into the ground. It took four steps down to the polished white marble flooring, and the steps wrapped all the way around the room, much like an arena—except for where the center stage would be, there were tables. A door in the middle of each wall gave access to the Hall. Even without the presence of any windows, the white walls and two big chandeliers made the space look bright and airy. Four columns on each of the narrower sides of the rectangular room supported a balcony from which banners hung, embroidered with the king's crest.

Boran only briefly looked at Lucas when he approached the table. The king gave an approving nod to a staff member, after which they showed Lucas to an empty seat. King Boran's guards remained close enough, until he told them they could go.

"You look well," commented Boran. "I take it you were able to sleep?"

"I did, thank you," replied Lucas, while discreetly scanning the various people seated at the table. He had already seen Finton and Eli sitting at the end and did his best to avoid making eye contact with them.

"Excellent," said King Boran, and he then proceeded with introducing the other guests at the table. Some were lords holding prestige and title, but most were senior-ranking officers. Lucas noticed that they were armed, and strategically placed around him. Finton was introduced as Lord Finton, giving him a title, but he appeared not to have a position within the army, for which Lucas was pleased. Eli, however, was introduced as an officer in charge of the second cavalry division, and an expression of sheer gloating covered his face as his title was made known to Lucas.

The individual Lucas was most interested in was the officer who had held the sword above his head to kill him. He could feel his eyes on him all the time and was likely seated next to Lucas as a precaution. Lucas listened with piqued interest when Boran finally introduced him.

"And the person on your right," said Boran, "is Grant. He is the commander of the guards."

Lucas returned Grant's nod and felt a cold chill run down his spine. He knew it had been Grant's position and uniform that had initially thrown him off from recognizing him outside the gates. But now, dressed in evening attire, with a grey mink cloak draped over his shoulders, he was unmistakably the mystery guest Lucas had seen at Lord Killeand's castle. At the order of King Itan, he had followed Finton and Eli to Killeand's castle and, with help from his circus friends, he had snuck inside. There, hidden from view, on a balcony above the dining hall, he had observed a banquet and seen Grant.

Lucas was puzzled as to why Boran would have him liaise with a lord, but then many things seemed to be run differently here than at King Itan's.

The last to be introduced was the priest, Eneas, who also acted as the physician, which made Lucas wonder if he was a true priest at all. His stare made Lucas feel uncomfortable—when the food arrived, and Eneas finally took his eyes off him, Lucas breathed a sigh of relief.

Among the colorfully dressed servants entering, Lucas recognized the young girl he had seen in his room. She stood at the back of the line and wore an elegant blue bell-sleeve dress that hung just below her ankles, instead of the plain brown dress he had seen her wear that morning in his room. She cradled a large jug in her arms. Lucas watched as the girl stopped beside King Boran and held the jug above his chalice to pour the wine. Her arm trembled under the weight, causing the vessel to drop and hit the cup's rim.

"Valora!" scolded Boran, his booming voice bringing instant silence to the table as the chalice toppled over. "You clumsy girl," he shouted, striking her across the face with the back of his hand.

Lucas began to rise from his seat but immediately felt Grant's hand press down on his shoulder.

"Don't," said Grant as Valora stepped back with tears in her eyes and the imprint of Boran's ring on her cheek. "She's a simple slave girl and not worth getting killed over."

Lucas sat back down when Boran picked up his chalice and held it up for Valora to fill.

"You paid too much for that girl," said Eneas once he had his cup filled and Valora had moved away. "She's weak, gangly, and will never make a good servant."

"We'll see," said Boran, glancing at Lucas while sipping his wine. "Every servant eventually serves a purpose."

After Valora and the other servants left, Lucas ate in silence. No one spoke to him, but he knew they were watching his every move. Lucas's position as either guest or prisoner that evening was not clear to him, and he could tell from Eli's demeanor that he felt similarly. When dinner was finished, Lucas left the table to be escorted back to his room, and Eli walked close behind.

As they approached the end of a hallway that would take them in separate directions, Eli called out to the guards to pause for a moment. He approached Lucas with a sneer, and stood with his hands on his hips. "I don't know how you managed to weasel your way to the king's table tonight," said Eli, "but I would assume that Boran still wants to kill you. Your time here is running out."

"I guess we will have to wait and see," replied Lucas, turning away as the guards began to move him along.

He was locked up in the same room that night, and this time left for several days with only an occasional servant entering to tend to his needs. He could think of no other reason than Boran had yet to decide what to do with him. Or he was planning to keep him locked up and out of the way for the rest of his life, as Nolan had warned. Lucas felt the first was more likely, and Boran was thinking of a way to test him that would determine what his decision should be . . . or would cause Lucas's death without awakening the curse, which could only be done if he died in an accident.

To deal with the worry and the boredom, Lucas decided to prepare himself for every possible scenario. He no longer cared to sleep on the bed, believing the comfort would make him soft and weak, and he started to sleep on the hard stone floor instead. He kept his mind strong with meditation and his body with strength exercises.

The only distraction came when Valora brought him food in the evenings, which she carefully laid out for him on the table. She always wore the blue dress he had seen her wear in the Hall, and he assumed she was to serve the king's table after leaving him.

On one such night, he was watching her from his meditation pose on the floor when the guard turned his back on them and stepped out into the hallway to converse with another guard. Lucas took the opportunity and got to his feet. He followed Valora to the table and waited for her to put the tray down before placing his hand on her arm. "Your name is Valora, isn't it?" he asked softly.

Valora flinched under his touch and peered over her shoulder to the door before turning to him. "How?" she asked.

"I heard King Boran speak your name," explained Lucas, gesturing to the fading yellow bruise on her cheek. "Before he . . ."

"Ah, yes, of course," said Valora, blushing as if ashamed, taking the plate off the tray and placing it on the table.

"Does he often hit you?"

"Only when I do something that displeases him," answered Valora, "which is not often. He is usually tolerant and likes me near him. The other girls even tease me that I am his pet. I am the one he chooses to attend on him during his private meetings."

Lucas had gathered by now that Valora was likely overhearing conversations, and could perhaps give him some insight on his captivity, but this was better news than he had expected. "Do you know why he keeps me locked up here?" he asked. He peered over his shoulder, as it seemed that the conversation between the guards had ended.

Valora nodded, then followed his gaze. "I'm sorry," she said, picking up the tray when the guard turned to face the room. "I wish I could tell you, but the king . . ."

"Hey," grumbled the guard, stepping into the room. "Don't talk to him."

"She didn't," said Lucas, backing away from Valora with his hands up. "I spoke to her."

Valora looked at Lucas, her eyes soft and filled with an inner glow.

The guard stared from one to the other, then stepped aside to let Valora through.

Lucas watched the door close behind her and listened to the key turn—locking him in for the night. No one came to his room the following morning, and when the door finally opened again, Grant walked in with guards.

Grant looked at the floor, studying the blanket and pillow Lucas had pulled off the bed for a moment, but he said nothing. Instead, he called a male servant to enter the room, who handed Lucas a new set of clothes, different from the previous ones.

"I need you to change into these," said Grant, "and then you will have to follow me."

Lucas looked at the garments handed to him. Simple brown trousers, made of a durable but stiff woven wool, and a white cotton shirt. He waited a moment to see if Grant and the guards were going to give him privacy to change, but when they didn't, he knew his suspicions had been right.

He wasn't a guest—not in the least.

"Where are we going?" Lucas asked while changing.

"You will see, momentarily," answered Grant.

Lucas picked up the clothes he had been wearing and moved to lay them on the bed, but a guard stepped forward and took them from him.

"We will take those," said Grant. "You will not need them anymore."

The clothes he was wearing now were comfortable, and although plain, they were perfectly tailored and exactly his size. Knowing Boran liked to see people well-dressed in his presence, Lucas suspected he was to see him soon. He was starting to put together what was about to happen. He tied the laces of his boots and then stood up to face Grant. "I'm ready," he said.

He was escorted outside, into a large arena, where hundreds of heads turned to look at him as he squinted in the bright sunlight. It brought him back to four years ago, when he was led out of the hole to take the chosen test. The sun had also been too painful for his eyes at first. His twelve-year-old body had been weak then and his steps slow and painful. But this time, at sixteen, his body was strong, his steps firm, and his mind eager to complete whatever test they had in store for him.

He walked alone, towards the center of the arena, and gave a respectful bow to King Boran, who was seated on a large, high platform. The king was surrounded by everyone Lucas had been introduced to and more, including women in beautiful dresses and children who stared down at Lucas as if he was about to transform into something evil or godly.

Boran stood up to address the crowd, and all whispering stopped. "To all who have gathered here," he shouted, raising his arms, "let me introduce Baelan, the true king's protector and bringer of the peace, sent by the gods to be by my side at long last."

As the crowd erupted in a cheer, Lucas caught sight of Eli, who sat off to the side and stared at him blankly. Lucas quickly averted his eyes and prepared to listen to King Boran again, who had calmed the crowd.

"Baelan possesses skills beyond that of any warrior, which he will elucidate for us in two demonstrations today. Having him fight one of my best warriors will do him no justice, so, in the first demonstration, he will not fight one, but twenty-five of my best warriors."

Lucas followed the king's hand to where he saw the crowd disperse to allow the warriors to enter. They formed a large circle around him, and every one of them was holding a wooden sword that appeared to have been dipped in red pigment of some sort. Lucas frowned when he saw this and, as he did so, caught Boran's smile.

"As we do not want to see anyone killed here today," he continued, "the weapons have been colored and will simulate a wound when flesh is touched. If the wound is to be deemed mortal, then that warrior will leave the fight, and another will take his place."

After Boran finished his speech, Grant walked up to Lucas to hand him a wooden sword coated in a wet, blue pigment. Lucas took the sword but was suspicious that he did not have to fight to the death.

He prepared himself for whatever might come.

The first warrior stepped forward and started to fight him. When Lucas's sword left a blue pigment behind across his stomach on his white shirt, he gave a respectful bow and retreated to his spot. Lucas admired the thought behind the pigment, which seemed to work well, and the second warrior retired after a third wound was deemed mortal. He continued to fight warrior after warrior, only receiving minor wounds himself on either his arms or shoulders. Every now and then, when the pigment on the sword's blade dried out, he was made to reapply it.

When only ten warriors remained, Boran stood up to pause the proceedings and ordered Lucas to be blindfolded to fight the last ten. "As it is now evident that one warrior at a time is no match for Baelan," the king announced, "he will fight the remaining warriors simultaneously." The crowd cheered and raised fists in the air with excitement, but then just as quickly fell silent when Lucas started to walk blindfolded in small circles to invite the first warrior to come forward. A warrior approached, and so did a second, then a third, and soon Lucas was engaged with all ten. Cheers came from the crowd as he fended them off, sometimes by kicking, sometimes by ducking or leaping over them, until the last warrior was on the ground, a blue mark across his neck.

Lucas removed the blindfold and raised his sword in victory. He knew he had met their expectations of a warrior sent by the gods when the cheers became louder. The crowd hooted and whistled and chanted his name. His eyes fell again on Eli—the blank stare Lucas had been met with earlier was replaced with a sinister smile.

Lucas lowered his sword. He turned away from Eli and saw the magpie perched on the wall behind King Boran, who now stood at attention, seemingly enraptured by the massive wooden gates, which were now opening. Lucas then watched in horror as a large iron-barred cage on wheels was pulled towards the middle by two rows of soldiers holding a rope. The cage was two horse carriages wide. At least twenty men could comfortably stand inside, but it held no person. Instead, a large cougar inhabited the space, and Lucas knew he would be expected to join it.

"The second demonstration," bellowed Boran, "will show you the power of the gods by bringing together both the gatekeeper and the son of the afterworld. The cougar and Baelan!"

Lucas turned towards Boran and glared at him, and the king, in return, looked back at him placidly before sitting down again.

Dangerous and calculating, Nolan had told him. Nothing like Itan, and not to be underestimated. He had been right. How was he going to get out of this one? Boran had outsmarted him. You could not order a cougar to kill someone, and if the wild creature killed Lucas when he entered that cage, it would not be at Boran's hands.

"Lucas?" he heard a frightened voice enter his mind. "Lucas?"

He was breathing hard and backed away from the cage as it came to a stop. He put both hands on his head and tried to block the voice out. Davis could not have known what was happening but must have felt his fear.

The cougar growled at the soldiers hurrying away from the cage and then started to pace restlessly in front of the bars.

When Lucas did not move, the king snapped his fingers at a guard, who then hurried over to him and asked what he was waiting for. "The king expects you to enter the cage and stand united with the cougar side by side," said the guard.

"Without a weapon to defend myself?" asked Lucas.

The guard shrugged his shoulders. "The king believes you will not have to defend yourself since you have both been sent by the gods. He also said that you may refuse, but that you will regret that decision later and will come to wish you had not."

Clever, thought Lucas—Boran had even gotten the guard to say he didn't have to go in. He was covering all his corners. Lucas took a deep breath and looked up at Boran one last time before walking towards the cage. With the cougar still pacing inside, he walked up to the door and knelt in front of it. Two soldiers with sticks came forward to keep the cougar away, and a third began to remove the lock off the latch. The cougar swiped at one of the sticks and flung it out of the hands of the soldier. The soldiers hastily retreated and left Lucas by himself, and the crowd suddenly became silent.

Remembering how he had been able to lure the dogs towards the chosen ones in the hunters' woods—the dogs had been sent ahead by Boran's soldiers to attack the hunters' village—Lucas again searched for the powers he knew were deep within him. But he didn't think he could simply command the cougar to submit as he had with the domesticated dogs. The cougar was a wild animal, and Lucas would have to take away its instinctive desire to kill him in order to survive. Something he'd never tried before—and even if he could do it, he had no idea how long it would last. Stepping into that cage could mean the end of him—but so did the alternative.

He was left no choice.

He closed his eyes and concentrated on entering the cougar's mind. It was, to Lucas's surprise, full of bewilderment. The animal lacked any rage and was simply determined to survive—its fearful thoughts revolved around escape. What looked like anger was indeed only the outward appearance of self-preservation.

Lucas took his time and managed to break through the resistance. He then removed its sight and its smell and slowly stood up to open the door. The cougar heard him but backed away when he entered, as he could not see or smell what was coming for him. Lucas paused by the stick left on the ground, but then stepped over it and slowly walked towards the cougar.

The poor beast let out a growl, but then calmly sat down when he was within arm's reach. Lucas kneeled and waited for the cougar to lay down before he placed his hand slowly on the animal's head and closed his eyes.

He took the cougar with him to the hill by the stone, where they stood, side by side. There were no people. The sun was setting, turning the sky into a myriad of colors—pinks, blues, yellows, and a deep purple.

It was the sound of the door opening and soldiers entering that took them out of their dream. "Is it dead?" one soldier yelled.

The soldiers, Lucas realized, had come to see if he had killed the beast.

The cougar opened his eyes and, with one swift movement, jumped up and over Lucas to grab a soldier by his throat. Knowing it was too late to help, Lucas pushed the other men out of the cage and latched the door. He sank to the ground, trying to catch his breath, and could do nothing but watch the cougar rip the flesh off the poor soldier.

CHAPTER 3

Lucas couldn't determine if Boran was pleased or disappointed as he stood before him unharmed, but as the crowd overcame their shock of seeing a soldier mauled to death in front of them and began to cheer for Lucas, the king did nothing to silence them. He gave Lucas an approving nod, allowing him to accept the people's cheers.

Lucas had no idea what his status was after the spectacle Boran had put him through. He was returned to his room and left alone, except with the door unlocked. The clothes he was originally given—clothes befitting a person of high standard—were returned to him.

He was lying on the plush bed, exhausted from the ordeal and unable to shake images of the cougar from his head, when Grant came to tell him he was expected at dinner in an hour.

"Expected at dinner as *what*?" he asked, turning his head slightly. Grant was standing in the middle of the room and had left his guards outside. He stood relaxed, with his hands folded behind his back, and Lucas was suspicious of what appeared to be yet another test. "It's not very clear to me at this point if I am a prisoner or a guest."

"King Boran hopes that, in time, you will be neither," answered Grant. "But he wants to take it one day at a time. For now . . . a guest.

You are free to leave your room and walk around the grounds as you please."

"But I am not allowed to exit through the main gates?"

Grant shook his head. "No," he answered. "I'm afraid not. You will also not be permitted to carry any weapons or enter any rooms other than your own, unless invited in."

Lucas sat up and swung his legs over the side of the bed. "Sounds like a prisoner to me," he responded.

"One with benefits, perhaps."

Lucas looked up, and saw a faint smile appear on his face. He liked Grant. He seemed duty-bound and honest, but Lucas was unsure if he could trust anyone in Boran's castle. Lucas watched him make his way to the door. "We shall see you at dinner, then," Grant said, and left without waiting for a reply.

The guards posted outside his room said nothing when Lucas left to go to the Hall that night. They followed him down the hallway and pointed to direct him when he stopped and pretended to be disoriented. In truth, he had been mapping the layout of the castle in his head from the moment he'd set foot through the gates.

Lucas sat himself down at the dinner table next to Grant, where he had been seated the first night. He saw Eli turn his head away but could feel Finton's stare on him. Cold chills ran down his spine, and he had to remind himself of why he had come. Finton was not the reason. It was Boran's trust he needed to gain. If it meant having to endure Finton, then he'd have to learn to do a better job of that. He was glad for Grant's effort to make polite conversation with him while they waited for Boran to arrive, which wasn't long. Everyone rose and remained standing until Boran gave a nod of approval to those in attendance. Lucas had changed back into the blue tunic and trousers.

"I am glad to see you accepted my offer to come to dinner tonight," said Boran after everyone sat down.

"I didn't think I was given a choice, sire," said Lucas, glancing sideways to Grant.

Boran followed his gaze. "No," he said, eyeing Grant up. "I am sure you weren't." He paused when the food arrived. Unlike at Itan's, where the food was placed on platters in the center of the table, here, each person received an individual plate. There was no distinction between the plates, and everyone received the same combination of meat, cheese, brown bread and wine to wash it all down.

Lucas watched Valora as she made her way around the table and served the wine, her grip on the jug's handle firm and steady as she held it above the cups. When she came behind him and Grant, Lucas leaned to his left to allow her more room to bring the jug between them.

"I apologize for the delay of your release," continued Boran, after the servants delivering their food left them to eat. "It was not easy to come by a cougar. They are elusive creatures."

"Where is it now?" asked Lucas, watching Valora pour his wine.

"It was returned to the wild," answered Grant, as Boran had just taken a bite from his food. "No harm was done to it."

Lucas looked up and smiled at Valora when she finished pouring his wine. "Thank you," he said, pausing to see her smile back shyly before he turned to face the table, his heart racing alongside the fluttery sensation in his stomach—not one he had ever felt before.

Boran finished chewing and nodded. "It was Grant who got hold of one," he said, taking a sip from his ale, "after Finton convinced us that you would not enter the cage with a wild cat. Toroun had the gift with horses, not cougars."

Lucas looked briefly at Finton before turning back to Boran. "Well, I am not Toroun," he said.

"No," said Boran. "You showed us that today. I think your qualities were underestimated by those who claim to know you well." He had spoken firmly and directly to someone at the table. Lucas didn't have to follow his gaze to know it was Finton. There was a silence at the table. Lucas waited to see if Finton was going to defend himself, but he didn't. Finton was a different person here, subdued and unopinionated.

"Well," said Boran, breaking the silence. "Let's eat, shall we?"

In the days following, Lucas was permitted to walk around unescorted. Grant also invited Lucas to join some of Boran's forces in training during the day. Upon accepting the invitation and attending, Lucas was surprised to discover that he was treated as an equal.

At times, he felt Grant was too kind, as if he had an ulterior motive, but Lucas suppressed the uneasy feeling inside of him. He could do with a friendly face, having left all his friends behind. The only other person in the castle who was warm towards him was Valora. She smiled when he saw her in the hallways, but he never stopped to talk with her—either other servants accompanied her, or he was walking alongside Grant.

In the evenings, he ate dinner at Boran's table, and that was the only time he was close to either Finton or Eli, but they avoided any interaction with him. The other people at the table spoke with him openly and Boran treated him with respect, but Lucas knew that he had not completely won his trust. There were areas within the castle he was barred from entering, and when Boran rode out of the back gate to the valley and mountains beyond the castle and was gone for hours, no one spoke of the reason for his absences. Boran traveled too far for Lucas to see anything other than a narrow mountain road leading to another valley.

"How are you enjoying my hospitality?" asked Boran when Lucas was walking the front wall with him one day.

"You are very generous, sire," answered Lucas politely. "I am being treated well." He had to adjust his steps to Boran's—the king was walking slowly with his hands folded behind his back in a leisurely fashion. As a king, he projected an air of relaxed confidence. Lucas had seen him wandering alone, greeting people he met along the way, a smile on his face, a kind word or warm joke on his lips. A king that gave others the fleeting impression that they were an equal, even if they knew they were far from that. Having seen him lash out at Valora and other staff, Lucas was aware that there were two sides to Boran. It was never a good idea to cross him, or to get on his bad side. It was fear that was driving the castle and the people in it. As long as one did what was expected of him, and no one stepped out of line, everything would go the way it was supposed to.

Boran had taken no queen. He had told Lucas a queen only caused a king to be distracted, but Lucas had seen plenty of women around the castle, and some frequented the king's lavishly furnished chambers.

"You still seem to be tense . . . and on guard," said Boran. "I don't blame you for that. I made you believe you were a guest in my house, and then I tested you. But that's long since done. It's time for you to get to know me. Is that not why you came?"

"Yes," answered Lucas.

"You will find that I am not like my father or his father before him. I look after the people, and I give to the poor instead of taking from them. I claim no taxes and only accept donations and gifts from people who give at their own free will. The people love me, Lucas. When I go into town, they gather in the streets to welcome me, to get a glimpse of me. They try and touch me, as if I am their god." When Lucas didn't say anything, Boran turned to him. "You do not believe me?"

"No," answered Lucas, "it's not that. It's just hard to picture it, when I have only ever seen people keep their distance as King Itan passed through a village."

"Ah," said Boran. "Then, I will have to show you." He smiled and gave him a friendly slap on the shoulder as they continued their walk.

The stroll with Boran reminded Lucas of the many times he had accompanied King Itan on his walks. The fact that it felt somewhat pleasant also felt somewhat confusing to Lucas. He was attempting to distract himself from the conflicting emotion by inhaling the fresh mountain air and letting his eyes wander toward the town when he suddenly sensed his friends. The longing he felt to connect with them was more powerful, by far, than any pull a king could have on his feelings.

He reached out to Davis with his mind. "Have you heard from Orson?" he asked. "Do you know if King Itan received my message?"

"No, not yet," answered Davis. "Why? Are you alright?"

"Yes," answered Lucas. "I'm ready to get out of here, but I'm fine."

As promised, Boran invited Lucas to ride alongside him the next time he went into town. Even though he claimed the people loved him, Boran took no risks and assembled a large party to accompany him.

When they entered through the town gates, Lucas was surprised to discover Boran had not exaggerated the people's reactions to his presence. Men, women, and children alike cheered and waved to them from second-story windows of buildings as they went past. The people filled the streets, and foot soldiers had to push the crowd aside to make a path for their group to get through. Children waved flags embroidered with cougars.

It was clear that the people recognized who he was, so Lucas could only assume that news of his arrival had long since reached the town. Boran smiled from ear to ear. "Lighten up, Lucas," Boran told him, reining his horse in to avoid hitting people. "Smile! Enjoy it. They are shouting your name as well. Let them touch you. You are a god and they admire you. They want to be close to you."

Lucas tried to relax, but to him, that many people meant chaos, and he was there for another reason. He needed to make contact with his friends and, even as Boran showered him with flattery, he was trying to get a glimpse of them in the crowds. He finally spotted them standing off to the side, at the corner of an alleyway, with Dastan. Lucas leaned forward over his horse's neck and shook the hands of the people reaching for him, smiling all the way to pretend he was finally enjoying the attention, but at the same time, he was sending a warning to Davis that Eli was riding in the back. When he sat back up in the saddle, he watched them disappear down the alley, into the shadows.

"He seems to love you," he heard Davis's voice say a short time later. It sounded far away, and echoey, and for one weak, painful moment, he longed to see Davis before him.

"He doesn't," replied Lucas. "He's playing a game, and so am I. I need you to set the plan we talked about in motion. The town is the perfect place for it. The sooner I have Boran's trust, the better."

"I'll talk to Dastan."

They came to an open square, where they stepped their horses off to the side. The soldiers parked the large wagon they had brought along with them in the middle of the square. They pulled the canvas away and revealed loaves of bread, which they then started to hand out to the people, who stood in orderly lines as if accustomed to the ritual.

"You do this every time, sire?" asked Lucas.

"No," smiled Boran. "Only when I am in the mood for it."

From there on out, Lucas rode with Boran each time he went into town. It was the only time he was able to leave the castle. He pretended to enjoy the attention he was getting and waved at the people as they rode through the streets. It was a distant reminder of his time with the circus, when they arrived in a new town. While he smiled at the people and stopped from time to time to shake a hand, Lucas was learning the pattern of the route Boran took. He studied every building, the number of people in each street, and routinely communicated with Davis, who was always following Lucas and Boran from a safe distance. On one particular day, when he was riding through a commercial section of the town, Davis reached out to him.

"This is the area Dastan wanted you to see," said Davis. "On market day, the stalls set up here make these streets too narrow and thus prevent horses from being able to get through."

"And Boran has been seen to walk here?" asked Lucas.

"Yes, he visits once a month, on market day," answered Davis. "Dastan informs me of one street in particular where fresh produce and wares from faraway places are sold. He says Boran always gets off his horse there to walk some of the way, and never passes up tasting and smelling the fruits and spices. There is a building in that street which has a slate tiled awning that is in desperate need of repair."

"Bad enough for it to collapse and it to be seen as an accident?" asked Lucas. "With time enough to let me and Boran escape from under it? Remember, the whole point is that I gain his trust."

"With a little help, yes. We can make it appear that you have saved his life."

"Then that sounds to be the best location for our plan," said Lucas. "When is the next market day?"

There was a moment of silence before Davis answered. "According to Dastan . . . next Saturday."

"In six days," said Lucas. "Does that give you enough time?"

"We'll be ready."

"Then go ahead and set the plan in motion," said Lucas. "And remember, we want Boran trapped—compromised—but not killed. It is not up to us to determine the true king."

The bailey was crowded with a variety of staff members on the morning of the market day, all waiting for Boran.

"Are they all coming along?" asked Lucas, turning to Grant, who had just mounted his horse.

"Yes," answered Grant. "Boran completes many purchases at the market, so he needs staff to assist him. That's why I am coming along as well," smiled Grant. "I get to hold the king's purse."

Lucas looked over to the castle entrance, where he saw Boran step out and mount his horse near Finton and Eli. Lucas had not seen much of either in recent days, as Boran did his best to keep him away from them.

"Are you ready to gaze upon the treasures of the market, Lucas?" asked Boran, riding up to him.

"I am," answered Lucas.

"Then let us not wait any longer," said Boran, and he gave the order to open the gates.

Lucas was relieved to see that Boran did indeed dismount at the appointed street. He followed closely by his side as Boran strolled from merchant to merchant, picking up things along the way and occasionally tasting the food. Grant paid for the things the king bought, and the staff collected the items and passed them down to a wagon to be taken back to the castle. Lucas kept a careful eye on the mass of people all around, which was no easy task given how crowded and bustling the street was. When he spotted Arne, a friend of Dastan's, in front of him, he knew he was getting close.

He could see the building Davis had told him about ahead on the right. It was a two-story structure that had indeed seen better times. Some of the daub was missing, exposing the woven twigs in the panels between the timber frames. The large awning at the front, held up by wooden posts, was sagging under the weight of the slate tiles. Under the overhang were rolls of the finest cloth, all neatly stacked up against the wall, and a large ox was tied to one of the posts. No one would suspect anything was awry if the ox happened to move and thereby pulled the post from underneath the overhang. All Lucas had to do was position Boran and himself beneath it, with himself close to the edge for an easy escape once Lucas saw the ox begin to move.

A young boy no more than six came running from the building towards them and was stopped by a soldier before he got too close. With trousers held up by breeches and sleeves rolled up to make the oversized shirt fit him, he also wore a large-brimmed hat that concealed most of his face.

"Sire, sire!" the boy yelled, determined to be heard when he was pushed back.

Lucas tapped Boran on the shoulder to get his attention and directed him to the boy.

"We have the finest fabrics for sale over there, sire," said the boy enthusiastically. "Best prices, too! You will not find cloth like ours anywhere else. We have the finest!"

"You do now, do you?" asked Boran, looking at the rolls of cloth the boy pointed at. Lucas could see he was interested, but not in a rush to immediately make it over there, as he had yet to reach a stall with baskets of fruit on display.

"Why don't we go and have a look," said Grant suddenly. "The king can join us shortly." He had placed his hand on Lucas's shoulder and was waiting for Boran to permit them to move ahead. Lucas shuddered when he felt Grant's touch. It was unexpected, and it made him feel uncomfortable. They were so close to carrying out their plan. Had Grant caught wind of it? Had he recognized any of Lucas's friends, or even Dastan, during one of their trips to town?

"No," he heard Davis project. "And Dastan doesn't know him either."

Boran had turned to them and looked from one to the other. Lucas smiled congenially and did his best to look relaxed. "Of course," said Boran. "You two go up ahead."

Lucas was relieved when Grant finally took his hand off his shoulder and started crossing the street ahead of him. Lucas followed close behind, along with the two soldiers, who were there to protect the money Grant was carrying.

When he had made it halfway across the street, Lucas heard the shrill chitter of the magpie and suddenly stopped. Time stood still as he turned around to see King Boran reach down to push away a lid that was covering one of the baskets. Having not been allowed to carry any weapons, he reached for the soldier's dagger that was closest to him and pulled it from his belt. Lucas was vaguely aware of people screaming as he charged towards their king with the blade. He shoved Boran aside just as Boran removed the lid of a woven basket, revealing the hissing serpent hiding beneath it. Boran stumbled back just before the serpent was able to strike, and guards rushed to his aid to pull him away. The crowd had backed away from the fruit stall, and they all stood silent as they watched Lucas step aside. The dead serpent hung limply over the side of the basket.

Boran looked from the snake to Lucas, whose heart was racing as he dropped his eyes to his hand. There, on the back of his left hand, were the two puncture marks left by the serpent's fangs, with small droplets of blood seeping out.

As the dagger clattered to the ground, Lucas heard Davis's panicked voice telling him it had not been them that planted the snake. Then everything began to go dark, and Lucas collapsed.

CHAPTER 4

Davis was sitting in the small cellar of the safehouse near the town's gate with his elbows on a table and his forehead resting in his hands. Jars, bowls, and jugs of different sizes were stored in crates along the walls belonging to the potter who owned the house. In a room above, a baby started crying, and he could hear the floorboards creak under the weight of someone walking. When the footsteps disappeared and the crying stopped, Davis raised his head and inhaled a deep breath. He looked at Dastan and Warrick, who sat opposite him, and then turned his head toward Zera, who was pacing in front of the door that gave access to steps leading out into the street. "Will you please sit down?" he asked. "You're not helping my concentration."

Zera stopped. "I'm worried," she huffed. "Lucas didn't look well when they loaded him on that wagon."

"Are you getting anything from him?" asked Warrick, looking at Davis. "Any sign that he's alive?"

Davis shook his head. "No," he answered. "The connection I had with him is broken."

"Hasn't that happened before?" asked Dastan. "Like when Lucas entered Boran's castle? You were worried then too."

"Not like this," answered Davis. "When Lucas or I intentionally disconnect or get separated by distance or some massive distraction—as was the case with the castle—we can still feel each other's existence." He sighed and pushed back from the table.

"Are you saying you think he's dead?" asked Zera with a watery gaze.

"I think we would know if he was," replied Warrick before Davis could. "You and I may not share the same connection with Lucas, but as chosen, we are connected to him in other ways. When Lucas leads us in practicing our fighting stances, we move as one because he is guiding us. And remember when Boran's army advanced through the forest toward the hunters' village? We all knew what Lucas wanted us to do then, without him speaking a word to us."

"That's different," said Zera, finally sitting down. "I never hear his voice in my head or feel him like Davis does."

Warrick shrugged. "It's a connection we have with him. I sense he is still with us."

Davis could feel the tension in the room and was about to reassure his sister that Lucas was alive when all four of them looked apprehensively towards the door as it swung open—it was Arne and his young son.

"What did you discover?" implored Dastan.

"Not much," said Arne. "We took the ox back to the field closest to the castle and waited until some soldiers came by and inquired about Lucas. They asked why I was interested, and I told them the whole town was buzzing over how the king's protector saved the king, and eager to know his status. They told me they didn't know how bad it was, but that the king's physician was still working on him."

"You mean that so-called priest, Eneas," muttered Dastan.

"Oh no," breathed Davis.

"What priest?" asked Warrick.

Dastan took a deep breath. "Boran has a priest who also acts as his physician," he finally answered. "Some say he uses dark magic to heal."

Warrick shrugged. "Does that matter? If he can reverse the effect of the poison and keep Lucas alive?"

"We don't know what else he will do, now that Lucas is in his hands. They say he can break into people's minds. Make them comply, control them somehow."

"What I want to know is how that snake got in the basket," said Arne. "It's not native to this area or the region where the fruit came from. The vendor seemed as surprised as everyone else."

"Yes," said Zera. "Poor man. The way Boran's soldiers dealt with him . . . when it was clear he had nothing to do with it."

"It cannot have been a coincidence," said Dastan. "There is someone who wants to see Boran dead. Someone close to him, who knows him well and would have succeeded if Lucas had not been there."

"Why did Lucas save his life?" asked Arne. "It would have resolved the issue of two kings if Lucas had left him to the snake. What if he now dies as the result of saving Boran?"

Dastan looked at everyone sitting quietly around the table.

Davis raised his head. "He would only do that," he said, "if Boran is the true king."

"No," said Zera, shaking her head wildly. "Lucas isn't going to die, and Boran can't be the true king." She paused before turning to Davis. "Please don't tell me you believe this?"

Davis looked at his sister. She was staring at him with a watery gaze and biting her lip while waiting for him to answer. He wished he could reassure her.

"Has Lucas told you that Boran is the true king?" asked Dastan, breaking the silence.

Davis took his eyes off his sister and inhaled a deep breath. "Lucas doesn't know," he answered. "But he thinks it's possible."

CHAPTER 5

Lucas blinked several times, until everything slowly came into focus. He was in a room of exposed brick that was dark and damp. Dusty shelves full of jars and bottles lined the walls. Some of the jars looked to have dead things inside of them, and from the spiderwebs in between, he could tell they had not been opened or touched for a while. He found himself lying on a cot in the middle of the room, his swollen hand bandaged and placed on his stomach. He knew exactly where he was, though he had not been there before—or at least not physically. The room was only accessible by a stairway leading below the castle, the entrance of which was guarded by soldiers.

"How long have I been unconscious?" he asked.

Eneas was standing by a table, pouring liquid into bottles. When Lucas spoke, he stopped what he was doing and came over to him.

"A few days," he answered while checking him over. "You were very lucky. If the snake had been able to release all of its venom, we would not be having this conversation."

He was surprised to hear he'd been out that long over a snakebite, given that the venom had not been strong enough to stop his heart, but he felt weak and did not question the strange contradiction any further. He watched Eneas walk back to the table and choose one of the bottles he had just filled and return to have him drink from it. The liquid had a strong smell and tasted bitter, and its effect made Lucas's eyes roll back and his head spin.

"Sleep," he heard Eneas say as he collapsed back onto the mattress. "I will inform the king you have woken."

With blurred vision, he watched Eneas leave the room, and he suddenly felt sick. He retched over the side of the cot and threw up some of the liquid he had just been given. There was a stain on the floor where it looked like he had thrown up before, but he could not remember doing so. Too weak to get up, he laid his head back again and watched the walls close in on him. He had a hard time focusing on everything around him but did notice something odd in the dark corner of the room, something he had not seen in his mental mapping of this place—a small sliding door of ancient oak that had been left ajar. A set of stairs went further down, and he followed it with his mind to another underground room, which was lit by a few torches. A table with restraints attached to it stood in the middle and strange devices hung from the walls, giving the impression of a torture chamber.

Two prison cells stood at the far end of the tomb-like chamber, and he tried to concentrate harder to see behind the iron bars. He saw the outline of a man lying motionless on the floor in one of them and noticed movement in the other. A man was sitting with his back against the wall, sliding his feet back and forth in a nonstop rhythm. His clothes were dirty and his hair long and unkempt. He didn't appear to be of sound mind. but there was something familiar about him that Lucas recognized before he drifted back into darkness.

When he woke again, Lucas sat up and saw Eneas back in the room, the floor now clean where he had thrown up. He looked to the corner where he had seen a door but was puzzled when, in its place, stood a heavy cabinet.

"How are you feeling?" asked Eneas.

"Like I've been kicked in the head by a horse," answered Lucas, "instead of being bitten by a snake."

Eneas gave him a sympathetic smile. "Yes, well," he said, "it may have been the medicine I gave you to recover. It can do that to you. It can also make you see things that are not there, but it will wear off soon."

Lucas sighed and prepared himself to get up.

"Would you like me to summon guards to help you to your room?"

"No, thank you," answered Lucas. "I'll be fine. Thank you for helping me recover."

Lucas felt uneasy and unsteady on his feet, but wanted to escape the strange, underground room as quickly as possible. He climbed the steep stairs back up to the surface, stopping a few times to catch his breath. Once he was above ground again, he leaned against a column in the hallway and took in the fresh air.

"There you are," he heard a loud voice say, and looked up to see Boran approaching him. "Eneas told me you had regained consciousness."

Lucas pushed himself upright to face him.

"You saved my life," said Boran when he stopped in front of him. "If it wasn't for you, I might not be here, so I thank you."

"You're welcome, sire," answered Lucas.

"How did you know the snake was there?" asked Boran after a moment.

"I didn't," answered Lucas. "At least not until seconds before, and then I just knew."

Boran nodded understandingly. Lucas thought he was probably coming to his own conclusions right now. But there was something that confused Lucas and didn't make any sense. Why was he able to save the lives of both kings, when he was only supposed to protect one?

By the time Lucas made it to his room, he felt much stronger. He was pleased to see that his sword had been returned and was on the desk waiting for him. With his sore and swollen hand, he was struggling to fasten the belt around his waist when he heard a familiar voice behind him, coming from where he had, in his dazed state, accidentally left the door open.

"I should probably congratulate you on becoming another king's pet—another king who is ordering everyone to treat you like something special . . . who has threatened everyone not to lay a finger on you."

"I was wondering when I would see you up here," said Lucas. "Did your father send you?"

"My father doesn't dictate my every move," said Eli.

"Is that what you keep telling yourself?"

"Don't mock me, Lucas."

"Then why don't you just tell me what you want?" asked Lucas with a sigh.

Eli remained silent and looked around the room for a moment. Then he looked directly at Lucas. "I found out that the dark order were the ones who tried to take you from Itan's castle when we were boys." He shifted his weight against the doorpost and unfolded his arms. "When you were found at the bottom of the well?" he added, as if Lucas might have forgotten.

Lucas finished strapping his belt on and made sure his sword was hanging in the right place. He turned to Eli and stared at him.

"I always thought my father was the one who gave that order. To deliberately kill you, or maim you badly enough that you would never be able to fight again," continued Eli. "It never crossed my mind that others could be responsible."

Lucas reached for the dagger that was lying on the table and tucked it in between his belt and his waist. When he did not respond, Eli continued.

"I'll get to my point. I need to know if my father was involved, and if he was the one who let them in."

"What difference would that make to you?" Lucas replied.

Eli shrugged. "If he helped them, then it means he knew who you were, and if he did, he was making me hate you, pushing me to want you dead . . . all the while knowing he was sending me to my grave if you died because of me."

They stared at each other silently for a moment. Lucas could see, by the haunted look in Eli's eyes, that he was deeply troubled by the possibility of this. All his life, Eli had tried to make his father proud. He idolized him, would kill for him, and believed his father would do the same for him. The thought that his father had used him made him feel betrayed, and Lucas knew he could use this to cause a rift between the two if he wanted, but he wasn't going to. Eli stood patiently, waiting for Lucas to tell him what he needed to hear.

"No," Lucas finally answered. "I already took care of the man who was responsible for that. Your father, though he never wanted to believe I was anything but unwanted trouble and a threat to your future, had no role in what those men came to achieve. But I doubt your father has changed his opinion of me, and I don't know what his intentions are for you now."

He watched Eli processing the words he had spoken. Eli nodded, letting go of the doorpost, and left without saying another word.

When Lucas showed up at the table that night, everyone rose from their seats and clapped to welcome him back. He felt flustered by the attention and was glad when he could sit down. He noticed Eli and his father were not sitting next to each other and, even though Finton avoided eye contact with him, Eli gave him a nod of acknowledgment.

"I have no idea how you did what you did," said Grant, who sat next to him. "It was impressive."

"It was the work of the gods," said Eneas. He turned to face the king. "They have spoken, sire."

Boran grinned. "Well," he said. "If that is the case, Eneas, then the gods also gave you the knowledge and power to save him, and I will drink to that." He raised his chalice and waited for everyone else to do the same. "To Lucas and Eneas," said Boran.

"To Lucas and Eneas," followed everyone in a chant.

Lucas looked at his food before him. He had not eaten for days and was starving. His stomach was hurting, but he couldn't tell if it was because he had gone without food for so long, or there was something else gnawing away at him. He raised his head and saw everyone else had started to eat. He felt Eneas watching him but when he looked at him, he turned his head and started a conversation with an officer next to him. Lucas picked up a chicken leg and took a bite. His head started to spin, and he put it back down. He waited a moment for his head to clear and started chewing the bread instead. It, too, was unappealing, and he dropped it back on his plate.

"Are you alright?" whispered Grant.

"I don't know," answered Lucas. "My head's spinning."

"Drink something," said Grant. "You might be dehydrated."

Lucas nodded and took his advice. His stomach was churning as if it was crying out for sustenance, but his head told him differently. He tried the goat's cheese this time, which made him feel even worse.

Boran looked at him when he pushed his plate away from him. "Anything wrong?" he asked, concern on his face.

"The snake's poison may still be affecting him," said Eneas, before Lucas could answer.

Everyone else turned their heads and stared at him. "May I be excused, sire?" asked Lucas. The air felt stifling, and he had a strong desire to leave.

Boran nodded. "You may," he said. "We probably assumed too soon you were well."

Leaving the Hall, Lucas made his way to the bailey and felt much better when he breathed in the fresh air. The moon was full and lighting his way when he climbed the stairs to the wall. He walked as far as he could and sat himself down in between the merlons.

"We've been worried about you," he heard Davis say. "Are you alright now?"

"I'm not sure," answered Lucas. "How long do you think it would take for the snake's venom to leave my system?"

There was a pause before Davis answered. "Dastan says anywhere from a few hours, but no more than a week, depending on the snake."

"Then Eneas could be right," muttered Lucas.

"Boran's priest?" asked Davis. "Why?"

"I couldn't eat tonight," explained Lucas, "and he said it could be that the venom is still inside of me."

"Dastan doesn't think Eneas is to be trusted. He wants you to be careful."

"I'm getting that impression as well."

"You should try and get out, Lucas. There has to be another way to find out what Boran is up to."

"No," said Lucas. "I've done what I set out to do. Now I have to see it through."

After some time had passed, he began to feel more like himself. He stood and began making his way to his room, until he caught a glimpse of Finton and Eli standing outside the Hall. Without stopping to think, he ducked out of sight, concealing himself in a shadowy nook. They didn't see him and continued talking.

"You can't tell me what to do anymore, father," he heard Eli say. "I am going to make my own decisions now." Eli made to walk away, but Finton grabbed him by the shoulders and turned him back around.

"Eli," he said forcefully. "We have to stick together on this. Trust me."

"No," said Eli. "I am done. I'm out."

Finton took his son more firmly by the shoulders, as if physically restraining him would change his mind. He gave Eli a good shake. At this point, Lucas decided to step out from the shadows and made his way towards them, in the direction of his room. It was clear Finton was about to say something else, but noticed Lucas as he drew near. At this moment, Eli broke loose from his father's grip and walked the other way.

"One day," said Finton to Lucas as he went past, "you will regret you ever crossed my path."

CHAPTER 6

And so it came to pass that Eli and his father no longer sat together at the dinner table, and avoided all eye contact with each other. It certainly didn't make the evening meal any more pleasant. Lucas tried to stay as long as he could at the dinner table for the next two nights, but became violently ill each time he ate.

On night three, he could barely look at the food on his plate. "May I be excused?" he asked when a wave of intense nausea came over him. He crossed his arms and pressed them against his stomach, hunching over in pain.

"You look as pale as bone exposed to the sun," said Grant, turning to him. "Are you feeling sick again?"

Lucas nodded. It was all he could do to keep the contents of his stomach from coming up. His skin felt clammy, and droplets of sweat were rolling down the side of his face.

King Boran looked at him with something akin to mild alarm in his eyes. "Valora can help you back to your room," he said, "and I will further excuse you from attending my table until you are feeling yourself again."

"Thank you, sire," mustered Lucas, rising unsteadily from his seat.

Valora rushed to his side and pulled his chair clear when Lucas bumped into it. "I'm here," she said softly, holding him up by his arm. "Let me help you."

Lucas was aware of the silence in the Hall behind him and was relieved when he finally made it out the door. He leaned against a pillar in the hallway and emptied the contents of his stomach onto the black and white marble floor tiles.

"Don't worry," said Valora when he looked at the mess on the floor. "I'll clean it up."

"I'm sorry," said Lucas, swallowing the bitter bile burning the back of his throat. "I don't know why I keep getting sick after I eat at night."

"You weren't sick after the breakfast I brought you this morning?" asked Valora, helping him upright.

Lucas shook his head.

"Could the meat pie have made you sick?" asked Valora. "I've known people to get sick after eating chicken."

"It's possible," answered Lucas, although it seemed that the sickness had come on too fast for it to be food poisoning. He pushed himself away from the pillar and started walking toward the stairs. His head was throbbing, and he felt dizzy. All he wanted was to get to his room and lie down.

Lucas didn't attend dinner for several days after, and, when he was finally able to return, Eli surprised him by taking the seat to the left of him. Boran had not come down yet, and Finton was not yet in attendance either. In the past, when Lucas had been anywhere near Eli, it had resulted in a confrontation, so he was naturally wary. He instinctively moved away a little, but Eli said nothing and didn't even acknowledge him. Instead, he casually picked up the chicken wing from his plate and put his teeth into it. He avoided the angry stares from his father as he took his seat, and made polite conversation with an officer on the other side of him as he continued to eat. Lucas decided to ignore what was happening until he noticed Eli had scooted closer to him.

"What do you want?" asked Lucas softly.

Eli looked around the table before whispering, "Meet me in the chapel after dinner. We need to talk." He then picked up an apple, and casually bit into it.

Lucas picked up a slice of buttered rye bread from his plate and did the same.

"I'm happy to see you eating," said Boran as he sat down. "Are you feeling better?"

"Yes, sire," answered Lucas, swallowing a mouthful of bread away. "I feel like my old self again."

Boran pressed his lips together and nodded. "Good," he said before turning his attention to two officers who were talking about the status of the armory.

Lucas took another bite from his bread and half listened to the discussion and the request for an additional bladesmith to fulfill the demand of new swords. He watched Eli while he ate, and wondered what he could possibly want to talk to him about, but he didn't catch his eye until the end of dinner.

"Meet me," mouthed Eli as he got up, and Lucas waited until Eli had left the Hall before he followed.

The chapel was dark and empty. The few candles lit in sconces on the pillars cast long shadows over the stone floor. There was no moonlight to illuminate the images of past kings on the stained-glass windows behind the altar, and no one occupied the pews. Lucas had pondered over Eli's request to meet him throughout the rest of the dinner—he worried that Eli could be up to his old tricks to try and get him into trouble. He had nearly decided not to go, but then his curiosity got the better of him.

Lucas had not yet been inside the chapel, but he understood straight away why it had been Eli's choice to meet him there. The alcoves and columns on the sides were perfect places at night to hide anyone who did not want to be seen. Lucas knew Eli was standing in the shadows behind one of the columns but he continued walking down the aisle until he heard him call out in a whisper.

"Psst, Lucas . . . over here." Eli looked nervously towards the door to see if anyone else had come in.

"Don't worry," said Lucas. "I wasn't followed."

Eli nodded, but the way he shifted back and forth nervously showed he was still not at ease. "We both already know how my father feels about you," he whispered. "That is not why I am here." He paused and again made sure no one was coming through the door before he continued. "I'm here to warn you. He has found someone who hates you even more than he does."

Lucas stepped closer towards him. "Do you know who?" he whispered back.

"He didn't give me a name," answered Eli hastily.

"Why are you telling me this?" he asked.

"Because I am no longer the one who wants you dead," answered Eli.

"And this other person does?"

"My father seems to think so."

Lucas nodded and dropped his gaze to the ground. Hearing that Finton still wanted to see him dead came as no surprise to him, nor did the possibility of someone else wanting him dead, but Finton pairing up with this other person . . . this he had not seen coming. Finton no longer held the prestige that he had when he was with King Itan and making a move against Boran's wishes would be very bold, unless . . . the other person was of rank.

"Does anyone in particular come to your mind?" Lucas asked. "Someone your father speaks highly of, perhaps?"

"I don't . . ." Eli stopped when he heard footsteps in the hallway outside the chapel. They both waited with bated breath. Lucas used his mind to see it was only the chamberlain, probably returning to his room after finishing his duties after dinner. Eli, who did not have the knowledge Lucas had, remained on edge and kept listening until it was quiet again. "I have to go," he said hastily and slipped out of the chapel.

Lucas waited for Eli to be gone, then turned around and walked down the aisle toward the altar. He stepped inside the third pew and sat down with his back resting against the back of the bench. "It's all right," he said, looking at the seating in front of him. "You're safe. I won't tell anyone you were here." After a moment's pause, he heard a shuffle and a slender body emerged before him in an upright position.

"How did you know I was here?" asked Valora. The light of a candle illuminated her white skin to a soft yellow as she turned to face Lucas. She was still wearing the blue dress she had worn at dinner service but had loosened her hair and tied it in a ponytail.

"I saw the toe of your boot sticking out from the pew," answered Lucas.

Valora frowned and glanced down at her feet, which were tucked close to her body, but she didn't say anything.

"How long have you been hiding?" asked Lucas.

"A while," answered Valora. "I'm not allowed to be here, so I come at night after most have gone to bed to pray or to just be alone, but today someone came in shortly after me, and then I heard soft voices . . ."

"You heard me. And Eli."

She paused, her eyes grew wide, and her lips trembled when she spoke again. "I won't tell anyone what I heard," she said.

Lucas observed her quietly in the dim candlelight. Her face was ashen, and a vein in her neck pulsed visibly underneath her skin. "I hope you don't," he said when he realized she was scared. "You have nothing to fear from me. I would never hurt you, but I don't know about Eli."

Valora lowered her head and dropped her shoulders. "Thank you," she said in a soft whisper.

Lucas wished he could do something to improve her life, but he knew he couldn't. He still felt like an outsider in Boran's castle, and from what Eli had just told him, his own life was hanging in the balance. "We'd better go," he said, not wishing to leave her. "Before someone sees us."

Valora nodded and silently slipped from the pew.

Lucas watched her exit through a small side door on the chapel's side before taking leave to return to his quarters.

After Eli's warning, Lucas tried to watch Finton more closely, but he never saw him spend any time with any one individual in particular.

"His hatred for you will be his downfall one day," commented King Boran. Finton had wasted no time in making himself scarce when Boran requested that Lucas join him for a post-dinner walk in the back gardens.

"He blames me for many of the bad things that happened at Itan's castle," replied Lucas as they descended the steps.

They stepped onto the soft green lawn and walked underneath the cherry trees, towards an opening in the inner wall, which revealed a garden behind it. There were two walled gardens behind the castle—split by a narrow road that led to the back gate. Each garden was divided into different sections. It was a part of the grounds where Lucas had not been permitted to go as of yet. He silently followed, listening to King Boran, who was telling him about how his father was inspired to create the garden as they walked. Each individual section was unique in its own way and just as beautiful as the one before. With its orchards and its green grass, the first garden reminded Lucas of the hidden valley. The second garden had a neatly manicured lawn with flower beds and paths in between, much like the one at the monastery. It even had a cherry tree growing in the center of the garden, with a bench placed next to it. The third and last garden on the right side of the gate had a cloister, like the one from the warrior monks' training courtyard.

"The gardens are beautiful," said Lucas when they paused to watch a butterfly flutter from one flower to the next. "You must be proud of your father's creation. May I ask what inspired him to create them this way?"

"I am not sure," answered Boran. "My father was close friends with a traveling priest, who was also a healer. He would come and stay with us from time to time, and I know he had a role in the design. My father chose the assortment of flowers in this garden. He loved flowers."

Strangely, to Lucas, each garden they walked through seemed to represent a place from one of his own memories. He wondered if the priest could have been a warrior monk.

After they climbed the stairs that gave access to the back wall, they walked across the top of the gatehouse, and Boran stopped to look towards the valley with its snowcapped mountains. Lucas peered over the wall on the opposite side, where he could see the first garden in the new section from above. It was a replica of the courtyard that housed the black stone. There was an island with a similar amount of water around it, except there was no stone on it.

He went to join Boran and leaned on the wall to let his mind go as far as it would go, but even on the back wall, he saw nothing out of the ordinary. He caught sight of a road on the edge of the mountain and noticed dust settling on it. He followed the road back towards the castle and saw the rider making his way towards them.

"Are you expecting anyone?" asked Lucas.

"Why?" asked Boran, who followed his gaze into the distance.

"Because someone is coming."

Boran kept looking, but it was a while before he saw what Lucas had already seen. Calls from the gatehouse below confirmed that a rider was approaching. He came in at high speed and wore the king's colors of yellow and blue. There was no hesitation at the gatehouse on the part of the guards in receiving him, and Lucas could hear the single gate below swing open to let him in. Lucas watched the soldier slow down and ride through the narrow roadway that led towards the castle's bailey. He followed Boran down the stairs, but kept his distance when they arrived at the bailey, and the king exchanged some words with the soldier who had just ridden in.

Standing still, with his hands clasped behind his back, and his gaze on anything other than the king and the soldier, Lucas eavesdropped on their conversation.

"All is well, sire," he heard the soldier say. "They are ahead of schedule and want to know how you wish them to proceed."

"How far ahead?" asked Boran. "A few days?"

"A few weeks."

"Hm," mumbled Boran, rubbing his chin as if in deep thought. "Perhaps I should go and take a look for myself." He turned on his heels to face Lucas. "Would you like to accompany me on a long ride?" he asked.

"If you wish, sire," answered Lucas, as casually as possible. Deep down, he was both very curious and apprehensive to see where Boran wanted to take him.

A short time later, after a quick meal of fried fish and boiled turnip taken in his room, Lucas rode out through the back gate. He was positioned next to an officer, just behind Boran and Grant. Only a few soldiers accompanied them as they crossed the valley floor and continued on the road the rider had come from. When they reached a second valley, a smaller one that fed into the one they had just come down, the landscape suddenly changed. It was barren and, where trees once stood, now only stumps could be seen. They kept on following the road as it twisted alongside the mountain, but slowed into a walk when it narrowed. Lucas could hear the repeating thud of stones breaking in the distance.

Dust filled the air when they came around the corner, and people were seen moving around on the valley floor below. There was still a forest on the opposite side of the valley, where Lucas could hear axes and shouts warning others when timber was coming down. Oxen were pulling trees, secured with chains, down to the valley ground, where men stood waiting to strip the branches off. They turned the trees into thick poles that were then dragged towards a large deep opening in the side of the mountain. Small wooden carts pulled by donkeys and full of rocks were exiting the hole. The rocks were dumped on the ground outside, where men set to work to pulverize them into smaller pieces and load them onto different carts.

As they descended further down into the valley, they passed men, but also boys as young as thirteen, working on the side of the road. They were using the rocks that had come out of the mountain to widen and strengthen the road. Lucas recalled when the judge had sentenced him to hard labor in the mine once, and the grim thought occurred to him that it could have been him now if things had worked out differently. He looked more closely at those he passed and saw that, though they looked tired, they did not appear unhealthy. They bowed respectfully to King Boran as he went past—his black fur cloak swaying gently over the back of his horse. There were few soldiers around, and none were overseeing any work, which led Lucas to believe they were free men, able and willing.

"Who are these people?" asked Lucas, turning to Grant, who had switched with the officer next to him.

Grant shrugged. "Just laborers from all over the country," he answered.

"They're not prisoners?"

"What makes you say that?" asked Grant. "No, they are all here of their own free will."

"So, they are paid?"

"All those that work receive housing and food," continued Grant. "They are well looked after and will be rewarded monetarily once the work is finished."

"What work might that be?" He could now see a couple of buildings on the valley floor with smoke rising from the chimneys. The smell of fresh bread filled the air.

"You will see," answered Grant.

With the end of the road in sight, the opening into the mountain that loomed up in front of them also became more visible. Lucas marveled at the size of it. It was at least three horses high and wide enough for a column of soldiers to pass through.

"What do you think?" asked Boran as they dismounted and walked towards the entrance.

"You're building a tunnel?" asked Lucas, who couldn't help but marvel at the size of the opening.

"Yes," answered Boran. "How else can a final battle between kings be fought when you have a wild river and a mountain pass too high for an army to cross?"

Lucas stared at the entrance of the tunnel. He let the knowledge that this massive hole was going all the way to King Itan's land sink in for a moment before speaking. "A passage through the mountain . . . I would have thought it impossible. How long have you been working on it?" he asked.

"My father started it almost eighteen years ago. Not long before you were born, and the timing of its completion coincides with your arrival as well. We had not expected to see the end for at least another couple of months, but it appears we are close." He paused and let Lucas finish looking around. "I want you to ride by my side when I take the battle to Itan," said Boran, his tone earnest and enthused.

"Sire," interjected Grant, "we had discussed that—"

"What is it now?" scolded Boran, turning to Grant in frustration.

"Nothing," said Grant. "I apologize. I realize things have changed now."

Lucas looked from one to the other. He knew he had just come close to witnessing a side of Boran that put the fear into his people, but that the king seemed to refrain from further outburst when he saw that Lucas was watching him.

"They have," answered Boran in a different tone. "Have they not, Lucas?"

Yes, thought Lucas, they had. He saw the two men waiting for his reply and nodded. "I believe so," was all that he answered.

Boran walked him closer to the entrance of the tunnel, where they first had to step out of the way of a cart full of rocks hurriedly exiting the opening. The cart was emptied by the roadside and the donkey switched out for another. It was then turned around and taken back in with a different worker. Lucas watched the process with great interest—he'd never seen anything like it.

"It's a long way to the end," explained Boran. "Animal and handler are exchanged once they have made the journey twice—there and back."

Lucas saw workers building a timber frame around the entrance of the tunnel. He had already seen a group of men build what looked like an enormous gate panel on the ground outside and he wondered why. He could think of no possible reason why anyone would want to seal off an entrance—unless, of course, they were afraid of something or someone coming through after them. If Boran was planning on attacking, and coming out victorious, then a barrier didn't seem necessary.

When Boran and Grant started up a conversation with a foreman in the tunnel, Lucas decided to go back outside to confirm what he thought was an enormous gate. He watched how long planks were attached to an iron frame that was lying flat on the ground and observed the workers as they fastidiously toiled at the massive project before them. Some of them raised their heads to give him a glance as he stood watching, but most simply proceeded with their work as if he wasn't there at all.

Lucas walked past them towards a small stream and kneeled to touch the water as it flowed calmly past. He closed his eyes and let his mind follow the stream upwards as it flowed along a road to a narrow ravine. He saw two huge gate panels, like the one being built, hanging on either side of the entrance to the ravine, and workers coming and going from rows of wooden houses built along both sides of the rock wall. He continued to follow the stream between the houses until it turned a corner, and the ravine was blocked by a wall made of wooden beams laid horizontally on top of each other. Water was seeping through the bottom, which created the stream. He felt a hand on his shoulder just when he tried to see past the wall, and he quickly busied himself with splashing some water on his face.

"Anything interesting to see?" asked Grant.

"No," answered Lucas.

"You have been down here on your knees for a long time."

"Just wanted to wash the dust off and cool down."

"Well," said Grant, "the king is ready to return."

"I'm sorry. I won't be long," replied Lucas. He waited until he heard Grant leave before standing up. His mind was preoccupied with what he had seen, and it caused him not to pay attention as he turned around. He bumped directly into a man leading a mule down to the stream to drink. Lucas apologized and would have continued to walk if he had not looked into the man's face. "Winslow?" he muttered and stopped. He stepped back and looked more closely at the man's face. The man did not respond and stood motionless next to the drinking mule. He wasn't wearing soldier's clothing and his long hair and beard were unkempt, but to Lucas, he looked like Finton's man who had spoken up for him when he had first arrived . . . and who he had not seen for some time.

He also remembered the dream he had of the secret door in Eneas's room and the prison cells in which he had seen two men. This looked to be the same man he had seen move his feet back and forth, and if it was . . . then the dream might not have been a dream. If he was right and this man was Winslow, then Eneas could be the one Finton had mentioned to Eli.

Lucas whispered Winslow's name a second time but still got no response.

"You know that man?" asked Grant when he got back to his horse.

"No," lied Lucas when he saw Boran's eyes on him as well. "I bumped into him and wanted to make sure he was alright, and that he would accept my apology."

"No need to apologize," commented King Boran. "Some of the workers here are of simple mind, and they need to learn to watch where they are going. They're very fortunate that I give them work and house them."

"What will happen to them once the tunnel is finished?" asked Lucas as they started riding back up the road.

Both Grant and King Boran looked over their shoulders at him, but only Boran answered. "You don't have to concern yourself with their welfare," he said flatly. "They will be taken care of."

CHAPTER 7

Lucas caught up with Eli that night on his way to dinner, stopping him just before he entered the Hall. "Can I talk to you?" he asked. "Somewhere quiet?"

Eli looked surprised but nodded. "What do you want?" he asked, following Lucas into a small passageway off to the side. It was narrower than the main hallway and sparsely lit. Lucas knew it to be a servants' entrance to the solar room, which had not been in use since the passing of the late queen.

"Winslow," said Lucas. "Your father's man? Where did he go?"

Eli looked at him with a puzzled expression. "What do you mean?"

"I wanted to ask him something, but I haven't seen him since the day I arrived. I thought you might know if he was dismissed, after the way he spoke to your father."

"No," answered Eli. "We were told by King Boran to let that go, since Boran called on Winslow and he had no choice but to speak what he believed to be the truth, and so we did. I saw him afterward but, come to think of it . . . I have not seen him for quite some time now."

"Your father doesn't seem like the type to forget things quickly," said Lucas. "Could he have done something to him?"

Eli pressed his lips together and shook his head. "I think I would know if he had."

"What about the person who hates me more than your father? Do you have any idea who that could be?"

Eli shook his head. "I still don't know who that is. All my father told me was that he had found someone who wanted you out of the way even more than he did, but to be honest, I think he may have just been rambling." Eli paused and then continued by saying, "If you want me to, I can probably find out where Winslow is. The other men might know."

"No," said Lucas. He was now convinced Eneas was involved. "Don't ask anyone. I'm sure he will turn up."

They walked into the Hall together but went their separate ways at the table, and Lucas spent most of the evening keeping a close eye on Finton and Eneas. Only Eneas noticed being watched and their eyes briefly met. When Eneas looked away, Lucas sensed a darkness enter the room and felt the powers inside of him getting stronger in response.

He fell into a restless sleep that night and found himself standing in the water of the stream that flowed through the ravine. He felt the eyes of hundreds of workers on him. They stared at him from the water's edge, and from the windows and doorways of the wooden houses—each man just like the other—silent, with no hint of expression on their faces.

A young boy appeared in front of Lucas at the water's edge, and slowly raised his hand to point. Lucas followed his direction to the entrance of the ravine, where he saw the gate was closed. He looked back at the boy, whose eyes were pleading for help. He looked fearful, and Lucas wondered why he was the only one showing any emotion. Lucas took a step forward to ask what was troubling him, but the boy suddenly backed away.

When he felt the water beginning to rise, Lucas looked down at his feet. He realized with horror what was happening, but it was too late. A rumbling sound came from the back of the ravine, shortly followed by the deafening sound of splintering wood, coming from the first houses that were smashed by the wall of water.

With his visit to the tunnel several days behind him, Lucas stood on the wall overlooking the town in the distance, where little lights were fading as the night progressed and the residents were heading off to sleep. Guards passed silently behind him on their watch, paying little attention to him. They had seen him there before, gazing over the landscape and the town in the distance, taking in the scenic view—or so he knew it would appear to them. They could not hear the words he was speaking and the replies he was receiving from beyond the walls as he communicated with Davis.

King Boran had started to mobilize his army and, every day, troops of soldiers arrived, men who had been called back from other parts of the country where they had been stationed. The fields behind the castle had turned into the army's camping grounds. Lucas waited until the guards had passed before he connected with Davis again.

"We've noticed the preparations in town. Weapons are being made everywhere," he heard Davis say. "How long, do you think, before he will be ready?"

"Boran is planning on moving the entire army there soon, but he'll wait until everything is in place before breaking through the last bit of the tunnel. With the number of workers he has down there, he could have his entire army through in four weeks, maybe less."

"So, you want us to leave tonight?" asked Davis.

"Yes," answered Lucas. "Time is running out. If you leave now, you can get to the secret valley and be back with Nolan, the warriors, and the other chosen before the next half-moon."

He heard Grant speaking to some of the guards in the bailey, near the base of the stairs that led to the top of the wall, and quickly told Davis he had to go.

"Be careful," he heard Davis say, just as Grant reached the top of the stairs.

"Is the wide-open space calling you?" asked Grant before joining him. He rested his arms on the wall and took in the view.

"I like watching the lights of the town in the distance," answered Lucas. "Reminds me of glowing embers of a fire."

"Hmm," said Grant. "The way I see it, each light that goes dim over there has the potential to signify the start of a secret meeting . . . a plot against the king."

"But the king seems well-loved by the people."

"Yes," answered Grant, keeping his eye on the town, "but perhaps not all of them. And the fact remains—is he the true king?"

Lucas frowned and took a moment before answering. He wasn't sure where the conversation was heading. "I think you know I cannot answer that," he finally responded. "Toroun didn't know whose side he was to be on until the battle began and the gods told him."

"True," remarked Grant, "but did you not tell us once that you are not like Toroun? Is it possible that you already know?" Grant gave him a sideways glance as if he wanted to say something else, but then changed his mind and changed the subject. "The king wants you to take over the training of the cavalry's second division in the morning," he said.

"Second cavalry?" asked Lucas. "They are Eli's responsibility."

"Not anymore," answered Grant. "The king wants to put them on the frontline when the battle begins, and he wants you to lead them."

Lucas stared at him silently. That was the position Toroun had held at the start of the Great Battle.

"You did say you were going to be with him during the battle, did you not?" Grant looked at him with narrowed eyes and waited for an answer.

Lucas sighed deeply. He didn't know how much he should tell Grant. "I have no intention of not being there," he finally said. "So, if it pleases the king, I will train the second cavalry, but do know that the road to the battle is not yet clear to me."

"Good," responded Grant. "They start training at dawn, so be there bright and early." He pushed himself away from the wall and walked away.

"What about Eli?" Lucas called after him. He had not seen him at dinner that night or the two nights prior, and maybe that was why. The second cavalry was Eli's life now—and the reason why Lucas saw very little of him. He would have been devastated to lose command over them.

"He will be given another assignment," answered Grant.

Lucas got up early the next morning and made his way to the arena where Boran had tested him with the cougar. The podium chairs were empty, and the gate from which the cage had been pulled was closed. As he walked towards the center of the arena, he couldn't help but let his eyes drift to where the poor soldier had met his untimely death. The area had been cleaned. The soiled sand, from the blood that had seeped from the cage, was either removed or covered up.

Lucas found the second cavalry ready and waiting for him. They were dressed in full uniform, which consisted of dark blue riding pants, matching jackets with gold-plated buttons and black boots. Their scabbards, engraved with Boran's shield, hung on their left side from their belts, the swords inside at the ready. He had watched them train with Eli a couple of times. They were a group of fifty young soldiers who were fit and eager, but nowhere near experienced or trained enough to be in the frontline of battle. He felt they would be slaughtered instantly by Itan's cavalry, which had already proven itself in battle.

The second cavalry stood in a neat line, mounted on their horses, when he approached. Eli was not with them, but he should have been. Even if his feathers were ruffled, it was customary to have a formal handover of a unit from one officer to another, and Eli was a stickler for military rules.

"Where is your former commander?" asked Lucas of the nearest soldier.

"We have not seen him for the last three days, sir," answered the soldier. "We assumed that was the reason for the handover."

"Sir," Lucas then heard someone say behind him. Lucas turned to see a stable boy had stopped behind him. The boy was perhaps fifteen years old and holding the reins of an elegant black destrier horse. Destriers were the finest warhorses but they were costly, and Lucas had only known King Itan and Verron to ride one, until he had come to Boran's castle.

"A gift from the king, sir!" the boy said, handing him the reins. "He told me he wanted you to have the best horse of the stable."

Lucas took the reins and stroked the horse over the nose. At first, it jerked its head up and down, but eventually settled down and started to nuzzle his hand.

"He is a bit of a wild one," said the boy, "but strong and fast, if ridden properly."

"You trained him yourself?" asked Lucas.

"No, sir," answered the boy. "I am tasked with his care only, but I have seen how he rides."

"Then I am sure he will be great," said Lucas. He mounted his new horse and felt the force beneath him when it trembled and kicked up its feet. Lucas held the reins and ignored the horse's excitement. When the horse had settled for the second time, the boy turned and walked away.

"Fall into formation," called Lucas as he turned his horse to face the cavalry. "I want you to give me a demonstration of what you can do. How fast can each of you draw your sword and strike at an enemy without lopping your horse's ears off?"

Lucas watched the soldiers ride single file alongside the perimeter of the arena and then turn simultaneously to ride side by side as they crossed the arena. "Again!" he shouted, when each had stabbed at an imaginary enemy. He had them repeat the exercise until he had seen enough and called them back to the middle, where he paraded his horse in front of them. They all stood silently as Lucas took his time riding past each of them, sizing each rider up individually. He then told several soldiers to dismount and swap horses. Although confused, most obeyed the order, except for one.

"This has been my horse for several months now, sir," said the soldier, refusing to hand over the reins. "Why do we need to change?"

Lucas rode his horse over and stood before him. "Who put you on that horse?" he asked.

"No one, sir. I picked him myself."

"And why? Why did you choose that horse and not another?"

The soldier looked somewhat confused. "I don't know, to be honest," he answered. "He is strong and has a comfortable trot."

"He is strong," said Lucas, "but he spooks easily, and you are not able to control him. Perhaps with someone else, he would make a connection, but he is fighting you every step of the way and will throw you in battle if startled."

The soldier gave his horse another quick look and then handed the reins over without further argument.

When Lucas was satisfied that he had made the necessary changes, he had the soldiers practice formation the rest of the morning. By the end of the training session, he was pleased to see them all riding in a more orderly fashion, and more in control of their horses.

When he had finished for the day, Lucas handed his horse over to the boy in the stables. It was then, when he turned to leave the stable, that he noticed Eli leaning against the doorway. He didn't look like his usual self, with his hair uncombed and his clothes wrinkled. The buttons of his shirt were misaligned, and the shirt hung untucked on one side. He stared at Lucas when he saw him approach and then rolled off to the side to let him through without saying a word. Not wanting to antagonize him, Lucas quickly walked past.

Eli appeared again in the stables the following morning and stood behind Lucas when he was tacking up his horse. Lucas looked over his shoulder to acknowledge that he knew he was there but continued fastening the girth.

"I'm sorry I wasn't there to transfer the cavalry over to you properly," said Eli, after observing him quietly for a while. "I had no idea they had pulled me off the cavalry's command until this morning."

"No one's seen you in days," said Lucas as he finished tightening the girth on his saddle. "Where were you?"

"I was with Eneas," replied Eli. "Did he not tell anyone?"

"Eneas?" asked Lucas, taking the bridle from a hook. He moved to stand on the left side of his horse and put the bit into the horse's mouth before pulling the bridle over the ears. "What were you doing with him?"

"I became unwell a few days ago," explained Eli. "Couldn't keep my food down and was plagued by the most unusual fatigue. He helped me get better."

"Sorry to hear that," said Lucas. "I didn't know, and nobody told your men either."

"That's alright," said Eli. "I feel much better now."

Lucas looked at him and frowned. This was not the Eli he knew. He seemed much calmer and less aggressive. Lucas had thought for sure he was at least going to give him an earful about taking his job. "What did Eneas determine was wrong with you?"

"That's just it . . ." Eli walked to Lucas's horse and stroked the side of its head. "Remember how they said it was the snake's venom that made you sick when you ate?" asked Eli. "Well, I don't think it was the venom, because I got the same. I was fine to eat in the mornings but was getting sick after dinner two nights in a row. Then, on the third day, I could barely get out of bed, and Eneas took me to his room."

Lucas finished fastening the throat lash of the bridle and paused, staring at Eli. Alarm bells were going off in every part of his body. "What did he do to you?"

"Nothing," said Eli. "He gave me different medications, and for the most part, I just slept. I can't remember much. Why?"

Lucas took the reins in both hands and started leading his horse out. "I think he drugged you. That explains why you looked so dazed when I saw you yesterday."

"Yesterday?" asked Eli, surprised. "I didn't see you yesterday."

"You did. I thought you behaved a bit strangely, and you had . . ." Lucas thought about the strange look he had seen on Eli's face. The same vacant look he had seen on Winslow. He stopped in his tracks and turned to Eli. "Winslow," he said. "Did you say anything to your father or Eneas about Winslow?"

"I asked my father. Why?"

Lucas took a deep breath and shook his head. It was careless of him to have said anything, and he should have thought it through better.

"What's wrong?" asked Eli. "What did I do?"

"Did you mention that I asked you about him?"

"No," answered Eli. "He became so defensive when I mentioned his name that I walked out on him."

"How long after that did you get sick?"

"Maybe a day after?" he said, shrugging. "I can't remember. Why?"

Lucas's horse nickered when other horses went past and distracted him for a moment. He waited until the other horses were gone and continued. "Did you go to Eneas when you got sick?"

"No," answered Eli. "I was too sick even to leave my room. My father came to me and he eventually got Eneas to come and take me to his quarters. But why you are asking me all this?"

Not wanting to draw any further attention to the two of them talking in the middle of the bailey, Lucas started walking again. "I believe Eneas is the man your father spoke of," he said when Eli followed. "I have no idea what he would want from you, but it can't be a coincidence that we were both struck with the same ailment. You were poisoned, as was I."

Now it was Eli who suddenly halted and grabbed him by the arm. "That implies that my father is involved." He shook his head, then looked around to see if anyone was listening. "Why?" he asked with much urgency. "Tell me."

"All I can think of is that you asked about Winslow."

"But Winslow is gone. No one knows where he is."

"He's around," answered Lucas. "I have seen him, but he is no longer himself."

"What is that supposed to mean?" asked Eli. He had a wild look in his eyes.

"Look," said Lucas, trying to calm Eli down. "Give me some time. I'll figure this out. You're fine now, and so am I. Let's keep our heads down and stay away from Eneas for the time being."

"Eneas is a priest." Eli took a deep breath. "Why would he want to harm you? He serves the gods."

Lucas shook his head. "No," he answered. "He doesn't."

CHAPTER 8

Training the cavalry was proving to be more difficult than Lucas had anticipated. They didn't feel him like the chosen or the warriors of the valley had, so he had to explain everything more thoroughly, and sometimes repeat his demonstrations several times. It kept him busy and gave him little time to see what else was going on in the castle.

At the end of each day, he was exhausted and returned to his room reluctant to change into different clothes for dinner. His bed looked like an inviting alternative over the discussions of officers at the king's table and being in Eneas's presence. Aware of his watching eyes, Lucas could feel every fiber in his body warning him to leave. He had tried to avoid dinner with the excuse that he had to work on training schedules, but Boran would not allow it. Eli, on the other hand, had been more successful in not attending. With his tousled hair and disheveled clothes, he had not made it past the inspection by the door for the last three nights.

Taking his usual seat at the table, Lucas quickly glanced around to see who was present. "No Eli again, I see," he remarked quietly to Grant.

"No," answered Grant in an equally soft tone. "And if he knows what's good for him, he will not show up tonight. The king has banned him from his table."

"Why?" asked Lucas. "Because he's not adhering to the dress code?"

Grant nodded. "By doing so, he has openly disrespected the king, but that is not the only reason."

"What else has he been doing?"

"I can't disclose that," said Grant, "but you should stay away from Eli before the king questions your loyalty as well."

"Eli and I have nothing in common," responded Lucas. "Everyone knows that."

"You may not like each other," answered Grant, "but you were both raised under King Itan's rule. That binds you together, whether you like it or not."

Lucas pulled himself upright as soon as he saw Boran enter the Hall. Finton followed close behind. By the looks on their faces, it was clear that they had been engaged in a bitter discussion. Boran looked far from pleased, and when Lucas saw him stare in his direction, he quickly smoothed the creases of his tunic. It was probably in his best interest tonight to pretend he was happy to be there. He quickly entered a discussion about battle strategies with the two officers on his left.

The confirmation that Eli had been doing more than merely disobeying the dress code reached Lucas the following afternoon. He had just returned from the fields behind the castle, with the cavalry in tow, when he saw Valora come towards him. She waited until all the horses had come to a stop before walking up to him.

"The king has summoned you," said Valora. "He wants you to meet him in his private quarters."

"Right now?" asked Lucas, taking the reins over his horse's head. When Valora nodded, he handed his horse over to a stable boy. "Do you know what it's about?" he asked, taking his gloves off and following her.

“No,” answered Valora, “but he has had several outbursts toward staff today.”

Lucas slowed and looked at Valora. She was walking beside him with her chin lowered and her eyes directed at the black and white marble floor tiles. “Did he hurt you?” he asked. He was relieved when she shook her head.

“No,” answered Valora. “He’s been kind to me lately.”

They continued to walk in silence and stopped before Boran’s room.

“Is there anything else you need, sir?” asked Valora while the guards opened the door.

“No,” answered Lucas. “Thank you.”

Valora gave him a courtesy bow and turned to leave, and he entered the lavishly furnished chamber with all its ornate chairs and benches. Looking to his right, Lucas saw him standing by a polished oak table with a map stretched out before him. Grant stood next to him. Both had their heads down and were looking at the map.

Lucas approached them and stopped when he was a short distance away, not sure if he was to proceed. Boran only briefly glanced up but quickly returned his attention to the map. Grant was leaning on the table with his forearms covering a large section of the parchment and did not acknowledge he was there.

Lucas didn’t have to get closer to know that they were looking at a map of the area behind the castle. He could see the entrance of the tunnel clearly marked. The most northern part of Itan’s land lay just west of mountains, and a dotted line drawn on the map indicated the direction of the tunnel towards it. The line moved north first, then curved gradually to the west. Boran had one finger on the proposed exit of the tunnel and another on a large open terrain on King Itan’s land—the most likely place for a battle. Lucas frowned. He let his mind go back to the memory he had of the tunnel. Something wasn’t right. When he had stood inside the entrance, he had been sure that the tunnel had continued much further north than shown here on the map. Either the drawing was incorrect, or the tunnel did not finish where Boran believed it did.

"Sire," said Lucas, after waiting a few minutes. Grant jolted when he heard him speak and looked over his shoulder, as if deep concentration had prevented him from realizing Lucas had entered the room. Startled, he stepped aside, and Lucas did his best to look casual when an area on the east that he had not been able to see yet was exposed to him—revealing the ravine and that what lay beyond. "You requested to see me?"

"Yes," answered Boran, now acknowledging him. He dismissed Grant with a wave of his hand and backed away from the oak table to walk in the direction of a drink cabinet.

Lucas met Grant's fleeting glance as he hastily rolled up the map and brushed past him to take his leave. It made him wonder if there was something on the map he was not supposed to see.

After the door closed behind Grant, Boran poured some wine into a chalice.

"Would you like some?" asked Boran, holding the chalice out to him. When he saw Lucas's hesitation, he added, "Or perhaps something else? Mead, or ale?"

Lucas was worried about offending the king, but he rarely drank. Wine had a taste that he had not yet acquired, and ale and mead affected his body in a way he'd rather do without. "I'm grateful for your hospitality, sire," he answered, "but I am still on duty."

Boran gave him an approving smile. "So you are," he said, and brought the chalice to his lips. He walked over to his gemstone chair and casually rearranged the cushions. The action suggested informality but Lucas knew that no meeting with the king was ever informal, no matter what was suggested in gestures such as this one. Lucas waited patiently for the king to sit down and to address him again. Boran's eyes were sizing him up from top to bottom as he took another sip of his wine. Lucas shifted uncomfortably from one foot to the other—he was beginning to wonder if he had done something wrong.

Boran finally rested the chalice on the armrest. "Eli has not been himself lately," he started. "Last night, he left to go into town." He paused and waited until Lucas nodded to acknowledge he was listening. "I need someone to find him and get him back. I was going to send you, but I have since been told that you may be the cause of Eli's strange behavior. That, somehow, you have influenced his thinking."

Lucas froze, careful not to show any emotion. "I'm not surprised," he said, "that Finton would lay that blame at my feet."

"It wasn't Finton," said Boran. "It was Eneas."

"Oh . . ." Lucas frowned. "Eneas?" he asked.

Boran nodded. "Yes," he said. "Eneas has been telling me that you, too, have not been acting yourself lately—that you and Eli may be conflicted about your calling and the gods you both serve."

Lucas felt the muscles in his back tense. He was about to say that Eneas was lying, but the king raised his hand to stop him from speaking. "Eli has been asking questions about Eneas in the soldiers' mess hall," Boran continued, "when he should have been sitting at my dinner table, had he been appropriately dressed. A smart ploy, if that was his intent. Something I would expect you to come up with, not Eli."

"And you believe I set him up to that?" interrupted Lucas. "I am the last person who would be able to convince Eli to do my bidding. I have no idea what made him do these things. Whatever Eli is doing, he's doing on his own."

"I have been misinformed, then?"

"Yes, you have," said Lucas.

"Good," said Boran, "then you will have no problem locating him for me. Find out what he has been up to in town, and bring him back."

Lucas took a deep breath. It was hard to believe Eli could have been foolish enough to ask questions about the king's trusted priest. He must have known that the king's eyes would be on him as soon as he started to disobey his protocol. And Eneas, Lucas realized, had finally made his first move by trying to discredit him in the eyes of the king. He wondered what his true agenda was. "No, sire," he answered. "I have no problem with that."

"You hesitate in your response," remarked Boran. "Why is that?"

"If Eli is somewhere in town and you are sending me out to look for him," explained Lucas, "then that requires me to leave the castle without your presence and supervision. Something you have not allowed me to do yet."

"Yes . . . I am well aware of that," replied Boran. "Are you telling me that will be an issue?"

"No," Lucas replied. "It will not."

"Good," said Boran, his tone suddenly lighthearted. "That is settled, then. Besides, you will be supervised by me indirectly, by two of my most trusted men." He stood up and walked over to the window, where he looked out over the valley and the mountains behind it. "How is that horse I gave you?" he asked.

"He is exceptional, sire," answered Lucas, glad for the change of subject. "I am grateful for such a horse. He is fast, strong . . . agile."

"I knew you would like him," said Boran. He paused and momentarily turned around to look at him. "After all," he continued, "that horse is a direct descendent from the stallion Toroun rode into battle. The one he was captured with."

Grant informed Lucas that Malcolm and Isaac from the second cavalry would accompany him into town. Isaac was a soldier with black skin, one of a few who served King Boran, while Malcolm was fair skinned with reddish brown hair. Both men were strong and had shown him substantial respect in the short time he had known them. He knew they would protect him if needed, but he was also aware that they were loyal to the king. Especially Malcolm, who would no doubt be asked to give a full report once they were back.

Fortunately, Lucas had nothing to hide. His friends had already left the town. All he had to do was find Eli and bring him back.

They had left their horses at a guard station inside the town to traverse the streets on foot, asking questions along the way of anyone who might have taken notice of a tall, blond-haired soldier of roughly eighteen. With so many stores, houses, inns, and taverns, it seemed like an impossible task. He had no idea what Eli's intention could have been in going into town, or where even to start in searching for him. They had checked the inn closest to the castle, which was mostly frequented by soldiers, even though Lucas didn't buy the notion that Eli may have gone to drink somewhere. Least of all on his own. As far as Lucas knew, he didn't have any friends at Boran's. He wondered if Eli missed the camaraderie of the elite borns as much as Lucas missed the company of the chosen ones.

Malcolm was leading the way, and Lucas could tell he was becoming more and more irritated by the congestion on the street. He had already pushed a man aside roughly. The man had been struggling under the basket of corncobs he was carrying, and some of the corn fell to the ground as he swayed, regaining his balance. Lucas understood that Malcolm, having been cavalry all his life, wasn't used to having people underfoot.

"It would have been easier if Eli was wearing his officer's uniform," remarked Isaac, "instead of the street clothing the guards said he wore when he left. And too many travelers frequent this town for the locals to stop to take notice of anyone out of place. Do we even know why Eli came here?"

"No," answered Lucas, dodging out of the way to avoid a collision with a handcart pushed out of an alleyway. "That would make it too easy as well." He was glad he was wearing plain officer's clothes, instead of the more colorful and flamboyant clothes he had worn when he visited the town with Boran. No one recognized him as Baelan, and only a handful of civilians here and there glanced at him with a mild degree of interest.

"We should check The Tangled Net," said Isaac.

"What is that?"

"A tavern situated near the water, right next to a fishmonger's shack," explained Isaac. "Smelly little place. Dark, too. Perfect place if you want to have a quiet talk with someone, or so I have heard."

"I doubt we'll find Eli there," said Malcolm. "Hardly the place a king's soldier is welcome."

"He's not in uniform, remember," commented Isaac.

Lucas recalled his memory of the Black Log Inn, where he had worked. The hushed conversations, the discreet handshakes under the tables. It was exactly the kind of place you would go to if you wanted covert information or just wanted to remain out of sight—two options he had contemplated as a possible reason for Eli's disappearance. "Let's go and check it out," Lucas said.

Malcolm looked over his shoulder, a cautious look on his face. "We may need to get some reinforcements then. Three of us may not be enough if we encounter trouble. People may suspect we have come to arrest them."

"No backup," said Lucas. "We'll be fine."

As soon as they veered off the main street and onto the less crowded back streets, Lucas saw a familiar face up ahead. The small boy, who they had used to lure Boran underneath the awning at the market and who he knew was the son of a friend of Dastan, was casually leaning with his back against a wall—he wore the same large-brimmed hat as before, and Lucas had noticed the boy following him a few streets back and had wondered where all this was going. Just before Lucas passed him, the boy looked down to his feet and discreetly cupped his hand behind his ear—an innocent motion that looked like he was scratching his ear, but Lucas knew what it meant.

"Tangled Net," mumbled Lucas, a little more audibly than he would have normally done.

"What about it?" asked Malcolm, turning around slightly.

"The place where we hope to find Eli . . . fitting name if it is next to a fishmonger," Lucas said. "But also if Eli is weaving lies." He gave the boy a quick look in passing and saw that he was already turning on his heels and running off into a side street. It was clear to Lucas that it was no coincidence that the boy had been there. He had run off as if he was going to report where they were going . . . but to whom? His friends had all left town. There was no sign of them, and Davis had not connected with him since their last conversation. And yet, he trusted the boy.

The visit to the tavern was unsuccessful. Eli wasn't there, and the tavern owner was less than cooperative in answering their questions regarding who had been visiting his establishments recently. "Who wants to know?" he had asked from behind the bar. He was a heavyset man wearing a sleeveless tunic that showed off his bulging muscular arms. Lucas imagined he would probably do quite well in a log throwing competition. He was pretending to be busy wiping cups down with a rag, but had cast a warning eye to the four customers who were inside. All talking ceased, and heads were lowered. One customer slipped out the door.

Lucas rested his arms on the bar and looked over his shoulder to each one before turning back to the tavern owner. "The king," he answered firmly.

"Well, you can tell him that no one fitting that description was here last night."

"Did I say last night?"

The owner shrugged his shoulders. "When else do soldiers get time off?"

Lucas wanted to continue interrogating the bartender, but Malcolm and Isaac had become restless. Two new customers had come inside and had taken a seat at a table. Their eyes were fixed on the owner, who had given them a subtle shake of his head.

"We should go, sir," insisted Malcolm.

Lucas reluctantly agreed. Even though he sensed the tavern owner was lying, Eli wasn't there. He pushed himself away from the bar and followed Malcolm and Isaac out the door.

As soon as he stepped outside, he spotted the boy close by. He sat crouched on the ground next to a few other kids, who were playing a game with little sticks. They had them piled up like a tiny bonfire, and each child tried to remove a stick without moving another. If successful, that child could keep the stick. Whoever had the most sticks in the end won.

Lucas remembered playing the same game with his friends on a few occasions when they were outside King Itan's castle grounds and were able to get hold of sticks. He remembered how Warrick had hidden some in his bedroll once so they could continue to play in their dorm room. They had done so for a few nights, until Verron nearly caught them when he came for inspection. Lucas had been engrossed in the game when he suddenly became aware of the officer coming up the stairs. Punishment for staying up would have meant a nightly run for all of them. Warrick had picked up the sticks and thrown them onto his bed before flinging himself on top of them and pretending to sleep. The rest of the boys and Zera had scrambled to get into their beds. There was no possible way that Verron did not suspect something was going on when he opened the door, but it had started to rain, and Lucas imagined he probably did not feel like getting wet—he would have had to supervise the run.

The stick game was never played in the dormitory again, but he wondered what Warrick had done with the sticks. He would ask him next time they were together again.

"Whether Eli was there or not," said Lucas, loud enough for the boy to hear, "that man knew who we were talking about."

"Then we should check all the inns close by and see if he has taken up lodgings at any of them," said Malcolm. "He wouldn't have gone to the town without taking coin with him."

Lucas pretended to be in deep thought while resting his eyes on the group of playing kids. The boy had not taken a turn, and Lucas was sure that he was listening. "Alright," he said, turning back to Malcolm and Isaac. "That sounds like a good plan." In his peripheral view, he saw the boy get up and disappear around the corner.

As they moved through the town, Lucas led the way through the streets, while Malcolm and Isaac kept a close eye on their surroundings, as Lucas had instructed them to. This freed him up to focus on the boy. The boy was small, and with him zigzagging between the crowd of people, it was hard for Lucas to keep up. He finally saw him dash into an alleyway and disappear down the steps of an inn with its entrance in the storeroom of a tall building. Lucas turned into the quiet narrow street, his two men behind him.

"There's another inn," said Isaac, pointing towards the small hanging sign above the entrance.

Lucas let Malcolm step around him to lead the way and followed him down the five steps into the partially underground inn. He bent his head to get through the low door and then stepped past Malcolm into the dimly lit room. The small, street-level windows didn't allow much light to pass through. The tables were all occupied. It was late in the day, and evening meals were being served. He saw the boy come towards him—eyes down—a bowl of soup clutched between his hands. The boy purposely bumped into him. The contents of the bowl spilled onto Lucas's clothes.

"I'm sorry, sir," the boy apologized. "Please forgive me."

"You fool," Malcolm scolded the boy, raising his hand to lash out.

Lucas grabbed his arm. "Don't," he said, calmly but firmly. Several people had pushed their stools back. "He's just a small boy and no harm has been done. I'm sure he knows where I can get myself cleaned up."

"Yes, sir," replied the boy eagerly. He righted himself from the cowering position he had taken up. "There is clean water in the kitchen, sir."

Before Lucas followed the boy, he turned to Malcolm and Isaac. "Why don't you check the rooms upstairs," he said. "I'll return shortly."

"Yes, sir," said Isaac and headed for the stairs, but Malcolm remained.

His body tense, Malcolm looked at the patrons silently watching them, then settled his gaze upon the kitchen door.

"Go with him," said Lucas, gesturing to Isaac, who had stopped and was waiting for Malcolm at the bottom of the stairs. "We need to find Eli and I don't want it to take any longer than necessary."

Malcolm slowly nodded while keeping his eyes on the door, but then turned around to follow Isaac.

Lucas waited until he saw them both go up the stairs before pushing open the double swinging doors. There, in the hallway, Dastan stood waiting.

"What are you doing here?" Lucas whispered as soon as he saw him. He put a hand on Dastan's shoulder and walked the two of them further into the kitchen. "I thought you had returned to the valley?" A few members of the staff looked up at them, but they continued working.

"Don't worry," said Dastan, seeing his worried look. "This place is run by people known to me. When your friends left, I thought it was best that I stay behind to keep an eye on things. But what about you? I was surprised to hear from Arne's son that he had seen you arrive in the town and instructed him to follow you. I thought you told Davis you were not allowed to leave the castle?"

"I wasn't," answered Lucas, "but General Finton's son, Eli, has gone missing. He was seen to go into town but failed to return. I was sent to find him."

"Well, I am glad you were," said Dastan. "I've been pondering on how to get a message to you. You're not going to like it."

"What's that?" asked Lucas. He took the rag the boy held out to him and wiped the soup from his trousers. It had been too watery to leave a stain, but he would make sure to clean it properly once he got back. For now, the rag did its job by absorbing most of the liquid.

"I saw someone," continued Dastan. "Someone who we all thought to be dead."

"Who?"

"The last member of the dark order. The fair-haired one."

"Byram?" asked Lucas. The last time he had seen him was just before a hunter's arrow took him down from his horse. Byram had been the one who had led a hundred of Boran's soldiers into the forest to attack the hunters, and now Lucas wished he had checked to make sure he was dead. At the castle, he had not heard the dark order being spoken of, but if Byram was still alive, why would he not have returned? "Are you sure it was him?"

Dastan nodded. "I only got a glimpse of him, but he's not a person I'd likely forget."

"No," responded Lucas, "you're right. Where did you see him?"

"Here in town," replied Dastan. "Two days ago. He came out of the tavern next to the fishmongers."

"Why does that not surprise me," muttered Lucas. "Was he with anyone else?"

Dastan shook his head. "Not that I saw. I waited a while, and even went inside the tavern, but . . . if he had been there to meet someone, that person could have left before him."

"That's true," said Lucas. "That is one more person I have to watch out for." He handed the rag back to the boy and was turning to leave when he felt Dastan's hand on his arm.

"You don't have to go back to Boran," he said, his face full of worry. "You can leave out the back door, and I can have the two cavalrymen taken care of."

Lucas shook his head. "Boran will have considered that possibility when he sent me. I cannot risk it."

"Nolan will not be pleased that I let you go with Byram close by," said Dastan, letting go of his arm. "You better know what you're doing."

"I think I do," said Lucas, although he was starting to wonder if he had been missing important clues to Boran's true intentions for him.

Dastan took a deep breath and let go of his arm. "If you are looking for Eli," he said, "I heard that it's common knowledge here in town that The Tangled Net is a gateway to prison and has often been the last place visited by many of those who have disappeared."

Lucas nodded. "It seemed to be the kind of place where silence could be bought."

They had been walking along the sloping ground for some time, under a low, arched ceiling, and the moss-covered damp walls indicated they were now significantly below the foundation of the town. The sound of their boots clacking on the stone floor was the only noise to be heard in the otherwise deathly silent prison. There was no potent smell of human waste, no rats, and no desperate hands of prisoners reaching through the bars. The cells were all empty, which Lucas found strange.

The sentry fumbled nervously with the keys on his belt as he led the way down the dark tunnel. They had caught him sleeping upon entering the small prison's office, which was built inside the town wall. Its entrance was located on the opposite side of the town, facing the castle and the road that ran parallel from east to west. Isaac had kicked the sentry's chair to wake him up. He had jumped up, his expression groggy and bewildered all at once. When Lucas told him why he was there and gave a description of Eli, it had sent him in a whirl of excuses and apologies.

"How was I to know?" he had said, throwing his hands up. "No one told me he was an officer. He wasn't wearing a uniform, and I trusted the tavern owner to be truthful when he complained about someone breaking mugs and being belligerent, and then passing out from intoxication."

"When were you made aware of this?" asked Lucas.

"In the early hours of this morning," stammered the sentry.

"Did he not tell you himself who he was?"

"He wasn't conscious," explained the sentry, "and he hasn't said anything since."

They walked to a cell at the very end of the hallway. The sentry's hands trembled when he stuck the key in the lock. He had seen what they could all see—Eli was lying motionless on the hard, stone ground. By the position of his body, it looked like he had not even moved after being dropped onto the floor. There was no way Eli had been drunk.

Malcolm and Isaac did not wait for Lucas's orders to go in as soon as the door opened. Throughout their search in town, Lucas had noticed the deep respect and concern the two cavalrymen had for their former officer. Respect that had been earned and not demanded. It showed that Eli had come a long way since their time together at Itan's.

They both had.

Lucas stayed outside the cell and waited for his men to tell him that Eli was alive before going in himself. The space was cramped, and Malcolm and Isaac stepped back out to allow Lucas to enter.

He kneeled next to Eli and rolled him onto his back. His body felt limp, but the movement caused his eyes to flutter.

Lucas could tell he was trying to speak. "What is it?" he whispered, leaning in. With no sound coming from his lips, Eli slowly mouthed the word *pocket* to him.

"Do you think he is sick?" Isaac asked. "Should we get Eneas?"

"Or Grant?" asked Malcolm.

Eli looked up at Lucas and parted his lips again. This time, he mouthed the words *don't* and *trust*, before closing his eyes.

Lucas contemplated Eli's words as he stood up and then shook his head. "No," he replied. "They were right—he is drunk." He noticed the disbelieving look Malcolm gave him, so he continued. "The smell of ale is all over him. See what you think." He stepped back against the wall to let the two men through and secretly put the crumpled note he had found in his trouser pocket.

It was clear to Lucas that whoever had set Eli up had been careful to cover their tracks and had poured alcohol on Eli's clothing. After the two men agreed that there indeed was an odor of ale, Lucas gave the order to have Eli carried out and watched them do so. He then addressed the sentry who had remained at a distance—no doubt because he had feared to be in serious trouble.

"What would have happened to him if we had not come here, and you had not discovered he is a king's soldier?" Lucas asked. Dastan had said people disappeared from the tavern, but he had also mentioned once that people disappeared from the prison. The emptiness of the cells would prove that. With the size of the town, the prison should have, at the very minimum, a handful of prisoners at any given time.

The sentry cleared his throat before answering. "He would have been sent with the next collection."

"When was the last one?" asked Lucas. He directed his eyes to the empty cells all around him and understood that the sentry was referring to a prisoner roundup.

"Less than a week ago."

"Really?" asked Lucas, having a hard time containing his surprise. If prisoners were sent to work on the tunnel, they would have had to pass through the castle to get there. He had not been aware of this happening. Unless there was another way into the valley or they had been taken elsewhere? He waited until Malcolm and Isaac were out of earshot before risking questioning the sentry any further. "I was not aware that the king had ordered for more tunnel workers to be sent," he stated casually.

"I would not know about that, sir," answered the sentry. "I don't receive my orders from the king."

"No, of course, you don't," said Lucas, and followed the sentry out of the prison. He could think of only one person trusted enough to speak in the name of the king, and it was becoming clear that he was up to something.

CHAPTER 9

Byram directed his horse off the eastbound road and onto a rocky path leading up into the mountains. His job was done, for now, and it was time to head home.

It was a shame, he thought, as he left the town below him, what was going to happen to the teenage boy, Eli. His father had sold him as being ruthless, determined, and driven—all the qualities he demanded from those who were to ride with him. Attributes that were running through Byram's own family's veins since the beginning of time. His bloodline was the purest. Any baby or child showing signs of weakness had been destroyed, a necessary sacrifice so that one day his family could reclaim what was rightfully theirs.

He recalled the day he was ten years old and in front of his parents' house. The house was built in the shadows of a cliff and had an ominous look about it. Sunlight could not reach it. He was chopping firewood with his two younger brothers. Only a day before, his mother had given birth to a fourth baby boy. An occasion that should have made his father happy, but instead, Byram had watched him leave the bedroom with a solemn look on his face.

"Your new brother is frail," his mother had explained when he had gone to see her, "but he will soon grow up to be big and strong." She had given him a weak smile and asked if he wanted to hold the baby.

He had sat down at the edge of the bed, and his mother had placed the baby in his arms. He had cradled it, held its little hand, and looked into the newborn's eyes. To Byram, the baby had been perfect, but to his father, he was the runt of the litter. Later, he had heard his parents argue and watched his father become more ill-tempered throughout the night. Byram had woken his brothers early the next morning and kept them out of the house by doing chores.

They had already cleaned out the stables—fed the chickens and were halfway through splitting the logs into firewood—when their mother's piercing cry reached them. It had made the hair stand up on the back of his neck, and he had frozen, the ax he'd been using wedged in the log that was on the chopping block. His brothers stood still as well and watched their father exit the house with a small, wrapped parcel in his arms. Byram realized the mistake he had made when he caught his father's angry eyes before he disappeared into the woods—he had shown weakness by letting his mother's anguish affect him. That night, he had received a beating that had caused him to never react to another human cry again and had made him into who he was today.

"We all made sacrifices," his cousin Grant had said to him just a few nights ago, as they shared stories of their childhood, "and now it is time to finish this." They were sitting at a table in the corner of a tavern where money still bought silence and secrets remained secrets.

"I'm sorry you must live in hiding," continued Grant, "but Boran still assumes you died alongside the hundred soldiers in the hunters' forest, and we gain nothing by changing that. Especially now that Lucas has made himself known to the king and taken his place beside him."

"And we *will* finish it," answered Byram. "Baelan—or Lucas, as you call him now—was the obstacle in the road. I was ready to die for the cause by leading the attack on the hunters." He took another sip from his ale and watched his cousin look at him sympathetically.

"I know you were," said Grant. "But it would not have been on Boran's orders, and you would have given your life for nothing."

"Then why did you not finish it when he gave you the order?" asked Byram, his tone harsh. "You said yourself that you had the boy on his knees. All you had to do was bring the sword down."

"It wasn't as easy as you make it sound," said Grant. "Boran retracted the order almost as quickly as he had given it, and then Eneas . . ."

"What about Eneas?"

"Eneas advised against killing him."

"What?" gasped Byram. "I thought he wanted him dead more than any of us?"

"He did, but he changed his mind. He claims there is another way."

"Another way to what?" asked Byram. "He doesn't think Lucas has to die to stop the prophecy? We were all in agreement that his death is the only path to success."

Grant cleared his throat. "We were, but what if Eneas is right and he's found a way to keep him alive? It would avoid the release of a potential curse."

Byram didn't like what he had just heard. He had spent the last several years of his life trying to accomplish the one task he'd been given and had lost dear friends in the process. "And you agreed that this would be best? You voiced your approval?"

"Yes," answered Grant reluctantly. "I did."

Byram stared at his cousin. He saw something else he didn't like—compassion. An unfortunate character flaw that ran in Grant's side of the family. He wondered if that was the true reason for allowing the boy to live. "You let that boy get to you," scolded Byram. "You like him."

Grant sighed. "There isn't much not to like about him."

"He's dangerous . . . and intelligent," said Byram. He leaned back in his chair. "I'd be surprised if he hasn't got you all figured out yet."

"Why would you suggest that?" asked Grant. "I've given him no reason to distrust me."

"I told you we nearly caught him near Lord Killeand's castle," said Byram. He shuddered at the memory. It was where he had lost his friends. Itan's decision to send the boy out alone to spy for him after his general had left him had given them the perfect opportunity. They had caught him unawares by a stream, where he was washing his hair. If only that horse of his had not come charging and they'd not made the mistake of splitting up in their pursuit. "You were at that castle," continued Byram, "to make a deal with the mercenaries."

"So I was," said Grant, "but so were Finton and Eli. It would have been them he followed there. We all know that it didn't take Itan long after that to conclude that Killeand was betraying him."

"Hmm," muttered Byram. He was not convinced, but then again, Grant was Boran's commander and handled the king's communication. Even if Grant had been seen by Lucas to go in, Grant could be right in believing Lucas thought he was nothing more than the messenger between Killeand and Boran. "You said that Eneas *thinks* the boy does not have to die to stop the prophecy," continued Byram. "Which suggests to me . . . that he is not sure?"

"No," said Grant. He paused and glanced around the tavern to make sure no one was watching or listening. "That's why I need you to do something for him." He reached inside his pocket and pulled out a small brown glass bottle that he held in the palm of his hand for a moment, before pushing it across the table.

"What is this?" asked Byram, taking the bottle. He could see the liquid inside of it and instinctively checked to see that the cork was secure. Eneas was known to experiment with poison.

"Eneas wants this tested. Eli is the subject of choice."

"Finton's son?"

"Yes."

"Why?" asked Byram. "I thought I was to take him with me when I leave here? He will be no good to me if he is compromised in any way."

"It is too late for that," said Grant. "Eneas has already been using him, and substantial damage has already been done."

"I suspect he did not tell you?"

"Of course not. Eneas knew I had other plans for Eli."

Byram rolled the little bottle around in his hand and watched the liquid move from one side to the other. "Will it kill him?" he asked.

"It shouldn't, but that's why it needs testing. Eneas believes Eli is the key, since he is an elite born and Finton once told him that King Itan believed Lucas to be one as well."

Byram put the bottle in his pocket and leaned closer towards his cousin. "What's the plan?" he asked.

CHAPTER 10

Lucas stood in front of the fireplace in his room and carefully unfolded the note. It had been important enough for Eli to direct him to it, and he felt it must have something to do with the state he had found him in. He was glad for Father Ansan's persistence in teaching him to read and write so that he could now read the words meant for Eli's eyes only.

> *I can tell you what you want to know, but not within these walls.*
>
> *Meet me in town, at The Tangled Net. Eight o'clock tonight.*
>
> *Come alone, and tell no one.*

Only nobles or those that held a high position within the army were educated, knew Lucas, and would have been able to write the note—narrowing it down to only a handful of people residing in the castle. He read the words again and studied the writing until he realized who the author was.

How foolish of him! He had been blindsided by friendly words when he should have trusted no one. He should have heeded Davis's advice to get out when he still had a chance. Especially now that Byram was alive and nearby. He was certain Byram was involved in the net that was closing in around him. But why had he not returned to his king?

He took a deep breath and dropped the note in the fire to let the flames grab hold of it. It was too dangerous to keep in his possession. If he was going to make it through this himself, he had to pretend he knew nothing of the trap set for Eli.

Lucas rested his arm on the mantel and watched the note burn. When the last piece of parchment had fallen as ash between the logs, a knock on his door brought him back from deep thought. "Come in," he called, even though the door was already opening and he knew who was entering. "The last time you came to my room, I ended up in a cage with a cougar," said Lucas. He remained to stare at the fire with his back towards the door. He was afraid that if he turned around now, Grant would notice the worried look on his face.

"Are you sure I have not stopped by for a friendly visit since then?" asked Grant.

"Not to my knowledge," answered Lucas.

"There's a first for everything, I suppose," said Grant, approaching the hearth. "Anything interesting to see in those flames?"

"It's the only moving thing I can look at," responded Lucas. He turned around and forced an innocent smile. "No window," he said, gesturing towards the outside wall.

Grant nodded and began inching his way around the room as if looking for something. He paused when he noticed the pillow and blanket on the floor and turned with a faint smile on his face. "Still sleeping on the floor?"

"From time to time," answered Lucas. "Only when I have to get up early in the morning, and I know the comfort of the bed would stop me from doing so."

“Sensible,” remarked Grant. “Maybe I should try that one day.” He walked over to the desk and glanced at the stack of parchment neatly stacked in the middle of it. He lifted a sheet from the top and held it in the light of a candle, then placed the paper down again and let his finger trace the edge of the stack to size it up.

It was obvious to Lucas that Grant was checking to see if he had used it, or maybe to determine whether he was familiar with the written word. He wondered if somehow Malcolm or Isaac had seen him take the note from Eli’s pocket and reported this to him. Fortunately, not a sheet would be missing from the stack, because Lucas never needed to convey a message in writing with Davis nearby. The parchment had appeared in his room one day, and he was pleased not to have even scribbled on it.

Seemingly satisfied, with every piece of parchment accounted for, Grant sat himself down on the edge of the desk to face him. “I heard you found Eli in the town’s prison?” he asked. He was trying his best to be his usual friendly self, but Lucas looked right past that now and finally saw the mysterious guest he had seen before. A calculating man who had been at Killeand’s to achieve something, as was the reason for his presence now. Whether it was to do Boran’s bidding or his own, Lucas had a feeling he would find out soon.

“I did,” answered Lucas. He knew Eli was the true reason why Grant had come to see him.

Grant folded his arms in front of his chest. “What made you go to the prison?”

“Just a hunch,” replied Lucas casually. “I was locked up in prison once with men charged with the crime of public disturbance and intoxication.”

“You suspected him to be drunk then?” asked Grant.

Lucas shrugged his shoulders. “Why else would he have gone into town?”

"Have you seen him drunk before?" asked Grant.

"Eli and I had a completely different upbringing," answered Lucas. "I was a chosen, and he was an elite born. They had privileges we could only dream of, fine liquors being only one of them, yet I never had the pleasure of seeing him miserable from the effect of too much ale, until yesterday, when the king asked me to find him."

"Did he talk to you?" asked Grant, not letting the subject go.

"Who?" asked Lucas, trying his best to sound oblivious.

"Eli? Did he say anything to you?"

"No," answered Lucas, raising his voice as to give the impression that he was getting frustrated. "I am sure Malcolm could have told you that." Lucas saw a bewildered look appear on Grant's face and realized he might have reacted too strongly. "I'm sorry," he apologized, sighing deeply. "It's been a long day, and I'm exhausted. The last thing I needed this afternoon was rescuing Eli from the depths of darkness when I must be fit and ready to train the cavalry again first thing tomorrow."

Grant unfolded his arms and placed his hands on either side of him on the edge of the desk. "You are right," he said, and pushed himself off. "I'm sorry for keeping you from your sleep." He walked towards the door and gave Lucas a friendly slap on his shoulder—an innocent touch that suddenly caused a flash of images to enter Lucas's mind. The same thing had happened to him when King Itan had touched him after the king's mark ceremony.

The images came fast and made him feel dizzy. It took all his strength to remain standing. He could not let Grant know what was happening to him. "Did you see Eli?" he asked, before Grant could leave the room.

"Not yet," answered Grant. "I only spoke with Finton, and he did not seem pleased after speaking with his son."

"Eli is awake, then?"

"Yes," answered Grant. "Confined to his room until the king decides if he is to receive any punishment."

"I probably should have left him where he was then," commented Lucas. "Eli will be furious with me for bringing him back."

"Best to stay away from him then," replied Grant, grabbing the door handle. "Goodnight, Lucas."

Before the door was even closed, Lucas dropped one knee to the ground. He placed his elbows on his other leg and supported his head in his hands. He could no longer hold the image off that tried to push itself into his mind. He closed his eyes, allowing himself to see—he was standing in the bailey of Boran's castle with his back towards the gates. People were emerging from every building, confused as to what was going on. They glanced around as if to seek answers from those who had already formed the crowd in front of him and were staring in his direction. Lucas saw Grant stand near him—his eyes wide and his mouth dropped open as he looked at the ground before Lucas. Behind Grant, King Boran halted, his face red with anger. Next to the king stood Eneas, smiling a wicked smile.

Lucas lowered his head and stared at the sword he was holding in his hand—blood dripping from the blade. He let go of the hilt and watched it slowly fall to the ground, as if time had slowed. When it hit the sand, grass sprouted up around the sword, and Lucas knew he was no longer in the bailey—a second image had come into his mind. A wind was blowing, and he could feel the warm sun on his skin. He looked around at the unfamiliar landscape of green rolling hills, rocky outcrops, and the bodies of soldiers strewn all around—Boran's soldiers.

Lucas held his breath, taking in the massacre that had taken place. Boran's army looked to have been caught unaware, with some soldiers not even having time to pull their swords from their sheath before being slaughtered. A gentle breeze was tugging on loose pieces of clothing and banners attached to poles placed into the ground. Lucas stepped over a dozen bodies until he came to a fallen soldier who was clutching something in one hand. He kneeled beside him and pulled on the green material until it came free. It was an intricately woven piece of cloth that had been torn from another soldier's tunic, no doubt in the last moments right before death . . .

Lucas lay on top of the covers on his bed. He felt hot, and the heavy feeling in his chest was preventing him from falling asleep. He had tried to erase the images of dead soldiers with throats slashed from his mind for hours, but he had not been able to. He decided he might as well get up and swung his legs over the edge of his bed. He ran his fingers through his hair and sighed deeply before standing up to get dressed.

The halls were empty when he stepped outside his room a short time later. Through the windows on the landing, he could see it was not dawn yet. His stomach growled, having missed dinner the night before, and he decided to try the kitchen to see if the basket of apples was left out, as it sometimes was. If he were lucky, he might find the kitchen staff already at work, and he could get an early breakfast.

He made his way down the spiraling stairs of the tower and turned right at the bottom, entering a wide hallway. He walked past the chapel and glanced through the open door. The sun had started to rise over the mountains, and its rays were shining on the pictures of Boran's descendants on the stained glass windows. Lucas stopped in his tracks and stared at the clearest picture of them all. A king on his horse, a green and blue banner flying high above him. That was not right. Boran's colors were blue and yellow.

His hunger forgotten, Lucas entered the chapel and made his way closer to the windows behind the altar. He looked at the last picture on his right, where a king stood in a garden surrounded by flowers—Boran's father. It was hard to imagine that a man who devoted his life to creating the beautiful gardens was also the man responsible for the death of his parents and the destruction of their village. The picture before him had to be that of King Rodin. Filled with greed, he had made the people work in the mines instead of farming the land to provide food for their families. This had been the cause for the rising of another king, Itan's grandfather. Rodin was sitting on a throne Lucas recognized all too well—the one with the inlaid gems Boran used in his private quarters. Before him, different kings had ruled—all protected and defended by the mountain people, but why? What was their connection?

"Lucas?" asked someone in a soft tone behind him. "What are you looking at?"

Lucas peered over his shoulder to see Valora push herself upright in one of the pews and rub her eyes as if she had just woken. "The kings in these pictures," he answered as he turned back to the stained-glass windows. "My people used to defend them."

Valora scooted her bottom along the bench and stood beside him as he looked up at the last panels on the right. "Do you know why?" she asked, following his gaze.

"No," answered Lucas. "That's what I'm trying to find out. The story of my people started with a fight over leadership between two brothers. There was a warrior by the name of Yric who killed his older brother and angered the gods. That same night, a large black stone fell from the sky, and Yric himself died the next day when he set out to destroy what the gods had sent. Arak had been the first leader chosen by the stone, but he wasn't a king." He paused and glanced along the windows. "I never questioned how the first king came about," he said.

"The kings are in the order of succession," said Valora. "I look at their pictures every night, and I think you might like to see the first window on the left."

Lucas followed Valora as she walked toward the left and paused by the picture of the king on his horse. Again, he noted the colors of the banner. Green and blue. The two kings who succeeded him had the same colors. Then it changed to just blue, and by the time Rodin came to power, the banner's colors were blue and yellow. "The king's colors change," remarked Lucas.

"Yes," said Valora, looking up as she continued to walk. "The oldest kings all have blue and green as their colors, except for the second king, where the banner is a solid green."

Lucas recalled the piece of cloth he had pulled from the soldier's hand in his dream. "What about the first king?" he asked.

"He doesn't show any colors," answered Valora, stopping beneath the windows on the far left. "Unless you want to count the color of his tunic." She stretched her right arm and pointed upwards. "Does that image show the story of your people?"

Lucas stopped beside her and gasped. "It certainly does," he answered, looking at the window that was the only one split in two. On the lower half, he saw a man dressed in a plain green tunic, kneeling before a warrior holding a sword. Above it, the nightly sky with a fireball falling to the ground—the stone.

Lucas gasped. "That's what I was missing when considering how the first king came to be," he said excitedly. "It wasn't by choice of the people. It was the stone. Not only had it chosen the leaders of my people, but it had chosen the first king." He looked at Valora. His heart started racing, and the fluttery feeling in his stomach returned when he saw her soft eyes and caring smile. Before he could stop himself, he pulled her closer and lifted her chin to kiss her tenderly on the lips.

Valora placed her hands on his chest as if wanting to push him away but then gave in and returned his affection.

For what seemed like an eternity, Lucas held Valora as if time stood still and nothing mattered, but then let go and stepped back. "Valora," he said. "I'm sorry, I . . ."

"No," said Valora. "Don't apologize. I wanted it as well. It's just that you and I, we can't . . ."

"Maybe not now," said Lucas, "but one day."

Valora shook her head. "Don't make promises you can't keep. King Boran will never let me go." She averted her eyes and gestured to the first stained glass window. "You think the warrior holding the sword is Arak?" she asked, changing the subject before Lucas could say anything else.

Lucas slowly took her eyes off her and nodded. "I think so," he answered, looking up.

"And the man kneeling before him . . . the first king?"

"Yes," said Lucas. A thought came to him, and he looked around before directing his eyes to the stone floor. In between the smaller tiles, he saw larger ones with inscriptions—names, and dates of kings who rested in their crypts below.

"What is it?" asked Valora when Lucas lifted a torch from a sconce on one of the central columns.

"I need to find the tomb of the first king," he answered, aiming the light across the floor as he walked up and down. There was no order in the dates. He read the names of every past king, but was not sure what he was looking for. The names meant little to him. He then counted the windows and the number of crypts below the floor. "They don't match," he spoke out loud to himself.

"What doesn't match?" asked Valora, who had followed him.

"The number of windows and the tombs of kings," answered Lucas. "There's one extra window. One more king should have a grave below, but for some reason, doesn't." He rested with his back against a column and let his eyes glance over the long wall of the chapel. It was bare of the sort of plaques or statues that were so vividly present in other parts of the castle. Likewise, these walls were not covered with plaster, exposing the stones that built them. Large, solid blocks that one would use to build a defensive outer wall for a castle or a town. The chapel was located deep inside the castle. There was no need for such thick walls. Unless . . .

Lucas stepped away from the column and turned to follow it upwards. Every column inside the chapel was plastered and connected with an elaborately decorated arch. None of them gave any support to the ceiling, suggesting it was built much later and only for the intended purpose to transform a plain chapel into something more awe-inspiring. It could explain why the first king was not underneath the chapel. The crypts could have been a much later addition as well. His grave would be outside or, just maybe . . . Lucas looked at the altar that was covered with a blue silk sheet and rushed towards it. It had the unmistakable shape and length of something he had seen before in the monastery chapel.

He grabbed the edge of the silk sheet and pulled it off to reveal the sarcophagus underneath. Lucas stepped back and stared mesmerized at the family crest engraved on the side of it—a double-headed battle axe over a green background. Not Boran's family crest. Or at least not the one they were using now. He got down on one knee when Valora stopped behind him and let his fingers follow the outline of the battle axe blade. "I've seen this crest before," he mumbled. "Three times, to be exact."

"Where?" asked Valora, looking over his shoulder.

"The first time was when the stone showed me the history of my people during my ceremony to become a master warrior," answered Lucas. He remembered standing on top of the stone as Yric approached him. He had held his sword in one hand, but in the other, he had been holding a shield with the same crest that was on this sarcophagus. It could not be him who was resting here. The timing did not fit, but the family crest had lived on after the stone killed him. Had there been another brother . . . or a son?

"The second time," he continued, "I saw this crest on a banner belonging to Lord Hammond. Hammond had come to King Itan's castle to renew the alliance treaty." Lucas recalled helping him off his horse. He had been friendly and kind—for a lord. Lucas had discovered the plot that was to see Lord Hammond poisoned, and so prevented his murder. He had suspected Lord Killeand to be responsible but always wondered what his motivation could have been.

"What about the third time?" asked Valora. "Where was that?"

Lucas lowered his head to think and stared at the floor. He couldn't believe he had not made the connection. Not once in all these weeks that he had been around Grant had he thought of it—the wax seal that he had found in the lining of the saddlebag when he had searched his room at Killeand's castle. He had discarded it, and had only made an imprint of the seal that had turned out to be Boran's. Why would Grant have had Hammond's seal?

"Lucas?" asked Valora when he didn't answer.

"It doesn't matter," answered Lucas, rising to his feet. He thought it best not to mention Grant, lest he endanger Valora by entangling her in something sinister. "I saw it on something at another lord's castle—a long way from here."

Valora gave a fleeting glance toward the exit of the chapel when the sound of an iron bucket swinging on its hinges as it was carried passed by in the hallway. "The first maids' shift is starting," she said. "I must go and clean the ashes from the hearths and light new fires in the rooms before everyone gets up."

Lucas nodded and watched her leave. He liked Valora. She was the first girl who moved him in ways he had never felt before. If only their circumstances were different. He sighed and pushed the thought of Valora from his mind. He walked around the sarcophagus and read the name engraved in large letters on the other side—*Ulmerson.* The name meant little to him, except that the town was called Ulmer. He would have to find a way to get some answers to his questions. But first, he had to deal with the hunger that churned in the pit of his stomach, and he covered the sarcophagus up again.

It was still early when he entered the kitchen. Only a handful of staff members were present and had started the preparations for the day. A single pot of porridge was already bubbling on the stove, leftovers from the day before, given to early risers and guards coming off night-shifts. The king always requested fresh bread for breakfast, and Lucas could see the fires already burning inside the chambers of the ovens. It would be at least another hour before the ashes could be removed, and the ovens would be hot enough for baking.

Lucas grabbed two wooden bowls and spoons from a cupboard and walked over to the stove. No one was paying him any attention or coming over to assist him, but it was not unusual for officers to help themselves. Their busy schedules often prevented them from attending the posted eating times. The cavalry's early morning schedule of late had made Lucas a regular visitor to eat in the kitchen. Except that, this morning, he had no intention of going straight to the stables after. He needed to speak with Eli first.

He used a ladle to scoop porridge in each bowl and added honey to sweeten it. A luxury for the privileged he had only recently become accustomed to since arriving at Boran's castle.

He settled at a small table and ate fast, since he did not have much time. The rest of the castle would be waking soon. He placed his empty bowl in a large sink and picked up the other bowl to take with him.

The guard outside Eli's room was dozing against the wall but immediately stood to attention as soon as he heard Lucas approach.

"Breakfast," said Lucas, "for Eli."

"I will make sure he gets it," replied the guard, "but I cannot let you in."

"That works for me," said Lucas. "I'll stay outside, and you can go in and watch him eat."

The guard looked at him, confused. "Why would I do that?"

"Did they not tell you?" asked Lucas.

"Tell me what?"

"Eli has this condition," explained Lucas. "It compromises his breathing, which causes him to pass out. It's likely what contributed to the debilitating attack he experienced when in town. There is still a chance he has not fully recovered, and he could choke on his food, so someone has to watch him."

"And what if he chokes?"

Lucas shrugged his shoulders. "Then you will have to help him. You do know how to stop someone from dying when they choke, right?"

"Of course," answered the guard resolutely, yet his body language showed differently. He looked worried and took a step back when Lucas held the bowl out to him. "Maybe you should do it," he said. "It's best if I remain on my post." Before Lucas could respond, the guard had already opened the door and stepped aside.

Eli's room was twice the size of his own. The bed that stood in the left corner was a large four-poster with a blue canopy, and he had ample space for both a desk and a table. By the fireplace stood a comfortable chair, and on the opposite wall was a large window, which Eli stood in front of. When he realized Lucas was alone, he began to approach him, but Lucas gestured to the door behind him and put a finger to his lips. He could see the guard on the other side with his ear pressed against the door.

"I brought you breakfast," said Lucas, loud enough for the guard to hear. "You must be hungry," he continued and put the bowl down on the table with a thud.

"Thank you," said Eli. He scraped the chair over the floor as if he were going to sit down. Lucas waved him over to the far corner on the right side of the room. Once there, they huddled close together, so that their voices would not carry.

"Does anyone know you're here?" whispered Eli.

"Only the guard outside," answered Lucas. "No one else."

Eli nodded, wringing his hands. His face looked clammy from sweat, and he was trembling.

"What's wrong?" asked Lucas. He was not used to seeing Eli like this.

"Someone jumped me in an alley and forced one of Eneas's elixirs down my throat," replied Eli angrily. "I know everyone thinks that I was drunk."

"I don't," said Lucas. "I found the note in your pocket, and I know it was a setup. You had ale spilled on your clothes to make it look that way. Grant even came to my room last night to see if I believed that story."

"Grant?" asked Eli, surprised.

Lucas nodded. "He was the one who wrote the note. I recognized his handwriting."

Eli shook his head. "My father told me last night that your days here are numbered—after first giving me a lecture on excessive drinking. I think the original plan had been for me to go inside the tavern and have the elixir slipped into my drink. I would never have known what happened and would probably have believed him when he told me I passed out drunk."

"Then your father knew about it?"

"Clearly," answered Eli. "I was suspicious of that and knew it could be a trap. I was curious to see who would be sent for me to meet, so I watched the tavern from the alley across the road. I had no intention of going in. But they must have spotted me, and it changed the plan. Someone snuck up on me, and before I knew it, I was thrown to the ground and pinned down. The elixir was forced down my throat." Eli averted his eyes to avoid looking Lucas in the eye, as if embarrassed to admit his defeat.

"Did you get a look at your attacker?" asked Lucas. He was surprised someone had been able to take Eli down. He was lean and muscular, and on top of that, he was a highly trained soldier. Not an easy target for just anyone.

"Yes," answered Eli, "but I didn't recognize him. He was dressed in all black, extraordinarily strong, and I remember his eyes to be very blue."

"Byram," concluded Lucas. It also explained the success of the attack. He had nearly been taken down by members of the dark order, in the woodshed of the Black Log Inn, a long time ago. "You were taken down by a member of the dark order."

"Dark order?" asked Eli. "They're all supposed to be dead."

"Yes," answered Lucas, "only this one appears to be hard to kill. During the ambush in the forest, I saw Byram go down with two arrows in his chest. They had looked fatal, but now I regret not checking to make sure he was dead myself. I left it up to the hunters to go through the fern field and kill every soldier still alive."

"He can't have been with the dark order," said Eli, shaking his head. "Boran would have had him return to the castle."

"I don't think Boran knows Byram is alive, but Grant clearly does," said Lucas. Then a thought came to his mind. "Did you tell your father about the attack?" he asked.

"Of course," answered Eli. "I wasn't going to let him lecture me on something I wasn't guilty of. I told him I knew he was involved with Eneas and that I needed him to tell me what he had gotten himself into."

"What did he say to that?" asked Lucas. He wished Eli had played ignorant and kept quiet, but could sense by the tone of Eli's voice that he had more to tell.

"He squirmed a little, and tried to deny it at first," said Eli. "I wanted the truth. I told him I was ready to confront Eneas about everything and he told me to keep quiet. That it was all over, and I would be fine as long as I didn't say anything. He told me I had been a necessary sacrifice for Eneas to find a way to take you down."

"With what?" asked Lucas. "He knows he can't kill me."

"He's not going to," answered Eli. "When I didn't react to my father telling me that Eneas was planning to stop you, my father must have assumed I still hated you. He started telling me everything. Our mutual hatred for you is what bonded us in the past, and I think he relished the thought that we were back there." He paused and looked Lucas directly in the eye. "I don't hate you—not anymore. We have both been misled and betrayed."

"I'm listening," said Lucas.

"My father told me that, years ago, Eneas found a way to control people's minds with an elixir that he created," started Eli. "They laced the tunnel workers' food with it—that's how they work as hard as they do. They don't even need to be supervised by soldiers. It takes their willpower away. Makes them compliant. Boran ordered the same elixir to be put in your food on the first day you arrived here, but they were all shocked when you were not affected by it."

"That explains the invitation to dinner that night," said Lucas. "I found it odd to be treated as a guest when other signs indicated me to be very much a prisoner."

"Yes," said Eli. "I remember being confused about that."

"Did they know *why* it had no effect on me?"

"Not at first," answered Eli. "They tried it for two more days with the food that was brought to your room, but then Eneas wondered if it was your different blood that made you resistant. My father told him that he had always suspected you to be an elite born—not a chosen. If that were to be true, then my blood would be the same as yours."

"Let me guess," said Lucas. "They tried it on you?"

"Yes," answered Eli. "Without me knowing about it."

"When was this?"

"Before they put you through the test in the arena."

"The elixir didn't work on you?" guessed Lucas.

Eli shook his head. "No," he answered, "it didn't."

"Then what happened?"

"Eneas set out to create a much stronger, more potent elixir that would affect our blood," continued Eli. "When you impressed everyone with the cougar, Boran changed his mind and told him to stop."

"Except he didn't?"

"No," answered Eli. "My father said that it made Eneas even more determined to improve the elixir. There was a fine line to navigate between disabling the victim and killing them. The new, more potent formula needed testing, and the king was not to know about it. That's when my father became involved. Eneas knew my father hated you and that one of my father's men had just betrayed him. My father agreed to let Eneas try the new elixir on Winslow since he cared little about the effect it would have on him. The elixir proved too strong for Winslow. My father said it made him lose his mind completely." Eli stopped and looked at Lucas for a reaction. "But you already knew this?"

"I saw Winslow near the tunnel," answered Lucas. "It was clear to me that he was not of sane mind, but I didn't know what had happened to him, except that his sudden state of insanity couldn't be a coincidence."

"Yes, and now Eneas was ready to try it on you," explained Eli. "According to my father, he was excited when they brought you to him with the snake bite. It gave him the perfect opportunity. If anything had gone wrong, he could have blamed it on the snake's venom."

"If he tried it on me," said Lucas, "it didn't work."

"Oh, it did," corrected Eli. "Eneas told my father that it had made you sick because your body was working hard to reject it. It made him believe he was getting closer, and so he kept making it stronger. Remember how you kept getting sick at dinner for days?"

"I do," answered Lucas, shuddering at the memory of it. "He told me it was the effect of the snake venom lingering in my system."

Eli nodded. "But you became doubtful of that, and so did the king," continued Eli. "Eneas knew he had to stop. That's when they switched the testing over to me."

"Your father agreed to this?" asked Lucas. He knew Finton's hatred for him ran deep, but to allow Eneas to test a poison on his son that would make him sick or, even worse, could have him end up like Winslow was more than Lucas could ever have expected. "I'm sorry," said Lucas when he noticed Eli's somber face. "I had no idea. If I had known . . ."

"You weren't to know. Only my father and Eneas knew."

Lucas stared at him, confused. "Grant wrote the note to you, so he must have known what Eneas was up to?"

Eli shook his head. "Grant didn't become involved until a few days ago when he noticed me acting differently. Like you, he saw me at the stables and made the connection that Eneas was responsible. He was furious that Eneas had gone behind the king's back, but Eneas convinced him that it would solve the problem of keeping you away from Boran during the battle with King Itan. If Itan gets killed, Boran will be the only king left. Eneas told Grant he had one final test to do, and it was Grant who came up with the idea to do it away from the castle."

Everything was starting to make sense now. "We need to get you out of here," Lucas told Eli. They had been talking for a while, and the guard outside was growing restless—Lucas could see him shifting his weight from foot to foot and glancing over his shoulder towards the door.

Eli reached out, placing a hand on Lucas's forearm. "It's you who needs to leave the castle as soon as possible. They have what they want now. This last elixir they tried on me, it's the worst. It made me black out, but then I found myself in a nightmare from which I could not wake. I could hear everything said around me, but couldn't move. It was like being trapped underneath the wheel of a wagon with your mouth sewn shut."

"I can't leave," said Lucas. "Not yet at least. Boran will have the army start heading towards the tunnel in a few days. That will give me time to deal with Eneas."

"What about Grant?"

"He's the reason why you need to get out of here—today!"

Eli looked perplexed. "Why?" asked Eli. "I will just keep my head down as my father told me and not say anything."

"That may have worked if you had gone inside the tavern and had accepted that you had simply become drunk," said Lucas. "But you did not, and you saw Byram. If I'm right and Grant knew Byram was alive but did not share this with Boran, he has a reason for it. He'll want to keep it that way."

"I have a guard outside my room," said Eli. "How am I supposed to escape?"

Lucas walked towards the window and looked out. "You will have to climb."

"Are you out of your mind?" asked Eli, joining him to look outside. "It's too far down."

"You'll have to climb up," said Lucas, looking up at the edge of the roof that started not far above them. Eli would be tall enough to reach the stone rain gutter if he stood on the windowsill, and strong enough to pull himself up.

"You want me to climb onto the roof?" asked Eli. "And then what? The castle walls are guarded and too high to jump off. Even if I could manage all that, I'll never make it without a horse."

"That's why you will start climbing as soon as I leave this room," said Lucas. "Head towards the stables and hide between the hay bales on the loft. In less than an hour, I'll be taking the second cavalry out for training. We'll be the only ones out. As soon as the men are gathered in the arena, I need you to get on the horse I will have saddled for you and ride towards the gates."

Eli shook his head. "You think they will just open the gates for me?"

"No," answered Lucas. "But you won't be asking. Every morning around seven, the gates are opened to allow the delivery of milk and eggs from the farm. When that happens, you'll have to be ready."

"That sounds too simple," said Eli. "It will never work."

"I don't think you have a choice," said Lucas.

Eli sighed and peeked out of the window again. "How long do I have?" he asked. "To make it to the stables?"

"No more than twenty minutes," answered Lucas.

Eli stretched his arms and rolled his shoulders to loosen them up. He breathed out loudly through pursed lips. "I'd best start climbing then."

Lucas nodded and was starting to leave the room when something else came to his mind. He turned back around and saw Eli already sitting on the windowsill, looking up to see how he was going to tackle the climb. "Eli?" asked Lucas. "Who will be taking over from Lord Hammond if he dies?"

Eli lowered his head and frowned. "His brother," he answered. "Eylgar Hammond."

"Have you met him before?"

"No," answered Eli. "I don't think I have. Why?"

"There's no time. I'll have to tell you later," said Lucas, and headed to the door.

CHAPTER 11

Lucas was the last one to walk his horse into the arena. After returning the emptied porridge bowl to the kitchen, he had consumed a cup of hot milk while following Eli's precarious climb with his mind. The act delayed him from saddling his horse while the cavalry was there and would allow him to saddle a second one without anyone seeing him do so. He was glad for the rigorous training King Itan had put them both through, for Eli had made it look relatively easy—careful with choosing crevices between stones but fast in pulling himself up once he had made his choices. Confident Eli was going to make it to the stables unseen and before the changing of the guards, Lucas finished his milk and stepped out into the bailey to head over himself. He let his eyes wander towards the distant high cliffs in front of the castle and then upwards to the still-visible moon in the sky. Half-moon was in two nights, when Davis was to be back.

Lucas stopped when he reached the center of the arena and turned his horse around to face the entrance like the cavalry behind him. He took his time checking his horse's tack, all the while watching the cavalry with his mind. Malcolm observed him with interest from the first row. Lucas was not surprised—he had never been late.

He stifled a fake yawn to make it look as if he had just woken not long ago as he glanced at the lined-up cavalry.

"Late night, sir?" asked Isaac, a compassionate smile lingering on his face. He was sitting on his horse next to Malcolm.

Lucas turned to him. He had one foot in the stirrup when he heard a guard shout from the wall to open the gate for a delivery. Lucas froze for a second—the wagon was earlier than expected—then continued to pull himself up into the saddle. "Prepare to ride out," he ordered loudly. He could only hope Eli would hear him and wait until he had taken the cavalry out of the arena and past the stables to the back of the castle before taking his chance to escape through the front gates. He shortened his reins and was ready to spur his horse forward when he saw a horse and rider leave the stables opposite the arena. Eli.

Lucas stopped his horse and turned it sideways to block the view of the bailey, but he was too late.

"Sir!" called Malcolm. "Was that Eli who just rode past?"

"I don't know," lied Lucas, leaning over and pretending to adjust the stirrup strap. "What if it was?" He could hear the gates starting to swing open and the wheels of the farmer's wagon rolling in.

"Eli is not allowed to leave the castle, sir," replied Malcolm.

"By whose orders?" asked Lucas, turning his horse around to face Malcolm and the rest of the cavalry. He had not considered Malcolm. No cavalry would have dared to speak to their officer the way Malcolm just did unless they were taking direct orders from higher up, and Lucas didn't think it could be the king's orders—when told of Eli's intoxication the night before, Boran had expressed not wanting to waste another minute of his time on Eli. He would have been glad for Eli's self-imposed riddance. Malcolm was Grant's man—there was no doubt about it.

"Commander Grant, sir," answered Malcolm, confirming Lucas's suspicion. "He gave specific orders that no one was to leave the castle until he returns."

"Grant left?"

Malcolm nodded. "He went into town and is due back later this morning."

The news that Grant was not at the castle came as a surprise to Lucas, and he wondered what business prompted him to ride out after dark, but if he was due back anytime, it could jeopardize Eli's escape. Lucas looked at the waiting cavalry and Malcolm's watchful eyes. A gentle wind started to blow, playing a game with the sand. Some of the horses tossed their heads in the air to avoid sand entering their nostrils. He took a moment to think, then quickly dismounted. He would have to find another way to get Eli out.

Lucas walked his horse over to Isaac and handed him the reins. "Have everyone walk their horses around the arena to warm them up," he told him. "This will not take long."

When Lucas walked into the bailey, he could see Eli's horse prancing in front of the guards who were blocking the way. Eli himself tried to hold it together, but sweat droplets on the side of his face showed he was nervous and eager to get going.

"Eli!" called Lucas.

Eli turned and rode over to him, his face pale and drawn. "The guards won't let me through," he said quietly. "Grant's orders, apparently."

Lucas grabbed hold of the horse's bridle and stepped closer so no one could hear. "I know," he said. "Malcolm just told me he gave that order last night. We must find another way to get you out."

Eli shook his head wildly. "No," he said. "I'm in danger here. You told me so yourself." He looked at the guards, who had started to close the gates. "You're an officer," he said, turning back to Lucas. "Tell them the order doesn't apply to senior staff and to let me through."

"You know I can't do that," hissed Lucas softly. "I don't have that kind of authority, and even if the guards did obey me, Grant will know I was involved in your escape."

"Then come with me."

Lucas looked at the farmer's wagon, which was coming back after having dropped off its cargo. He was tempted to get his horse and follow Eli out, but Malcolm was likely under order to stop him. "I can't," he said. "Together, we won't make it far, but you should go."

He took a step back when the farmer's wagon rolled past him and signaled to the senior guard. "Open the gates to let the wagon out."

"Sir?" asked the guard, gesturing to Eli still sitting on his horse.

"My apologies. I understand I am not to leave," said Eli, taking his feet from the stirrups. He dropped the reins on his horse's neck and held his hands high to show his intent to dismount. "I must have misunderstood the order given last night, but Lucas just explained it to me."

Seemingly convinced, the guard turned around and gave the signal for the gate to be opened.

"Get ready," said Lucas when the guards grabbed hold of the wooden gate panels. "You'll have to be really quick."

Eli nodded and subtly rested his boots back on the edge of the stirrups. "If rank had not divided us," he said softly, "we might have made a half-decent team."

"It's not too late for that," said Lucas as the gate opened and the road outside the castle came into view. "Stay safe, and we might meet again."

Eli gave him a nod and gripped his reins when the farmer's wagon started to leave. He was ready to ride out when a booming voice echoed behind them and made them both look over their shoulders. Finton was coming across the bailey with long strides—waving his hands at the guards and shouting for them to close the gates immediately.

"Go quickly," said Lucas. The guards, likely confused, had turned their heads and were looking at the wagon, which was driving leisurely through the entrance. "You can still make it."

He watched Eli spur his horse forward and waited for him to be on his way before turning to face Finton. How he was going to handle this one, he had no idea. Finton was red-faced and wide-eyed with fury now that his son was headed for the gates.

"He has made his choice, Finton," Lucas called out. "Let him choose his life's path."

Finton diverted his gaze from the gates and looked at him with more hatred than Lucas ever recalled seeing in him. Even the rage he'd shown after the chosen had rebelled against the elite borns was nothing compared to this. Finton marched towards him, pulling his cloak aside to reveal a dagger. Lucas held his breath and contemplated his options. Backing away and calling for guards to intervene was the most sensible thing to do. Boran didn't approve of any fighting amongst his men, and he could not afford to get into any trouble. With Finton approaching fast, Lucas was about to call for assistance when he noticed Eli had halted his horse just outside the gates. He was looking down the road, his horse prancing nervously beneath him. Following his gaze, Lucas saw what had made him stop—it was not his father, but Grant, approaching the castle at full speed. Eli peered over his shoulder, unsure of what to do, but Lucas had no time to worry about him. With Finton now upon him and too late to call the guards, Lucas put his hand on the hilt of his sword.

Just then, a horse came running up from behind, and he saw Eli jump from the saddle as it passed by. Eli landed directly in between Lucas and Finton, stumbling and falling forward against his father's chest. At that moment, Lucas felt everything around him stop.

Eli and his father stood frozen for a moment, staring at each other. Then, Eli stepped back, and they both looked down. Shock flashed across Finton's face as Eli dropped to his knees with his hands pressed against his stomach, before falling to the ground.

Lucas stared at the blood on the dagger in Finton's hand. When he raised his head to look him in the eye, Lucas saw no sadness, no remorse—only darkness . . . and blame. Finton was blaming him for what had happened to his son. He watched him raise the knife and point it towards him.

In the sky above, dark clouds were forming, and thunder clapped in the distance.

"Don't do this," said Lucas, lowering his hand towards his sword when his warning found no ears. He saw people emerge from every door of every building and heard the cavalry ride out of the arena, alarmed by Finton's earlier shouts to close the gates.

Finton let out a scream of rage and, with his face contorted by the years of built-up anger and frustration, he charged like a mad man. Lucas felt he had no choice but to respond in the only way he could.

Stopped by the sword that pierced his body, Finton stood only inches from Lucas. He no longer showed any rage and stood calm, as if life had already left him. He looked down to where Eli lay on the ground and heard his soft groaning.

"He will live," said Lucas quietly. "The wound is not a mortal one."

Finton slowly turned his head towards him. "You know this to be true?" he asked. His face looked pale, and he struggled to breathe.

"I do," answered Lucas. "His death will serve me no purpose."

"I was never a believer of the prophecy," stammered Finton. "And Eli . . ." Finton spat blood from his mouth and was unable to finish the sentence.

"It doesn't matter what you believe," said Lucas. "Every one of us has a role to play to see the prophecy fulfilled."

Finton slowly nodded. There was total silence in the bailey when he directed his gaze towards the storm above and took his last breath.

Lucas released the hilt of his sword, catching Finton in his arms and lowering him gently to the ground.

Grant rode in and jumped from his horse. His eyes grew wide when he stopped and saw what Lucas had done.

Behind Grant, King Boran halted, his face turning red with anger. Lucas knew he'd just lost what little trust he had gained from either man. Next to the king stood Eneas, a subtle smile tugging at the corners of his mouth.

Lucas lowered his head and stared at his sword laying on the ground—Finton's blood still dripping from the blade. It was as if time stood still. Then the heavens opened, and lightning flashed through the sky.

With the kitchen staff and servants running to seek shelter from the rain, Lucas heard his horse's loud neigh and raised his head. He connected with his horse, watching as it broke free from Isaac's hold. As Lucas urged the horse across the bailey, Boran shouted for the guards to close the gates. Lucas turned to face his fast approaching horse and, as he did so, he felt his legs kicked out from underneath him. He fell to the ground, lifting his head to watch his horse run past and make its narrow escape through the closing gap between the gates. All he could hope for now was that, with the chaos at hand and Eli needing immediate medical assistance, no one would feel inclined to go after his horse and find out where he had just sent it. He tried to push himself up, but someone was pinning him down with a knee on his back.

"I don't think I can allow you to leave the castle," he heard Grant's voice say.

"What gave you the impression that I would?" asked Lucas.

"You made your horse break free."

"Horses spook."

"They do," said Grant, taking his weight off and helping Lucas up. "But not when you can control them, and I know you do."

Lucas said nothing and let the silence hang between them. He saw Boran staring at him from across the bailey and watched as he abruptly turned around to go inside. With the rain turning the bailey into a muddy mess, Lucas watched as Finton's body was scooped up by his arms and legs and carried off like a sack of grain. It was a sad sight. He had been a respected general with Itan but had never regained that prestige under Boran. Even with all that Finton had put him through, Lucas felt he deserved better.

Grant told him to follow and had two guards walk closely behind him. He glanced at Eli, who was being loaded onto a stretcher as they went past.

"I understand he was trying to leave this morning," said Grant, looking back over his shoulder. "That is what brought you to the gates?"

"It was," answered Lucas.

"Did he give you a reason for his hasty departure?"

"Not with too many words," answered Lucas. It was clear to him that Grant suspected he could be involved. He would have to be careful with his response. "Just that he needed to get away from his father."

"And you allowed the gates to be opened?"

"Not at first."

"What changed your mind?"

"Don't know," lied Lucas. "I guess I didn't mind seeing the back of him. He has caused me enough headaches over the years. But he seemed so desperate, like he feared for his life, and a part of me pitied him."

They stepped inside the castle and were silent the rest of the way. When they reached Boran's private quarters, Grant instructed Lucas to wait outside with the guards, and went in alone.

Lucas expected he would be asked to enter soon after, but that did not appear to be the case. He paced a little, with the guards watching his every move. It reminded him of when he first came to the castle, and he was unsure of Boran's intentions. Except for this time, he didn't think it was the king he should be watching. Moving closer to the door, he casually leaned against the wall. He could hear talking inside and focused his mind to listen.

"I am telling you," said Eneas, directing his words to the king, who was pacing back and forth from his chair to the window, "the forces of darkness were at play here. They have possessed him, are controlling him, and he will become more dangerous if you do nothing. It may well be that he was sent here by the gods—to fight by your side as you have come to believe—but that changed when the serpent's venom entered his body and affected his mind."

Boran stopped pacing and scratched his neck. He turned to Grant, who had been standing quietly with his hands folded behind his back. "You have spent a great deal of time with him. What do you think?"

Grant let go of his hands and shrugged. "To be honest," he started, "I'm not sure what to make of this morning's events. It would have been easy for him to deflect Finton's attack with his fighting capabilities, and I don't know why he didn't. We all know the history between the two of them, but I never expected Lucas to kill him."

"Then you don't believe he acted as himself?" asked Boran.

"It's possible," answered Grant. "He's been acting unusual of late, more quick to react, so last night I went to see him in his room."

"And?" asked Boran, sitting himself down in his chair.

"I didn't notice anything amiss," said Grant. "He seemed preoccupied with something, maybe, but claimed he was tired. I left it at that."

Having heard enough, Lucas pushed himself away from the wall and walked over to a window on the opposite side. The storm had passed, and the sun was shining behind the yellow stained glass. He rested his hands on the windowsill and pressed his head against the cool glass.

When the door to the king's room opened, and he heard the request for him to enter, he followed the guards inside. Boran was now seated, and Eneas and Grant were standing off to one side. Their eyes were on Lucas as soon as he entered the room and stopped before the king.

Boran only briefly looked down at Lucas before he spoke. "With a battle to prepare for, the last thing I expected this morning was a quarrel between Itan's cohort, one of which is now dead, one of which is wounded, and . . ." Boran stopped when he was interrupted by the sound of the door opening without proper announcement.

It was Malcolm who entered—supporting a guard with his clothes in disarray and blood all over his face. It was the guard who had let him inside Eli's room that morning, and it was clear someone had beat him.

Grant rushed over to Malcolm and listened to the hushed words spoken to him. When Malcolm finished, Grant turned to the guard. "Do you see the person who attacked you here?" he asked.

The guard raised his head towards Lucas and nodded.

"Sire," said Grant, turning away from Malcolm and the guard. "This man was posted outside Eli's room last night. He was found severely beaten and claims it was Lucas who attacked him in the early hours of this morning." Grant paused and looked at Lucas with indifference. "If this is to be true, then I am afraid Eneas may be right, and we should not allow him to walk free."

Lucas looked from Grant to Boran, who had curled his lips and was giving him a hard stare. "Do not believe the lie, sire," Lucas said, raising his voice in frustration. "I did not harm this guard. I couldn't have. The blood is still seeping from his wounds. As for Finton . . . he had every intention to take my life. I had no choice but to take his." He waited for Boran to respond but saw he had no intention to do so when he waved his hand to have the guards move in on him. Lucas resisted when they grabbed him by the arms, and Eneas was coming towards him—an aura of darkness surrounding him.

"You are not yourself," said Eneas, lifting his hand to touch Lucas's forehead. "The serpent's venom allowed the forces of darkness to corrupt your mind, but I can help you."

Lucas jerked away, nearly elbowing a guard in the face. "Don't come near me," he hissed. He was angry but also felt a panic come over him. "It's you who has been tainted by evil, not me."

"Lucas," scolded Boran, rising from his seat. "You will not speak out of tone to my priest."

"He is no priest," shouted Lucas. "He never was." He felt threatened and wanted Eneas to go away but saw him step even closer now that the king and Grant were coming towards them.

"At this point, the king has no sane reason to believe you," said Eneas, stepping aside to let Boran through.

"For a while, Lucas, I believed you were to be by my side in battle," said Boran, "but darkness or no darkness, I no longer think that is the case. Seeing what I saw this morning and watching you now—"

"I'm not the one you need to be concerned about," spat Lucas. "Ask Eneas and Grant what each of them will gain from keeping me from your side."

Grant's eyes grew wide at the mention of his name, and he took a step toward Lucas, but Boran stopped him from going further by putting his hand on his chest.

"Grant and Eneas only fear you may turn on me," replied Boran. "As Toroun did to my grandfather."

"You'll be making a big mistake if you let Grant lead your army," said Lucas. "He knows what lies beyond the exit of the tunnel, and it's not . . ." He had been looking deeply into Boran's eyes and did not see the blow to the side of his head coming. The guards gripped him tighter when his knees gave way, and they laid him on the ground. With blurred vision, he saw the faces of Boran, Grant, and Eneas looking down on him.

"I'm sorry," apologized Grant, addressing the king. "Maybe you would have liked to have heard the fable he was about to tell you?"

"No," answered Boran. "We have wasted too much time already. I was going to tell you this morning that I want the entire army moved to the tunnel—today."

"Today?" asked Grant.

"You heard me correctly," answered the king. "One day earlier should not matter. I'm keen to get this over with." Boran gave Lucas one last look, then turned his back and walked away.

"What about Lucas?" called Grant after him.

"No longer my concern," answered Boran. "I trust you will do what is right."

Those were the last words Lucas was able to make out before everything went dark.

CHAPTER 12

Lucas came to as they carried him down a steep and narrow staircase. They were taking him down into Eneas's room. Eli's words played in his head, and Lucas knew what would be waiting for him down there. He noticed his hands and feet had been tied, but he struggled nonetheless, making the guard holding him by the shoulders lose his grip on him and fall against the wall. He let out a cry of pain when his back hit the stone steps.

Eneas was rushing up the stairs with a bottle in his hand. "Hold him," he shouted, putting his knee on Lucas's chest to help pin him down. "It is most unfortunate that you regained consciousness so soon," he said, uncorking the bottle that he then forced between Lucas's lips.

Lucas gagged as the vile tasting liquid was poured down his throat. He could feel the elixir take an almost immediate effect on his body, numbing all sensation in his muscles. With one last effort, he lifted his head and slammed into the bottle. The unexpected move had the bottle fly from Eneas's hand and shatter on the steps as it landed.

Rage flashed across Eneas's face as he watched the remaining liquid ooze down the stairs. He gripped Lucas's neck as if to strangle him until Lucas was no longer able to put up a fight. It was as Eli had described, thought Lucas. He felt trapped inside a body he could not control.

"Bring him," ordered Eneas, standing up and leading the way down the stairs.

Lucas struggled to regain movement as he was carried into Eneas's room. The guards briefly stopped, and he heard something scrape across the floor. He was aware of a tall cabinet next to an opening in the wall and stairs leading deeper underground. As they carried him down into the second underground room, he remembered what he had then thought was no more than a dream.

Lucas half expected to be locked up in one of the two cells, but they remained closed. Instead, Eneas instructed the guards to lay him on the table in the center of the room, where they secured a leather strap at each wrist. When the restraints were in place, Lucas heard Eneas dismiss the guards and walk from one side of the room to the other before appearing by his side.

Eneas frowned when he looked down at him. "You can hear and see," he muttered, "but I don't think you can move or speak, or you would have done so already."

Eneas walked over to a shelf on the wall and came back with a small knife. He ripped Lucas's shirt open and pressed the tip of the knife into his chest. Lucas closed his eyes in pain as the knife sliced through his skin. No sound escaped him, though he tried to cry out. Eneas's eyes lit up. "Not even a flinch," he said. "That is good, but what about your ability to make a sound?"

Eneas was leaning over him, a sparkle in his eyes, seemingly taking pleasure in what he was doing. He had gone insane, thought Lucas. When he felt the knife pierce his skin a second time, he could hear footsteps coming down the stairs and Grant's voice asking Eneas what he was doing.

"Making it look convincing for the king that I am expelling the darkness from this boy," answered Eneas.

"Why?" asked Grant, coming down the last steps. "You heard the king. He wasn't buying into your story that the forces of darkness possess him."

"Just making sure he will not cause you any trouble then," said Eneas.

"Put the knife down," scolded Grant, "before I begin to believe what Lucas said about you." He came to stand by the table and looked down.

Lucas was thankful his eyes were focused upward, and he didn't have to look at Grant directly. He felt disgusted with himself for thinking there was any sort of mutual respect or friendship between them. What a fool he had been.

"Did you give him the elixir?" he heard Grant ask.

"Yes, I did," answered Eneas.

"Then why is he still conscious?"

"I don't know," answered Eneas. "Maybe I did not get enough inside him. He resisted and had me drop the bottle on the stairs, but there is no need to worry. He is under my complete control and will not be fighting in the battle."

Grant shook his head. "You need to give him more. I don't like the look of this."

"I wish I could," sighed Eneas, "but all I had was in that bottle. It will take time to brew more."

Lucas struggled to keep his eyes open. He was tired but determined not to give in to the desire to sleep, for he was afraid he might never wake up. Grant averted his eyes from him. If he had any sympathy for Lucas, or any remorse for handing him over to Eneas, he was resisting it. Grant was another, thought Lucas, who had deceived him by portraying himself as someone other than who he was. If only he had remembered the wax seal belonging to the Hammonds sooner.

Grant stepped away and headed back towards the stairs. "How long?" he asked. "Before you can have more of your poison?"

"I need to collect a few more ingredients first," replied Eneas. "Then it will take a few hours at least."

"Then you better get started," said Grant. "I don't think Boran will come down here, but if he does—I cannot have Lucas speak of the tunnel."

"What secret is it that you are withholding there, I wonder?" asked Eneas. He had put the knife down and started to follow Grant out of the room.

"You would do better not to question me," replied Grant. "Don't forget that it is me who is allowing you to keep him here—as long as you don't kill him and release the curse." As their steps disappeared further up the stairs, Lucas heard Grant speak to Eneas again. "I will have one of the slaves bring the ingredients you need. After you set the elixir to brew . . . go and see to Eli. I've decided he could be of use after all and want to take him with me."

Lucas heard Eneas shuffling back down the stairs and across the floor. He was losing the will to keep his eyes open.

"You are strong," remarked Eneas. "I gave you more than Eli. Even before the rest of my creation went down the steps, but yet . . . here you are. Still fighting the poison. How long will you be able to keep that up, I wonder?"

His feet shuffled across the floor again, telling Lucas he was coming closer. He felt Eneas's breath on his face as he came to lean over him to check the pupils of his eyes, prying Lucas's eyelids open roughly. "Hm," muttered Eneas. "I may have to do something else before I can have more of the elixir ready. We would not want you to cause a scene, now do we?" He continued to mutter, more to himself this time, looking around for something he had lost. When he found what he was looking for, he grabbed Lucas's right wrist.

A sharp sting and a drop of warm liquid rolling off his hand told

Lucas that his fight against the darkness was only just beginning—Eneas was trying to weaken him by draining his blood. One drop at a time.

Satisfied, Eneas put the knife down and looked up when someone called down from the top of the stairs. "Father Eneas?"

Lucas recognized the girl's voice and forced his eyes open. They seemed to be the only part of him still under his control.

"Father Eneas, are you there?" called Valora, coming down the stairs. "I was informed to bring you these ingredients without delay and—" Her last word trailed off as she reached the bottom steps.

"Valora!" answered Eneas, standing upright. "Just set them—" Eneas stopped and followed her startled gaze to Lucas, a devious sparkle forming in his eyes.

When he saw the devil's grin come over Eneas's face, Lucas wanted to scream and tell Valora to turn around—to run—but no sound passed his lips.

"How charming," said Eneas. "I had no idea you favored her." He paused and glanced at Valora before turning back to Lucas. "I wonder if you have spent time alone with her?" he asked. "And if not, perhaps you would like to watch when I have my way with her?" Then, without hesitation, he reached for Valora, and she spun around to retreat.

Tears came into Lucas's eyes as he fought against the elixir in his blood. He heard Valora scream and try to escape. He could tell by the skirmish he heard on the stairs that she had failed, and Eneas had managed to grab her. He envisioned Eneas pulling her back down the steps by the hem of her dress and could only hope she could break free from the clutches of the deranged priest. He tried to use his powers of seeing, but they, like the rest of him, had been disabled.

"Please, sir," cried Valora. "Please let me go!"

Eneas grunted something inaudible before Lucas heard what he could only assume were Valora's boots scaping and slipping on the steps. Then there was a loud thud, followed by silence.

"By god's bones," said Eneas, stepping back. "Look what you have done now, you little witch."

Tears flooded Lucas's eyes when he realized what had just happened. Filled with grief and helplessness, a hard lump formed in his chest as he listened to the wretched sound of Eneas dragging Valora's body across the stone floor. "You're no lightweight," he said casually between pants, finally dumping her body in the corner of the room as if her life had not mattered. "I always thought Boran was too good to his slaves, and you are clearly no exception."

At that moment, Lucas vowed to avenge her, forcing his sadness into anger and the will to survive. He closed his eyes when Eneas stepped back from the corner to prevent him from seeing the hurt there, no doubt still visible.

"A pity," mumbled Eneas. "Such a pretty girl." Lucas could feel Eneas's eyes upon him. "Rest assured," he said as he made his way to the stairs. "You will get to join her soon." He then disappeared up the stairs, leaving Lucas with slow drops of blood dripping from his wrist. He came back down from time to time to check on him and reopen the wound when it started to heal. Lucas slipped in and out of dreams, waking each time the cabinet at the top of the stairs moved back and forth, telling him someone was coming. He fought the elixir in his system and tested for any movement in his body before Eneas's footsteps reached the bottom steps. When he started to feel a tingling sensation in his legs, he knew that the poison was finally wearing off. Whatever had made his body behave the way it did, it wasn't going to win.

Eneas noticed the slight tremble in his body when he entered the room and picked up the knife from the shelf. "I was afraid this might happen," he said.

"Don't," said Lucas softly when Eneas grabbed his other wrist. His throat was dry from thirst. "The king . . ."

Eneas looked alarmed when he spoke but relaxed when he saw he struggled to keep his eyes open. "The king has left," said Eneas, letting go of his wrist after making a tiny cut. "Moved his army out some time ago. It's just you, me, and a garrison of guards who are left behind these castle walls."

"Then . . . why?" stammered Lucas.

"Why do I continue to try and take your mind now that the king has left?" asked Eneas. He put the knife down and walked back around the table. Lucas followed him by moving his head slightly. "Because this isn't for him," continued Eneas. "It's for me. I want you to suffer for what your family did to mine. I want to destroy Toroun's name and legacy. When the prophecy he foretold does not come true . . . only then will I be at peace."

"You have an ancestor who died," said Lucas. His head was becoming clear, and he focused on the knowledge presented to him in his mind.

Eneas jerked his head to look him in the eye. "Yes," he replied. "He was Toroun's executioner. He was the first to die from the curse, but he did not deserve it. All he did was do his job. He was the royal court's butcher, and the task of executioner was bestowed on him because no one wanted it. He had no choice in the matter. After his death, his wife and children no longer had a home on castle grounds and were treated as outcasts by the rest of the town. They were forced to live in poverty outside the town walls, as families of executioners had done before them."

Lucas could feel the fingertips of his left hand graze the knife Eneas had carelessly left by his side. With some control of his body returning, he inched his fingers forward when Eneas started pacing the room. "Except for you," Lucas said, trying to distract Eneas with the conversation. "You have done well for yourself."

"An unfortunate event helped me escape a lifetime of misery," responded Eneas. "I left home to fend for myself at an early age. I worked, stole, begged. Whatever it took to stay alive. Then, when I was around thirteen years old, a king's horse bolted into a street where I happened to have my eye on a baker's cart. I didn't get out of the way quickly enough, and the horse trampled over me. When asked by an officer where my parents were, I told him I was an orphan."

"Which was a lie?"

"I might as well have been. At that point, I no longer had contact with my parents. They were happy to have one less mouth to feed."

"Then what happened?" asked Lucas. He wanted to keep Eneas talking for as long as he was willing to do so. His fingertips were touching the heft of the knife.

"I was taken to the castle to heal my injuries. When I developed a fever and was near death, a traveling priest, who happened to be visiting the late king, came to sit with me and prayed. He convinced the king to let me stay and gave me the responsibility of taking care of the chapel. After I recovered, being at the castle made me consider the better life I should have had. I grew bitter. The priest noticed my anger, and he listened to my story of how my family had come to suffer under Toroun's curse. He was the only one who ever cared and wanted to help me built a different life for myself. He was a healer, and willing to teach me the art of healing. I continued my studies in his absence and, year after year, he made regular trips back to the castle to assess my progress."

"Did that priest have a name?" asked Lucas. He was sure Boran had spoken of the same priest when they had walked the gardens.

"Father Oswall," answered Eneas. "You may have heard his name spoken. He came from the same monastery Finton told me you lived at."

"I have heard of him," answered Lucas. With the knife now in the palm of his hand, he was trying to cut through the leather restraint. He remembered Father Ansan telling him Oswall was the name of his teacher. Oswall was also the one who received the message from the stone informing him of Lucas's upcoming birth. He had left the monastery soon after and taken that knowledge with him without sharing it. Now, it was clear to Lucas where Oswall had gone . . . and how Boran's father had come to know about Lucas's birth. "He taught you to be a healer, not a priest?"

"He refused to let me take the vow," answered Eneas. "Oswall knew the darkness was growing inside of me after I found a book about the prophecy and learned Toroun's descendants were still alive. He told me to pray to the gods. He had me praying with him in the chapel for hours, until my knees were stiff and my mind restless with thinking."

Lucas lay perfectly still when Eneas stopped talking and was coming towards him. He had almost cut through the leather strap, but the effort had caused more blood to seep from his wrist. His face felt clammy, and it was becoming harder to breathe. Seemingly happy that he was finally becoming weaker, Eneas continued. "He had me pray to the very gods who caused my family's demise. Looking back, I think that was the end of our friendship."

"He was trying to help and turn you away from the darkness," Lucas said, his voice a hoarse whisper.

"Yes," answered Eneas, "but the only good that came from all that praying was that it made it easier to convince the king I was Oswall's apprentice after he left. Oswall did not return for quite some time, and in his absence, I became the king's priest. When Oswall eventually returned and found out, he threatened to inform the king of my secret unless I agreed to immediately leave the castle. Of course, I could not."

Lucas felt the leather restraint break away from his left hand. With Eneas standing on the opposite side, he would only be able to free his other hand if he left, but time was running out. He had little strength left and couldn't allow Eneas to get the elixir. "What did you do?" stammered Lucas, staring hard at Eneas. "To Father Oswall?"

"He was the first I tried my elixir on," answered Eneas. "Made him go mad. He kept rambling on about a descendent of Toroun who would come and be the end of me if I did not fight the evil festering my mind." He ran his hand through his hair and stared down.

"You did not believe him?" asked Lucas weakly. He needed Eneas to believe he might be slipping away.

"They were the ramblings of a desperate man who knew his gods had left him in his hour of need, as they have left you now. Where are those gods to help you fulfill your destiny? They could have struck me down with thunder and lightning, but they didn't. Why not?"

Lucas did not answer. Instead, he kept his eyes closed and his body slack. Eneas stepped closer to touch his face, then looked to the ground, where Lucas knew the puddle of blood would be significant right now. "No . . . no," murmured Eneas. "You are not allowed to die." He tried to lift Lucas's wrist to stop the bleeding, but when the restraint prevented him from doing so, he frantically unbuckled the strap.

Lucas waited until his hand was free and Eneas was reaching for a cloth to tie around the wound. He bolted upright and threw his arm around Eneas's torso, who let out a scream in surprise. With his other hand, he pressed the knife against Eneas's throat. "You have made several mistakes," he told him. "The first was believing your ancestor had no choice in taking Toroun's life. The position of executor was voluntary. Even when Toroun told him what would happen, he did not hesitate."

Eneas struggled to get loose, but Lucas, determined not to let go, tightened his grip.

"The second mistake," he continued, "was thinking Eli and I are of the same blood. I am not an elite born, and your elixir would never have worked on me." He pulled Eneas closer and spoke quietly in his ear. "Your third mistake? Believing the gods abandoned us."

"Go ahead," hissed Eneas. "You may kill me, but I know you're too weak to make it out of here alive."

“There you make another mistake,” replied Lucas. “I’m not the only one in this quest to set things right.” With his last bit of strength, he pulled the knife across Eneas’s throat. “This is for Valora,” he said and let the false priest drop to the floor.

He laid back down on the table and stared at the vaulted ceiling until he slowly felt the cold air filling the underground room—dropping the temperature to near freezing. He then watched the torches’ flames go dim before closing his eyes. There was nothing left to do except wait.

CHAPTER 13

Davis was sitting on a rocky outcrop on the high cliffs overlooking Boran's castle. Warrick was seated not far from him and had stopped playing with the dung beetle. Davis had not taken his eyes off the castle for some time now and he startled when he heard the sound of pebbles crunching underfoot behind him. The forest's edge was only a few feet away, and he watched as Nolan and Dastan emerged and stopped near the cliff's edge. Both brothers stared into the distance where, the day before, they had all seen Boran's army disappear around the corner of the mountain.

Davis looked at Nolan. He was half a head taller than Dastan and the sterner looking of the two. Davis remembered Lucas telling him that it was Nolan who had visited him at the monastery after his father had died. And it was Nolan who had convinced the warrior monks to teach Lucas their ways. Nolan was also the leader of the mountain people, and in charge of the warriors now waiting in the forest behind him.

Davis was looking back towards the castle and continuing to listen for any sign of Lucas when Nolan broke the silence to speak to his younger brother.

"I don't think it was ever Lucas's intention to meet us," said Nolan. "Boran would not have allowed him to leave voluntarily, and if Lucas had planned to escape, he would have done so by now. It's time for us to head towards the river to make the crossing. If we leave now, it will give us plenty of time to get there before the battle between Boran and Itan takes place."

"Why not give him another day?" asked Dastan. "Half-moon is tonight. That's when Lucas told Davis to be here. He and the other chosen will not want to leave before then."

"I'm not going to give them a choice," replied Nolan. "If Lucas has gone with Boran, the chosen need to be with us." He stepped away from the cliff's edge and met Davis's eye when he started walking back to the forest.

"He did not go with Boran," spoke Davis. He stood up and turned to face Nolan. "I would know if he had."

"Then where is he?"

"I'm not sure." Davis had felt a faint connection with Lucas the moment he arrived at the top of the cliff, like a candle that was flickering and never came to a full flame, and it had still been there long after the army had marched off. Then, in the early hours of the morning, he had lost it, and he had not wanted to accept the possibility of the reason why.

"I cannot hold everyone here on a hunch that he may still be down there," said Nolan. "Get the chosen ready to move out." He gave a stern look and continued to walk into the forest, and Dastan gripped Davis gently on the shoulder in passing as he followed his brother.

Warrick came to stand next to him. "I want nothing more than to see Lucas ride out of those gates as well," said Warrick, "but I think it is time we face the fact that he isn't going to."

"You want to follow Nolan and the warriors to the river?" asked Davis.

"Do we have another choice?"

"Maybe not," answered Davis reluctantly and started walking towards the forest. "Let's go and inform Zera and the others."

They followed a deer track and caught up with Nolan and Dastan as they walked down the forest gully, where the mountain warriors and hunters were sitting by small campfires. Orson rose from one of them and came to meet them.

"No sign of him?" asked Orson, looking first to Davis and then to the two brothers. The task of being the hunters' leader was showing on his face—his people were used to fighting off small attacks in the forest now and then, and Davis knew the full-fledged battle that lay ahead put their entire group at risk.

"No," answered Nolan. "The castle has been deserted, except for a watch on the walls."

"He has gone with Boran, then?"

"It looks that way," answered Nolan. "We'll be ready to follow you to the river as soon as we have broken camp here."

"Fair enough," replied Orson, then gestured towards Davis. "You don't seem too keen?"

"I'm not convinced Lucas has left the castle," answered Davis.

Orson furrowed his brow and turned back to Nolan. "Should we not make sure of that first?"

"How?" asked Nolan. "Storm the castle? We—"

Before he could finish, a shrill neigh from a horse in the distance broke the forest's silence. Hunters wearing fur clothing and warriors with leather armor rose from their resting places, and Nolan raised his hand for everyone to be still and listen.

Zera, Archer, and the other chosen had been making their way towards Davis but now stood frozen and waited for his instructions. Davis looked up towards the ridge. He knew Orson and Nolan had placed a watch all around, and if there was to be a surprise attack from Boran, they should have known already. But perhaps not—the gully chosen as camp hid the many warriors and horses from sight while they rested, but it would be a challenging place to defend. Davis motioned to Zera to get the chosen back onto the ridge, and he followed them with Warrick, picking his way around warriors and hunters resting in small groups. They then began the tedious climb up the slippery slope of moss and rotting leaves.

When they were some distance from the gully, another neigh echoed through the trees. This time it sounded clearer, and Davis could tell it was coming from further down the mountain.

"It's the same horse calling," commented Zera.

Davis nodded. "I agree."

"What would it be doing here by itself?" asked Archer.

"There's only one way to find out," answered Davis. "Let's spread out in a line, two horse lengths apart, so we can keep an eye on each other, and head down the mountain."

He used a hand signal that was passed down the line to have the others stop from time to time and determine if anyone had heard anything. Zera was next to him, her eyes reduced to slits as she concentrated on her surroundings. Each time they came to a stop, he looked at her, but she would only shake her head. There was no news, and they carried on, gradually moving further down the slope. When they heard nothing for quite some time, and the forest floor became too dense for a horse to have come through, Davis signaled to return to camp.

It was then that they heard a soft whinnying nearby. The chosen all lowered themselves down to the ground and slowly closed in on a black horse that appeared to have lost its rider. It was standing in some brambles and restlessly throwing its head up into the air.

Fearing it could be a trap, Davis ordered a sweep of the area before moving in on the horse. It was skittish and tried to back away when they approached, but the reins got tangled around some deadwood.

Davis spoke calmly and stretched his hand out towards the horse. It snorted when he touched its nose but settled down when he gently stroked it. He reached down to untangle the reins and then moved it to a small clearing where the chosen stood watching. The horse shimmered in the dappled light filtering in through the canopy of leaves above.

"That's a destrier and not a common horse," commented Warrick. "I wonder where its rider is?"

"Doesn't look like he had one," said Archer. He was coming back with a few of the chosen after following the horse's tracks further down. "At least not while coming up the mountain. There is no sign of anyone having fallen off a horse."

"Must have escaped then," concluded Warrick. "There's an initial on the saddle deck."

"It's a B," said Davis. He didn't quite know how to read, but he had learned the letters that made words from Lucas. "It could stand for Boran." He looked at the horse, standing quietly next to him, then let his eyes go back to the embroidered initial. The stitching seemed relatively new. "Zera?" he asked. "Do you recall anyone in Boran's entourage riding with a letter on their saddle deck?"

Zera looked at him, confused, then nodded. "One or two," she answered. "But different letters."

"You didn't see a B on King Boran's horse?" Davis asked.

Zera shook her head. "No," she answered. "Where are you going with this?"

Davis turned to Warrick and the group of boys who, like Zera, were looking at him with anticipation. "I think that those who rode with an initial were special to the king," he said. "I don't think this B stands for Boran. I think it stands for Baelan. This is Lucas's horse, and he sent it here for us to find—he's in trouble."

"If so, why doesn't he connect with you?" asked Zera.

"He may not be able to," answered Davis. "And if something bad happened to him before yesterday, I wasn't here. I would have been too far away."

Warrick looked from the horse to Davis. "What do we do?" he asked. "Nolan was clear this morning that he will not act on a hunch from any of us. How are we to convince him this is Lucas's horse and that Lucas needs us?"

Davis stroked the horse's nose. It was much calmer now and playfully nuzzled his arm. "Maybe we should talk to Dastan first," he answered. "He's more inclined to go with his instinct and may be willing to back us up when we talk to Nolan."

"You have agreed to *what* exactly?" Nolan asked his brother. The space between his dark eyebrows narrowed as he stared down at the shorter Dastan.

Orson stood next to Nolan, staring at the ground as if deep in thought, his broad shoulders slightly slouched.

Davis had stayed with the chosen, a small distance away, listening and watching the three men hopefully.

Before returning to camp, the chosen had gone to find Dastan and Orson to discuss the possibility of the horse belonging to Lucas. When Dastan told the chosen that Arne's son had seen Lucas arrive in town on a black horse when he had come in search of Eli, Davis became more convinced that Lucas needed his aid, and he was able to convince Dastan of the same.

The trick was in getting Nolan on board. Davis anxiously watched the three men as they talked.

"I told the chosen I would help," said Dastan. "If that is the horse Lucas has been riding, then I think Davis may be right about Lucas sending it here with a purpose. The only way to find out is to get inside that castle."

"How?" asked Nolan. "The walls have been left well-guarded. Even with our numbers, we will face a substantial loss of life if we try to breach them."

"There will be no attack," said Dastan. "Well, at least not until we are inside."

Nolan looked from Dastan to the group of chosen. Davis could see the tight line of his mouth. "You already have a plan?"

"We do," answered Dastan.

"A good one?"

"Best we could come up with."

Nolan looked to Orson, who had been standing quietly next to him. "What do you think?" he asked.

"Ah," answered Orson, scratching the back of his neck. "Sneaking into castles is not in my realm of expertise, and I would have to say anyone attempting Boran's castle may not be of sane mind. That said . . . I've seen what Lucas is capable of, and I think he may very well have sent that horse here. The reason is anyone's guess, but I think it's worth finding out."

Nolan sighed. "Alright," he said. "I know when I'm outnumbered. Let's hear it."

Davis had his back pressed snugly against the wall. He was listening to the guards walking around above him. Each time he felt it was safe to do so, he waved another chosen over. They were hiding underneath hay in a wagon Arne and his young son had driven into a field near the castle's gates. The field, full of black cows, was used for grazing, so the presence of the haycart drew no attention. When all the chosen had scrambled out from under the hay and made it to the wall, Arne began to drive the wagon away. Davis watched as the boy, standing up in the back of the wagon, dumped the last of the hay out for the herd of cows.

He looked at Zera beside him, who had tied her long black hair in one braid that rested along the middle of her back. She turned to him and gave him a nod. He then looked at Warrick, pressed up against the wall on Davis's other side. Warrick rubbed the side of his nose as if he had an itch and stood himself up a little straighter, gestures Davis assumed meant Warrick was feeling nervous, though he could only imagine what his friend was thinking—the last time they had breached a wall, Tanner and Lucas had been with them. Losing Tanner was something they did not talk about, but it was a grim reminder of the risk they were about to take. "Are you ready for this?" he asked, reaching for a polished silver coin in his pocket.

"Yes," answered Warrick. "I wish we were breaching under cover of darkness as we did at Lord Meloc's castle, but I'm ready."

"I know," replied Davis, taking the coin between his fingers and tilting it towards the sun. "But at this time of day, the guards are least likely to suspect anything amiss. And we may be running out of time, if Lucas is in trouble." He let the sunlight reflect onto the coin and aimed the beam towards the town before putting it away to watch the road. A moment later, he caught a glimpse of movement and saw Dastan and twenty warriors casually approaching the castle gates.

Hearing the guards' footsteps along the wall as they moved towards the gatehouse, he gave a signal to two chosen boys to start climbing. Without ropes to assist them, their progress was going to be slower, but he could not risk throwing a hook on the embrasures. He watched them climb with relative ease until they were halfway and then focused his attention on Dastan and his group, who had stopped some distance from the gate. He could hear a guard shout down to them to identify themselves and strained his ears to listen.

"Northeast patrol," replied Dastan. "We have come to answer the king's call to arms."

When no reply came from the guard, Warrick looked at Davis. "Is there such a thing?"

"No idea," answered Davis. "But I'm sure Dastan knows what he's doing."

"I hope so," mumbled Warrick.

Dastan had relaxed the reins on his horse and was patiently waiting for the guard's reply. The warriors behind him had done the same. If Davis didn't know any better, the group did not look like they would pose a threat. He could only hope that Boran's guards thought so, as well.

"Where are your colors?" asked the guard.

"We don't ride with any," answered Dastan.

"You are mercenaries?"

"We used to be," replied Dastan, "but not since King Itan killed most of us off in the battle with Lord Killeand. Now we work solely for King Boran. Why don't you go and ask him? I am sure he'll be happy to see we have arrived."

"I am afraid you've come too late," said the guard. "The king has already departed, and we have orders not to let anyone pass."

Davis looked up and saw Zera and Archer reach the top and disappear over the wall. A moment later, ropes were lowered, and the other chosen started climbing. Davis was glad Lucas had informed Dastan how Meloc's castle's siege had been able to take place. The mercenaries' involvement with Killeand seemed to have preceded them, and the guard sounded less hostile. Davis grabbed the rope and began to climb.

"When did the king leave for the tunnel?" he could hear Dastan asking.

"Yesterday," answered the guard. The guard wasn't questioning

Dastan's knowledge of the tunnel's purpose, and it made Davis believe its existence had to be well known among Boran's men.

"Then, we are not too late and can still catch up to him. My men are quick, and eager." Dastan waited a moment, but with no reply given, he continued. "Look," he said. "I'm happy to turn around and avoid fighting another battle for the king, risky business as it is, but if I do, my men don't eat. And it's on you when the king finds out we were here, and you refused to let us through."

Davis reached the embrasures and saw Zera and the rest of the chosen crouched on the stairs on the north side of the wall-walk. The guards were all standing on the walk directly above the gates to his left. Most were watching Dastan—others were in discussion, but all stood with their back towards the chosen. The guards outnumbered the warriors two to one, with likely more guards taking breaks in barracks close by, and could easily have refused entry, but Davis doubted, after Dastan's last remark, that they were going to risk a court-martial and demand the warriors leave. He quickly unhooked the ropes and let them fall the long way down before making his way to the stairs. The chosen followed him down into the deserted bailey and spread out, their main goal to get out of sight as quickly as possible. Davis managed to hide behind some barrels just when the order to open the gates was called, and the guards that had been stationed on the wall-walk rushed down the same stairs he and the chosen had used only seconds before.

Davis's heart was beating fast when Dastan and the warriors rode into the castle, stopping their horses when the gates closed behind them. He could see Zera and a few other chosen behind a wagon to the right of him, their hands ready on the pommels of their swords.

"Why are you stopping?" asked a guard, marching up to Dastan. "You are to take the road out the back gates and continue to the tunnel."

"Change of plan," answered Dastan, throwing his leg over the saddle and jumping off. He pulled his sword and aimed it at the guard. "In truth, we are here for a friend of ours."

The guard looked confused until he saw the rest of the warriors jumping off their horses and pulling their swords. Realizing they were under attack, he cried out for help but was too late to defend himself. With other guards now alerted and charging towards the warriors, a bitter battle of life and death quickly unfolded. Davis whistled, and the chosen sprinted out from their hiding spots to join the fight, putting the odds in their favor when the guards were taken by surprise a second time.

Davis leaned over a mortally wounded guard who looked like he did not have long to live. "We are here for Lucas," he said. "Or Baelan, as he may be known here. Do you know where he is?"

The guard stared at him with a blank expression and remained silent.

"He is not going to answer you," said Dastan, coming towards him and kneeling by the guard. "At least not willingly." Without hesitation, he put his hand on the wound in the guard's stomach and pressed down on it. The guard cried out in pain but still refused to speak. "You don't have much longer for this world, but it's up to you how you are going to leave it," continued Dastan. "Now, answer the question, or you will suffer longer. Where is Lucas?"

The guard locked eyes with Davis, a plea for help in his glistening eyes. "I will not stop him," Davis said, gesturing towards Dastan and ignoring the uncomfortable sensation in his stomach. "So you better talk, and quickly."

"Press him harder, Dastan," said Zera, as she approached. Her chest heaved as she tried to catch her breath. "He has to know where Lucas is."

"I have no idea where he is," gasped the guard. He groaned when Dastan pressed down. "It's the truth. No one has seen him after he killed that former general of Itan's. Finton."

"Lucas killed Finton?" asked Davis. "When?"

"Yesterday," answered the guard. "They got into an argument. Finton's son tried to escape, and—"

"We don't care about that," interrupted Dastan. "What happened to Lucas after?"

"I have no idea. He followed the commander inside the castle, and that was the last time I saw him."

Dastan looked up at Davis before turning back to the guard. "Was he killed for it?"

The guard shook his head. "I don't think so . . . there was a rumor."

"What rumor?" urged Dastan, leaning closer. The guard was struggling to get his words out, and it was apparent that they were losing him.

"The priest," answered the guard with his last breath. "Underground room . . . trying to save his soul."

Dastan jumped up and turned to the warriors and chosen who were standing around him. "I need the lower floor searched for any stairs leading underground," he shouted. "Open every door and every hatch you come across to find it, but do not go down until you have support. This priest is not to be trusted, and we don't know what we'll be dealing with."

Davis watched everyone rush off in small groups. He followed Dastan inside the castle with Zera right behind him, carefully opening doors as they went along. Davis was aware that some guards could still be hiding, but they found no one—only a few slaves cowering inside a storeroom in the kitchen. With the castle quiet and the hallways empty of activity, it had an eerie feeling to it and sent shivers up his spine. When they rounded the corner of one of the hallways, he spotted Warrick and Archer on either side of an arched opening in the wall, their heads aimed into the open space—listening.

"What is it?" Davis asked when he got near but asked no further when Warrick put a finger to his lips.

Davis peered into the doorway and saw the steep stairs leading down. Not able to see what lay beyond the stairs, they waited until more chosen and warriors joined them before carefully making their way down.

They found the physician's room empty, and the chosen began looking around. "Do not touch anything," warned Dastan. "Eneas has a reputation of being more than a healer, and we have no idea what he was brewing in that bottle."

Davis followed his gaze towards a table where he saw a bottle on a stand with a candle holder underneath. The candle had long gone out, but whatever was in the bottle was releasing a terrible odor. The darkness and the room's exposed brick reminded Davis of the cold cellar at his ancestral house. It was where his mother would store all the pickled food, but he didn't think there was anything edible in the jars Eneas had on his shelves.

"It's cold down here," murmured Zera.

"Colder yet over here," replied Archer, who was standing near a large cabinet by the wall. "I can feel an icy draft of air . . ."

CHAPTER 14

Lucas was vaguely aware of the sound from the cabinet as it was sliding across the floor. He thought for a moment that Eneas was coming down but then remembered what had happened. He listened to the soft whispering of voices and the footsteps that followed, and worried that guards were coming down to check on Eneas, or worse—that it was Grant. His body was cold and stiff, and he felt in no state to defend himself. It wasn't until they were close and he felt someone touch him that he knew his friends had arrived to save him. He tried to connect with Davis but was too weak to do so.

"He is freezing and covered in blood," said Davis. "Is he breathing?"

"Barely," answered Dastan, leaning over Lucas. "The cold must have kept him alive, but we need to get him out of here and warm him up slowly. The blood looks to be mostly the priest's, fortunately."

"There's a girl on the floor in the corner," said Zera.

"Is she alive?" asked Dastan. "Is she breathing?"

"No," answered Zera. "Her skin is pale and her eyes open and fixed."

Lucas wanted so badly to speak, to tell them what had happened to Valora and him, but even simply remaining conscious was no longer possible, as he felt himself slipping away into a deep, dark hole. The more he tried to escape it, to join his friends, the further the hole sucked him in, until he gave in and slept.

He didn't know how long he stayed like that, but it was the smell of campfire smoke that brought him back and made him open his eyes. He stared at the stars in the sky above and took a moment to realize where he was. As a young boy, he often woke under the starry sky while traveling with the circus, but he could see the spire on the castle's tower and knew he was in Boran's bailey. He was lying on top of a pile of furs, his body weighed down with blankets and his wounds bandaged. Davis and Warrick were busy stoking up the fire, and Zera sat nearby with her head in her hands.

"You were not too late," he spoke softly. "You found my horse and came as fast as you could."

Zera raised her head. A faint smile of relief appeared on her face but was quickly replaced with a sterner look as she knelt by Lucas's side. "You had us all worried," said Zera. "Davis blamed himself for not being able to connect with you. What if we had not made it in time? You would have frozen to death."

"I knew bringing in the cold air was what I had to do to stay alive," replied Lucas. He turned his head towards a wagon when he heard a thumping noise and saw the bodies of dead guards loaded up to be driven away by warriors.

"You always know what to do," continued Zera. "But what if one day you get it wrong, and what you believe will happen does not?"

"Then, that will be the day my story ends," answered Lucas. He paused, watching everyone stop what they were doing to approach him. "Zera?" he asked, turning back to her before his other friends came closer. "What happened to the girl's body you found in the underground room?"

"Don't worry," answered Zera, who had followed his gaze to the wagon. "She'll not be buried with the guards or that priest. Dastan has told his men to make sure she is returned to her family for proper burial." She then moved aside and allowed Dastan to kneel beside Lucas.

"How are you feeling?" asked Dastan. He propped Lucas up and put a hot drink to his lips.

"Glad to be out of that dark place," answered Lucas, sipping the broth. He tried to sit up, but Dastan placed a hand on his chest, stopping him.

"You need to rest," said Dastan. "It will take some time for your muscles to get their strength back."

"I can't," said Lucas. "How long has it been since Boran left with his army?"

"The day before yesterday," answered Davis.

"Then maybe we are not too late," muttered Lucas. "I need to get to the tunnel."

"I am not allowing you to go after Boran," said Dastan. "From what he did to you, it's clear he knows you are a threat to him. He won't let you get near him."

"It wasn't Boran who ordered Eneas to do what he did. Boran has been deceived and played as much as I have, but it's not because of him that I need to get to the tunnel. It's something else that's pulling me in that direction."

Lucas tried to get up again, but Dastan was right—his body was not yet strong enough. Frustrated, he laid back down and turned his head to Davis and Warrick. "I need you to find something for me," said Lucas. "A map." He described what it would look like and gave them directions to Grant's room.

He drank more of the hot broth that had been brewing above the fire and rested with Zera by his side until Davis and Warrick returned. Davis held a parchment roll under his arm that he spread out on the ground in front of him. Helped by Zera and Dastan, Lucas sat up. It was the map he remembered seeing Boran and Grant examining. Only now, he was able to see what Grant had covered with his arm before.

He pointed to several circular lines in the mountains east of the tunnel valley. "What are these?" he asked.

"Quarries," answered Dastan. "Open-pit mines for marble, limestone, building stones—among other things. Most are from the time of King Rodin, and no longer in use."

"What about this one?" asked Lucas. He followed the ravine where he had seen the workers' houses with his finger until it came to a quarry marked differently than all the others. "There's a downward pointing triangle drawn inside it—the symbol for water."

"I don't know," answered Dastan. "Maybe it got flooded."

"The ravine . . ." said Davis. "Is there a river that runs through it?"

"More like a stream," answered Lucas. He paused and looked at Davis, suddenly recalling the dream he had of standing in the ravine with the water rising.

"What is it?" asked Davis. "You look like you've seen a ghost."

Lucas shook his head and hurried to stand up. He could feel blood rushing to every part of his body, and he felt the urge to vomit. He staggered and would have fallen if Dastan had not jumped up and caught him.

"You're in no state to get up," said Dastan, laying him back down.

"I have to," said Lucas. "They're trapped."

"Who?" asked Warrick and Zera at the same time.

"The tunnel workers," answered Lucas. "We need to get them out of the ravine. Where's Nolan?"

"He stayed on the cliff with the warriors and hunters," answered Dastan. "We signaled to him a few hours ago that we found you, and he'll no doubt be heading to the river right now, as was the plan. But if you need them here, I can send someone to get them. They can't be too far."

Lucas knew the ride to the valley to be a couple of hours, and he could see the sun to be already rising by the orange glow in the eastern sky. In his dream, it had been the noon hour. "You can send one of your men to get Nolan," Lucas said, "but we have no time to wait. Have him meet up with us at the tunnel as soon as possible."

Dastan looked at him in silence, then nodded and started to give orders to those around him.

"We can do this without you," said Dastan when he saw Lucas needing assistance to get onto his horse.

"I'll be fine once we get going," answered Lucas, trying to find his balance in the saddle. After eating some hot porridge and putting on the clean clothes he had sent a chosen to get from his room, he already felt a different person.

Dastan waited until Lucas had found his reins and had his feet in the stirrups before he gave the sign to open the back gate. He sent two of his warriors ahead to make sure the road ahead was clear, while the rest of them rode as fast as Lucas could.

When they reached the stretch of road that cut into the cliffside, one of the warriors came riding towards them. "We heard a loud noise," he reported. "About an hour ago."

"Like rockfall?" asked Dastan.

"No," answered the warrior. "More like something slamming shut. There was a massive echo. I've never heard anything like it."

Dastan looked over his shoulder to Lucas and frowned.

"It was the door to the tunnel," said Lucas. "The last of the army to enter was to close it behind them. We need to hurry."

They increased their speed until the road went down, and the tunnel's entrance came in view—sealed from the inside by a large door. There was no sign of life anywhere on the valley floor. Tools were left scattered, mining carts stood abandoned on the side of the road, and no smoke rose from the chimneys.

"Where is everyone?" asked Zera.

Lucas looked toward the creek. "This way," he said, spurring his horse to take the lead. He followed the road along the stream with the others close behind until he came to a ravine closed off by a two-story double-door gate. It was the biggest door he had ever seen, fit for a giant to come lumbering through.

"Are they behind it?" asked Dastan.

"Yes," answered Lucas. He stayed on his horse while Dastan ordered his men to remove the crossbar. When the gate swung open, he rode his horse through the shallow creek just as he had done in his dream. Wooden shacks, built on top of each other with little space in between, lined the rock faces on either side of the ravine. He saw simple ladders or footholds were used to reach the upper floors. The others followed him in and stared at the many workers watching them from every door and every window.

The workers started stepping out of their houses, apprehensive and confused. Lucas gathered they had not been fed in days, and the poison had started to leave their system.

He rode until his horse started throwing his nose into the air and was lifting its feet higher out of the water. He looked down at the water level, but already knew what was happening.

"It has begun," he shouted, turning in his saddle and waving his hand. "Get them out of here!" He saw Dastan staring at the rising waters, a look of alarm on his face, before springing into action. Warriors and chosen rushed up to the cabins to get people out and started driving them out of the ravine. Some jumped off their horses and went inside the houses to pull people out. It wasn't until the water had risen high enough and was coming over the creek bank that the workers became fully aware of the danger they were in, and they started running towards the exit.

Lucas spurred his horse to go past the cabins and around the bend of the ravine, where he was stopped by the first of three dams he had seen on the map. His horse pranced nervously in front of the wall of logs that towered above them. Water was rushing through cracks between logs. Lucas could see that the dam had been tampered with recently—fresh cuts that looked to be made by an axe were making the logs bulge and splinter under the pressure of the water behind them.

"Come on," called Davis, who had followed him. "We have to go. It is about to burst."

Seeing it was too late to repair the damage, Lucas turned his horse around and charged after Davis. They rode at full speed through the abandoned workers' housing, where the last of the workers were being ushered out of the ravine. When he neared the gates himself, Lucas looked back one last time, reining in his horse when he noticed movement by one of the cabins. It was the boy he had seen in his dream—who had warned him of the water rising. The boy was tugging at a man's arm, trying to get him to move, but the man Lucas recognized as Winslow was not aware of any danger and kept looking aimlessly up at the sky.

"He won't move!" called the boy.

Lucas brought his horse alongside the boy and reached down. "Take my hand," he urged. "We have to go."

"What about him?" asked the boy. He had let go of Winslow's sleeve but was hesitant when he saw him walk further into the ravine.

Lucas shook his head. "I'm afraid he is lost," he answered. "He can't be saved." He grabbed the boy's hand when he finally reached up, and pulled him behind his saddle.

As his horse raced out of the ravine, Lucas heard the explosion of the dam, followed by cabins snapping to pieces and the thundering sound of water closing in behind him. Realizing his horse was struggling under the weight of two people and losing ground, Lucas told the boy to hold on to the saddle and dropped his feet out of the stirrups.

"Whatever happens," Lucas shouted at the boy while pulling himself up to a standing position on the saddle, "don't let go!"

Lucas waited until he saw a low tree limb and jumped. Hanging over the branch on his stomach, he saw that the boy had managed to stay on, and his horse gained speed as it made its escape. Lucas swung his leg over and looked at the road to see that everyone else had made it to higher ground. He then wrapped himself around the branch and braced for impact.

The wall of water hit Lucas hard, nearly making him lose grip of the tree. He was lying flat on top of the limb, with his legs and arms wrapped around it, and his head and body tucked away on the side not facing the incoming water, to protect him from getting hit by debris. Holding his breath, he held on as the water rushed over him.

Only when he felt the worst was over did he let go of the tree and swim to the surface. He pulled himself up on a piece of wood that was floating past and looked around while catching his breath. The entire lower valley had turned into a tumultuous, muddy-brown lake—with every tree and building now submerged. Even the tunnel's entrance, he saw, was underwater—taking away Boran's only means of escape should he decide to retreat, once he discovered what was waiting for him at the other side.

CHAPTER 15

Eli looked over his shoulder when he heard the second bang coming from behind. The first time he had heard it, they had been closer to the tunnel's entrance. At the sound of the second bang, some of the foot soldiers looked back, but no one stopped or slowed down—they had sealed off the opening, and Eli imagined it would be no easy task to open the large wooden barricade from the outside. He glanced over to Grant, who was riding next to him, looking unconcerned.

Settling back into the saddle, Eli couldn't decide if he was lucky to be riding through the tunnel or if he would have been better off having died on his father's sword. He was not looking forward to being put to battle against his former friends. Would he have to face Baldric, Milton, or even Carleton? No doubt Carleton would be leading the elite borns. Eli swallowed the bitter thought—it would have been him if Lucas had never come to Itan's castle, which had ultimately caused his father to leave Itan, taking Eli away from all he knew.

Eli had feared death after his attempted escape from Boran's castle. The guards had taken him to a secluded room and left him alone to bleed out. Or, at least, that was his assumption, until Grant had shown up.

Grant had stood over him, his face stoic. He seemed unmoved by Eli's struggle to stay alive. It was the same Grant he remembered from Lord Killeand's castle. The one who had stared him down with cold eyes and made him feel insignificant. He had been wary of him when he first arrived at Boran's, but Grant had appeared a different person—especially after Lucas came, and Eli had watched the two become friends. He had felt jealous of their camaraderie. Lucas had a way of getting along with people.

Believing his fate already sealed, Eli decided he would not give Grant the satisfaction of knowing he was feared and looked up at him with defiance. "If you have come to watch me die," he had told Grant, "then you may have to wait a while. I'm not ready to leave this world just yet."

"What makes you think I wish for you to die?"

"I'm sure the fact that I tried to escape today didn't improve your opinion of me." Eli didn't mention the other possible reason. If Grant didn't know he'd spoken to Lucas and discussed his attack in town, it was best not to make him aware of it.

"Well," responded Grant, after a moment of silence, "what if I tell you that I can arrange for you to live far beyond this day."

"At what price?"

"I can make you a deal," answered Grant. "The same deal I had with your father before Lucas killed him."

He must have looked surprised, because Grant had smirked. "Ah," he said. "You were not aware of this yet."

Eli shook his head. He had fallen to the ground soon after his father's dagger had stabbed him. "How?" he asked.

"In cold blood," answered Grant. "No hesitation whatsoever. But don't worry—I'm not letting him get away with it. He's being taken care of as we speak."

"Good," replied Eli, turning his head towards the wall to hide his true feelings. He had been at odds with his father for some time, and the betrayal involving the elixir he had been poisoned with was unforgivable. But if Grant found out he had turned against his father for that reason, he was as good as dead. He had to convince Grant he was still his father's son. Eli took a deep breath and turned back to face Grant. "What was it that you offered my father?"

"Land, property, wealth," answered Grant.

"In return for?

"Everything he knew that would help in taking Itan down," responded Grant. "Now it can be yours, if you are willing to do the same."

Eli thought for a moment, then nodded. "My future was as good as gone the minute Itan laid eyes on Lucas and became infatuated with him. I do not owe Itan anything. I'll agree to help, but what I want in return is what I have worked for all my life—to become a general, like my father."

"If I can make that happen," answered Grant, "do we have a deal?"

"Yes," answered Eli. "Unless I die in the meantime." He briefly lifted the hand he had pressed to his wound to remind Grant of the crisis he was still facing.

Grant nodded and turned to face someone just beyond the door. "Have the wound sealed," he ordered, and exited the room when Malcolm stepped in.

Eli had not seen Grant again until the army was moving out and he was put on a horse next to him. King Boran was riding up front, and he could not see him now for the tunnel's darkness. The only light source came from a single flaming torch carried every couple of rows—just enough for the foot soldiers to see where they were putting their feet—but Eli could not help but try and make out Grant's face in the dim glow, as if the man's very expression could give him some sort of answer.

Grant glanced at him. "Something on your mind?" he asked.

"I just heard a noise coming from the entrance," answered Eli. "I was wondering what it could be."

"Nothing that is of any concern to you," answered Grant.

"You heard it as well, then?"

Grant turned his face away and resumed staring ahead into the darkness. "I just told you. It is not your concern."

CHAPTER 16

Lucas shivered, pulling the fur cloak more tightly over his shoulders. He was standing on the castle wall, looking toward the town, where hundreds of people had gathered before the town gates to welcome back their loved ones.

Nolan had met up with Lucas and Dastan as they were returning with the workers from the valley. They had decided to send scouts ahead, with word of their arrival, and the happy news had spread to the surrounding countryside. People had gathered in masses for the reunion.

Seeing so many people now fall into each other's arms with tears of joy put a smile on Lucas's face. It was perfect, like something out of a dream or storybook, until he spotted a woman pulling a young girl along by the hand. She was weaving through the crowd, pausing to question each tunnel worker she came across. Lucas kept watching, hoping she would find the person she was searching for, but with every headshake she received, he knew her chances were getting slimmer. When she gave up and started to walk away with her head hung, he took his eyes off her. Men had gone missing from this town who were still unaccounted for, and he needed to give the people answers to what happened to them.

Lucas sighed when Davis came to stand beside him. "Last time I stood here," said Lucas, "you were in the town, and it was Grant who joined me here."

"That seems like a long time ago," remarked Davis.

Lucas nodded. "It does."

"You feel betrayed by him?"

"Not as much as Boran will when he exits the tunnel and finds out who is waiting for him there. Grant was the only one he truly trusted."

They gazed toward the town in silence before Davis spoke again. "Dastan wanted me to let you know that the body of the girl we found dead alongside the priest has been taken to the town's cemetery for burial."

"Valora," said Lucas.

"Was that her name?"

"It was," answered Lucas.

Davis sighed. "Zera seems to think she was more to you than a friend," he said. "Is that true?"

"She could have been," answered Lucas honestly. "I liked her, but she was a slave girl and we never got the chance to become close." He turned around when he became aware of Warrick and Zera climbing the stairs behind them.

"We're ready to go whenever you are," said Zera, joining him on the wall-walk. "But Nolan wants to see you before we leave. He just finished his talk with the town officials. They finally admitted not knowing what to do in case of an invasion. None of them come from a military background. They have agreed to have the warriors stay to protect the castle from looters—or whoever might return victorious from battle to claim the castle—and for Nolan to lead them in council."

"Good," said Lucas. "Wisest decision they've made in a long time, no doubt." Lucas had been in the meeting earlier to inform the town officials that Boran had been deceived by Grant and possibly others close to him. "I told the officials," Lucas said, "that the king is not responsible for the sabotage of the dam—that he's been lured into a battle that he has no chance of winning. And that it's therefore left up to them to protect the people and to prepare for any possible outcome. But they only seemed interested in pointing fingers as to who might have conspired with Grant, instead of coming together to make decisions in the absence of the king." Having no interest in listening to the group of well-fed, grown men argue, and seeing Nolan putting his hands through his hair when even he could not get a word in, had made Lucas decide to walk out and leave them to it.

"I wonder how they got the job as town officials?" asked Davis. "They don't seem to be the brightest bunch."

"Grant probably had a hand in appointing them," answered Lucas, leading them down the stairs. "You don't put the smartest in charge when you are planning to take down the king."

"You don't think any of them are in cahoots with Grant?"

"No," answered Lucas, looking over his shoulder. "Grant was smart. He did well to keep his plan and identity a secret from those who had access to the king. Even Eneas had no idea and thought Grant acted against me to protect Boran."

He was pleased to see that the town's officials had left when he entered the Great Hall and only found Nolan and Dastan there. Both were standing by the table with Grant's map spread in front of them.

"Are you sure you need to do this?" asked Nolan when he saw him approach. "It will take you at least two days to cross the mountain on horseback and reach the other side."

"I am sure," Lucas answered. "I saw Boran's army defeated in a vision but did not see the king himself, and I need to know what happened."

"Are you sure you don't want one of us to come?" asked Dastan, gesturing to himself and his brother.

"I am only taking the chosen," answered Lucas. "With Boran gone, the people need protection. I don't think you would go through all this trouble to take a king down and not take his place. Grant flooded the valley to prevent Boran from returning through the tunnel, but that means the army that defeats him won't be able to use it either and must come here another way."

"You believe the Hammonds are coming?" asked Nolan. "If you think Grant is related to them . . ."

"I—" started Lucas, but Dastan shook his head and stepped back from the table.

"Something doesn't add up," said Dastan. "The Hammonds are in alliance with Itan. Would Itan not know they are planning to take Boran down for him?"

"Maybe he does," answered Nolan. "The Hammonds have a castle in the northern part of Itan's land, closest to the tunnel, and a large army at their disposal."

"Then why send Lucas and the chosen here to find out how Boran was to come across to battle him if Itan already knew Boran was building a tunnel?"

"I don't think he knew," answered Lucas when Nolan raised his head and was looking at him questioningly. "I don't think Lord Hammond does either. Someone else is behind all this."

CHAPTER 17

Eli followed Grant and the second cavalry towards the end of the tunnel. They were going to exit ahead of the king to make sure all was clear. Eli had no desire to fight against King Itan, and thought perhaps he could try and make a run for it—except Grant kept a close eye on him, and he didn't think he'd get far. If he did manage it, he could run into Itan's army, and there was no telling how they would receive him. Eli remembered hearing vivid stories about Egon, told to him by older elite borns when he was young, about how Egon tortured every deserter, traitor, or spy, and made them talk, only to kill them once they'd given him the information he wanted. When he became in charge of the elite borns, Eli had passed on those stories, even though he had no idea how much was true.

Eli was surprised when he saw Grant take no caution in exiting the tunnel, riding out at a trot and heading straight for a hill without even looking around. Grant would only do that if he already knew there was no danger, or if he was overconfident. Careless was the word that sprung to mind—that, or plain stupid. Eli reined in his horse and took in the unfamiliar surroundings of rolling hills and rocky outcrops.

He noticed the cavalry behind him closing in, and pushed his horse into a canter to catch up with Grant and Malcolm.

"Where are we?" asked Eli when he had drawn near them. "This doesn't look like Itan's land."

While Grant ignored his question, Malcolm gave him a sinister look as they rode to the top of the hill. What Eli saw next was not what he had expected. The sight took his breath away.

With banners blowing in the wind, two armies stood motionless on the other side of the hill, as if expecting them. The army on the left carried a green color. The color of the Hammonds, who Eli knew were under an alliance with King Itan. Could it be true that Grant was betraying his king? Was that why he and Lucas had been close? Had Lucas and Grant been working together to lure Boran into a trap? Had the whole deal with Eneas just been an elaborate cover, and Eneas was in on it too? But then why was Lucas not here now? Eli's mind was overflowing with questions and conflicted answers. If the Hammonds were here to fight against Boran, then where was King Itan? Or Lord Aron? He did not see Lord Hammond himself either. At the front of his army was a middle-aged man not nearly as old as he remembered Lord Hammond being.

He looked to the soldiers on the right. They were dressed in all black and were waving a banner he'd never seen before. As with the Hammonds, their leader stood at the front—an older man with white hair reaching past his shoulders and a beard parted by two braids. He looked to be a fierce warrior despite his age—someone who commanded respect from his army and the commander by his side, who he recognized all too well. With his fair hair and lean build, he was unmistakably the man who had attacked him in the alley and who Lucas had called Byram.

Grant stopped halfway down the hill and waited for both armies' leaders to come forward on their horses. Eli could feel his heart beating in his chest and looked anxiously at the cavalry around him. None of them seemed alarmed, and all sat relaxed in their saddles, except for Isaac. He was biting his lip, and his horse was reacting to him by prancing around. Isaac noticed Eli looking at him but quickly averted his eyes when both leaders stopped before Grant.

"Uncle Eylgar," said Grant, bowing his head to the man who had come from the left. He then turned to his right and greeted the older man dressed in black. "Hakon."

Hakon returned the greeting by giving a slight nod.

"It is good to see you, Grant," said Eylgar. "It has been a long time. I take it that Boran does not suspect anything?"

"No," answered Grant. "All should go smoothly."

"I am pleased to see you brought the boy," said Hakon.

Eli felt Hakon's eyes on him, sending shivers down his spine.

Grant looked over his shoulder to see who Hakon was looking at and then shook his head. "Ah, no," he replied. "That is Eli, Finton's son. He is replacing his father."

"Then the boy rides with Boran?" asked Hakon, abruptly breaking his eye contact from Eli to stare at Grant. The news seemed to displease him.

"He does not," answered Grant. "I had an opportunity to leave Lucas behind, and I thought it was best to do so. It was clear to me that he had come to respect Boran as a leader, and I didn't want to take the risk of bringing him."

"I hope you have not made a mistake," said Hakon sternly. "The people believe he is the protector of the true king. They need to see him by my side if they are to accept me as their king willingly."

"Yes, and he will," replied Grant. "But for now, Eneas is keeping an eye on him for me. As for the people—they will no longer see Boran as their king when they find the bodies of their drowned loved ones. They will believe it was him who gave the order to trap them in the ravine and destroy the dam holding the water in the quarry. I have already sent scouts to spread word of Boran's responsibility, and when the map detailing the plan is discovered, those rumors will be verified.

I made sure the map carried Boran's signature, and left it in plain sight, in the former king's quarters."

Eli nearly choked. So that was what the noise had been that he heard in the tunnel, and why Grant and his men had looked unconcerned.

"It pleases me to hear Yric's blood still runs through your veins," said Hakon, his demeanor relaxing, shifting into a wry smile. "Your cousin had told me he thought you might have become weak when you showed compassion for the boy."

Eli saw Grant look towards Byram, but it was Eylgar who replied. "Your side of the family may have inherited Yric's brute force and thirst for blood, Hakon," said Eylgar, "but Grant and I inherited his cunning ways of deceit. Don't forget that, without us, you wouldn't be standing here."

Hakon stared at Eylgar with hard eyes—he didn't look as to take kindly to the insult and seemed ready to pull his sword. Eylgar did not seem to be affected, and returned the stare with a firm expression. Eli could feel the tension between them mount. Then Hakon suddenly gave a mischievous grin and raised his hand in the air—bringing the army behind him into motion. "Then, you best stay back, Eylgar," said Hakon, "and let us do what we do best."

With Hakon's army fast approaching and Eylgar riding back to his command, Grant turned the cavalry around and rode them back to the top of the hill. There he halted and dismounted. He took his canteen off his saddle and sat down on a rock. The cavalry followed his lead, spreading out and dismounting. Eli stayed on his horse, feeling sick to his stomach all the while. He had heard enough to understand an unfair battle was about to take place. In front of him, he could see the tunnel's exit and the first of Boran's army exiting. Behind him, he heard the rustling of armor from soldiers making their way up the hill. Trapped between the two, Eli was uncertain of what to do. Then Isaac grabbed him by the arm and pulled him from the saddle.

"Don't show your hesitation," whispered Isaac. "You'll be dead the minute Hakon sees you are unsure of whose side you are on."

"I am not . . ." muttered Eli. He was not sure of Isaac's intentions.

"It's all right," said Isaac, pushing him to the ground and making him sit like the rest of the cavalry. They were to have the appearance of casually resting soldiers, and that was all that Boran would see when he came over the hill. Everything was becoming perfectly clear—how had he been so naive?

"Relax yourself," Isaac added. "I know you're not here by choice, and this isn't your battle to fight."

Eli glanced over to Grant. He appeared to be talking with Malcolm, who was looking at the tunnel exit, but then noticed the hand signals he was giving to the army lying in wait on the other side of the hill. "Why have a battle?" asked Eli. "If they want Boran dead, could Grant not have done so at the castle? He would have had plenty of opportunities."

"Old family code," answered Isaac. "The one to rule is to make the kill. It's not Grant who is supposed to be king. Only Hakon can kill Boran."

CHAPTER 18

The wind was blowing, but Lucas could feel the warm sun on his skin. He raised his head and looked at the bodies of soldiers strewn all around—Boran's soldiers. Holding his breath, he could feel his heart beating in his chest when he took in the carnage of the massacre that had taken place. The stench of blood, flesh and human excrement had some of the chosen retching and covering their noses. Some soldiers had been taken by surprise—their swords either still in their scabbards or only half drawn. A soft breeze ruffled his hair and was tugging on banners attached to poles placed into the ground. Lucas looked down at a fallen soldier by his feet who was clutching a torn strip of fabric in one hand.

Zera walked over, a black scarf wrapped around the lower part of her face to cover her nose, and stopped beside him. "What's he holding?" she asked, looking down.

"Confirmation," answered Lucas, kneeling. He bent his arm to cover his nose when the nauseating smell of rotting flesh came towards him and pulled on the green material the soldier was holding until it came free. He already knew that the intricately woven piece of cloth was torn from one of Hammond's soldiers, no doubt in the moments right before death. He stood up and showed it to Zera. "Now we know for certain that the Hammonds were here."

"He's not here," said Davis, stepping over bodies as he approached. "Could he have escaped?"

"Not likely," answered Lucas. "Boran would have been near the front when the attack happened."

"Well," sighed Davis. He looked at the piece of cloth Lucas was holding in his hand. "The Hammonds must have taken his body then."

"I don't think he's dead."

Before Davis could respond, Warrick called out to them, and they turned to watch him come down the hill—carefully avoiding the slain soldiers on his path.

"The Hammonds were not alone," said Warrick when he reached them. "We found tracks of another army coming and leaving to the east."

"How big?" asked Davis.

"Big," answered Warrick. "At least a thousand soldiers. Mostly on foot."

"And the Hammonds?" asked Lucas.

"Similar in size but more horses."

"How far out do you think they are?"

"No more than half a day—they would have stopped somewhere to rest after the battle."

Lucas looked around and nodded. There were flies around the bodies. The battle had likely taken place two days ago, and if the men had camped for a day to recover and tend to wounded before heading out, then they still had a chance of catching up to them.

"Who do you want to go after first?" asked Davis.

"The Hammonds," answered Lucas. "If they're on horseback, they'll be faster in moving. If they don't have Boran, then we can still catch up with the army going east."

"You're not curious as to who they are?" asked Zera.

"I am," answered Lucas. "But I have a feeling we will meet them soon enough."

The following day, they caught sight of a large army camp on an open field ahead of them. By the wear on the terrain, Lucas could see that the tents that were set up looked to have been there for some time—there were already paths worn in the dirt from people walking in and out of the tents, and in the spaces between the tents that had become thoroughfares. This army had set up well before the attack.

"There are hundreds of tents," said Davis as they lay spying from a rocky outcrop. "It will take you hours to check them all with your mind."

"I don't think I'll have to," replied Lucas. "If Boran is alive and inside a tent, he won't be in any of the smaller ones. They would keep him in one of the larger green ones located in the middle of the camp. Likely with guards posted by the entrance."

Retreating into the clearing where the other chosen were resting, they waited until nightfall, when most soldiers would have settled in for the night. The four of them—Lucas, Davis, Zera, and Warrick—then moved closer to the camp under cover of darkness. Two large fires had been lit at either end of the camp to keep the wolves at bay, and they made sure to stay hidden within the shadows it projected, stopping when they reached a collapsed rabbit warren that gave them something to hide behind.

Laying flat, with his friends at his side and keeping an eye out for any soldier who might be strolling in their direction, Lucas let his mind wander through the camp and checked every tent that caught his interest. The larger tents were set up around an open circle in the center, and he noticed that most housed officers. He then caught sight of three silk tents located right next to each other. Each of them had guards posted by the entrance. The first one had a four-poster bed in the center, a richly carved oak desk on the side, and animal furs covering the floor for warmth. Its occupant appeared to be absent. The second tent was much the same, except for a seating area near the entrance around a small fire pit. By the light of the fire, Lucas could see two people occupying the chairs. One of them was leaning comfortably back in his chair with his feet resting on a small stool, and a drink in his hand. He did not seem to have a care in the world, which made Lucas cringe.

"What is it?" Davis asked. "What do you see?"

"I see Grant," muttered Lucas. "He's here."

"What about Boran?"

Lucas shook his head and concentrated on getting back in the tent. The second man, sitting opposite Grant, he did not recognize. His brown hair was curly and cut at shoulder length. He wore a dark green tunic with the crest of the Hammonds embroidered in the center. He was resting and had his eyes closed. With nothing of interest happening between them, Lucas left the tent and moved on to the last of the three, which he noticed was different. The floor had a minimal covering, with only a runner from the door through the center. There was no seating area or desk, and there were two beds instead of one. There was someone sleeping in each bed, and he recognized who they were straight away. Running out of energy to continue the concentration, Lucas pulled back.

"Did you find him?" asked Zera. "Did you find Boran?"

Lucas shook his head. "No, but I think I've found someone who can tell us what happened to him."

"Who?" asked Davis.

"Eli! He's in one of the bigger tents."

"Alone?"

"No. Someone from the second cavalry, Malcolm, shares the tent with him. Grant's right-hand man. Guessing he's there to keep an eye on him."

"Is your plan to go in when everyone in the camp is sleeping?" asked Warrick. "Sneak in from the back?"

Lucas looked at Warrick. The thought of doing something dangerous had brought a sparkle into his eyes—a challenge always motivated Warrick. It was the only time Lucas saw him focused and not fooling around or playing with sticks or rocks.

"I think that's a good plan," said Zera, moving from laying flat to a crouching position. She was always ready for action.

Davis, on the other hand, looked concerned. "I don't like it," he said, his lips pursed. "Even if we do manage to sneak into the camp, which will be risky on its own, how do you know that Eli won't call for guards the second he sees you? I know you told me that he saved your life, and the two of you had established a truce, but you did kill his father, and you don't know how he feels about you now."

"I understand the risk," said Lucas, "but it's one I must take. Hopefully, Eli can tell us what happened and what the Hammonds are up to. If they're after the entire kingdom, they won't stop with Boran. He was just the first on their list."

"Hammond has an alliance with Itan," said Davis. "He didn't seem the type to break an agreement like that."

"Lord Hammond's not here," said Lucas. "Another Hammond is leading this army. I asked Eli who was to take over from Lord Hammond when he died, and he told me it would be his brother, Eylgar Hammond. I believe it is him I saw with Grant . . . in one of the tents."

"Then Lord Hammond must be dead?"

"Possibly," answered Lucas. "Someone tried to poison him when he was at Itan's a few years back, there to sign the new alliance. I thought, at the time, that Killeand was behind it, to weaken Itan's backup in the event that Boran invaded. Now I think it was part of a much bigger plan."

Davis took a moment to think, then nodded.

"Do you now see why I have to try and talk to Eli?" asked Lucas.

"Yes," answered Davis, sighing. "But any sign of trouble from Eli—promise you will allow me to deal with him?"

"If it comes to that," answered Lucas, standing and peering out over the rabbit warren, "I will do it myself." He walked back down and gathered the chosen around to inform them of his plan. He couldn't talk to them with his mind as he could with Davis, but they sensed him, and he could direct them to avoid danger or to come near his side in the face of it. "Zera, Warrick, and Davis will come with me," he told them, "and I'm going to need you near in case something goes wrong." They nodded their agreement, and Lucas sent them toward the camp, one at a time.

He had opted to enter the camp from the side so they would be able to get to Eli's tent from the back. There were only a few sentry posts on the outside perimeter, and none of the soldiers were on high alert. They were either sitting down or standing by the fires to keep warm, and none watched the surrounding countryside. Being in their territory—or at least close to it, as far as Lucas remembered from studying the map—and with no enemy nearby, they were complacent in their job, and every chosen managed to sneak past in the shadows. When all of the chosen were in place, Lucas and Davis made their move.

When they reached Eli's tent, Zera and Warrick were already there. "We've cut a seam in one of the cloth panels near where Eli is sleeping," Zera whispered. She held the panel open for Lucas and Warrick to slip through.

The boys waited a moment to make sure no noise had woken Malcolm before crawling over to the side of Eli's bed.

Eli's eyes shot open wide when Warrick tapped his arm. He stared at Lucas in disbelief and began to speak, but Lucas put a finger to his mouth, urging him to be quiet. Lucas then motioned for him to get off the bed, and when he did, Warrick slipped in his place under the covers. He put a pillow over his head to hide his hair since he was close in size to Eli but not as blond. "I'll stay behind to be near Warrick in case he's discovered and needs help," Zera told them.

Eli looked confused when he saw Warrick take his place but then understood what was going on. "This is not a rescue mission then?" he whispered, after following Lucas and Davis into an empty supply tent.

"Do you need rescuing?" whispered Lucas, attempting some humor. "It doesn't look like Grant is treating you badly."

"No. He isn't, at the moment." Eli looked at Davis. "When did you and your sister and Warrick leave King Itan?"

Davis shrugged, indicating he had no intention of answering. It was clear he was not going to let his distrust and contempt of Eli go anytime soon.

"The chosen have always been close by," Lucas answered for him. "Itan sent them with me."

"How many?"

"Twelve of us in total."

"Isaac told me you were left behind with Eneas. How did you manage to get away from him?"

"That's a long story," answered Lucas. "One for which we have no time." He also didn't know how much he could tell Eli. "And the less you know, the better it is for both of us. But, speaking of Isaac . . . I know the second cavalry is here, and Malcolm, but where is Isaac?"

"Probably dead now, along with Boran and all the others who were captured by Byram," answered Eli. Lucas held his breath and let him continue. "There was another army waiting with the Hammonds—led by a man named Hakon, but under the command of Byram. I've never seen an army like it. Every soldier was highly skilled and moved like lightning. Boran's army stood no chance. Grant lured Boran up the hill by waving to him that all was clear. When he was close, these soldiers, dressed in black, swarmed over the crest of the hill like ants going in for the kill. Grant had us all hunker down as to not be in the way, but Isaac stood up and rushed towards Boran."

"Was he trying to protect him?" asked Lucas. Whereas Malcolm had been under the influence of Grant, he had felt Isaac's loyalty had always been with Boran. Perhaps Isaac had felt pressured, along with the other cavalry members, to follow Grant's command, but his heart had stepped in at the moment of darkness.

"It looked that way," replied Eli. "And after the battle, I saw him on his knees with his hands tied behind his back. Grant looked to be angry with Isaac. He paced in front of him and then hit him before walking away. I don't know what happened to him after that. All prisoners, including Boran, were given to Hakon."

"For what purpose?"

Eli shrugged. "Eylgar, he is the one leading this army." He paused to make sure Lucas knew who he was referring to, and Lucas nodded that he did. "He didn't want to deal with any of the prisoners, as it is Hakon who is planning to take over."

"You mean Hakon is the one trying to become king?"

"That is what Isaac told me before the battle. Eylgar and Hakon are bound by a family code that states that the one who is to take leadership is the one who must kill the rival."

"Eylgar and Hakon are related?" asked Davis. He was listening while keeping an eye on what was happening outside the tent.

"They all appear to be," answered Eli. "I heard Grant call Eylgar his uncle, and Hakon referred to Byram as Grant's cousin. I also heard them mention a man named Yric."

Lucas looked at Davis, whose expression was grim, his lips a tight line.

Eli must have noticed. "You know who that is?"

Lucas nodded, sighing. "Yes," he answered. "He has to be their ancestor somehow."

"Did you know Yric left behind a child?" asked Davis. He had come to learn the stone's story and knew Yric was the one killed by it.

"No," answered Lucas, "but I'm sure there is much I still don't know. It's all becoming clearer, though." He turned back to Eli. "Do you know if Hakon killed Boran?"

"From what I heard, they were taking prisoners back home with them," answered Eli. "Malcolm told me they use prisoners for entertainment—have them killed in games. I would not like to be in their shoes. Hakon and Byram will show them no mercy."

"I guess we will have to see for ourselves." Lucas glanced over to Davis.

"What?" asked Eli. "You are not thinking of trying to rescue Boran, are you? What about Itan?"

"What about him?" asked Lucas.

"The reason why Grant took me along is so I can give him the information he needs to get to Itan," said Eli. "They're planning on taking him down next. I thought Itan was the true king you're here to protect, not Boran?"

"No one knows who is to be the true king," answered Lucas. "But I do know that Hakon is not on that list."

"Take me with you," pleaded Eli.

Lucas shook his head. "I can't. When Grant notices you've disappeared, he'll come after all of us, and he's not to know I'm no longer in Eneas's custody."

"Then what am I to do?"

"Stay near Grant. Gain his trust by giving him the information he asks for, and he will treat you well. Use your best judgement—when you can, try not to relay knowledge that will compromise the king or anyone else living in his castle."

"He might become suspicious," said Eli. "I've not been very forthcoming with information, and I think he knows I hate him for what he's done. Do you know he killed all the tunnel workers? He had a dam opened, and water directed into the ravine that housed them, and made it sound as if the order came from Boran."

"No," answered Lucas. "I didn't know that." He didn't want to tell Eli that the workers were safe. It was another thing he was better off not knowing.

"That doesn't bother you?" asked Eli, narrowing his eyes. "Are you not here to be the people's hero as well as the king's?" There was sarcasm in Eli's voice, and Lucas felt he was probably lashing out—he'd been transferred to the Hammonds like a pawn, and Lucas understood his rage.

"I can't be there for everyone," answered Lucas. "I can only try and stop more innocent people from getting killed. Do what you must to play Grant's game. Make him believe you loathe Itan, and you still hate me."

"That shouldn't be too difficult for you, Eli," interjected Davis. He stepped towards Eli, and the two stared at each other with hatred in their eyes. "I don't believe for a moment you've changed your ways and are not like your father. His hatred for Lucas ran so deep that in the end, it cost him his life."

Lucas put an arm between them. It was unusual for Davis to be aggressive, and he gave him a stern look. For a moment, he saw the old Eli in front of him. He sighed with relief when Eli took the first step back and let it go.

"One day, Davis," said Eli. "One day."

"I'll be ready," answered Davis, then, as to avoid a further altercation, he indicated it was time to go.

Lucas took Eli back to the tent and put a hand on his shoulder before letting him go inside. "Are we good?" asked Lucas.

"You mean, do I forgive you for killing my father?" asked Eli, looking at him with an expression of resentment Lucas remembered all too well. "No, I don't," he continued after Lucas nodded. "But for now, I hate Grant and Byram more than I ever hated you, so you needn't worry. I won't stand in your way until you've dealt with them."

"Fair enough," said Lucas. Then, he thought for a moment. He had to give Eli something, some kind of hope, and trust in him. "Eli, it's very important you keep this between us . . . can I trust you completely?"

"Yes," Eli grumbled, but gave a weak smile. "Like I said, I need you as much as you need me right now."

"Then know this—the tunnel workers are safe. We did manage to save them. But Grant must not know we have spoken."

Eli gave a somber nod, then disappeared through the tent's opening without another word. A few seconds later, Warrick came back out.

"How did it go?" asked Warrick when they slipped out of camp.

"As we hoped," answered Lucas. "We got what we needed, and Davis managed to remind Eli to hate all of us again."

"According to plan, then?" asked Zera.

"Yes," answered Lucas. "Hating me is the only way for him to be near Grant and stay alive."

CHAPTER 19

ith Hakon and Byram days ahead and a rainstorm washing away their tracks, it took the chosen some time to pick up their trail.

"Here!" shouted Archer excitedly, leaning his thin body down along his horse's neck and pointing at the ground. He and two others had ridden ahead of Lucas and stopped.

Lucas caught up with the three chosen and stared at the hoof marks and footprints left in the mud. "We will have to ride hard and rest little," he said. "Boran and his soldiers are likely to await death once Hakon reaches his destination." He was also propelled forward by the urgent feeling that he was supposed to be by their side when they were faced with their execution.

When the scenery around them changed, and the lush green gave way to a barren landscape of stones and sparse yellow prairie grass, Lucas sensed he was closing in on the army he was chasing. Hakon had kept his army moving—there were no signs of them making camp for the night.

The chosen were desperately in need of a break, and Lucas let them rest in the tree line, leaving them behind and continuing ahead with only Zera, Warrick, and Davis. After a considerable distance,

Lucas stopped and viewed the desolate land that stretched before him. The prairie grass was flattened by the soldiers' many footsteps, going straight across towards the east. Some distance away, he could see wagon ruts coming from the south that made a permanent trail going north, indicating there was civilization nearby.

Davis reined his horse in alongside Lucas. "We could be nearing their destination," he said. "But in this terrain, we'll be out in the open for anyone to see."

"Maybe we should wait until nightfall?" asked Warrick. He had stopped his horse on Lucas's other side and was sitting back to look around. "It's hard to imagine, though, that anyone would want to live here. Looks dry and miserable. What are they doing for food?"

Lucas turned to Warrick and shook his head with a smile.

"What?" asked Warrick, who noticed his attention.

"You," answered Lucas, continuing his grin. "You seem to be thinking a lot about food lately."

"Warrick thinks about food all the time," commented Zera. "Not just lately."

Warrick shrugged. "If you live on rations like we do, it's hard not to."

Lucas noticed Davis was still considering their situation. "I'm not surprised they chose to live here," said Davis, his expression stern. Lucas knew he didn't always appreciate Warrick's different point of view on things. "It's why we didn't know of their existence—no man would venture out here without a purpose. But I would like to know what brought them back, after the battle."

"What do you mean?" asked Zera.

"Eli told us that Hakon is to take over Boran's kingdom," said Davis. "If that is true, then why did they not follow the mountains around to go south and cross the river? Why did they come back here, where there is no visible way to enter Boran's land?"

Hearing his friend's words, Lucas let his eyes go back to the wagon tracks and followed them to the mountain range on his right. From a distance, they took the appearance of a wall—a wall surrounding a large pasture or a dividing fence between two kingdoms. Davis was right. What *was* here that had made them come back? Facing back to the track the army had made across the plains, he bit on his bottom lip. He was torn in his decision on how to proceed.

"What do you want to do?" asked Davis.

"We'll wait until dark," answered Lucas. "Then, we will change course."

Lucas leaned forward in his saddle and let his horse find his way up the steep slope. He was glad for the few trees that provided cover from anyone looking up from the plains but wished there were more. Behind him, he could hear the tumbling of loose stones and the heavy breathing of the horses as they made their way up. When he reached a ridge, he waited. The sun had just risen, and he could see a haze over the landscape below. It had taken them all night to reach the mountains, carefully avoiding a cluster of houses after they heard dogs barking.

When the last of the chosen reached the ridge, Lucas nudged his horse to walk again. Moving east, he kept sight of the land below and soon learned that his decision to no longer follow the army had been the right one when he spotted what he could only assume were watchtowers. Tall, black structures dotted the landscape, strategically placed to maximize their view of the plains. There would have been no way to avoid them, and he sighed with relief when he realized the kind of predicament they could have been in had they followed. Beyond the towers, he could see smoke rising and the contours of a large settlement in the far distance. He steered his horse away from the possibility of being seen and led the chosen away from the edge of the ridge and deeper into the mountain's foliage.

It was midday when the forest suddenly became thicker, and it became more challenging for the horses to find their way through the brush. Pushing forward, Lucas stopped when the sound of people echoed off the rock walls. "Dismount," he called softly, but loud enough for the chosen to hear.

Davis came to stand next to him and turned his ear to listen. He frowned when it became clear it was someone shouting.

"Sounds like someone giving orders," Lucas said.

"Soldiers?" Davis asked.

"Not quite," answered Lucas. He had let his mind go and caught the first glimpse of what was happening in front of them. Davis looked at him questioningly when he heard the unmistakable sound of a whip slicing through the air and hitting the ground.

Lucas motioned to the chosen to follow him, leaving two behind with the horses. The crack of the whip sounded once more. Crawling forward and peering over the edge of a narrow gorge, the chosen soon observed what he had already seen. A group of fifteen men, all chained together, were walking through the canyon below. A guard on horseback, holding a whip, rode next to them, urging them to keep moving.

"Prisoners?" whispered Davis. "What are they doing down there?"

"I think they're coming from wherever it was they were laboring," responded Zera. "They're filthy. And look exhausted."

"Prisoners finishing a hard day," remarked Warrick, his expression grim.

Lucas looked to his right. There was nothing in the gorge to indicate that they had been working nearby, but for them to be prisoners seemed plausible. He recalled having been sentenced to hard labor himself after killing the two dark order members at the inn. He shuddered to think he could still be on the chain if it had not been for

Officer Verron rescuing him from the prison transport that was taking him to King Itan's mines.

Watching the group disappear, Lucas crawled back from the edge and had everyone return to the horses. There were a few hours of daylight left, and he wanted to find out where those prisoners had been working. It meant a delay in finding Boran, but something gnawed at him. He either had to confirm his suspicions or put them to rest.

As they rode higher up the mountain, Lucas let his mind follow the gorge and soon noticed wooden ramps built inside the canyon. "They have constructed ramps," he said, turning around in the saddle and speaking to Davis behind him.

"Where?" asked Davis as he maneuvered his horse around a low bush. "Inside the gorge?"

"Yes," answered Lucas. "Where it is too difficult for men or horses to traverse large boulders."

"What do the ramps look like?" asked Zera, who was not far behind her brother. "Could those prisoners have built them recently?"

"Not recently," answered Lucas. "It looks like the ramps have been there for some time. Moss and algae have spread along their edges, in places where the canyon is damp and wet."

"Sounds like the canyon is an important thoroughfare," said Davis. "I wonder where it leads to."

Lucas nodded and turned back in his saddle. "So do I," he mumbled under his breath.

When they began to lose the light and the terrain became too treacherous for the horses in the dark, he had everyone stop and rest for the night.

At dawn, they continued and observed a second group of prisoners making their way down the canyon. Again, they were chained together, with a single guard riding next to them. This time, Lucas counted eighteen men and two boys who were similar in age as himself. With it being this early morning, he wondered if they had been working through the night. But on what?

"Could they be Boran's missing townspeople?" asked Zera. They had ridden away from the gorge to find water for the horses and were filling their canteens by a small waterfall.

"They could be," answered Lucas. "It's crossed my mind."

"Then there should be others," continued Zera. "Were there not hundreds who went missing over the years?"

"If they were brought here and are still alive, yes," answered Lucas. He stood up and put the wooden dial back in his canteen to close it. He then walked back to his horse and tied it to his saddle. When he looked over his shoulder, he saw most of the chosen still quenching their thirst or splashing water over their faces. Archer had taken his boots off and was washing his feet. He looked up and, when he saw Lucas, smiled at him before going back to scrubbing. Archer was the cheery one in the group, always making the best of every situation—even though he had to be missing Tanner. The two of them had been close. They had spent a lot of time together working in the stables at Itan's. After Tanner's death, Archer had grown quiet and subdued, but now he seemed his usual self again. Lucas didn't know why, but over these last few days, whenever he laid eyes on Archer, his heart felt heavy.

"Something's troubling you," said Davis, while tying his canteen to his saddle. He had spoken without looking at him. "And you're not sharing it with me. Why is that?"

"Maybe because I'm not sure and don't want to alarm you," answered Lucas.

"Since when has that stopped you?" asked Davis. He finished securing his canteen and put the reins over his horse's head.

"Since now, I suppose," Lucas replied.

Davis let out a sigh but asked no further and mounted up.

Having to find an easier route for the horses had slowly forced them away from the gorge. If it wasn't for the loud creaking sound of wood and the noise of a rope being pulled through a pulley, they would have missed seeing the end of the gorge and the structure built against the cliff wall. Now, lying on their stomachs, they watched the hive of activity as a massive platform carrying soldiers was heaved from the bottom of the gorge to the top by teams of oxen. When it drew level with the plateau above, the soldiers got off and marched away, using a road cut out through the mountain.

"There's our answer as to what those prisoners are working on," said Zera. "And how Hakon is planning on moving his army onto Boran's land. They are building a road."

"I wonder how far they've gotten," muttered Warrick. "And how many people they have working on it."

"There's only one way to find out," answered Lucas, backing up. The others followed his lead too abruptly, causing some stones to crumble away from the ledge. They all froze as the rocks hit the side of the gorge on their way down. Lucas saw them hit the ground, narrowly missing the men arriving by horse. One of them looked up, a lock of fair hair falling away from his cold blue eyes—Byram!

Lucas rushed everyone back to their horses as quietly as possible. It was clear that the structure was a lift, and he didn't want to be anywhere near Byram when he got off at the top—it would be a quick trip around the end of the gorge to where the chosen were gathered. He didn't think Byram had seen any of the chosen, but he thought it best not to wait and find out. He rode away from the gorge until they came across a path going in the same direction as the much wider, newly cut road they had seen at the top of the lift. This path was narrow, allowing only single file. It appeared that, up until recently, the path had been well-traveled—young plants were sprouting up where horses' hooves and footsteps had left their mark in the ground.

"A trader route?" asked Davis. "Or a shepherd path?"

"Or the trail used to smuggle people off Boran's land," stated Warrick. "They would have had a way to get them here in the first place."

"It could also be the way the dark order traveled," said Zera.

Lucas only half-listened to his friends discussing the possible uses of the path. He knew enough of Hakon's plan to get into Boran's land. Now it was time to stop him from having the right to take it. Which meant he had to find Boran before it was too late. He led the chosen down the path until they came across a road running along the side of the mountain with fresh cartwheel tracks. Lucas stopped to listen.

"Do you hear anything?" asked Zera, pulling up next to him.

"No," answered Lucas, shaking his head. "The road seems clear."

"I think it's too dangerous to continue," commented Davis. "Judging by the number of fresh ruts in the road, it will only be a matter of time before we come across someone."

"I don't disagree," said Lucas. He peered over his shoulder and looked at the chosen, who were sitting quietly on their horses. "We'll camp for the night," he said, backing away from the road, "and try to find a better way to continue in the morning."

They found a shallow cave some distance into the forest, where they built a small fire and roasted the two squirrels that Archer and Zera had managed to kill with their bows. It would have been Tanner left to that task with Archer in years past, thought Lucas, as he chewed on the meat. He couldn't help but long for Tanner's company from time to time, impossible as that was. He knew everyone still missed Tanner, but they hardly spoke his name these days. His death only reminded them of their own vulnerability, and no one wanted to follow in his footsteps.

The chosen sat quietly. Each enjoyed the few bites of food—not nearly a large enough portion to fill their stomachs, but none complained. Throwing a bone into the fire, Lucas reached for Grant's map, which he had folded and packed up before leaving Boran's castle, and

Davis had now fetched from his saddlebag. Lucas spread it out in front of him, smoothing out the creases. After studying it, he took a half-burned stick from the fire and blew out the flame at the end.

"What are you doing?" asked Davis.

"Trying to determine where exactly on Boran's land the road they're building will enter."

"How would you do that? Hakon's land and this part of the mountain range are not shown on the map."

"I don't need them to be," answered Lucas. "If we had traveled at normal speed, and not as fast as we have done over these last three days, how long do you think it would have taken us from the exit of the tunnel to where we saw what looked to be Hakon's settlement?"

"At least another day," answered Davis. "Making it four."

"Four days . . ." mumbled Lucas. He continued to study the map, using the charcoal from the stick to mark dots on it and to draw lines from Boran's castle to the east. He ignored Davis's further questions, provoking a few annoyed sighs—at some point, Davis got up to go and sit by Warrick. After a while, Lucas yawned. He suddenly felt tired and folded the map. He had a few hours to rest before midnight, when they planned to head further down the mountain. He placed the map under a rock next to him and lay down to close his eyes.

Alone, and aware he was dreaming, Lucas looked up when the clouds moved in front of the moon, taking with them the light that had shown him the entrance to a dark and narrow passageway. Standing before the entrance, in total darkness, Lucas had no choice but to step inside. If he wanted answers, it was the only way. He walked forward, putting his hands on the walls on either side to guide himself. He could feel the rough texture of thick-sawn planks and the horizontal grooves in between. Lucas sensed he was not alone in the tunnel. He paused to listen and felt his heart pounding when he heard the unmistakable low growl of a wolf behind him. Looking over his shoulder, he could see nothing in the darkness, but the growling became louder and closer. He reached for his sword, but it was not there, and neither was his dagger. Panic came over him, and he increased the speed of his steps. When he could see the tunnel's end, he began to run toward it, but found it closed off by an iron gate. He gripped the bars to push it open. Nothing. When he pulled at it, it would not budge either. With the clouds moving away from the moon, he could see a dark arena on the other side of the gate. With high walls surrounding the sandy floor—he knew that even if he managed to open the gate, there was no escape from what was coming for him . . .

Lucas woke when he sensed the danger and jumped to his feet with a sword in hand, but he was too late. With his back to the mouth of the cave, he could do nothing but watch Byram step from behind the trees and into the light of the moon. Surrounding him were the same men Lucas had seen Byram with in the gorge, their black clothing making them almost indistinguishable from the night as he blinked to make them out. To Lucas's horror, two of them had their arms around Warrick and Archer—and each of his friends had a knife at their throat.

"Well, well, well," said Byram. He was grinning ear to ear. "You are the last person I expected to find when we followed the tracks down the path, and so easily, I might add. After we found your horses, all we had to do was wait for these two to show up. You've lost your touch, Lucas. Did you not sense me coming?"

Lucas couldn't help but curse under his breath for letting his guard down. He should have checked to see where Byram was going after he used the lift. All the other chosen had jumped to their feet, swords in hand. Zera was standing closest to him, her eyes fixed on the scene before her. The only person he didn't see was Davis, but then heard his voice and saw him with his mind—Davis was hiding in the shadows with his back against a boulder that was obscuring him from sight. He had his bow ready and was peeking around the stone to find his target.

Byram gestured at the sword Lucas was holding. "You might want to drop that if you want your friends to live," said Byram. "You know it's you I want."

"Let them go first," said Lucas. The men holding them were large and muscular, and Lucas could see Warrick and Archer struggling to breathe under their restraint.

"I don't think so," said Byram. "I know what you and your friends are capable of, even with your backs against a wall. Surrender or these two are the first to die." To add to the threat, Byram took his knife and grabbed Archer for himself. Archer resisted only for a moment, his boots scuffing at the ground as he writhed in Byram's grip.

"Lucas," muttered Zera, her voice full of panic. "We have to do something."

Byram tightened his grip, and Archer's eyes filled with fear. Lucas threw his sword onto the ground. Around him, the chosen did the same. Zera was the last to do so.

"Sensible," said Byram, looking at Zera. "Now, before you get any ideas in your head . . ." His eyes were stone cold as he stared at Lucas. Then, with one abrupt, automatic movement, he cut Archer's throat and threw him to the ground. It happened so quickly and so suddenly that all Lucas could do was gasp when he watched Archer's body fall. Archer kicked a leg out, as if to fight the pool of blood forming around him, but then was still. The chosen stared in shock, but none dared to move—Byram now had his knife pointed at Warrick.

"Why?" was all Lucas managed to get out. He swallowed hard,

pushing down his emotions, knowing that Byram would only respect him if he showed strength. He had to remain visibly unfazed by what had just happened to someone who had been like a brother at his side. He saw Davis lower his bow. "I did as you asked."

"You did," said Byram. "And now you will make sure that you will keep doing so. Now get on your knees, or another of your comrades will die."

Knowing now that Byram would not hesitate to carry out the threat, Lucas slowly sank to his knees. He put his hands on the top of his head and let a member of the dark order tie his hands behind his back. When he was secured, Byram lowered his knife and pushed Warrick onto his knees next to Lucas.

"I'm sorry," whispered Warrick as the other chosen were being tied up. "They were already waiting for us by the horses."

"It wasn't your fault," replied Lucas.

"Where is Davis?" asked Warrick.

Lucas gave a small shake of his head—Byram was making his way over to them. The only hope they had now was to keep Davis's presence a secret.

"The only thing that would give me more joy than having you on your knees," said Byram, "is to see a sword go through you. Just as our Garam had a sword go through him."

Lucas lifted his head and stared up at Byram. "I don't know which of your men Garam was, but if he was the one who killed my father . . . then he got what he deserved, and on that score, we are even." He then gestured to Archer. "As for him . . . we are not." For a moment, he thought Byram was going to erupt with rage and regretted provoking him—he had the other chosen to think of—but Byram only turned his back on Lucas and made an upwards motion with his hand, signaling all the chosen to get up on their feet.

As they were escorted away, the chosen lowered their heads when passing Archer. It was all they could do to respect their friend and mourn their loss. Lucas swallowed a lump in his throat and heard Davis's voice in his head.

"I'll see to his burial," said Davis. "Then, I will come for you, find a way to free you, and you can kill Byram."

"Byram will pay for what he did," answered Lucas. "But I don't want you to try and come for us. You are needed on the other side of these mountains, with Nolan and the warriors, when Hakon invades." He paused to concentrate on something else before getting back to Davis. "Take the map. I left it under a rock by the cave. On it, you will see a spot I marked—be there when Hakon comes."

"What about you?" asked Davis. "What about my sister?"

"I will try and keep everyone alive," Lucas replied.

When they reached the spot where the chosen had left their horses, they found them scattered and wandering away. Byram's face contorted with anger when he saw the rope the horses were tethered to lying on the ground. Taking significant strides and crushing branches under his feet, he marched over to Lucas.

"I don't know what you are playing at," hissed Byram, grabbing him by the collar and pulling him close. "I warned you not to pull any stunts, and you better get those horses back."

"Are you saying I gave the horses a signal of some kind?" Lucas spoke as gently as he could. "Told them to do that?"

"That's exactly what I am saying."

"If that was possible, don't you think I would've had those horses come barreling down by now, and had you kicked out of the way? That is, if I was indeed responsible for them getting loose?" asked Lucas, meeting Byram's hard stare. He knew he had to bluff his way out of this. He had set the horses wandering to get Davis's horse away but now needed to put Byram at ease before he lashed out again.

"I can get them back," Lucas said calmly, "but know I had nothing to do with this. They more than likely got spooked." He wasn't sure if Byram believed him, but he kept his expression stoic and, after a moment of silence, Byram let go and stepped back.

Lucas looked around, giving Byram the impression he was determining where the horses might be. He then whistled a few distinctive tunes to make it appear as though he was trying to get them to come. He didn't want Byram to know that, in truth, he was concentrating on bringing the right horses forward and to ensure his horse stayed in the night's shadows, along with Davis's. Davis would need two horses if he were to have the best chance to escape, and the destrier that had been given to him by Boran was the fastest and most robust, making him the obvious choice. Lucas also preferred that his horse didn't become someone's trophy, and he couldn't rule out that this could be the end of the line for him. He only hoped that if it came to that, the others could walk free. Or break free.

Byram was becoming impatient. Lucas was pretending as if he had to whistle a different tune for each horse, and he took his time doing so. Byram paced before him, demanding Lucas hurry up, but Lucas ignored him—hoping that Byram's mounting frustration would have him overlook a horse whose rider had been killed. When he felt Byram could take no more, Lucas brought the last horse forward, allowing it to step into the clearing. It looked like Byram was looking for another horse to appear for a moment, but when he saw all the chosen mounted, he pushed Lucas hard in his back.

"Get on," snapped Byram. "You've wasted enough of my time."

Without a word, Lucas walked to the dun horse that had been Archer's. He had to wait for an order member to help him up, since his hands were tied behind his back. He watched as Byram mounted his horse, a proud gleam of triumph plastered over his face.

Byram had Lucas ride in front of him, behind two of his soldiers. The chosen were surrounded by the rest of the order, some distance behind him. They rode in silence after several attempts from Lucas to ask where they were going went unanswered. He could only assume Byram was taking them to Hakon.

He mourned the loss of Archer as they followed the path down the mountain. He could have prevented it. Deep down, he had known something was going to happen to Archer. That was when he should have turned the chosen around, proceeded alone with Davis. Even though each chosen had been aware of the risks and had accepted their fate, come what may, now they were all in hot water.

Byram had them stop at a sandy rock pool to let the horses drink as they reached the bottom of the mountain. He had his comrades dismount to quench their thirst while leaving Lucas and the chosen on their horses to watch. They sat unmoved, each trying to look unaffected by the inviting water, though Lucas felt their desire. The pool had a sparkle to it because of the light-colored sand beneath its surface and the sunlight shining on it. It was the only inviting thing Lucas had seen during their time in this region. He saw Byram kneel by it, taking his time to drink and then dunk his head into the refreshing water—no doubt he knew he was watched and wanted to prolong their agony. When he stood up, he calmly put his hands through his wet hair, stretched his arms, and turned around.

"Best place to refresh yourself," said Byram, as he passed Lucas on his way to his horse. "Used to come here all the time with my brothers."

"You have brothers?" asked Lucas. He half wished Byram had not told him that. It meant he would have more of Byram's kind to kill, once he was able to escape.

Byram paused and looked up at him with a calm stare that unnerved Lucas more than the cold eye he had been getting from him. Byram smirked and shook his head as he continued to his horse—it was clear to Lucas that he was enjoying every minute.

"So, tell me something," said Byram as he mounted. "The last thing

I heard was that you were down in Eneas's dungeon, strapped to a table in a trance-like state, unable to move or speak. Yet . . . here you are. I'm curious as to how you achieved this."

"Did Grant tell you this?" asked Lucas. "I know he's the one getting you to do his filthy work for him."

Byram narrowed his eyes. "Was what he told me not true?"

Lucas wanted to say that it wasn't. Grant had fooled enough people with lies, including the king he worked for. Who was to say he had remained truthful to his cousin, but the pause in Byram's movements and the tensing of his muscles told him that the possibility of Grant's disloyalty had already crossed his mind, and this was not what he wanted to hear. Now was not the time to put doubts in Byram's mind about family loyalty, Lucas decided. He had the chosen to think of and needed to keep Byram's dark side at bay to keep them out of harm's way. "When Grant saw me," he replied instead, "Eneas had only just given me his elixir. He didn't come back to check to see if it worked."

Byram continued to mount and gave his warriors the signal to move out.

"Did you kill Eneas?" he asked, and waited for Lucas to answer. "I know he would never just let you go."

Lucas didn't answer.

"It's alright," continued Byram. "You saved me the trouble of having to do it myself."

CHAPTER 20

It was only an hour later when they left the mountain path and reached the dirt road leading to the plain's large settlement. As they approached, Lucas could see that every house and building was black, just like the watchtowers he'd seen days ago. He could now see that they were made of blackened wood, giving the whole place a sad look. The houses were spread out over a large area, with no walls around them for defense and no road system—as if each house had been built wherever the owner pleased.

There were plenty of people about, all wearing black and going about their business, and taking little notice of the group riding through their town. Lucas wondered if the two groups of prisoners he had seen in the gorge had been brought here—it seemed, by the lack of reaction or surprise in the people around him, that observing the transport of prisoners was a daily occurrence in the people's lives.

Byram took over the lead when they passed all the houses and were riding towards a group of larger structures on the settlement's outskirts. These buildings were the only ones built with thought and purpose. Each one was connected to another by a covered walkway and there were courtyards in between. The central building was the grandest and most ornate, with double doors and columns that held up the roof over its entrance.

Byram stopped when they reached an open area with smaller buildings along the side. There were training fields with pelts and climbing structures in the distance, but what Lucas saw before him had his immediate interest. On the ground lay square panels, the size of a wagon floor, constructed of wooden beams tied together in a crisscross pattern. And each trellis covered a pit.

Busy trying to comprehend what he was seeing, Lucas was caught by surprise when someone pulled him off his horse. He lost his balance when his feet hit the ground, and fell backward on top of one of the trellises. Rolling over onto his stomach to get back up, he looked down and saw twenty or so confused pairs of eyes staring up at him from the hole below. He took in their dirty and blood-crusted faces and recognized the only dark-skinned man below him.

"Isaac," whispered Lucas.

It took a moment before Isaac realized who it was calling his name. He jumped to his feet. "Lucas!"

"How many in total are here?" asked Lucas.

"This is it," answered Isaac. "They took the strongest to do hard labor, or so we've been told."

"Where's Boran?" Lucas asked. He heard Byram shout behind him, and he felt the trellis bow slightly under the weight of the two large men who stepped on it. He was grabbed under his armpits and pulled off before Isaac was able to give him a reply.

Standing back on solid ground, Byram stood before him.

"Where is the king?" asked Lucas.

"Boran is no longer king," snapped Byram.

"Was he killed?"

Ignoring his question, Byram spoke to his men. "Put them in one of the holes at the far back. I don't want him anywhere near the soldiers."

Having experienced that a trellis was strong enough to hold the weight of three people, Lucas noticed it was heavy as well when it took two men to lift one off a pit furthest away from Boran's soldiers. A ladder was lowered down into the hole, and the chosen had their hands freed one at a time before being told to climb down. Lucas was the last in line and rubbed his wrists while turning around to step onto the ladder. He saw Byram watching him from a distance. He turned and walked away as Lucas began his descent.

When the trellis dropped closed, dirt crumbled off the sides and fell onto the chosen standing against the walls. They had lowered their heads to prevent it from getting in their eyes.

Zera brushed it off her hair.

"Now what?" asked Warrick, standing next to him.

"Now we wait," answered Lucas, finding a space against one of the walls for himself. He stretched his legs and looked up at the blue sky visible through the openings in the trellis. If it were to rain, they would all get soaked, but he doubted it was to happen. There was no evidence of water ever dripping down these walls. They were smooth, dry, and rock hard.

Zera came to sit next to him and followed his gaze towards the sky. "I didn't see Davis when Byram captured us," she said. "Nor did I see his horse afterward, and you left yours behind. He's not trying to come and rescue us from this death trap, is he?"

"No," answered Lucas. He'd not been able to speak with Zera or Warrick since their capture. "We're alone in this one."

They continued to sit side by side, listening to the abundance of sounds around them—soldiers marching, officers shouting, horses trampling the ground in the nearby corral as they ran along the fence, the opening and closing of doors. When nightfall came, those sounds disappeared, and it became quiet.

"I never thought I'd be able to say that it's too quiet for me to fall asleep," said Warrick. "The silence is unnerving. I can't even hear the guards moving around."

"That's because there aren't any," said Lucas.

"What? No guards? None at all?"

Lucas shook his head. "No one is watching us."

"Well," sighed Warrick, looking up at the framework high above, "I guess they are safe in the knowledge that no one can get out."

"Yes," replied Lucas. "It's the most secure prison cell I've ever seen."

"While I was waiting to climb down," continued Warrick, "I saw the people imprisoned close to us. They looked like the workers we saw marched through the gorge."

"I believe they are," said Lucas.

"What do you think they are doing here?" asked Zera.

"I wish I knew," answered Lucas. "I also want to know where Boran is. I can't see him anywhere."

In the far distance, dogs started to bark a chorus, and Lucas noticed Warrick slumping over and falling asleep. After suppressing a yawn, Lucas decided it was best to give in to his own desire to rest.

Once again, Lucas found himself in the narrow tunnel that led to the arena. He could hear the deep growl of the wolf as it came closer in the darkness, but this time, he didn't run. He knew the exit was barred, and there was no way out. He would face what was coming for him. As his eyes adjusted to the dark, the black shape of a wolf came forward from the shadows. It approached slowly, with its head down and yellow eyes locked on Lucas. Lucas could feel his heart pulse in his chest when the wolf stopped and showed its white teeth in a deep and threatening snarl. "You may try and take me," said

Lucas, "but I am going to fight you all the way." He planted his feet firmly on the ground and braced for the wolf's jump . . .

It was early in the morning when commotion near the other pits woke Lucas from his dream. He jumped to his feet and got the chance to stand just as the trellis was lifted. A man appeared near the edge of their hole with a bucket that he emptied above them. A watery liquid of corn, cabbage, and soggy bread fell to the ground before them. Scraps one would only feed to pigs, and even then, the mixture would be poured into a trough.

"Don't touch it," warned Lucas when the trellis closed again. "None of us should be eating this. They are trying to make us sick."

"What if we're given nothing else?" asked Warrick.

"Then we go without food. We've all done this before." He stepped forward and turned around to look at each of his companions. They were all staring at him and waiting to hear what he had to say. "Every one of us experienced the hole at King Itan's," Lucas began. "We all remember going without food and water for days before the fight to determine if we were a chosen one or not. What did that do to us? Did it weaken us as intended, or did we become stronger and even more determined to prove our worth?"

"Stronger," answered the chosen in unison.

Lucas nodded. "Where the average man will fall, we rise. That's what it means to be a chosen."

"You think they will have us fight?" asked Zera.

Lucas nodded. "I do."

"Against whom?"

"I think we will find out soon."

CHAPTER 21

Lucas used the heel of his boot to scrape dirt over the liquid seeping towards him from the pile of slop in the center of the pit. He hoped that their agony was not going to last much longer. It had been three days, with no sign of Byram, and no sign of anyone coming for them. At first, their spirits were high, and they made a conscious effort to keep them that way. Warrick had even played little mind games to distract everyone, but now everyone was quiet.

Lucas let himself doze until Zera nudging him woke him up. She was gesturing upwards. Lucas watched as the lattice framework was lifted and pulled away, and a wooden ladder wrapped at the joints with coarse rope was lowered down. The face of an officer from Hakon's army appeared and its owner peered down at the group for a moment before requesting that Lucas get on his feet.

"Just you," said the officer when Lucas looked around at the chosen.

"I'm not going anywhere without them," said Lucas, and remained standing at the base of the ladder.

"It's you he wants to see," said the officer. "Not anyone else."

"Who?"

"King Hakon."

“King?” asked Lucas. “Since when?”

Ignoring his question, the officer backed away from the ladder. Several soldiers appeared along the edge of the pit, holding long spears in their hands.

“You better go,” said Warrick. “I think he was serious when he told you to come with him.”

“I think you might be right,” said Lucas, and grabbed the ladder with both hands. When he was above ground, they tied his hands behind his back again and walked him to the building with the double doors and wood columns.

With the outside of the building dark and uninviting as it was, Lucas had guessed the inside would be no different. His hunch was confirmed when he entered and found himself in a room that was tall and narrow, with nothing of color that he could see. Small windows ran along the top of the walls, but they let little light through. If it wasn’t for the candles and torches hung from the walls, he didn’t think he would be able to see much of anything.

Towards the end of the narrow room, he saw a raised platform covered with animal fur and a throne of black granite from which an older man was watching him approach with great interest. It was their leader, Hakon. His snow-white hair and beard, parted in two braids, would have drawn anyone’s attention, but all Lucas had eyes for was the fur of a black wolf hanging off his shoulders.

He was stopped and roughly pushed down onto his knees when he had made his way about halfway down the room. Behind him, footsteps sounded from someone approaching. Lucas didn’t have to look to know that the black pair of boots stopping beside him belonged to Byram.

He could feel Hakon’s eyes upon him as he remained kneeling with his head down and his eyes directed at the floor. He was not allowed to look up. The couple of attempts he had made to do so, he had felt a kick in his side from the officer standing behind him. It seemed Hakon had a strict protocol in place on how he wanted things done. Even Byram, as he stood motionless beside Lucas, seemed to respect the leader before him, and Byram, of course, was known to bow to no one.

When Hakon was finally ready to address him, Lucas felt another kick, but this time it was to make him look up.

"I know who you are," said Hakon. "I also know it is hard to get to you—I've lost good men trying. It had me puzzled when I learned of your easy capture this time, but now . . . I wonder. Have you come to recognize me as the rightful king, or could it be that you simply made a terrible mistake?"

Lucas didn't know how to answer. He had no idea why it had been so easy for Byram to apprehend him either. Perhaps it was part of the prophecy, and his capture would have been the only possible way for him to get close to Hakon—just as staying behind with Eneas had allowed him to save the tunnel workers. Taking too long to speak caused him to feel another boot, this time against the back of his leg. He looked up at the officer, annoyed, before facing Hakon. "I was not aware that the time to recognize a new king was here," he replied. "Should I assume Boran is dead?"

"I defeated Boran on the battlefield," said Hakon. "His soldiers are now mine. His land will soon be mine. His people will be honoring me as their king, and I require you to do the same."

"For a king to lose everything to a rightful other . . ." Lucas began, pausing to choose his words carefully. He had to play this smart. Hakon had avoided telling him that Boran was dead, which meant he might not be, and he needed to know for sure. ". . . that king needs to have died or fallen from grace, making him no longer worthy of the title."

"Fallen from grace?" asked Hakon.

Lucas nodded. "If for whatever reason a king is not strong enough to lead his people, he would be deemed unfit to rule."

Hakon rubbed his top lip with his finger for a moment and then stood up. "Bring him here," he shouted and stepped off the platform.

Lucas could hear doors opening and the sound of someone dragged in with their legs trailing behind them. He held his breath when he saw the figure dropped on the floor before him. Tied with his hands behind his back, and with his mouth gagged, lay the king. Lucas barely recognized Boran. He was wearing an ordinary pair of brown trousers and a white undershirt, stained with dirt and blood. Gone were his flashy, vibrantly colored clothes. His usually perfectly groomed beard was now matted with the same substance that covered his clothes and skin. His eyes looked hollow, and Lucas could see there was little life or spirit left in them. No wonder, thought Lucas, that he had not seen him. This was not the man he had been looking for.

Hakon stepped towards Boran and grabbed him violently by the hair to turn his face toward Lucas. "Is this a man you would still call king?" yelled Hakon.

Lucas saw Boran stare at him, his eyes desperate. For all the mistakes Boran had made as a king, all the people he had wronged, and all that he had planned to do, Lucas still could not bear to look at him and turned his head away.

"Look at him," shouted Hakon. "Look him in the eye, and tell me this man is no longer worthy of being king."

When Lucas refused to comply, Byram and the officer grabbed him by both arms and pushed him closer to Boran, bringing them face to face. Only inches away, Lucas could smell him, and shook his head in protest. It was the same sour smell of someone living unkempt on the streets. Hakon released Boran from his clutch and turned to Byram, and the two men made their way towards the fur-covered platform, where they continued to vent their rage over Lucas's refusal to admit he had the right to be king. While they were busy bickering, Lucas whispered to Boran, "Stay strong. It's not over yet."

A spark of life came back into Boran's eyes for just a brief moment, before Hakon had him removed from the room.

Lucas, who was still being held by the officer, searched his captor's face for anything resembling mercy, but there was only determination and rage. Hakon's eyes, wild and dark, shifted restlessly as he paced the floor. He was an imposing figure, tall and robust, with age not having affected his agility. Lucas understood why Byram was subdued in his presence. Hakon looked like a man who could break another man's neck with his bare hands and would not hesitate to do so.

He saw Hakon stop and look upwards to one of the windows. "You will join your friends in the arena tomorrow," Hakon said without looking at him. "There, you better do as I tell you."

The iron gate groaned on its hinges as the last chosen was put inside the holding cage outside the amphitheater. The metal bars reminded Lucas of the cage Boran had used for the cougar, except this one was smaller and could barely fit all ten of them. Lucas watched as, shirtless and painted with black lines on his torso, Warrick joined the others, who were also painted. Zera was wearing a black sleeveless top she was given, and only her arms were painted.

"They've made us look like them," Warrick remarked, looking down at the markings on his body and the black trousers he was wearing. "I'm only glad they used paint and didn't make this permanent. Have you seen what some of their warriors have on their bodies?"

"Yes. It must take hours to do that," Zera answered. "I suppose we are not worth the time."

Warrick's ramblings and Zera's responses to him were registering in the background for Lucas—he was paying more attention to what was happening a few yards away inside the amphitheater. Using his mind, he watched people arrive and clamber over the rows of wooden benches constructed above the circular arena's wall, all of them eager to find the best possible seats. He could feel their excitement and hear their muffled discussions over the upcoming entertainment they had come to see. It brought him back to his time with the circus, when he would anxiously await his turn to go on stage to impress the audience with his sword. Their cheers, their clapping, their calls for more had always driven him to do his best. Only today, he would take no pleasure in the performance he was to give them—they had come to see real blood.

"What do you think it means?" asked Warrick, drinking from the jug of water given to them, along with proper food. "That they have made us as one of them?"

"It means they want to make us appear to the audience as the good guys," answered Lucas. "The ones they will be cheering for."

"You reckon we are to fight them?" asked Zera, gesturing to a group of men just arriving on the grounds outside the arena. The men stopped opposite the chosens' cage, right next to a door that Lucas knew gave access to a tunnel located underneath the stands. There were several doors along the outside wall of the arena, and the tunnels all led to the same place—the staging ground in its center.

Lucas looked at the group and recognized them as prisoners from one of the pits. Some looked terrified when handed a weapon before entering the narrow tunnel, while others looked to have accepted their fate and took their weapon calmly. He followed them with his mind as they passed through the dark tunnel and made their way into the sun-lit arena. Dust circled around them as they settled into place. When drum rolls sounded, the doors fell closed behind the group of prisoners. Shortly after that, Lucas heard a person announce a series of games, and the crowds cheered when several gates in the walls of the arena opened.

Lucas turned his mind away from the arena and, as he did so, he heard the first clashes of metal upon metal, and the cries of dying men commenced. He joined the chosen, who were sitting quietly on the ground with their backs against the iron bars, and tried to block out the images forcing themselves into his head.

Two more times, he heard gates open for a fight that was over before it had even begun. The tired and weakened prisoners were no match for Hakon's soldiers. Then, the crowd fell silent, and the voice of the announcer echoed through the theater.

"To celebrate the victory of our king, we have now come to the main and final event."

Lucas stood up when two rows of soldiers lined up in front of their cage, and the heavy gate was opened. He was the first to be ushered out to make his way between the rows of soldiers towards an open door of one of the dark tunnels underneath the stands. He took the sword and shield he was given at the entrance of the tunnel and made his way to the closed gate at the end. Through the bars, he could see the announcer standing in the center of the circular arena, busy describing the event about to take place. He was an academic-looking man, a clerk perhaps, or a scholar. Every now and then, he had to pause to push his glasses further up the bridge of his nose—he was moving about dramatically, waving his arms to add animation to the story he was telling the audience, much like Lucas had seen Everett do time and time again when he was about to reenact Toroun in the great battle. Except this wasn't a story of a warrior from a long time ago—this was about Hakon, and how he rose to be a fearless leader.

"Unfazed by the size of his opponent," shouted the announcer, "Hakon charged with his sword raised and, using another man's crouched back as a step, he leaped through the air to let his blade remove the enemy's head from his neck."

Lucas listened with half an ear as the fight was described, with plenty of blood and gore to dramatize it—he had no interest in listening to a story that made the evil man he craved to destroy sound noble and courageous. He cast his eyes toward the stands to watch the people's reaction. They hung on every word spoken and reacted with oohs and aahs.

When the announcer came close to the end of his story, he paused in a theatrical effort to build tension and suspense. The excitement among the people was a palpable thing and Lucas could feel it closing in on him. The tunnel walls and ceilings were trembling with the stamping of feet on the wooden stands above.

"Why this incessant enthusiasm?" asked Zera, who was directly behind Lucas. "Have they not seen enough blood already?"

"That was not the blood they came to see," answered Lucas, approaching the gate and gesturing at the last of the bodies being removed from the arena. "Those men were workers for the road. They were not fighters and not the entertainment promised. We are the ones to provide the show they've come to see." He saw that the announcer was facing the tunnel's direction, and Lucas gripped his sword and shield in preparation for what was to come.

"And so I give you," called the announcer, "our *warriors*!"

A roar rose from the crowd, and the gate in front of Lucas lifted before him. He stepped through the opening and onto the sand of the arena, which was blindingly bright after the darkness of the holding pen and tunnel. The noise of the people was deafening as he and the chosen made their way further inside. Looking around, he could see the hundreds of people in the stands, pumping their fists in the air as if the chosen were in fact their true warriors. If this was a show in a circus, thought Lucas, then the speaker had done a great job in getting the audience drawn into the story.

He saw Hakon and Byram staring down at him from under a covered seating area. He continued towards the center of the arena, where the announcer was eyeing him somewhat nervously. Lucas couldn't blame him. He was standing alone, surrounded by walls twelve feet high, all exit gates closed, and approached by ten boys and one girl with swords, none of whom wanted to be there.

"Stop," said the announcer, holding his hand out. His voice was trembling. "Don't come any further. If you try anything, some of you will die." With a wave of his hand, he directed Lucas's gaze to an area at the top of the walls where archers were standing ready. "Have your friends line up behind you. You are to reenact Hakon, leading his warriors into battle."

"You mean Byram?" asked Lucas. He already knew from Eli it had been Byram against Boran, and he didn't think any leader would risk his life on the front line of battle.

The announcer pushed his glasses up his nose again and looked towards Hakon. The expression on his face was that of sheer confusion.

"It doesn't matter," said Lucas, seeing that his delay in complying had already caused Byram to stand up. "Where do you want us to take up position?"

"Right there is just fine," answered the speaker. He waited for Lucas and the chosen to take their places, pushed his glasses up his nose again, and raised his hand to silence the public. "And so," shouted the announcer, "answering Eylgar's desperate plea for help when he learned of Boran's planned attack on him—"

"Now that's just a flat-out lie," muttered Lucas.

The announcer gave him a warning look not to interrupt again. He cleared his throat and continued. "Hakon marched his warriors across the plain to aid him in their defense. Tired and hungry, they stopped not once to rest. It was on a cold and damp morning when Hakon finally caught sight of Boran and his army . . ." The announcer stopped and spoke quietly to Lucas and the chosen. "Defense position. Shields up, swords ready."

Lucas looked over his shoulder to the chosen. They were ready and waiting for him. He sighed and moved into position—planting his feet firmly on the ground and raising shield and sword. Behind him, the chosen followed in unison, inciting some scattered clapping from the crowd.

The announcer gave a nod of approval and then ran towards the wall, where a ladder had appeared.

"Where is he off to?" asked Warrick.

"He's getting out of the way," answered Lucas, having watched the hasty retreat. "I don't think he's the type to wield a sword."

"That's a shame," muttered Zera. "I had planned to make him my first victim."

With the announcer safely over the wall, a gate slowly opened, and the crowd erupted with boos when Boran stepped through the opening with Isaac and his other soldiers.

"Oh no," said Warrick. "They can't be serious? They want us to fight them?"

"Oh, they *are* serious," answered Lucas. "I was afraid this might happen."

Boran stepped from the shadows onto the sands of the arena. He was wearing clothes fit for a king, but his face was pale, his eyes sunken, and he struggled to put one foot in front of the other. Some of the soldiers behind him did not fare much better. There were twenty of them, but half of them did not look like they would last long in a fight. They were leaning heavily on their swords when they came to a stop some distance away. Boran looked in his direction. It was clear he knew what he was there to do and that he was sizing up the group of boys and Zera before him. He had never met any of the chosen, and Lucas didn't think Boran saw him until Isaac whispered in his ear, and a questioning look came over his face.

"Death to the false king," shouted a man from the stands with a raised fist. He repeated the chant and was soon followed by others in the crowd.

Hearing the people's shouts to slay Boran and his army, Lucas lowered his sword and relaxed his stance. He wasn't going to answer their call. "Stand down," he ordered the chosen. "We are not going to do this."

"They'll have our necks if we don't," responded Warrick. He was looking at the crowd that had fallen mainly silent, but some words of anger echoed through the theater.

"Warrick's right, Lucas," said Zera. "It's them or us."

"No," snapped Lucas. He glanced over his shoulder to add weight to his words. He understood where she was coming from, but this wasn't up for a debate. "We're not fighting them."

Zera lowered her sword and raised herself upright. "I hope you know what you're doing."

Hakon rose from his seat. "Do your job!" he shouted at the announcer, who Lucas could see was already hastily descending the ladder to sort this out and get the fight started. The announcer's fear of Hakon had to be more significant than the risk of putting himself in an arena with armed prisoners, thought Lucas, as he watched him step off the ladder.

"What are you doing?" shouted the announcer as he ran over. "Is it not clear that you are to fight Boran and his soldiers?"

"It's clear," answered Lucas. "But those men are not fit to fight. They can barely stand on two feet, let alone wield a sword. It would be against our code of honor."

The announcer looked over his shoulder to the seating area above the wall. Hakon was watching with intense focus. Byram was standing next to him and was showing his impatience by crossing his arms. "You don't have a choice," he said, turning back to Lucas. "I'll be a dead man if I don't deliver the entertainment promised to the people."

"Sounds to me like that is your problem, and not mine." He looked to Boran and his soldiers, who had not moved from their spot.

"It will be your problem as much as it will be mine. Regain your position to start the fight," continued the announcer, "and I will tell Hakon your delay was due to some misunderstanding."

Lucas dropped his sword and shield. "There is no misunderstanding. If it is entertainment you are to deliver, then tell Hakon to provide me with an opponent who is fit to fight."

The announcer's face turned red with anger. "Pick up your sword," he yelled when Lucas turned his back. "Or one of your friends will die every minute that you don't."

Lucas paid little attention to the announcer's words. After all, how much power could he hold over the people's fate in the arena? It would be Hakon's call. He continued to walk towards the chosen when he became aware of his mistake and heard the sound of an arrow released from a bow. "Shield cover," he shouted. "Now!" The chosen raised their shields overhead in unison and kneeled to the ground, locking themselves together in a tight cluster.

The crowd gasped as they heard the thud from the arrow as it hit Warrick's shield. With no time to think, Lucas spun on his heels and reached for his shield, which lay on the ground a few feet away from him. When a second arrow was released and coming towards Zera, he dropped to his knees before her and, hiding behind his shield, braced for impact. The arrow splintered the wood but stopped with only the tip of the point coming through. Lucas pulled the arrow from the shield, and it was in that moment when he noticed the announcer raising his hand to order another release. Turning the arrow around in his hand, he pulled his arm back and threw it.

No more than a weak gurgling sound escaped the announcer's mouth as he tried to speak. He had grabbed his throat in an effort to stop blood gushing from the wound, and he sank to his knees. His eyes were soon lifeless, and his glasses slipped from his nose when he hit the ground.

Total silence took hold of the theater. Only the gentle flapping of the silk cover above the imperial box where Hakon was sitting could be heard. The archers stood motionless—their bows still aimed at Lucas, but Hakon had raised his hand to stop them from releasing more arrows. The crowd remained quiet, their eyes directed at their leader when he spoke.

"You took a life that was not yours to take," called Hakon. "Tell me why I should not have you and your cohort hanged for it?"

"The killing was my doing," answered Lucas, rising to his feet to face Hakon. "If anyone is to answer, it should only be me, but you may consider that I did you a favor."

Hakon leaned forward to the edge of his seat. "How so?"

"He told me he'd be a dead man if I refused to fight Boran and his men," answered Lucas. "I just did the job for you." He followed Hakon's gaze to Boran and his soldiers. With weary faces and some trembling with fever, they looked far from the ferocious warriors they once had been.

"You *did* do me a favor," replied Hakon. "You showed me what you are capable of, but you also made it clear that you'll only fight to protect those closest to you." He turned sideways in his seat and spoke a few words to Byram. Moments later, several gates to the arena opened, and six groups of ten soldiers marched in. They followed the arena's outer perimeter to encircle the chosen and the people erupted with excitement.

"Now they are going to get what they want after all," said Zera, who was near and looking up at the stands.

"Hakon was one step ahead of you," said Warrick, walking up to Lucas. "He anticipated you wouldn't be willing to fight Boran." The three of them watched as some of the soldiers stepped forward to drive them towards Boran.

"Refusal to fight will not be an option," sounded Hakon's voice above the crowd. His eyes met Lucas's. "If you want this fallen king to remain alive."

With calls for Boran's blood coming from the crowd, Lucas picked up his sword. He saw Byram making his way into the arena to meet with the soldiers' leading officer and avoided his gaze.

"What happens if you get killed?" asked Warrick. "Does Hakon not know about the curse?"

"He does," answered Lucas. "And I'm sure Byram will instruct his men not to take me down with fatal blows. It's Boran they want dead, not me."

"Sire," said Lucas when he reached Boran. "Isaac."

Isaac nodded in return.

"I have no idea how you got to be here," said Boran to Lucas, looking at the chosen. "But if this is supposed to be a rescue mission, then I hope this was part of your plan?"

"No, it wasn't," answered Lucas. "For now, the best we can do is try and keep you alive."

"It'll be two to one," said Boran. "The odds are not in our favor."

Ignoring Boran's comments, Lucas pulled Isaac aside. There was no time to discuss their precarious situation. Byram was already lining his soldiers up. Thirty were standing in a semicircle with a second row not far behind them. "I need your help," Lucas said after assessing the situation.

"Anything," answered Isaac.

"Good," said Lucas. "Select the strongest men from the group and have them form a tight unit around the king. Hold it, whatever may come. If the circle breaks, they'll get to the king, and we can't let that happen."

"Boran will want to fight," Isaac said.

"He'll get his chance," Lucas said, "but we need to change the odds first."

"You only want to use the strongest to form the defense around the king?" asked Isaac. He looked towards the soldiers. "What about the rest?"

"Place them wherever you think they may be of use. I'll take the front line with the chosen and try to keep them away from you for as long as we can." He waited for Isaac to nod that he understood and started to walk to the chosen when he felt Isaac's hand on his shoulder.

"If we don't make it out of here alive," said Isaac, "I want you to know that my loyalty has always been with King Boran. I had no idea of Grant's plans until it was too late."

"I know," said Lucas. "That's why I'm letting you protect him."

Lucas stood in the center of the line with the chosen spaced apart on either side of him. Looking over his shoulder, he saw that Isaac had formed an inner circle with eight soldiers, standing shoulder to shoulder. As Lucas had suspected, Boran occupied one space in the circle, not wanting to miss out on the fight. He could only hope he would soon come to his senses and retreat inside of it, or the need to keep him alive would all be for nothing. He saw that the weaker soldiers formed an outside circle. They would be the first to fall once Hakon's soldiers made it past the chosen.

"Remember," said Lucas, looking left and right of him. "This is what we trained for, and our bond makes us strong. Let's take them down, for Archer."

"For Archer," replied the chosen.

"If only Byram were brave enough to fight us," said Warrick softly next to him.

Lucas watched Byram leave the arena and take his place next to Hakon again. "He thinks his men are capable of the task without his help," he told Warrick. "We'll make him regret that decision."

The noise from the audience was deafening, with shouts of "Death to Boran!" and "Kill them all!" Lucas saw how it made the soldiers in front of him feel more confident with the support in their favor. They had their shoulders rolled back, their chins held high. Lucas focused and connected with the chosen. He cleared their minds and blocked any sound from distracting them. Then he brought a gentle breeze down into the arena to lift the sand and let it swirl just above ankle height. The audience calmed and watched the display before them. Lucas could see that some people looked at the banners hanging motionless from the poles above the stands. When no more sound came from the crowd, the sand settled back down, and Hakon signaled for the fight to start.

A roar came from the first row of soldiers as they charged towards the chosen, who stood as one, with swords raised and ready to strike. In strength, Hakon's soldiers were superior to Lucas's comrades, but their skill and speed outweighed their shortcomings. Quick and light on their feet, they avoided the first blows by ducking away and following up with fast and precise counterattack strikes aimed low. Soldiers were falling all around them—their leg muscles and arteries cut. As their blood stained the sand, Byram's voice roared from the stands to the second row of soldiers. "Don't just stand there!" he cried. "Take them down!"

With the rest of the soldiers joining the fight, and each chosen engaged in combat, some of those soldiers managed to get past the line. Lucas looked over when he heard the crowd cheer and saw Boran's soldiers in the outer circle falling fast. With more of Hakon's soldiers pushing through to get to Boran's circle, Lucas finished his fight with the two soldiers in front of him and helped the other chosen finish theirs. He then regrouped them behind the enemy line. The fighting was now happening in front of him, with Hakon's soldiers fighting Boran's.

"Spread out!" called Lucas, before leading the charge once again. The chosen ran towards the fight, slashing their swords through flesh. With less than half of Hakon's soldiers left standing, Lucas shouted to Isaac. "Break!"

Isaac broke the circle and had his soldiers join up with the chosen to surround Hakon's soldiers, leaving Boran on the outside. As the fighting continued, Lucas could see in his peripheral view that some wounded soldiers were rising to seize the opportunity to get to the king, and he quickly abandoned his place to help Boran. Finally, the last of Hakon's soldiers surrendered, dropping their swords on the ground before them.

Wiping away blood from a cut above his eye, Lucas counted the chosen. He was relieved to see they had all survived. Some had wounds that needed attending to, but they would live. From Boran's soldiers, only six were left standing, including Isaac. They stood with the chosen and looked up to where Hakon had risen from his seat. Hakon looked down at them, an angry expression on his face—and left the stand.

A moment later, the gates in the arena wall rose again, and guards holding shields and spears marched in. Lucas found himself, as well as Boran, separated from the chosen. They were forced to lay down their weapons. Once Lucas and Boran were disarmed, the guards lowered their spears and came closer to escort the two of them out of the arena.

CHAPTER 22

Nolan was walking out of the stable block at Boran's castle when he heard Dastan calling out that a rider was approaching. It had been several weeks since Lucas and the chosen had left to cross the mountain, and no news of their whereabouts had reached them yet. He ran up the stairs to the wall-walk, skipping every other step. When he reached the top, Nolan saw his brother already there. Dastan had taken charge of all security of the castle and spent most of his time on the wall.

"Just one rider?" asked Nolan, joining him.

"Yes," answered Dastan.

Nolan, straining his eyes, stared down the long road leading to the castle gates. He could see a black horse approaching, but it was hard to make out who the rider was.

"Your eyesight is better than mine," he said. "Is it Lucas?"

"No," answered Dastan, sighing. "It's Davis . . . riding Lucas's horse."

"Open the gates!" Nolan shouted down to the guards stationed below. He hastily ran down the stairs into the bailey with Dastan on his heels and waited anxiously for Davis to ride in. He grabbed the reins of Lucas's horse before it had come to a stop while Dastan rushed up to Davis, who looked as if he was barely holding on.

"What happened?" asked Nolan. "Where is Lucas?" When Davis struggled to answer him, he handed the horse off to the guards to assist Dastan in bringing Davis inside the kitchen block. They sat him down at one of the tables and gave him a mug of water that Davis downed in one go. He tried to clear his throat, but only after finishing a second mug could he finally get his words out.

"Lucas sent me here," said Davis. "To warn you."

"He's alright?" asked Dastan before Nolan could. Nolan knew his brother still felt responsible for Lucas's well-being, even though Lucas was now grown. "You had me worried when I saw you riding his horse."

Davis shook his head. "I'm not sure." He proceeded to tell them everything until the moment he saw Lucas and the chosen riding away with Byram. His voice trembled and tears came to his eyes at the mention of Archer, and he wiped them away. "I rode as fast as I could," said Davis. "My horse tripped after becoming fatigued, and I had to leave him behind. If it wasn't for Lucas giving me his horse, I wouldn't have made it here."

"The road," said Nolan. "Do you have any idea where it comes into Boran's land?"

"I have the map," said Davis, holding his cup out for more water. "It's in the saddlebag."

"I'll go and get it," said Dastan, and rushed out of the kitchen.

Nolan sat himself down next to Davis. "I'm sorry about Archer."

"I don't understand how Byram could have survived the hunters' woods," said Davis. "We saw him go down."

"We believe he must have crawled under some brush after being wounded and later found aid at a farmer's house near the edge of the forest," answered Nolan. "It was found burned down a few months ago. Before the fire, neighbors reported hearing the farmer's wife speak of a sick cousin staying with them. They allowed no one to enter the house."

"You believe it was Byram?"

"It was no doubt a tale to protect her family, as a result of being threatened," said Nolan. "But it did her no good. The entire family was found murdered inside the smoldering house."

Nolan took the map from Dastan when he made it back, and spread it out on the table.

"Here," said Davis and pointed to the circle Lucas had made on the map. "This is where Lucas believes they will come through. He said he couldn't be sure, but given the direction the road was going in, and how long it took me to get back here, I think he might be right."

Nolan used his fingers to mark the distance from the castle. "That's three days from here."

Dastan leaned in closer to have a better look and then gasped.

"What is it?" asked Davis.

"Nolan . . ." said Dastan.

"Yes, I see it," answered Nolan. "If they follow the valley the road comes in on, they will walk the plateau we use to get home."

Silence fell over the warriors who had slowly trickled in to gather in the kitchen with them. Davis swallowed uncomfortably. They all knew what it meant. With the fog gone, the entrance between the rocks was now visible, which left their loved ones in danger of being discovered.

"What are we going to do?" asked one of the warriors.

"The only thing we can do," answered Nolan. "We'll have to try and stop Hakon from getting that far."

Nolan put his finger on a second circle, faintly marked and smaller than the first. He looked at Davis. "Is this where Lucas wants us to be?"

"Yes," answered Davis.

"Did he speak from a vision?" asked Nolan. "Will he be with us?"

Davis shook his head. "He didn't say he was going to be there. All that he told me was that he trusted me to help you and the warriors in his place."

CHAPTER 23

Separated from the chosen, Lucas rested his back against the dark tunnel wall. The guards were waiting for the patrons to finish filing out of the amphitheater before leading the prisoners away.

Lucas was exhausted. The fight had taken the last bit of energy from him, and he tried to recover. He knew their plight was far from over.

"Grant betrayed me," spoke Boran. He was standing next to Lucas, looking up at the ceiling to watch the wood planks above them trembling with the marching of dozens of people exiting through the main entrance. Boran had fought to defend himself when the soldiers around him had fallen, determined not to die as entertainment. "I did not know he was a Hammond," continued Boran, "but judging by the last words you spoke to me at my castle, it seems that you knew?"

"I figured it out when it was too late," answered Lucas. "He had me fooled as well."

"What about Eneas?" asked Boran. "He and Grant appeared to be having conversations in hushed tones in the past weeks."

From Boran's carefully spoken words, Lucas could tell that he dreaded to hear that another person close to him might have betrayed him. "Eneas was loyal to you until his end," he replied. "His motive to conspire with Grant to keep me away from you was personal."

Boran gave him a sideways glance. "His end?"

"He took the life of the servant girl, Valora," answered Lucas, "and would not have hesitated to take mine. He deserved what was coming to him."

Boran sighed profoundly and nodded that he understood. Above them, the sound of the last footsteps disappeared, and the guards were getting ready to move again. "Those boys and the girl with you," continued Boran, "they are Itan's chosen ones?"

"They are."

"When did he send them?" asked Boran. "Recently?"

"No," answered Lucas. "They were already with me in the battle against Byram in the hunters' forest and were never far from me when I came to you."

"Byram," grunted Boran, upon hearing the name. "Now, there's another I would like to get my hands on."

Lucas wanted to respond, but the guards at the front had started moving again. He followed them out of the tunnel and back through the town towards Hakon's dwelling, where soldiers stood gathered in the courtyard. They had formed several rows in a semicircle before the building on the right. When Lucas and Boran approached the formation from behind, the soldiers formed an aisle, stepping aside in either direction to let them through. When they reached the front of the semicircle of soldiers, the guards raised their shields and stopped them. Lucas saw five of Hakon's soldiers—the ones who had survived the fight—standing side by side in the center of the courtyard. They stood to attention with their heads up and eyes fixed in front, silently waiting. Standing in a line directly behind them were Boran's soldiers and Isaac. Behind them were the chosen.

Lucas caught Zera's pained look. He instinctively stepped forward when he saw she was bleeding from her shoulder, but two spears crossed in front of him stopped him. He backed up and took his place next to Boran. As soon as he did, he noticed Byram near the building entrance, giving the guards the order to stand down. A moment later, the solid wood doors swung open, and Hakon walked out. His face was still contorted with anger when he stopped underneath the entrance roof. Broadening his chest and tucking his thumbs behind his belt, Hakon came forward, all the while examining the five defeated warriors who stood before him as if mulling over some sort of decision. Everyone assembled in the courtyard had their eyes on them as well, and Lucas sensed they knew what was to come.

Hakon's booming voice echoed through the courtyard as he addressed the warriors. "Today, you showed me your weakness," Hakon declared. "You brought shame to your families. You all know what that means." He paused to add weight to his words before continuing. "For those who wish to die with honor, step forward!"

There was a moment's hesitation, but then the first warrior stepped forward, followed by the rest. They were each handed a dagger, and kneeled on the ground. Lucas held his breath when he watched the warriors aim the blade to their chest with both hands. When Hakon came towards them, each one carried out their sacrifice, dropping themselves on the blade before Hakon—all except for the last one. Seeing his comrades fall before him, that warrior hesitated and met Hakon's sword instead.

Lucas heard Boran's softly spoken words. "Next time you fight his warriors," he remarked, "you might not want to leave any of them alive." After the bodies of the warriors were dragged away, Byram told Boran's soldiers to step forward. They complied, but the fear was visible in their eyes as they watched Hakon parade in front of them with the bloodied sword still in his hand.

Lucas saw that even Isaac, who had composed himself when Hakon killed the warrior right before him, was trembling. The chosen still stood unmoved, but he could tell their hope to remain alive was slowly fading from their minds as well. He then heard Hakon speak his first words to Boran's soldiers.

"Despite your disadvantage in health and numbers," Hakon began, "you defeated my warriors. You showed courage, strength, and perseverance. For that, I should grant you the right to live."

Lucas saw hope return to the soldiers' faces, until Hakon spoke again.

"However," continued Hakon, "you have also shown loyalty to a man who no longer has the right to call himself king." He paused to look over his shoulder at Boran. "Therefore, your fate is in his hands. Only if Boran bends his knee to acknowledge me to be your king will your life be spared."

Lucas turned to Boran, as did everyone else in the courtyard, and waited in anticipation to see what he would do. He saw him stare at his men and bite his lower lip—he had no intention to save their lives. "You are allowing them to be killed if you don't do anything," Lucas whispered to him when Hakon had turned back to the soldiers.

"They have already been condemned to die," answered Boran. "It doesn't matter what I say or do. Hakon will no doubt ask you to do the same for the chosen. It will be up to you if you let them die with their heads held high or bowed to a ruthless killer. Hakon will not stop until the last of our blood spills, and I will not give him the satisfaction to do so with my bended knee."

"Then I will have to do what you cannot." Lucas dropped to his knee and bowed his head when Byram stepped forward to push the first soldier down onto the ground. Hakon had his back to him and did not see him, but Byram did. Surprise flashed across his face, followed by a satisfying smile. He put his hand up to Hakon and stopped him from raising his sword.

"Well, well, well," said Hakon, turning around to see what Byram was gesturing at. "What has happened here? I did not think you would so easily bend the knee."

"It is my acknowledgment for you to be king that you seek," responded Lucas. "Not Boran's. But I am giving it to you only if you kill no further."

Hakon stared at him, then looked around at the gathered soldiers who were watching with great intent. For a moment, it looked like he was giving in to the demand but then shook his head. "I will spare the lives of your comrades," said Hakon, "but the fate of Boran's men is not in your hands."

"You're wrong," replied Lucas, raising his head to look Hakon in the eye. "I hold everyone's fate in my hands—even yours."

Ignoring Lucas's remark, Hakon turned around just as a dark shadow came over the courtyard. All eyes directed to the sky, where the moon moved slowly in front of the sun, blocking out its light and turning day into night. The guards stepped back from Lucas, and Hakon met him with questioning eyes.

Byram stepped next to Hakon. "The priest," he said. "It is as he foretold. It may be time to see what else he has to say?"

Hakon took another look at the sky and let out a deep sigh. "Fetch the priest," he ordered. "And bring the boy."

Once inside the narrow room, Lucas could see the sky lightening up through the small windows below the ceiling.

Hakon was pacing in front of his chair and only sat down when Byram entered the room. "And?" asked Hakon when he saw Byram had come alone.

"He's coming," answered Byram. "He doesn't move as fast as he used to."

Lucas peeked over his shoulder when he heard shuffling behind him and saw an elderly man make his way into the room. His back hunched, he was leaning heavily on a stick for support. The hood of his black cloak covered his face, but as he passed by, Lucas saw the old man turn his head as if to look at him, though the white cloud in his eyes revealed he could only have sensed Lucas's presence—he was blind.

"Oswall," called Hakon. "You took your time to get here."

Lucas's mouth fell slightly open when he recognized the name. Could this be the same Oswall who had been a warrior monk and priest for Boran's father? The priest who had played an instrumental role in his parents' death by telling Eneas of his birth? If it was him, he had to be nearly a hundred years old, and how had it come to pass that he was here? From Eneas's words, he had assumed Oswall had died after going mad from the elixir.

"I came without delay when I received the message that you summoned me," answered Oswall. "If you wanted me sooner, you should have called upon me earlier."

"Don't be smart with me," snapped Hakon. "You know I don't tolerate your snide comments."

Oswall stopped and rested both hands on the stick. He turned his head in Lucas's direction. "The boy before you?" asked Oswall. "It is him?"

"Yes," answered Hakon.

Oswall nodded as if he needed the confirmation, but Lucas felt he already knew who he was when he had stepped into the room. "He kneeled before you," continued Oswall. "When you did not accept this, the day turned into the night, yes?" When Hakon remained silent, Oswall spoke again. "You did not believe me when I told you that the boy would hold the power of the gods."

Hakon placed his hands on the corners of the armrest and leaned forward in his seat. He looked ready to lunge at the frail man before him, whose lecturing words had clearly angered him. "I may not have believed you," said Hakon, "but I was no fool to ignore all that you said. You told me you would know the future once the boy was here. It's the reason I let you live after Eneas handed you to me to be disposed of, and why I summoned you here now. So tell me what I need to know."

"I will have to get it from the boy," said Oswall. "It is he who holds the future. Allow me to get close to him?" A shiver ran along Lucas's spine when Oswall's blind stare bore a hole deep into his soul. It made him feel nauseous, and he turned his eyes away. A feeling to trust the priest came over him, but everything he had learned about him told him to do the opposite.

"How?" asked Hakon.

"By entering his mind," answered Oswall.

Hakon looked at Lucas with a firm stare, but Lucas could sense his uncertainty. It appeared he did not trust the situation, and waved his hand to have Byram step closer to Lucas. "Go ahead," said Hakon, when Byram was in place.

Oswall nodded and stepped towards Lucas. Fearing the old monk's approach, Lucas took a step back, but was stopped by the two guards behind him, each of whom took hold of his arms. He resisted their restraint until Byram's sword pointed at his chest, and he made himself be still. Looking past Byram, he saw Oswall come closer and mouth the words "trust me" before reaching out and placing his hand on Lucas's shoulder.

A bright light flashed before Lucas, forcing him to close his eyes. When he opened them again, he found himself standing in the foyer of the monastery where he had lived as a young boy. He saw the entrance door open, and two warrior monks stepped outside. One of them had a bag strapped across his back, indicating he was leaving.

His face looked somewhat familiar even though Lucas did not think he had ever met him, and he was older than the monk who stayed near the threshold. When the monk without the pack spoke, Lucas froze. He recognized it to be Father Ansan, and gathered the other monk to be Oswall from the words spoken.

"I have watched you leave many times before, but this time there is sorrow in your eyes," said Father Ansan. "This is to be a final goodbye, isn't it?"

Oswall nodded. "I am afraid it has to be."

"Can you tell me where you are going?"

"You know I can't," answered Oswall. "If I do, it will change everything." There was a moment of silence before Oswall spoke again. "Do you trust me?"

"You know I do," answered Ansan.

Oswall placed his hand on Ansan's shoulder. "Then I ask you never to doubt my reasons for what I am about to do," said Oswall. "Even when you are led to believe that I strayed from the path I was on."

Lucas watched Oswall take his hand from Ansan's shoulder and felt the weight removed from his. As the image faded from his mind, he could feel his body go limp and collapse in the arms of the guards. As he was laid down on the ground, a thick fog entered his mind, causing pressure in his head and blinding pain. From far away, he heard Byram ask Oswall if he had killed him and Hakon's roar that he had better not because of the curse.

"He sleeps," answered Oswall. "It is the only way I can enter the subconscious of his mind."

Lucas knew Oswall was kneeling beside him. He was still struggling with the pressure in his head until he felt a hand placed on his forehead, and Oswall's voice entered his mind. "We need to talk," he said.

"You tricked me," replied Lucas. "You showed me your last memory of Ansan to distract me."

"It was the only way," said Oswall. "You would not have willingly let me in. I also hoped that the exchange would show you that you can trust me."

"Why would I trust you?" asked Lucas. "Ansan spoke your name only once, and his words did not convey any kind of trust in you. He told me that before you left the monastery, the stone had revealed my birth to you. You withheld information from him, yet shared it with people who did not want to see the prophecy fulfilled. They killed my parents and the man who I came to love as a father." Lucas pushed aside the memory of looking through the forge window as a young boy and witnessing Einar die at the hands of the dark order. "He would not have died had I known who I was."

"I followed the path set out for me by the stone," answered Oswall. "All that I did was to step aside and allow you to become the person you are today. It was not just your birth that was shown to me. I saw your entire life, and mine along with it. From the time you were born . . . to us being here today."

"I don't believe you," said Lucas. "I heard what you told Hakon. You want to give him knowledge of the future to help him in his cause."

"Not his," answered Oswall. "Yours. Do you think the stone would have revealed your birth to me if I was to be the cause of your destruction?"

Lucas let the last words sink in. "No," he had to admit. But he had doubted himself and the reasons for coming across the mountains the moment Byram killed Archer. He felt lured into a trap from which there seemed no escape. "How are you to help me?"

"Give me an image of a future you want Hakon to see," answered Oswall. "Force his hand to act how you need him to—or you will have your friend and the warriors waiting on Boran's land fight for nothing."

Lucas thought for a moment. "Alright," he said, "but something tells me Hakon needs a great deal more than an image from the future to change the path he is on."

"Then we will give him that as well," answered Oswall. "Show me what you want Hakon to believe."

Lucas relaxed and opened his mind, to allow Oswall to follow him. He let his mind drift across the mountains and into the busy streets of Ulmer, where people were making their way to the center of the town. A stage had been built on the square, and he could see Hakon, standing tall and strong, with Byram next to him. Before them, kneeled near the edge of the platform with his hands tied behind his back, he saw Boran. Dressed in a plain cotton shirt, his hair and beard unkempt, Boran stared dull-eyed at the sky above him. He avoided looking at the people gathered around the stage and ignored their desperate calls. The crowd pressed forward, held back by soldiers that guarded the stage.

"King Boran!" called a woman. "Is it true that the army was defeated? My husband is a soldier. Where is he?"

"Why would the king give two rats about your husband?" another woman interjected. "Have you forgotten that he ordered the tunnel workers killed?"

A murmur of agreement could be heard from several people around them, and they looked up to see Hakon stepping forward.

"People of Ulmer," shouted Hakon, his booming voice silencing the crowd. "Standing before you today, I bring you the news that the battle, as foretold in the prophecy, was fought several weeks ago. With no consideration for the life of his men, Boran sent them to their deaths when he decided to invade my land, and the gods made their choice. As in the case of Toroun before him, the gods ordered Lucas, who you all know to be the true king's protector, to turn against Boran." Hakon stopped and gave a subtle nod to someone in the crowd.

Lucas directed his mind to the people closest to the stage, who turned to see the crowd behind them disperse to let a hooded individual come forward. He watched himself climb the steps onto the stage and uncover his head. He walked up to Hakon, pulling his sword from the scabbard, and laid the blade across the palm of his hands. "My king," he said, loud enough for the first rows of people to hear. He bowed his head and kneeled.

Hakon gave a satisfactory smile when he noticed the people in the square starting to kneel. He took the sword from the hooded figure. He then stepped beside Boran and raised the blade . . .

Lucas felt Oswall remove his hands from his forehead and sensed him sitting back. Oswall's breathing sounded labored. There was no doubt it had cost him energy to get into Lucas's mind, and to then stay long enough to receive the image he was to pass on to Hakon.

"And?" spoke Hakon. "Were you successful?"

"His defenses were strong," answered Oswall with a sigh of exhaustion. "But I did get a glimpse of what is to come."

"Then speak," ordered Hakon. "For you have taken much of my time already. What did you see?"

"King Boran," started Oswall. "You allow him to live much longer than I thought you would."

"It is true that I do not want to give him a quick death," said Hakon. "There is no satisfaction to be gained from that. I want him to suffer, knowing he has lost everything."

"Is that why you are taking him with you when you invade his lands?"

"No," answered Hakon. "His life will end as soon as we are done here."

"That is not what I have seen," said Oswall.

"Don't listen," interrupted Byram. "Boran needs to die before you can take his throne. It is how our family has taken leadership since the beginning of time."

"And he will die," interjected Oswall. "Just not here, and not today."

"When?" asked Hakon. Lucas heard the scrape of Hakon's chair as he rose to stand next to Oswall.

"In the town square of Ulmer, the town next to the castle," answered Oswall. "In front of his people who have kneeled before you."

"This is what you saw in the boy's mind?" asked Hakon.

"Yes."

"What about Lucas?" asked Byram. "Where is he in all of this? His bent knee means nothing, and his sole purpose for being here is to stop us somehow. What I saw today made it clear that he's more dangerous than I ever believed he could be."

"He may be holding the power of the gods," said Oswall. "But he is of flesh and blood—he can be stopped."

Oswall was smart, thought Lucas, and was playing his part well, but Lucas wasn't convinced Byram would believe him.

"How?" asked Byram. "He can't be killed without a great sacrifice on our part."

"No," agreed Oswall. "But I can block his memory of who he is and, by doing so, all access to his powers. The gods will no longer be able to use him to stop what you have planned. And you would be able to command him to stand beside you, before the people, when you deal Boran his fatal blow."

"I don't . . ." started Byram, but was stopped by Hakon.

"Do it," said Hakon. "But if this is all a lie, you will spend your last days staked to the pillars in front of my residence."

Oswall placed his hands back on Lucas's head and approached him a second time.

The grass was gently swaying on the hill around Lucas's feet, and the cool breeze played with his hair. The large black stone that had fallen from the sky lay in the distance below. It stood alone this time—Toroun and the warriors Lucas had seen waiting for him before were not there.

He heard a rustling behind him, and someone came to stand next to him. He watched Oswall remove the hood to reveal his shaven head. He had the distinctive look of a warrior monk, and his eyes were no longer white but blue, like the sky above them.

"I have stood on this hill before," said Lucas, fixing his gaze on the stone. "When death was close to me."

"It is not your death that has brought us here," said Oswall. "It's mine that is near."

Lucas narrowed his eyes. He remembered Tanner whispering to him, as he was dying after Meloc's battle, that he saw a large black stone in a field. Could it be that the stone was the last thing everyone saw before they departed from the living world?

"Only those directly connected to the stone come here," answered Oswall, as if reading his mind. "And the ones connected to you."

Lucas turned his head to look at the old man beside him. "You knew it would be your last day when we were to meet?"

Oswall nodded. "I lived far beyond my years to wait for you," he answered. "Now that my job is nearly done, it will be time for me to go." Lucas remained silent. "You still want me to set Hakon on the path you have laid out for him?"

"I do," answered Lucas. "It should bring me where I need to be and keep Byram at bay."

"There will be a great risk if you are not successful."

"I am aware," responded Lucas, "but I don't see another way." He heard Oswall take in a deep breath of the fresh air. He knew the old priest's time was nearly up, and it was time to leave.

"Has it been done?" asked Hakon when Lucas felt Oswall remove his hands from his forehead one last time. His voice sounded more distant now, and Lucas struggled to listen as sleep took hold of him.

"Yes," answered Oswall. "When he wakes, he will believe himself to be no different than the chosen ones he came with. He will be compliant and not resist any demand you put upon him as long as he is with them."

"Lucas cannot be reunited with those chosen," said Byram before Hakon could respond. "He needs to be separated from them."

"I didn't ask your opinion," snapped Hakon. "Speak out of turn again, and I will have to reconsider whether you are fit to lead my army."

"I apologize," said Byram. "I merely wanted to warn you about the risk you are taking."

A tense moment followed when Hakon did not respond. Finally, he turned to Oswall. "Tell me why I would not simply kill the chosen?"

Oswall tilted his head to one side. "That is a decision for you to make," he answered after a short silence. "All I can tell you is that Lucas's bond with the chosen is strong. The emotional distress of their loss, either by separation or death, could cause him to react in a destructive manner."

"But he may not?"

"No," answered Oswall, "but may I remind you that I have only blocked the memory of his powers. He can still use them, if pushed to do so." He paused as if waiting for Hakon to respond, but when he remained silent, Oswall continued. "Well," he said, pulling himself up on his stick. "Perhaps I should leave you two to discuss this. I will be in my room if you need me."

CHAPTER 24

Lucas slept a dreamless sleep and woke when a bucket of water was dumped in his face. He found himself lying on the cold stones of a prison cell. He blinked, everything gradually coming into focus as two soldiers pulled him to his feet.

"It's time to go," said one of the soldiers.

Remembering he was to act as if he was no longer himself, Lucas obeyed their command to stand still. He lowered his head and did not resist while they shackled his wrists and legs. When the soldiers were satisfied that he was secure, Lucas was led out into a dark hallway. On one side was a solid wall, but lined along the left were more prison cells. He noticed the cell next to his to be empty but spotted a lone figure sitting on a bench in the one after that. With his elbows on his knees and his face in his hands, Boran lifted his head as the guards led Lucas past. Lucas carefully allowed their eyes to meet and noticed the king's worried look. He wished he could put him at ease but, in truth, he had no idea how this was going to play out.

Near the end of the hallway, the soldiers stopped and stepped aside to allow a group of people to rush into a room where the door stood open. When they continued, Lucas glimpsed inside and saw that the space was someone's living quarters. He could see a desk with a chair, a small lit fireplace, and a comfortable bed with someone lying on it. There was no movement from the person, even when the group of people entered his room and hovered over him.

"What's going on?" asked one of the soldiers when they passed a guard.

"The old priest," answered the guard. "He took his last breath in the night."

"Really?" asked the soldier. "I'm surprised. I didn't think he would ever die. Was he not a hundred years old?"

"I think he was much older," answered the soldier behind Lucas. "The way he told his stories of times long gone, you would think he was there when it happened."

Lucas could not help but peer over his shoulder to give one last look towards Oswall's room. If he and Ansan were ever to meet again, Lucas would be glad to tell him that his old teacher had remained faithful till the end. If it weren't for Oswall, Boran would already be dead, and Lucas would have been locked away, never to see his friends again. Now he was relieved to see the chosen—all of them alive—when he stepped outside into the courtyard. They stood chained, along with the six soldiers belonging to Boran who had survived the fighting. Guards waited alongside them, with their swords in hand, and a group of soldiers were on horseback nearby.

Zera peered over his shoulder when he joined the line. "I'm so glad to see you," she whispered. "I was worried they would have us leave without you."

Aware of Byram's watchful eye, Lucas did not answer and let his head and shoulders drop.

"What's wrong?" asked Zera. "You're wet. What did they do to you? Where did they keep you?"

Lucas wanted to shake his head to signal to Zera that she stop asking questions but then heard Byram call his name.

"Baelan!" he called, bringing his horse closer. "Baelan!"

Lucas did not respond, and a guard poked him in the back with the blunt end of his spear to get his attention. "Answer the commander," shouted the guard when Lucas turned around to look at him.

Lucas gave the guard a puzzled look. "I apologize," he said, facing Byram. "I was not aware you called my name."

Byram tilted his head down to stare at him, then smiled a fake smile. "Very clever," he said. "But I'm not easily fooled. I have seen what you have become since I first laid eyes on you at the inn all those years ago. Hakon may have put his trust in the abilities of the priest, but I don't believe for a moment that you've lost your memory." Without waiting for Lucas's response, Byram gave a subtle nod to one of his men, who kicked his horse forward and drove it into the line of chosen.

Lucas had to restrain every muscle in his body from reacting and watched helplessly as Warrick and another chosen were knocked down to the ground. They were helped up by other boys, and Lucas was relieved to see they were not seriously hurt. He turned back to face Byram with a look of shock and surprise on his face.

Byram was still eyeing him suspiciously, but some of the intensity had faded from his eyes. He waited another moment before giving the order for the guards to move out, and brought his horse next to Lucas when the group was set in motion. "I'll be watching you," Byram said. "Make one wrong move, and I'll see to it that the blood of your comrades will be on your hands." He then kicked his horse and rode off with his eight soldiers.

"Can you tell me what that was all about?" asked Zera when Byram was out of sight.

"When we get to be alone," answered Lucas.

They marched for most of the day, until they reached the entrance of the gorge where Byram and his soldiers were waiting for them, and they were allowed to rest. With two guards always near during the march, Lucas had only conveyed enough to stop the chosen from looking at him for leadership. They now sat with their backs turned away from him, some quietly talking and others resting. Only Warrick and Zera sat facing him. Warrick had gathered some small sticks from the ground but, because he was hindered by the shackles, was stacking them in a pile with some difficulty.

"I don't think you have to be quite this docile for him to believe you are not yourself," said Zera when Byram's attention was momentarily diverted away from them. "You were never this quiet as a chosen at Itan's."

That's because I never believed I was one," responded Lucas. "And Byram doesn't know that. I'm having a hard time not returning his stare or, better yet, looking for ways to get my hands on a sword."

"That might prove difficult if they keep these on us," said Warrick, lifting his wrists to show the shackles.

"I hope they'll take them off when we get where we're going," replied Lucas. "It will be a challenge otherwise."

"I'm always up for a challenge," mumbled Warrick, placing the last stick down. "Ready to play?"

"Sure," smiled Lucas, taking the first stick from the pile without moving any others. Welcoming the distraction, he relaxed and became engrossed in the game. He paid no attention to what was happening around him until a boot landed on top of the sticks, and he looked up into Byram's cold blue eyes.

"The fun is over," snarled Byram as he kicked away the sticks. "Time to get back on your feet." When Lucas, Warrick, and Zera had scrambled to their feet, he turned on his heels and indicated to the guards to get everyone else up.

With Byram leading the group of prisoners and increasing their pace, the wooden structure Lucas knew to be at the end of the gorge came into view before nightfall. He saw a group of twenty soldiers standing on the platform. It was raised along the cliff wall by oxen pulling ropes on a pulley system, just as Lucas had previously observed. Other groups stood waiting as it came back down, but were made to step aside by Byram, who sent three of his soldiers to go up first. Their horses walked onto the platform with ease and remained calm when the platform went up, even though it did not look to be a smooth ride. The oxen had to pull hard, and from time to time, the rope got stuck on the pulley.

"You could make the horses panic," said Zera softly as she watched the platform rise. "Have one knock Byram off when he goes up."

"I can't risk it," replied Lucas. The same thought had already crossed his mind, but he didn't think Hakon would believe it to be an accident if his commander fell to his death. "I can't let them know I still have my powers. Not while Hakon has Boran, and we're all in shackles."

"Some believe Itan to be the true king," said Warrick in front of him, "but your effort to keep Boran alive suggests otherwise."

"I can't tell you who is to be the true king," said Lucas. "All I know is that the end of the prophecy is yet to come and Boran plays a part in it."

Lucas strained his neck to follow the platform all the way up and watched it come back down empty. It went up two more times before Byram led his horse onto the platform and joined the last of his soldiers going up. As soon as the platform came back down, the guards had all the prisoners step forward and loaded them on. They were made to stand close together, away from the edge, but Lucas saw Isaac making small movements away from them, inching his way towards him.

Isaac had been trying to get his attention a number of times that day, but with the chosen kept at a distance from Boran's soldiers, he had not been successful. He likely wanted to know if Boran was still alive, but Lucas couldn't risk being seen speaking with him. He caught Isaac's eye and subtly shook his head for him not to come closer.

Isaac frowned but stopped. He looked to the guards standing near the back of the platform—it was an ideal spot to be, as the cliff wall for the most part protected them from falling off. When he saw they were not watching, he moved his lips to form a name without a sound. "Boran?" he asked.

"Alive," mouthed Lucas back to him.

Isaac nodded, and turned away.

As Lucas suspected, Byram stood waiting at the top and had his eyes on him before he stepped off. Byram then directed his horse onto the cut road leading into the mountains.

The prisoners were pushed by the guards to form a single line, and were soon made to follow. Hungry and tired, and with daylight now several hours behind them, the group of prisoners struggled to keep going. Several times, Lucas heard the sound of a whip cracking and guards shouting for one of Boran's soldiers to get up. He worried it could soon be one of the chosen who would stumble and fall from exhaustion if they did not get to stop soon, but then he smelled the smoke of campfires. Soon the view of a high stockade loomed before him.

Walking through the wooden fortification's open entrance, he saw a settlement comprised of six large longhouses arranged in a circular fashion. The houses stood with their narrow ends and double doors facing an open center. Palisades had been built between the back of each house, preventing anyone from walking all the way around. It made for an empty space between the buildings and the outer stockade. Lucas felt the fencing and stockade were a later addition from when the settlement was first built—the wood from the longhouses looked to be darker and much more weathered than the fortifications surrounding them. A community like the one before him would house several shepherd families in one longhouse, but there was no sign of working families anywhere. Lucas only saw Hakon's soldiers walking in and out of the houses and occupying the central plaza.

An officer who had been standing by a campfire approached Byram as he dismounted. "I had not anticipated to see you for a few days yet," he told Byram. "Are we to expect Hakon here tonight as well?"

"No," answered Byram. "He will not come until everything is ready. I left in advance to make sure this group made it here without problems."

The officer followed his gaze to the group of prisoners behind Byram. "More of Boran's soldiers? I did not think—"

"Change of plan," answered Byram, handing the reins of his horse off to a squire who had rushed forward. He sounded irritable, and certainly not in the mood to have a conversation. He gave quick instructions to the guards and headed towards a fire, where a deer hung roasting on a spit.

The smell of food made Lucas's stomach rumble. He had not been given anything to eat in over a day. Boran's soldiers were staring longingly at the spit as well, but Lucas held no hope that any meat was going to be given to them. He watched as barricades were removed from two of the longhouses' doors, and guards started to push Boran's soldiers towards the closer building of the two. As Lucas followed the chosen towards the second longhouse, he became aware of one of Boran's soldiers' refusal to move. With eyes wild and focused on the roast hanging over the fires, the soldier thrashed about when poked with spears. He made loud grunting noises that drew everyone to look at him, including Byram, until several guards started beating him, and he fell to the ground.

"Hunger can make a person go mad," commented Warrick, turning away from the scene. The chosen had been stopped in front of the longhouse, where only their leg shackles were being removed. "Seeing that makes me glad we have proven to pass that test before." Warrick let his gaze wander inside the open door. "I'm just not sure if I'm ready for this."

Lucas struggled to keep his balance as his shackles were unlocked and pulled roughly away from around his ankles. He knew exactly what Warrick was referring to—using his mind, he had already seen the number of people sprawled on the floor inside. Stripped of any creature comforts, the longhouse before him was one big holding cell for the people forced to work on the road. There were no tables, no chairs, no beds—just a bare wooden floor. The only evidence that the longhouse was once home to many families was the dividing partitions and the two rectangular stone fire pits in the center aisle—now standing cold. The only light inside came from torches in sconces that hung from the posts holding up the pitched roof.

After all the chosen had stepped inside, the guards closed the doors. The sound of a beam falling into place on its brackets told them they were locked in.

"How many people do you think are here?" asked one of the chosen as they remained standing by the entrance. People were lying asleep everywhere. Some were in a sitting position with their backs propped up against posts and walls. A few had opened their eyes to the newcomers, but none looked too interested or cared to say anything.

"There must be at least eighty or a hundred," Warrick said.

Zera looked at Lucas. "And in the house where Boran's soldiers were taken?"

"About the same," answered Lucas, who had entered the space with his mind when Boran's soldiers were filing in. "Maybe slightly more." Carefully stepping over sleeping bodies, he led the chosen to the third partition, where he had seen space for some of them to lay down. He went to sit opposite them, with his back against the stone firepit. Warrick lowered himself next to him.

"How long do you think these people have been here?" asked Warrick.

"I don't know," answered Lucas. He looked across to his right, where he had noticed someone to be awake and observing him. "How long has it been for you?" Lucas asked of the man. His face looked somewhat familiar, but Lucas didn't think they had ever met.

"A few weeks," answered the man without delay. "But I'm one of the newer ones. Most have been here for years, and him over there—" he gestured towards the back "—he used to live here."

Lucas looked at the man pointed out to him. He was wearing a sheepskin vest and with his weathered skin and greying hair, he looked to be past the age of forty. When he turned back, he saw the man's eyes fixed on him once more.

"I know you," said the man. "You are the one they call the king's protector. I saw you riding next to King Boran some time ago, in the town called Ulmer. I heard there was a battle, and Hakon captured him. Are you here to save him?" When Lucas did not answer, he continued. "If your silence means that those outside do not know who you are, and you want it to remain so, then know your secret is safe within these walls."

"Thank you," said Lucas.

"Albert. The name is Albert," said the man before turning away. "If there is anything I can do, just let me know."

"Do you think he can be trusted?" asked Zera, casting a suspicious eye toward Albert.

"I don't know," answered Lucas. "We'll see."

Unable to sleep for most of the night, Lucas had only just closed his eyes when the doors to the longhouse opened, and guards raised everyone to their feet. They were brought outside in groups of no more than twenty, where ankle restraints replaced the wrist shackles.

"I wish they would take these off," complained Warrick, scratching his nose with his shackled wrists.

"I know," replied Lucas. He had been disappointed when the shackles from his wrist had not been removed the night before, but had noticed all the workers inside wore them. "Wearing these restraints can work to our advantage though."

"How so?" asked Zera, who was walking in front of him. She gave him a skeptical look over her shoulder.

"I let my mind drift outside last night," answered Lucas softly, "and it seemed that the soldiers feel secure in the knowledge that escape from the longhouse is impossible. No effort was made to check the doors during the night, and no watch was nearby. All we have to do is find a way to get these shackles off."

On a chain connecting them, each group walked past a large vat. Porridge was ladled into bowls and given to each worker. Lucas looked at the thick mixture in his bowl, which he saw was to be scooped out by hand.

"You want to eat it fast," he heard Albert say. "Before your bowl gets ripped from your hands and handed to the next in line." Albert took a handful from his bowl and stuffed it in his mouth. The chosen quickly followed suit when they saw bowls indeed taken away almost as soon as they were handed out.

Only Zera wrinkled her nose at the thought of putting her hand in her food and nearly had her bowl snatched from her. She twisted her body away from the soldier who wanted to take it from her. "Wait," she said. "I'll eat it."

"Best hurry then," said the soldier. "We don't have all day."

Lucas couldn't help but smile inwardly when he saw Zera fill her cheeks with food all while giving the soldier a death stare.

With little time wasted, all groups were led away from the settlement by soldiers on horseback. They walked for over an hour before the first workers were stopped and put to work hacking through the rock to widen the road. Lucas's group continued on until the sound of a river was heard, and they came to an open space where the construction of a bridge had begun. Near the riverbank, Lucas saw three large log panels built on top of rollers that would lead them towards the water. He could see stone piers built on both shores, to raise the bridge above the water. Lucas wondered how anyone could have gotten to the other side of this fast-flowing river until he noticed two chains just below the surface of the water that were fastened around large boulders on either side. Across the river, he saw the high cliffs, and the valley between them that narrowed into a canyon further off in the distance. It was what he had seen on the map, and he only hoped that Davis had been able to get to Nolan. Lucas had not detected any sign of his friend yet, and it worried him.

Placed with the logging detail, Lucas spent the entire day with the chosen, chopping trees down and stripping them of their branches before pulling them to the worksite. They were followed and watched by soldiers on horseback, who allowed them little rest.

He came to understand why none of the workers had woken when they had arrived the night before. All he wanted to do when he got back to the longhouse was close his eyes and sleep. His body ached in places he did not think possible. Even after a full night's sleep, he woke the next morning still feeling sore.

He saw little of Isaac and the rest of Boran's soldiers in the days following. They were on a different work detail, and Lucas only passed them in the mornings. The one he was happy not to cross paths with was Byram. He seemed to keep himself busy with the soldiers—who had started to arrive in great numbers—and not with the construction of the bridge. Lucas was therefore surprised when he suddenly showed up. They had just finished a long day's work, and all the workers were waiting to be lined up to return to the settlement when Byram arrived, stopping his horse near one of the officers in charge of the construction.

"I received word you are near completion of the bridge?" asked Byram.

"We are," answered the officer. "Two of the three bridge floors have been completed. We are ready to install them across the river tomorrow."

"Begin that work today," ordered Byram, casting his eye towards the line of workers. "There are still three hours of daylight left."

"Sir," replied the officer, "to install the first panel would require sending workers across the river with ropes to pull it across, and the river's current—"

"I know how it is to be done," interrupted Byram. "You don't need to tell me."

"Yes, well," stammered the officer, "then you understand the difficulty involved. After a long day of work, these workers are no longer fit for the task. In the morning, after they have rested, I will have the strongest men selected."

"No," snapped Byram. "Select them now. Hakon arrives in less than a week, and the bridge must be complete by the time he gets here."

"But sir," the officer objected. "It's impossible. We'll be set up to fail if we attempt it now."

Byram turned his horse to him in a threatening manner. "Do not disobey me!" he snarled.

Without saying another word, the officer approached the group of workers and started pointing at those he deemed to be the strongest—men in their mid-thirties, who were tall and built with muscle. Lucas sighed with relief when he saw that the officer was skipping over the chosen, but his relief was short-lived.

"Take those boys and the girl," said Byram, pointing at where their group sat together. "They are young and still fresh enough to continue."

"Of course . . ." murmured Zera, rolling her eyes. "This is the perfect opportunity to make us suffer more. Will Byram ever forgive us for what happened in the hunters' forest?"

"Not likely," answered Warrick. "And you're forgetting the men he lost to us in the arena."

Lucas heard the officer's sigh and saw him reluctantly summon all the chosen with a sweep of his hand.

Lucas found himself placed in the group that would push the panel from the back. Two other groups were designated to take the two ropes fastened to the front beam across the river, and pull once on the other side. Scanning to see where all the chosen had been placed, Lucas noticed Zera in a group that was to enter the water. From his time with the warriors and the outing he had taken with the chosen to a rock formation at the back of their valley, he remembered Zera, like her brother, couldn't swim. She had stayed back with Davis while Lucas and the other chosen had enjoyed jumping from a high cliff into the lake. With the river dangerous even for competent swimmers, he couldn't allow Zera to go in.

While the guards were still organizing the groups, and Byram talked to one of his soldiers, Lucas caught Zera's attention and made the quick switch with her. Shortly after, he began the single-file walk alongside the second group—also in single file—to the chains that hung over the river. The rope they would use to pull was draped across their shoulders, and the worker in front had tied it around his waist. It was the same with the second group, who would be responsible for the other rope.

Lucas saw that the river's current was powerful. Closer to the banks, foamy white eddies crashed into boulders that stuck out above the water. Stepping in, he found the temperature colder than he had expected.

"I have a bad feeling about this," muttered Warrick as he stepped in behind Lucas.

"Keep moving," said Lucas to the man in front of him, who was hesitating to go further. "If we stop, the cold will get to us and make it harder to hold on to the chain."

The man nodded, gripping the chain more tightly. He seemed scared of the water and possibly did not know how to swim, but even those who did would stand little chance if swept away by this river, thought Lucas. When he reached the halfway point between the two banks, where the water lapped roughly against his chest and he struggled to keep his feet in place, he looked over to the group on the other chain and bumped into the man in front of him. The man had stopped again.

"Keep going!" shouted Lucas, feeling the current was trying to take his feet from under him. "You can't stop now! You're almost there!" The sound of the river was deafening, and he didn't think the man could hear him—he remained frozen in the worst part of the river's rapids. "Go," he shouted again. He pushed the man, but he would not budge. Lucas looked over his shoulder to where Byram and the soldiers stood watching on the riverbank.

"Lucas, you have to do something," urged Warrick. "Slow down the river's current."

"I can't," said Lucas. "Byram will know I still have my powers."

"Then we have to go back," shouted Warrick. He struggled to hold on to the chain, and the men behind him were already backing up.

"Let me try and talk him through it," Lucas yelled back. He figured Byram wasn't going to be kind to those who gave up. Lucas turned back around to encourage him just as Warrick began yelling something, but the warning came too late—the current had swept the man in front of him off his feet. He flailed, grabbing Lucas by the arm in a panicked effort to save himself, and the hard tug made Lucas lose his grip on the chain. As the river took him and tossed him around like a ragdoll, he caught a glimpse of Byram and several of his soldiers kicking their horses into action.

Struggling to keep his head above water, Lucas saw the rising cliffs at the start of a gorge. A magpie flew upwards and landed on a ledge near the entrance. Below the bird, where the river narrowed, the man's body hit the rocks that jutted out from the bank.

Trying to avoid the same fate, Lucas started to fight against the current, but his efforts were futile. Just as he thought all was lost, he felt a hand grab the collar of his shirt—a soldier was lying flat on a rock above him, and was reaching down to help him.

"Stop fighting," shouted the soldier, lifting him from the water. "I have you."

Thrown onto the shore, Lucas coughed up the water that had tried to enter his lungs. Byram circled him, his hands on his hips and his face full of fury. For a brief moment, Lucas had seen compassion in Byram's eyes when he was pulled from the river, but that was gone now.

"What were you trying to do?" scolded Byram. "Trying to get away or have yourself killed?"

Lucas continued to cough. Why did Byram question his intent? Had it not been clear to him that it was an accident?

"Get up," shouted Byram. When Lucas failed to do so, he shouted again. "Get on your feet!"

This time, Lucas tried to push himself up on his elbows. He could hear the sound of hooves approaching.

"I was afraid this would happen," said the officer when he halted his horse. "That is the fifth worker we've lost to the river in the last two weeks alone."

Byram stared at the officer with anger. "This boy should not have been in the water," he scolded.

"Why? What is so special about him?" asked the disgruntled officer while Byram walked to his horse. "You yourself told us that all workers were expendable."

"Not this one," answered Byram while mounting his horse. "He's the only one we cannot afford to lose." As Lucas crawled to his knees, Byram turned to address the officer again. "Put him back to work, but keep him out of the water from here on out."

Lucas felt himself lifted to his feet by two guards. Byram shot him one last hateful look before riding off.

CHAPTER 25

Lucas sat with his back against the firepit. He was staring at the restraints around his wrists—he had been doing so for quite a while. Time was running out. They had nearly finished the road and bridge, and he had to come up with a plan to free everyone.

"You can stare at those for as long as you like," Warrick said, "but you'll need a key to open them."

"Maybe I don't," responded Lucas.

Warrick gave him a puzzled look.

"I grew up as a blacksmith's son," said Lucas. "I watched my father make many locks."

"I thought your father forged swords?"

"He did," answered Lucas. "But they didn't always put food on the table. He made all sorts of things. Doorknobs and hinges, nails, horseshoes . . . locks. I used to toy around with the mechanisms inside them."

"And you think you can open these shackles without a key?"

"Not exactly," answered Lucas. "I'll need something that could function as one. If you've noticed, when the key gets inserted to open these shackles, it doesn't turn. It gets pulled."

Warrick still looked confused. "What does that mean?"

"It means the mechanism is quite basic," explained Lucas. "All we need is something small and strong with a hook at the end to pull the spring." He looked at the longhouse until he spotted the iron sconces holding the torches. Lucas got up and walked over to the nearest sconce. Warrick was right behind him and took the torch from him after he lifted it from its holder. The bracket on the sconce that had held the torch was attached to the beam with two nails—if the bracket could be removed, the nails would come with it. Lucas examined it for a moment, then wrapped the chain of his shackles around the bracket and pulled on it with all his weight. It did not budge. He was preparing to try again when he heard a voice next to him.

"Anything in particular you're after?" asked Albert.

"The nails," answered Lucas.

"For . . .?"

"To make a key to get these shackles off me," he answered while pulling down again.

"Hm," mumbled Albert, "then allow me." He reached up and grabbed the sconce with both hands. It moved a little as he pulled on it, but not enough to break it from the post. Taking turns pulling and wiggling, they continued to loosen it. Around them, curious workers rose to their feet when word spread what they were trying to do. Some of them offered to help, and after some more force, the sconce finally came off.

Albert took the nails out of the bracket and handed them to Lucas. "I am sorry," he said. "They are not going to fit. These square nails are too thick to fit in the keyhole."

"I know," said Lucas. "We have to forge them to make them thinner." He laid one of the nails on the edge of the firepit and reached around to take back the torch from Warrick. "I need something to use as a hammer."

"How about this?" asked Albert, holding up the sconce.

"That might work," answered Lucas. "I also need as many human bodies as possible. Whoever is willing to help in blocking the noise, form a circle around me." He looked at the workers. They had been helpful up until then but now looked uncertain.

"You'll risk being heard by the guards," spoke a voice from the group of workers who had gathered around. "All to make a single key?"

Lucas looked to where the voice came from and saw it was the man wearing the sheepskin vest—Hallam, the settlement's original occupant.

"And what if you are successful in making this key?" continued Hallam. "Then what? Removing the shackles from our wrists will not set us free—it will have us killed."

"What do you think will happen to us when the road gets finished?" interrupted Albert before Lucas could respond. "Most of you come from Boran's land. How do you think the people will respond to Hakon when they find out he imprisoned you?" He paused and looked at the men standing around him, either shrugging or wrinkling their foreheads. "There would be rioting, total mayhem. We are a secret best buried. I can tell you what will happen," he continued. "Once our work is done here, Hakon will likely send us to the arena as entertainment for his soldiers."

"How does he know about the arena?" whispered Zera in Lucas's ear. "He told us that he'd only been at the settlement for a few weeks and indicated that he had arrived from Boran's land."

A mutter rose from the workers, and Lucas looked at Albert. Zera was right. By looking at those around him, he could tell that none of the other men knew about the arena. Before he could ask, Albert continued.

"That is what happened to those who have been released from this place," he said. "They were not set free, as they made you believe. They were given a sword, and hundreds of people got to watch as they tried to defend themselves against Hakon's soldiers. You can all guess how that went."

"How do you know this?" asked Hallam before Lucas could.

"Because I've seen it," answered Albert. "My home was not far from the arena."

"You are one of Hakon's people?" asked Lucas.

Albert nodded. "I was, but I left many years ago after I learned that my father killed my baby brother," he answered. "I was a child myself when it happened and only remember the baby to be crying a lot. Hakon, and other leaders in the community, viewed the child as a weak link in my family and provided my father with enough reason to be rid of it." Albert looked around at the silent workers. "Now," he continued, "I have no idea what Lucas here is planning, but if it will offer me a chance to live as a free man or die as one, I'm going to take that chance."

Lucas held the torch's flame underneath the nail's narrow end until it glowed orange from the heat. Using a rag so he would not burn his hand, he pulled the nail back onto the stone and hit the softened iron with the sconce. The process was slow and tedious as he tried to avoid making too much noise—he didn't hit the hot metal as hard as he had seen his father do. It was also an awkward movement with his wrists shackled together as they were. Albert and Warrick took turns to help when he needed to stretch his back and arm muscles.

When the nail was flat enough to fit into the keyhole, Lucas bent the narrow tip into a small hook. He then continued to do the same with the second nail.

"Why was it that we need two?" Warrick asked, but Lucas, focused on the task, only shook his head. The plan was slowly formulating in his head.

After several hours, he was finally holding the first finished product in his hand.

"Let's try it," said Warrick, holding his shackles up.

Lucas inserted the key into the lock and moved it around until he felt the hook catch onto something—he then pulled.

Warrick smiled when the lock sprang open.

"That is part one of my plan done," said Lucas, returning Warrick's smile.

"May I ask what part two is?" asked Albert.

Lucas nodded. He was going to need everyone's help. "I'm going to bring Boran and his soldiers one of the keys," he answered. "We will need them if we want to fight our way out of here."

Albert frowned. "And how are you going to do that?" he asked. "The two houses are kept separate with work detail. There's no way you will even get close to them."

"I'm aware of the difficulty," said Lucas. "It will have to be at night." He saw Albert glance towards the door with a puzzled look. It was the only obvious way in and out of the house but locked from the outside. Lucas lifted his head upwards in a quick motion towards the rafters above them.

"You are planning on using the roof?" asked Albert.

"Why not," answered Lucas. He put the shackles back on Warrick. "It's the weakest part of any building and rarely watched."

Having stayed awake all night to finish the second key while everyone else had nodded off around him, Lucas struggled to keep his mind focused on his work all the following day. He fell asleep as soon as they returned to the longhouse and woke when Warrick shook him by the shoulder.

"It's quiet outside," said Warrick. "Has been so for the past hour."

Lucas sat upright and held his shackles up for Warrick to unlock. He saw that Warrick was already holding the key—they had hidden it in a crevice between the floor and the wall before leaving for work that morning. After removing Lucas's shackles, Warrick handed him one of the keys, which Lucas put in his pocket.

"Good luck," said Warrick when they both stood up. "And be safe."

"Thanks," said Lucas. "I will." He took a deep breath and nodded to the chosen, who stood waiting. They moved to form a human wall that he climbed to reach the rafters. He pulled himself up and swung his leg over. Balancing across the beams, he made his way towards the back of the longhouse, where he could not be seen exiting the roof from the central plaza. Feeling the panels above, he searched for one he could break and found one that had been weakened by rainwater seeping through the gaps. Lucas pushed with both hands until it lifted upwards, creating a small hole to climb through. Once he was out, he crouched on top of the roof and put the board back. He counted which one it was so he could find it upon his return. It was the sixth panel down from the peak of the roof and the fourth from the edge.

With a quick look over his shoulder to make sure no one was standing in the plaza, he climbed over the pitched roof to the other side. He let himself slide down until his feet landed on the palisade that connected the two buildings. Lucas was thankful for the times he had climbed the monastery's roof and for his circus days, when Rosa had given him balancing lessons on beams that had been no wider than his foot. Thanks to her, the palisade was an obstacle he was able to cross quickly and with little effort.

Climbing onto the roof of the adjacent longhouse, Lucas searched for another loose panel and found one in almost the same place. It too appeared water damaged, and Lucas assumed it was a design flaw in terms of how the roof drained. He lifted it up and let himself slip inside. Workers raised their heads, and some of Boran's soldiers jumped to their feet when he moved over the rafters. Lucas brought a finger to his lips to tell them to be quiet and started moving to the center of the longhouse, where he could already see Isaac standing up. As the only Black man, he stood out among his fellow prisoners.

"What are you doing here?" asked Isaac, looking up at him.

"I've come to talk and to give you something," replied Lucas. He took the forged nail out of his pocket and held it up.

"What is that?" asked Isaac.

"It works like a key to open the shackles," answered Lucas. He was sitting in a crouched position on the rafter and held the flat part of the nail up so Isaac could see the tiny hook at the end. He then dropped it down for him to catch.

"How did you get it?" asked Isaac, turning the key around in his hand.

"We forged it last night," answered Lucas. "We made two. One for each house."

Isaac inserted the key into the lock of his restraints and tried to turn it to open.

"You have to locate the spring inside and pull once you feel you have the key hooked onto it," explained Lucas.

Soldiers and workers gathered closer to watch Isaac trying to open it. It took him a few minutes, but then he smiled and pulled the key. The crowd gasped when they watched his shackles open and fall to the ground. One of the workers tried to reach for the key in Isaac's hand, but Lucas's voice stopped him.

"No," said Lucas. "Not yet. You take the shackles off now with five hundred soldiers outside these walls, and we'll all be dead by morning."

Isaac reached for his shackles and put them back on. "What is your plan?"

"We wait until Hakon makes his way across to Boran's land," answered Lucas.

"And then what?"

"Then we break free from here."

"You don't think he will kill us as soon as the bridge gets finished?"

"He might," answered Lucas. "But Albert is convinced he will send us to our deaths in the arena." Lucas looked to the workers who had gathered around. Isaac must have told them about the arena and what happened there, because none of them looked surprised upon his mention of the place of death.

"King Boran?" asked Isaac. "He is still alive?"

"He is, for now," answered Lucas. "Hakon is going to take him to the town."

"Will you be trying to free him once we get out?"

Lucas shrugged, an involuntary smile coming to his face. "I can't just let Hakon kill him and take his throne, so yes."

Isaac looked to the other soldiers. "Then we will help in any way we can," he said.

"I was hoping you'd say that," said Lucas. Eager to get back to the chosen, he turned around on the rafter and looked down one last time. "Keep the key hidden until I find a way to let you know when to use it. Or all chaos breaks loose before I can manage that." He waited for Isaac to nod, then headed out.

Despite being pleased with the outcome and relative ease at which he had been able to make the trip into the other longhouse, Lucas took a moment to ensure he couldn't be seen from the plaza once he had climbed out onto the roof. He put the panel back in place and made his way to the palisade, concentrating on placing his feet in such a way as to make a fast crossing. Lucas was halfway across when he realized he'd made a mistake. He had only focused his attention on the open center of the settlement, and not the small space between the two longhouses. He should have anticipated that a guard or soldier could wander in to have a private moment. Lucas froze on the palisade when he saw a soldier come into view.

The soldier's back was to Lucas as he urinated against the side of the chosen's longhouse. Afraid to move and draw attention, Lucas wobbled to keep his balance. He could only hope that the soldier would remain too busy tucking his shirt back into his trousers to look up. For a moment, it appeared that way, but then the soldier stopped to secure his belt and began to look up. He turned his head, and right in Lucas's direction.

Knowing there was only one thing he could do, Lucas jumped from the palisade and lunged at the soldier.

Caught off guard, the soldier stumbled backward and fell to the ground with Lucas on top of him. Lucas had put one hand over the man's mouth to muffle his cries for help and was reaching for the dagger on his belt with his other hand when the guard grabbed Lucas by the shoulders and—since he was much larger—used his weight to throw him off.

Lucas found himself pinned to the ground with the soldier on top of him. The soldier's calloused hands closed in around his neck. Lucas tried to wriggle his body from beneath the weight and clawed at the hands that stopped him from breathing, but the soldier was strong and determined not to let go. Lucas felt himself blacking out, and in a final attempt, reached again for the soldier's dagger. His fingers touched the heft, but he couldn't get enough grip to pull it from its sheath, and his hands went slack at his sides. Accepting that this could be his end, Lucas was looking up towards the sky when a dark figure suddenly emerged behind the soldier. He saw the club swing at the soldier's head and heard the crushing sound of a skull breaking.

Free from the pressure around his neck, Lucas took a moment to recover before pushing the soldier's body off of himself. Still weak, he scrambled to get up. He was helped onto his feet by the person who had rescued him and he stared with relief at the familiar face.

"Orson?" whispered Lucas, surprised but delighted to see the hunter. "What are you doing here?" He saw two more hunters emerging from the shadows.

"Saving your life, by the looks of it," answered Orson. "We've been watching this place for the past two days, trying to find a way to get you out."

"Just you?" asked Lucas. He hoped Davis had come as well, even though he already knew the answer. There had been no connection with Davis.

"Other hunters are waiting nearby," answered Orson, "but I am afraid no one else. Nolan sent us to follow the trail Davis told us about, so that we might locate the road under construction. He wants to be sure he's going to be in the right location to stop Hakon. Now that you are out, we can go. And it may be wise if we hurry."

"I can't go with you," said Lucas. "I'm needed here, and I can't leave the chosen. Surely Davis would have told you that."

He heard the hunter's deep sigh. "I thought you might say that but hoped you wouldn't. We had discussed getting everyone out with Davis, but didn't realize how difficult that would be until we arrived."

They both heard a door open and listened to the muffled voices coming from a longhouse at the far end. Orson moved closer to Lucas and spoke softly. "Are you sure about this?" he asked, not pressing the matter further.

Lucas nodded.

"Then you best get back before more soldiers rise."

Lucas looked at the dead soldier on the ground. How was this going to be explained?

"Don't worry," said Orson, as if reading his mind. "We'll take care of him."

Lucas reluctantly turned to face the longhouse. He knew hunters had a way of moving around unseen, but removing a body from this settlement might prove too much of a challenge even for Orson. He wished he could go with them but dismissed that thought as soon as it entered his mind. There was no way he could let the chosen face the consequences of his departure. He reached for the top of the palisade and pulled himself up, Orson assisting him with a step up.

"Can you stay close?" asked Lucas. "In case I need you?"

"I have no intention of leaving you while chains restrict you," answered Orson.

Lucas made his way to the roof. He quickly found the loose panel and looked back before slipping inside. Orson and the two other hunters were gone, and so was the dead soldier, like ghosts in the night.

The following morning, before following the other workers out of the longhouse, Lucas pulled on both laces of his shirt to close the collar more snugly. He was trying to conceal the dark bruises that had appeared around his neck where the soldier's hands had squeezed him. It was Zera who had brought it to his attention, as there was no such luxury as a mirror to be found in the longhouse. Lucas didn't want anyone to see the marks and question him about them—least of all Byram, who was standing with his back to the door, only a few feet away. A group of officers stood gathered around Byram, and he was listening to one of them speaking. As Lucas stepped through the door, he picked up on their conversation.

"What do you mean, he's not here?" asked Byram.

"There's no sign of this man anywhere," answered the officer. "He was seen walking through the gates just before midnight. He told the guards he was suffering from muscle spasms and needed to stretch his legs. The guards swear they saw him walk back moments later. We searched the entire perimeter outside the stockade, in case they were mistaken and a cougar had gotten to him."

"I presume that was not the case?" asked Byram. "Or you would have told me so?"

"Yes sir. I can assure you he was nowhere to be found."

Byram glanced over at Lucas's group of workers as they went past, briefly resting his eyes on Lucas. Lucas was relieved he did not appear to have seen the bruise. It was when he was breathing a small sigh of relief that Byram jerked his head back in his direction, as if only now registering what he had seen.

"Wait!" shouted Byram, turning on his heels.

The guards halted, and every worker looked frightened as Byram marched towards them with significant strides. He went directly for Lucas and pulled down his shirt collar to expose the bruising around his neck.

"How did you get this?" asked Byram.

"It is nothing, sir," answered Lucas.

"It doesn't look like nothing," said Byram. "Whoever had their hands around your neck meant business." He let go of the shirt. "Who was it?"

Lucas lowered his head and declined to answer. With the soldier's body unaccounted for, there was no way of linking the two together, and Byram had to be thinking someone inside the longhouse was responsible.

"Someone better come forward," said Byram, looking down the line of workers, "and tell me who did this."

Every worker dropped their head, except for Albert, who was two spaces behind Lucas. "Why do you care, brother?" he asked. "You cannot lock a hundred people up together and expect there to be no disagreements."

Lucas saw Byram's body tense up, his attention now on Albert. He watched how the two men stared at each other—Byram with intense irritation and Albert firm and seemingly unafraid. Everyone around was holding their breath, and no doubt bracing themselves for the rage Byram was to release. Lucas, getting ready to get himself out of the way, did not expect Byram's next move—after an awkward moment of silence, Byram suddenly stepped back.

"Get these men moving," he told the guards, waving a hand to show his impatience. "We're wasting our time here."

With the line of workers set in motion, Lucas glanced from Byram to Albert. Byram had turned away, but Albert had not taken his eyes off him. The bravery surprised Lucas, but then the words Albert had spoken and the reason he had looked so familiar came to him. Albert's eyes and hair color were different, but his facial features—the high cheekbones, and the dimple in his chin—were unmistakable. He looked like Byram. And he had called Byram "brother"—but not in the general way of speaking, Lucas suddenly realized.

"You're related to Byram," said Lucas, when he was working next to Albert later that morning. The second bridge panel had been moved in place the day before, and they were securing it to the first panel with ropes. "He is your brother."

"Yes. My eldest," answered Albert, without looking up from his work.

"Your brother would allow you to be a prisoner here?" asked Warrick, handing Lucas another rope.

"I wouldn't be here if it weren't for him," answered Albert. "He's the one who locked me up." He stretched his back, looking around to see if any officers were near before continuing. "No one leaves Hakon and starts a new life elsewhere, but I made a mistake in thinking that Byram had done just that many years before—I followed him in his footsteps, and created a new life for myself as well. What I didn't know was that Byram had been sent on a secret mission to join a group of Hakon's soldiers who had infiltrated Boran's court and had remained loyal to Hakon. When Byram saw me in town a few weeks ago, he had me arrested and brought here. All made possible by Grant, who is a distant cousin of ours." Albert glanced sideways when Lucas did not respond. "Your silence tells me that you already made the connection between Byram and Grant. Now that you know who I am, you are questioning if you can still trust me?"

Lucas shook his head. "I don't doubt your trust when it comes to breaking free from these chains," he answered. "I only wonder whose side you will be on when faced with the choice between family and what is right for the people."

They finished securing the bridge, and Albert was called away by the guards to take his place on the ropes to pull the third and last panel across. Lucas and the chosen received orders to push at the back. As the workers heaved the last bridge panel across the river and let it fall into place, a cheer rose from the soldiers. The officers smiled triumphantly, slapping each other across the back. Only the workers stood silent. With the job almost finished, death was getting closer. Lucas noticed some of them staring at him, their eyes full of questioning. He turned and sent his focus across the river.

"Anything?" asked Zera, who knew he was trying to connect with Davis.

Lucas shook his head. There was no sign of him yet.

"He'll be there," said Zera. "He won't let you down."

It was dusk by the time Lucas and the workers arrived back at the settlement. Even from afar, Lucas noticed that the ground outside the stockade had undergone a transformation. That morning, a field of mountain grass had stretched as far as the rocks surrounding the settlement, but now an army camp with hundreds of soldiers occupied the land.

With his group usually the last to be back, Lucas would typically find the other workers already locked up, but tonight they stood waiting on the ground outside the gates. He saw them lined up in rows on either side of the entrance—forming a corridor for those entering. It appeared that everyone living at the settlement, whether by choice or imprisonment, was assembled outside the gates. Hakon's banners had been raised and were flying high above the entrance.

"It's finally happening then," said Warrick, when they and the workers that belonged to their longhouse took their places on the left side of the entrance. "Hakon's arrival?"

"It appears that way," answered Lucas. A feeling of dread came over him. There were far more soldiers than he liked to see. In the row of prisoners across from him, he saw Isaac and Boran's soldiers. Their clothes were dusty from pulverizing rock to widen the road, but he was pleased to see their spirits looked high. Boran's soldiers stood straight, their chins held high, unlike some of the workers who stood with hunched shoulders and sunken eyes. He could only hope they would not lose faith this close to the end.

A horn sounded, and Lucas watched Hakon's soldiers rush to take their place in rows behind the workers. When Hakon's procession came into view, Byram appeared at the settlement's entrance, several of his officers standing at his side.

With his long, white hair tied in a ponytail and his wolf cloak draped over his shoulders, Hakon slowly walked his horse through the corridor. His eyes were fixed forward as he headed towards the gates.

Behind him rode Boran, dressed in fine clothes and looking better than the last time Lucas had seen him. He was sitting tall with his head held high and was holding the reins of his horse lightly. No guards were riding next to him. If one did not know any better, they would think he was there of his own free will, until of course they noticed his pale face and the dark circles under his eyes. Boran was doing his best to keep what remained of his dignity intact, but Lucas could tell that he had all but lost hope. That was . . . until he noticed his men. Boran's soldiers raised their heads higher as he passed them by, and Isaac gave a quick nod in Lucas's direction. Boran turned his head slightly, and when he saw Lucas and the chosen, his eyes appeared to shine briefly with some hope.

When Hakon was halfway down the corridor of people gathered outside the gates, he turned his horse around and stopped. He let his eyes go over the crowd on either side of him. "The day we have been waiting for," he called out, "is almost here." He paused, and the flapping of banners in the wind was the only sound Lucas could hear as everyone waited for him to continue. "Tomorrow, I will take what is rightfully mine." He paused again. This time, Lucas could sense the excitement coming from the soldiers lined up behind them. "But tonight," continued Hakon, "we will have a feast and celebrate our victory!"

Cheers rose from the men, and as they chanted his name, Hakon rode through the gates of the settlement. When the last person of his entourage had entered, the workers found themselves urged to follow. With both lines of workers coming together, Lucas slowed his pace and weaved in and out of the conjoined line of people as inconspicuously as possible, until he was next to Isaac. Passing through the entrance, he saw the open space between the stockade and the palisade filled with supply wagons, all of them still hitched to horses. The wagons had been driven in on the right and brought all the way around for an easy exit.

As he walked onward, Lucas saw the doors of the longhouses open and noticed that guards were hurrying workers to get inside, occasionally prodding them with their weapons. No food was handed to them as would typically be the case, and one worker questioned a guard on the matter. "It seems, in the spirit of festivity," the worker pressed, "that you have forgotten our supper?"

"Why would we feed you," answered the guard, "now that your services are no longer required?

Another guard laughed at the joke, and more workers stopped to see what was happening. "You're all broken down, the lot of you," the second guard said merrily, "and I can't see Hakon investing what could be better spent on the livestock."

Lucas watched as workers who had listened to the response reacted with looks of horror and outrage. He moved closer to Isaac, and even though he had the distraction of the hungry and protesting workers to keep the guards' eyes off him, he was careful to keep his movements subtle. One wrong move and the plan would fail.

"Tell your fellow soldiers not to join the fight," he whispered when he was next to Isaac.

"What fight?" asked Isaac.

"Do it now," added Lucas, ignoring Isaac's question. He could see workers becoming agitated, many of them stalling or shuffling their feet, unwilling to give up on the notion of an evening meal. Arms were crossed over chests, and sullen glares were cast at the guards prodding them along. Someone threw a rock.

Guards were closing in around a group of workers that had stopped entirely, refusing to continue. Lucas watched as Isaac relayed the message to his comrades, telling them not to resist the guards, no matter what happened.

"Have we not given you enough?" one worker demanded. "Is toiling for you as slaves day in and day out not enough?"

"You will have us starve then?" asked another man, loudly enough for all to hear.

"That is not up to me," answered the guard. "Now, move!" He tried to move the man forward, but the man pushed back.

He struggled to stay close to Isaac when the guards began to use force to get workers to move. People were stumbling into one another and falling down all around them, and were they not in such a weakened state, Lucas would have feared a riot. Even still, he knew the workers were resilient despite their appearance, and the scene was making him uneasy.

"Is there a civilian in your house who acts as a leader to the others?" asked Lucas. "Yes," answered Isaac.

"Give him the key I gave you," said Lucas. The distance between them had become greater, and Lucas had to raise his voice. "Tell him not to use it until first light tomorrow."

"Why?" asked Isaac, but Lucas did not dare to answer him. Guards were coming in from the back—splitting the group to gain control. He saw Boran's soldiers move off to the side, their hands raised to show the guards they were not the ones causing trouble. The chosen did the same, and Lucas followed their lead, fully aware that Hakon and Byram watched from a distance.

Lucas had been listening to the heated discussion revolving around escape for some time. Many of the workers did not want to wait until first light to make their move. "First of all," said Albert, stomping towards a group of men talking near the back of the longhouse, one of which was Hallam, "it will be doubtful you will be able to get the key from those boys without getting hurt." He looked over his shoulder to where Lucas and the chosen were sitting. "But let's say you are successful," he continued, "and you get to remove your shackles. Then what? Wait for the doors to open and fight your way out of here?"

"We are only considering our options," answered Hallam. "Nothing more."

"You wish to fight without any weapons?"

"We would have the element of surprise," answered another of the group. "We can take the weapons from the guards."

Albert shook his head wildly. "You will get us all killed." He had raised his voice enough for other workers to pay attention to the discussion.

"You want us to do nothing and wait until we all starve to death?" asked Hallam. "Or hope to take our chance in the arena?"

"No," answered Albert. "We will listen to Lucas and do as he tells us to."

Now it was Hallam who shook his head. "You put too much faith in that boy."

"Lucas is the protector of the true king. Sent by the gods to see justice served to the people."

"So you have told us," said Hallam. "But what proof do you have of this?" He stared at Lucas. "I don't see anything special about him. He's just a boy and not even a stout one at that."

Lucas was sitting with his knees up, staring at the floor between his legs.

When no one gave any response, Hallam continued. "I don't believe he is the answer to our problems. We're running out of time and need to come up with a plan."

The men around him nodded in agreement.

Aware of everyone looking at him in the silence that followed, Lucas raised his head towards the group and locked eyes with Hallam. "There were five of them," he started. "Five men dressed in black." Albert looked confused, as did several other men, but Lucas knew Hallam knew what he was talking about. "You were chopping wood in front of the house opposite when you saw them ride towards you over the freshly fallen snow. There was no stockade to block your view as there is now."

All eyes went to Hallam, who was staring silently at Lucas. Having his attention, Lucas continued the story.

"They claimed to be merchants who had gotten lost in the snowstorm the day before. You had no reason to doubt them, as that scenario had happened in the past. You invited them into the home you shared with three other families. Your wife and the other women fed them over the next three days. The strangers helped with chores and even played games with the older children. Only your young daughter was scared of the one with the beard and the deep dark eyes—the one they called Garam."

"I should have paid attention to her," said Hallam, taking over from Lucas. "Seen the evil that was in his eyes, as she did. When they left after a few days, I thought I would never see them again, but I was wrong. Garam returned that spring with Hakon, and he—" Hallam stopped and took a deep breath to pull himself together. Tears had sprung in his eyes, and he wiped them away forcefully.

"Garam is the reason you want to break out of here tonight," said Lucas. "You think he has come here with Hakon, and you want revenge for what he did to your family." Lucas rose to his feet and took the key from the crevice by the wall. "Take it," he said, holding it out to Hallam, "but you will get everyone here killed for nothing. Garam isn't out there. Nor are any of his four comrades."

"How do you know?" asked Hallam.

"Because I watched Garam die as I thrust my sword into him," replied Lucas. He recalled the memory of the dark order chasing him through the woods on his way back from Lord Killeand's castle. "Two of his comrades died with him that day. The other two preceded him in death some years before when they came for me." He stretched his hand out further to see if Hallam still wanted the key, but he didn't.

In the silence that followed, laughter reached them from officers gathering in the plaza. The smell of fresh roast had already found its way through the cracks in the walls, indicating a feast would soon take place. Then voices were heard near the door outside, and everyone scrambled to sit back down. Lucas and Hallam were the last ones standing.

"The reason I am here," said Lucas, "is to stop what happened to your family from happening to others. You have to trust me when I tell you that I will get us out."

Hallam gave him a tight nod before turning away from him to find a place to sit.

Lucas sat himself down between Warrick and Zera just as the doors opened. He watched four guards stay in the doorway while two others stepped inside. They looked around until they spotted him.

"You," called one of the guards out to him. "Stand up and come over here."

Turning sideways to put his hands on the floor to push himself up, Lucas dropped the key in Warrick's lap. "I may need you to come and get me," he whispered. "You'll know what to do when it's time."

Warrick put a hand over the key to cover it up.

Lucas looked to the chosen sitting by the wall, his eyes urging them to remain calm and be ready for him, before standing up. He then stepped over several legs and other body parts blocking his path as he made his way to the guards.

Breathing in the cool night air, Lucas followed the guards to the central part of the settlement, where officers were sitting behind tables set up around the plaza. They were nibbling on nuts and dried fruits while conversing with one another. On a spit off to the side, a boar was turned over. Its fat sizzling in the fire below made Lucas's stomach growl. He had not eaten a decent meal in a long time.

Lucas saw Hakon seated at the head table, with Byram occupying the seat on his right. The two were in deep conversation and paid little attention to what was going on around them. To Lucas's surprise, on Hakon's left sat King Boran. He had a plate of food in front of him but wasn't eating. Hakon's tactics had changed. Instead of inflicting physical pain, he seemed to have resorted to making Boran suffer by showing him what he had lost—prestige, wealth, respect, and authority over his men.

Boran looked up when a guard stopped Lucas by the shoulder just as he was about to pass through a space between two tables. Their eyes briefly met, but then Lucas looked over his shoulder when he heard the shuffling of footsteps behind him. Isaac and the four soldiers who had fought in the arena were coming towards him. With their arrival, Lucas felt a nudge in his back, and the guard directed him to walk into the open area the circle of tables created.

"Ah," said Hakon, standing up when Lucas and the soldiers were made to kneel before him. "The last of our guests have arrived." Behind each table, officers stood up as well. Only Boran remained seated.

Isaac kneeled in front of Lucas, and half looked over his shoulder. "Do you know what the meaning of this is?" he asked.

"Are you asking me?" answered Lucas. He had Byram's eyes and ears on him and had to be careful with his response.

Isaac nodded.

Lucas shrugged his shoulders. "I have no idea," he answered, but he didn't think anything good was to happen. Seeing that the only soldiers brought before Hakon were the ones who had brought him humiliation in the arena by defeating his warriors in front of his people, he doubted any of them were to share in the feast. He watched Hakon pick up his cup from the table.

"I would like to bring a toast to our honored guest," said Hakon. He had turned to his left and looked down on Boran. "For if it was not Boran's desire to fulfill his grandfather's and his father's quest to regain the lands to the west and defeat King Itan, we might not have been successful in completing ours." He turned to Lucas and Boran's soldiers. "As for the condemned before us . . ."

Hearing Hakon's words caused the soldiers to lift their heads. Their worried looks were replaced with confusion as he continued. "You will be forgiven for your defiance in the arena and allowed to join us in our feast if you pledge your loyalty to me." He paused and looked around at the group of soldiers. Two of them were straightening their backs and looking hopeful. Lucas could tell they were ready to take the deal if it meant they would get to eat.

"Tell them not to do it," whispered Lucas, hoping Isaac could hear him. He then turned towards the table and looked at Boran. There was a glimpse of the king's former self as he stared angrily at the two soldiers who were ready to betray him.

Hakon was watching them as well. "Will you forsake the man once claiming to be your king," he asked, "for a chance to feast with us?"

Both soldiers nodded, one more reluctantly than the other. The soldier who hesitated had heard Isaac's warnings and looked to the rest of his group. When he noticed none of the others were taking Hakon up on his offer, he shifted on his knees and started to speak, but Hakon cut him off.

"Your loyalty is accepted," said Hakon. He smiled a devious smile and raised his cup towards the two soldiers. "You will be allowed to eat with us."

The soldiers were pulled to their feet by their armpits by several guards and moved a few feet away, where they were pushed back onto their knees. Only then did Hakon take his eyes off them and direct his attention to Lucas.

"What about you?" asked Hakon. "Is your loyalty still with Boran, or does your former pledge acknowledging me as king still stand?"

Fully aware that this was Hakon's way to catch him out, Lucas carefully responded. "I am not sure why my acknowledgment is of any importance, sire," answered Lucas. "My loyalty has never been with King Boran—it is King Itan I serve." He was aware of Boran's pained look and saw Byram's wide grin. Lucas couldn't tell whether Byram was finally satisfied that Lucas did not remember who he was and believed him to have spoken like a real chosen or that he enjoyed the game of making Boran suffer his defeat. Either way, Hakon did not seem to have questioned Oswall's abilities.

"Of course," replied Hakon, "but is it King Itan you wish to remain loyal to?"

"As a chosen one," answered Lucas. "I have little choice in the matter." He lowered his head to try and look uneasy with the situation. He was aware of Boran's intense stare before looking up to Hakon.

"What have you done to him?" asked Boran. His tone of voice sounded strong, like the king he was before his defeat. "That is not the Lucas I know."

Hakon placed a hand on Boran's shoulder as he stood over him. "We were able to achieve what your priest Eneas failed to do."

"You have altered his mind?" asked Boran, returning his gaze to Lucas.

"Only his memory."

"I doubt that is possible," remarked Boran. Lucas held his breath. The last thing he needed was for Boran to put doubt in Hakon's mind, but then he heard Boran give up the notion to argue as quickly as he had started it. "Unless Eneas was another who had me fooled all these years," he said. "Was he another of your family members I did not know about?"

"He wasn't," answered Hakon. "But he certainly served his purpose in our cause." With platters of meat arriving and set upon the tables, Hakon redirected his attention to his officers. "Feast," he told them, "with the knowledge that in a few days, you will dine in a castle with more riches than you could ever have imagined." He raised his cup and brought it to his lips, taking a sip after the officers saluted him.

Watching every officer drinking in excess, Lucas hoped plenty of ale was going around the soldiers camped outside the stockade. It might be enough to stop them from becoming aware of the figures approaching in the darkness.

CHAPTER 26

Still kneeled in front of the tables, Lucas lowered his head and stared at the ground. He no longer wanted to watch what the two soldiers who had pledged their loyalty to Hakon had to endure. They had been used for the officers' entertainment for the past two hours. The promise to share in the feast had been deliberately misleading. Hakon's men tossed bones and other food waste on the ground before the two soldiers, and they were forced to pick it up and eat it. When refused, it was smeared onto their clothes and stuffed in their mouths by officers cheered by their comrades. The laughter of the officers watching from behind the tables was deafening, and some of the men were standing up to watch as two of their cohort poured cups of ale down the soldiers' throats—a contest to see who could make their victim pass out first.

"Have a drink on us," someone shouted. Lucas looked over his shoulder and saw several officers raising cups.

"More, more, more," chanted the group when the soldiers started to gag on the ale. It was sickening to watch.

Hakon and Byram, having remained stone-faced for most of the night, were displaying an evil grin now and then.

Boran was picking meat from a bone and slowly bringing it to his mouth—ignoring what was being done to his soldiers. Lucas knew he would feel no sympathy for them. After all, they had betrayed him, and he would agree with Hakon that it was to be punishable by death in the end.

Isaac and Boran's other two soldiers were aware of this as well. With less attention paid to them, they had dropped to sitting on their bottoms, their heads hung and pressed against their knees. Beneath the noise of laughter, Lucas could hear the sound of wolves howling in the distance.

"Great," mumbled Isaac, looking up. "As if being surrounded by enemy soldiers is not enough. Now we have a pack of bloodthirsty wolves as well."

"These are friendly wolves," said Lucas softly.

Isaac turned to him. "There is no such thing as a friendly wolf."

"These are," said Lucas. He was always impressed with how precisely the hunters could replicate animals' sounds and communicate that way.

Isaac raised his eyebrows. "Are you familiar with this pack of wolves?"

Lucas nodded slowly. He was careful to keep an eye on Byram, who had started to lose interest in the two tormented soldiers.

"Will they dare to attack an army as large as this?" asked Isaac.

"I hope not," answered Lucas. "That would be suicide." He was happy knowing Orson had brought more reinforcements, but he worried for their safety.

"Then why are they here?"

"To assist if we need it," answered Lucas. "They'll wait and watch for now."

Isaac made sure no one was looking before scooting closer. "How do you think we can get ourselves out of here? We're shackled and have no weapons."

"Did you leave the key with someone you trust?" asked Lucas.

"I did," answered Isaac. "And I told him not to use it until first light."

"Good," said Lucas. "That gives me a few hours."

"To do what?"

"To get weapons," he answered. He shifted away from Isaac when he saw Byram stand up and walk around the table to stop behind the soldiers who were doubled over and groaning in agony. The two officers stepped aside when Byram took a dagger from his belt. The laughter died down—everyone sensed the game had come to an end. Byram stared down at one of the soldiers, who heaved and vomited. Then, as soon as the man finished, Byram grabbed him by the hair, pulled his head back to expose his neck, and in one swift movement, sliced his throat. He went on to do the same to the other soldier before he even knew what was happening. It brought an end to the soldiers' torture, but for Byram, Lucas imagined it was a routine killing—Hakon had grown bored.

The excitement and boisterous behavior of the officers soon dwindled. Some fell asleep with their heads on the table. Others staggered off to bed. Isaac and his comrades were lying down, and Lucas had done the same. No one seemed concerned that the small group of prisoners was still there. Even Byram, who was left at the table after Hakon excused himself to go to bed, did not attempt to see them returned to the longhouses.

Closing his eyes and pretending to be asleep, Lucas watched what was going on around him with his mind. Outside the stockade, the soldiers' camp had quietened down. A few fires were still burning food waste to prevent animals from coming near. The howling of wolves had not gone unnoticed.

Byram finished his drink and slammed his cup onto the table. Guards stood to attention when he rose from his seat and walked over to the group of sleeping prisoners on the ground. He stopped close to Lucas and looked down at him.

"Should we get them up and put away, sir?" asked a guard.

"No," answered Byram. "I cannot take the risk of opening the doors to the houses. By now, those men inside may have figured out the situation they are in, and with half the officers sheep-drunk, a revolt is the last thing we need. You can leave them here. Any sign of trouble—you may kill them." He pointed to Lucas. "Except for this one. Come and get me if he gives you cause for concern."

"Understood, sir," replied the guard before Byram walked away.

Hakon's men were settling in for the night, and Lucas waited until they were all asleep before he concentrated on entering the longhouse with his mind. He made his way to where the chosen were sleeping and saw Warrick open his eyes. Sensing Lucas was there and that it was time, Warrick reached for the key hidden beneath him. He unlocked his shackles and stood up to wake Zera and the other boys. In perfect silence, the chosen passed the key around and started to make their way to the rafters. When the last chosen was free of his restraints, Warrick woke Albert and handed him the key. Hallam and a few other workers got up and watched the chosen head to the roof's loose panel.

Refocusing his view on the area outside the longhouse, Lucas had the chosen wait to make sure it was clear before they emerged through the opening in the roof.

Warrick climbed through first, followed by the others. They carefully made their way down the roof and into the area of supply wagons.

Lucas reckoned no army this large would travel without spare weapons, and with their mission to conquer another land, they would need to recruit and arm more soldiers. All the chosen had to do was find those weapons. With Davis, he could have communicated in words which wagons he thought had the best chance of carrying weapons, but with Warrick, Zera, and the chosen, all he could do was direct them.

The chosen were moving from wagon to wagon, carefully lifting tarps and opening bags and chests until they found the wagons with the supply of weapons. There were three of them, loaded with trunks of swords. Zera and Warrick directed the other chosen to form a line back to both houses and started passing down swords and daggers to the boys left on the roof, who handed them down to Isaac and Albert inside, waiting below the rafters. When they finished, and all the chosen had returned safely inside the house, Warrick remained outside and replaced the roof tile. Lucas watched with his mind as he climbed back down, grabbed the two swords he had left lying on the ground, and made his way around to the other side of the settlement. Lucas rolled over on his side and watched Warrick scale the palisade closest to him. In the flickering light of a fire, their eyes met just before Warrick moved to hide behind empty kegs of ale stacked up against the house's wall. Once there, he settled in for the wait.

Lucas woke with the noise of loud footsteps and orders being shouted. He pushed himself up on his elbow and used the shackles on his wrist to scratch an itchy spot on his side. "What did I miss?" asked Lucas, seeing Isaac awake and looking towards the longhouses. Outside the stockade, he could see the camp cleared and soldiers lining up in formation.

"They are stacking wood against the walls," answered Isaac. He turned and looked at Lucas, his eyes wide and glassy. "I think they are planning to set fire to the settlement and kill everyone."

Before Lucas could respond, guards shouted for him and Boran's remaining soldiers to get onto their feet and step to the side—they were making way for riderless horses being taken toward the dwelling Hakon was staying in. Taking his time, Lucas glanced towards the house where Warrick was hiding. He was pleased to see the kegs were still there. He took his place next to Isaac and watched Hakon walk out of the center house, closely followed by Byram. They walked to their horses and mounted up. A moment later, Boran came out, accompanied by guards. He was looking annoyed and twisted his body in anger when shoved in the back to walk faster.

"It is time for you to return home, Boran," said Hakon. He had turned his horse to face him. "You will have the honor of telling your people they have a new king."

"You know I will do no such thing," replied Boran, stopping in his tracks. "You may as well kill me right now."

"I have no desire to do that yet," said Hakon. "Your people must witness your demise before their eyes. It will make them more accepting of new commands. You will do as I ask if you don't want your people's blood to stain the town square alongside yours."

Boran gestured towards Lucas and his soldiers. "Will they get to live?"

Hakon followed his gaze. When he shook his head, Isaac and the two soldiers jolted, and guards moved in to restrain them. They were pushed back down onto their knees, their resistance answered with force. Lucas had reacted by dropping to his knees before the guards got to him.

"What about Lucas?" asked Boran. "There is a curse on him. Killing him will mean death for all of you."

"I'm well aware," said Hakon. "He will stay here to watch his friends die and follow later."

"Sir," interrupted Byram. "Lucas shouldn't stay behind. I was planning on taking him with me, and personally keeping an eye on him."

Hakon yanked at his reins and turned to look at Byram. "Do not go against my orders," he yelled. "The boy stays. He caused me humiliation in the arena and will suffer for that. If you wish, you can stay here with him, and I'll see to it that you are relieved of your command."

"Apologies, sir," said Byram. He glanced over to Lucas as if to justify his concern. Lucas pretended to stifle a yawn and scratched his hip with his chains. "It was not my intent to question your authority. I merely wanted to point out that the boy shouldn't be left unattended."

"He won't be," replied Hakon. "A garrison of a hundred soldiers are finishing up here. Your concern has no grounds. The boy is harmless without his powers."

With all eyes aimed in his direction, Lucas was glad when Boran spoke, drawing the attention away from him.

"What about King Itan?" asked Boran. "You will have Lucas watch his death after he witnesses mine?"

"Itan is not my concern," answered Hakon. "He is Eylgar's problem. That was our agreement."

"Eylgar doesn't control all the Hammonds," said Boran. "His older brother does. That's why Eylgar only had a small army to help you attack me at the tunnel's exit. The last time I checked, Lord Hammond was happy to sign an alliance with Itan, which I am confident he will not break."

"Conflicts between brothers run in our family," said Hakon. "They are dealt with, even if one has to die." He looked to Byram, indicating to Lucas that Byram knew about Albert, but Byram turned his horse away from the conversation to begin handing out orders to the soldiers staying behind. Hakon turned his horse around as well and was ready to move out.

Boran had no choice but to follow when his guards pushed him to a waiting horse. He gave one last look to his soldiers after he mounted and, as he gripped the reins, gave them a somber nod of acknowledgment before riding out of the gates with Hakon. Lucas saw a softness in the defeated king's eyes he had never seen before, and it pained him to think what raw emotion the man might be experiencing.

After Hakon's departure, Byram rode his horse over to Lucas and stared down at him. Lucas kept his head down. He didn't want to give Byram cause to go against Hakon's demands. If he were to look up, he knew Byram would see the strength in his eyes and take him away from the chosen. Trying to concentrate on the feet of Byram's horse prancing on the ground before him, Lucas was relieved when a soldier came riding up.

"Sir," said the soldier, "the army is ready to move out. They're waiting for you to lead."

"I'm coming," Byram replied. He picked up his reins, and before he spurred his horse into a canter, he addressed one of the guards that stood behind Lucas. "Make him watch as you burn this place to the ground," he ordered. "When no more cries come from the fire, you kill these soldiers and bring the boy to me without delay."

With Hakon's army moving from sight, the remaining soldiers drove the supply wagons from the settlement onto the open ground outside the stockade and finished their preparations to burn the two longhouses.

Lucas watched as hay was stuffed beneath the wood piled around the bases of the longhouse. Soldiers stood greasing torches to be used to light the fire. They were moving much faster with their plan than Lucas had anticipated, and he had to push aside the feeling that he might not have enough time. He could sense Orson and the hunters closing in outside the stockade, and behind him, Warrick had already started approaching. Lucas glanced sideways to Isaac. Isaac had remained stoic, but Lucas could tell he was becoming anxious. "Are you ready?" he whispered, leaning closer to him.

"For what?" asked Isaac. "To die, or to watch others burn to death?"

"To fight our way out of here," answered Lucas. "Or at least die trying." He sized up the number of soldiers busying themselves inside the settlement. There were at least fifty, but they were scattered around, which would give them a chance to take at least a few of them down before they grouped to fight as one.

Isaac inhaled a deep breath. "Will the wolves we heard last night be helping us?"

"They're on their way," answered Lucas.

"Then I'm ready," said Isaac.

Lucas watched the soldiers walk towards the houses and place the torches between the woodpiles alongside the walls. He saw the hay soon ignite, and bright orange flames flare up to try and grip the thick log walls. Lucas knew the size of the logs with which the houses were built would buy him time. The thick logs would take longer for the flames to get hold of, but he was worried about the doors. If they were set alight, he would not be able to remove the barricade and free the workers. He saw Warrick crouch closer when the guards were distracted by watching the first flames. He stopped until he was only a few feet away.

"Now," called Lucas, and turned on his heels. Despite the shackles on his wrists, he jumped up and caught the sword that Warrick threw towards him. Using the momentum of the sword, he continued its movement, slitting the throat of the guard standing nearest him. When the guard dropped to his knees, he grabbed his sword. The other guards pulled their weapons when they saw their comrade on the ground, but the element of surprise was against them and proved fatal. As they fell, Boran's other two soldiers armed themselves with their swords and joined the charge towards the soldiers standing near the longhouses. With screams coming from panicked workers inside, and the crackling sound of wood burning, the first few soldiers did not hear their assailants coming and were struck from behind. While Isaac and his cohort engaged the soldiers who were countering the attack, Lucas and Warrick rushed to stop the soldiers who were igniting the woodpiles.

"Warrick!" shouted Lucas when he saw a soldier moving to ignite a woodpile by the door. With his wrists still shackled, he had his sword gripped between both hands and was limited in what he could do. Warrick, who was free of his, grabbed a dagger from the ground when he saw what Lucas was gesturing at. The dagger hit the soldier in the back, taking him down to the ground. The torch came to rest only a few feet from the wood by the door.

"Where are the others?" called Warrick. "We're getting overrun here." Soldiers from outside the stockade were coming into the settlement, alarmed by the sound of metal clashing.

"They're coming," answered Lucas. He had already seen Zera and the first boys emerge through the hole in the roof. From his peripheral view, he saw them running and jumping over the flames that reached the top of the walls to join the fight below. Workers followed close behind, and others could be heard trying to break down the barricaded doors.

Lucas had little time to assess the situation but knew he was running out of time. Smoke could be seen coming from crevices in the roof. If he didn't get the doors open soon, the workers would perish. Flames were already leaping towards the doors. Gathering all his energy, Lucas let his sword rip through anyone standing in his way. As he fought his way through, his arms tiring from using the sword with the shackles on, the creaking sound of two wagons driven fast into the settlement reached him. Looking over his shoulder, he saw Orson standing on one of them, a whip in his hand that he had used to run the horses but was now using on anyone who crossed his path. Both wagons stopped in front of a longhouse, with hunters jumping off on all sides.

"Let's go," urged Lucas, gathering enough chosen to charge for the doors. As the first door flew open, Albert and Hallam ran out, followed by others, all holding swords acquired by the chosen the previous night. Some workers were coughing from the smoke, but they were ready to fight.

Lucas saw Albert running in his direction—the key for the shackles in his hand.

"Allow me," said Albert after taking down two of Hakon's soldiers to reach him. Lucas held his wrists up while Warrick and two other chosen stepped in to cover him.

"Thank you," said Lucas as the shackles dropped to the ground. He placed the sword in his sword hand. "Now, let's finish this."

With a wind picking up, the flames were quickly jumping over to other houses, setting half the settlement alight.

"Get everyone out of here," shouted Lucas to Isaac when he caught sight of him. Only a few of Hakon's soldiers were left fighting near the rear of the plaza, leaving the entrance clear for people to escape. "Before the stockade catches fire." When he heard Isaac shouting orders for retreat, Lucas ran towards Zera, who was still fighting two soldiers.

"Go," he shouted, pushing her aside and taking over. "I have this."

"I don't want to leave you," said Zera, stepping forward and trying to get back in the fight.

Lucas blocked her to fend off an attack by the soldiers. "You have to," he pleaded, after he took one of the men down, but locked his sword with the other soldier. "There is no time. Go! Make sure everyone else is safe." He saw her hesitate for another moment until the noise of a roof caving in nearby made her realize they were about to be trapped within a giant ring of fire.

Taking care of the last of Hakon's soldiers, Lucas finally lowered his sword. He was breathing heavily from exhaustion and dripping with sweat from the intense heat of the burning buildings around him. Roofs were caving in, sending sparks high up into the air, and palisades were toppling over between the houses.

"We need to go," Orson called out to him. Lucas saw him pull his axe free from the chest of one of Hakon's soldiers. "The whole place will be ablaze soon."

"I have to stop Hakon!" shouted Lucas over the noise of the fires when he followed Orson out. "Where is Nolan?"

"Where you told him to be!" shouted Orson back over his shoulder.

As he ran from the burning settlement, Lucas saw that the supply wagons were getting plundered by workers searching for food. Crates and baskets were thrown off—their contents spilling on the ground. He saw the chosen busy unharnessing horses from the wagons' rigging and getting them ready to ride. Lucas could not blame the workers for behaving the way they did. They were free and wanted to still their hunger, but Lucas knew their plight was far from over if Hakon was successful with his plans to conquer Boran's land. He leaped on the back of one of the wagons and called out to the crowd to get their attention, but the men were so absorbed in trying to find anything edible that they did not hear him.

Making his way through the crowd, Albert demanded order. He grabbed men by the collars of their shirt to point them in the direction of Lucas. He then jumped onto the wagon himself and let his voice bellow over the group to silence the rest of them. "Be quiet!"

When every worker was facing Lucas and waiting for him to speak, Albert gave him a nod. "Go ahead," he said. "They will listen now."

Lucas nodded and glanced over the crowd. He had never spoken to such a large group before. He knew his voice was not as loud and commanding as Albert's, and he hoped he could get through to them.

"I know you are hungry, tired, and ready to go home," he began. "But as I speak, it is Hakon who is leading the way to your families. If he is successful in entering Boran's land and becomes king, there may not be a home for you to return to." He paused to make sure he had everyone's attention. "There is an army of mountain warriors waiting across the river. They are my people, and I will join them in their fight against Hakon, as will those who already fought for you today." He gestured to Orson, and the hunters grouped behind him.

Isaac and Boran's remaining soldiers were standing next to them. Orson gave him a nod of acknowledgment, and Lucas nodded back before facing the workers again. "I am not going to tell you to fight with us," said Lucas. "I am aware that not everyone will be able to." He looked to the men bleeding from wounds, and the elderly. "It will be your choice if you choose to fight."

There was silence from the crowd when Lucas finished. Then Hallam spoke.

"I am the last surviving member of the clan who built this settlement," said Hallam. "I have nothing left, but I will stand with you so that others will not have to experience what I have." He looked at those around him before stepping forward to stand by the hunters.

"Well," said Albert, "you already know whose side I am on." He walked over to Hallam to stand beside him. After a moment's hesitation, other workers followed.

CHAPTER 27

Lucas jumped off his horse and tied the reins to a tree limb, and Zera and Warrick followed suit. They then climbed to a higher point, from where they could view the bridge, which they had helped complete only the day before.

He and the chosen had traveled ahead of those who were making their way down the road on foot. Below, Lucas could see a steady flow of soldiers walking across the bridge to join the formation already on the other side. At the forefront, Lucas could see Byram with the soldiers assembled behind him, all on horseback. Hakon had yet to cross the bridge, as did Boran, who was next to him on his horse.

Lucas let his mind travel over the river and followed the valley until it narrowed and turned into a canyon. He turned a corner and felt great relief when he saw Davis, with Dastan and Nolan, waiting with what looked to be about a hundred warriors. Behind them, Lucas saw the bodies of the scouts Byram had sent ahead. Lucas turned to Zera and Warrick. "They made it."

"I told you he would be there," said Zera.

"Can you connect with Davis," asked Warrick, "or is he too far?"

"I can try," answered Lucas.

He focused again to let his mind drift over the rocky cliffs and into the gorge. It had been some time since they had connected, and Davis looked up in surprise. His sudden movement had caused him to tug on the reins, causing his horse to throw its head in the air. Dastan turned to Davis with a frown but then Davis spoke to him.

"Davis knows I am here," said Lucas. "But we're too far apart to communicate."

"Will Nolan know when to attack Hakon's army?" asked Warrick.

"No," answered Lucas. "I will have to tell Davis."

"How, if you are too far away?"

"I'll have to get closer."

Warrick scanned the valley, squinting in concentration. "Hakon will be able to see us if we cross the bridge too soon," he said. "The hunters are fierce but have already fought hard. The same counts for Boran's soldiers and us, and the workers—"

"I'm going alone," interrupted Lucas. "I can reach Davis from the bridge and have the warriors engage Hakon's army before we attack from the back."

"What if they see you?" asked Zera.

"They will only see me if they turn back or look behind them," answered Lucas, "which I can only hope they will not do."

They continued to watch the bridge in silence until Hakon finally crossed, and Lucas went down to meet the others on the road to tell them of his plan. When he felt Hakon was far enough down the valley, he walked onto the bridge, took a fighting stance position, and closed his eyes. It was time to put into action what he had trained the warriors for during his time with them in the secret valley. First, he would connect with Davis, and through him, connect with each warrior, until they became one and the fight against a thousand soldiers could begin.

Lucas could see that Nolan and Davis had dismounted and were standing in front of the warriors.

"Ready?" asked Lucas.

“We are,” Davis answered. He closed his eyes and took the same position as Lucas, and the warriors behind him did the same.

With Davis now guiding the warriors, Lucas redirected his focus. Before he would let Davis lead the warriors into the charge, there was one last thing he had to do.

Moving away from the canyon, Lucas watched Byram come closer. Byram rode in the center of the front line, with six men on horseback on either side of him. Seven rows of cavalry followed just behind. Byram had to have explored the route on one of his travels in the past. Thirteen horses abreast were all that would fit through the narrowest part of the canyon. Byram had his eyes fixed before him, no doubt listening for his scouts to return if there was trouble ahead. Lucas concentrated on the horses of Hakon’s cavalry before they reached the curve of the valley where it turned into the canyon, and connected with them. The horses’ ears went flat and their nostrils flared, and Lucas watched with his mind as their bodies tensed, his own body tensing with them. The front row reared, throwing some of their unsuspecting riders off while others desperately tried to cling on. Then the same happened to the second row, and the third, the fourth . . .

Hakon’s army was thrown into confusion.

“Now,” said Lucas to Davis. He watched as Davis raised his sword in the air and started to run. Dastan and Nolan spurred their horses alongside the warriors, running around the bend of the canyon. Their blades sliced through bodies not already trampled by horses running clear from the impending fight.

Lucas saw that Byram had managed to stay on his horse and was rushing towards the columns of foot soldiers. The soldiers had stopped and were looking confused with the chaos of rearing horses in front of them.

At the back of the army, closest to Lucas, Hakon had halted as well. He was leaning over to one of his officers, no doubt asking what was happening, but it was King Boran who looked over his shoulder towards the bridge. When he saw Lucas, he sprang into action and kicked his horse forward alongside an officer's horse. The officer turned in his saddle and tried to fend off Boran when he saw him reach for his sword, but he was too late. Boran had already pulled the sword from its scabbard and was swinging it to land a fatal blow.

Hakon, who had witnessed Boran take his officer down, raised his sword and let out a scream of rage as he sprinted his horse towards him.

Lucas redirected his focus from the primary fight to Hakon's horse. As he let it come to an abrupt stop, Boran turned in his saddle and saw Hakon coming. He charged, with sword stretched before him like a jousting lance, and struck Hakon in the chest. Hakon's eyes went wide as he stared at Boran, who swiftly retrieved the sword from his body. Before Hakon fell from his horse, he looked towards the bridge that trembled under the feet of a hundred men running past Lucas to join the fight.

"Will you be coming with us?" asked Zera when she saw Lucas was staring at the battle in front of him. Horses were running everywhere, and the sound of metal on metal echoed through the valley.

Lucas shook his head. "I have to find Byram. I need to know that he's been taken out, or this fight won't ever end."

Warrick put his hand on Lucas's shoulder. "If I see him," he said, "I'll take him down myself."

As Lucas watched his friends run after the other chosen, he let his mind go back to the warriors who were fighting shoulder to shoulder through Hakon's army, one row at a time. Each swing of their sword was like the other—precise, decisive, and determined to make it count. The way they fought, united as one, put doubt in Hakon's soldiers, who Lucas imagined were used to being the fearless ones. He saw Davis still leading them and let his mind go over the battlefield as he searched for any sign of Byram.

Then Lucas saw him, but it was not with his mind—there he was, in the flesh, riding with great speed, slashing his sword at anyone standing in his way. With the white showing around his horse's eyes and foam coming from its mouth, he pushed straight towards the bridge. Blinded by rage, Byram leaped from his saddle, knocking Lucas off his feet and sending them both into the frigid water of the river.

Narrowly missing the rocks in his fall, Lucas felt his body tumble underwater. When he recovered from the shock and regained his bearings, he pushed his head above the surface. Gasping for air, he saw Byram behind him, struggling to keep his head above water. Ahead of Lucas, the gorge, with its smooth rock walls, came closer. Water crashed into boulders by the gorge's entrance before the river could squeeze into the narrower path.

Lucas passed the boulder from where he had been pulled from the river before. There was no one to save him now. He stopped fighting the current and allowed himself to be taken instead. He could only hope he would not be thrown against the cliff walls. As the gorge began to narrow, its cliffs towering above him, he used his mind to take one last look at the battlefield. Hakon's soldiers were surrendering their weapons and, coming towards the river, he saw three riders. Davis's voice shouted, "Hold on!" Then, as he entered the gorge and disappeared, he heard Davis promise that he would come and find him.

The river's current was fast, and Lucas had no idea how far down the gorge he had gone before losing Byram behind him. Byram had continued to struggle to keep his head above water, and Lucas had seen him go under a couple of times only to resurface a few seconds later. Except for the last time, he had not. Thinking Byram had drowned, Lucas used his powers to slow the river's current when the gorge widened. As the waters around him calmed, he saw a boulder the size of a wagon sticking out above the water.

Exhausted, Lucas let his body drift towards the boulder. When he slammed against it, he reached for a crevice and pulled himself out of the water. As he clambered higher on the rock, he suddenly felt his ankle gripped by strong hands. Lucas peered over his shoulder and watched as Byram emerged from the water, a dagger clasped between his teeth. He grabbed Lucas's other ankle and started pulling him back down. Lucas kicked himself loose and climbed faster, but Byram caught up with him. He turned himself onto his back just as Byram launched himself on top of him, taking the dagger from his mouth and going for Lucas's throat.

With his head dangling over the edge of the boulder and his chest pinned underneath Byram's weight, Lucas grabbed Byram's wrist with his left hand, and with his right, he had caught the blade. A mistake, he knew as soon as he felt the sharp pain in the palm of his hand as Byram pushed the knife down.

"It's over," hissed Byram, foam coming from the corners of his mouth. "It is time to end your miserable life."

"You know I can't allow that to happen," gasped Lucas.

"You won't be able to hold on much longer," said Byram. He tipped his chin, indicating the blood dripping from the blade onto Lucas's shirt and grinning wickedly. "I have the upper hand here."

Lucas knew Byram was right. His hand was throbbing with pain, and he would not be able to hold him off much longer. As much as he had been glad to get out of the water, now the river was his only chance of survival. He turned his head to watch as the current became faster. Then the water became darker, and debris started flowing past.

"How well can you swim?" asked Lucas after Byram flicked his eyes upwards and noticed the change in the river. By the look in Byram's eyes, he could tell he knew what was coming. The changes were all the warning signs of a flash flood.

Byram stared at him. "I knew that priest never blocked your

powers," he snarled as a roar could be heard coming towards them through the gorge, "but there must be a way to stop you!"

"There is," answered Lucas, "but you'll not live to know."

Using all his remaining strength, he pushed against Byram's wrist while letting go with his left, just as the wall of water washed over them. The river lifted Byram off him, just before he was taken from the rock himself. As he was dragged under, he feared he had underestimated the power of the water when he wasn't able to surface. The noise of the water as it ravaged the gorge was deafening, and Lucas felt the panic return that had plagued him in nightmares when he was younger. He could see nothing but the white torrent of water and the pressure against his body made his chest feel as if it was about to cave in. His throat hurt as he gulped water into his lungs and images of his friends soon flashed before him.

He knew that if he wanted to survive the torrent of the river, he had to pull himself together. He wasn't that young boy anymore—he was the one in control of the future.

The current slowed after what felt like an eternity. When Lucas resurfaced, he was careful not to make the same mistake and searched for Byram, but there was no sign of him. The river was calm, almost tranquil. Debris floated past him like people in a hurry to get to the weekly market. He let himself go along with it on his back until he became too exhausted to stay afloat, and the fear of drowning became real once again. He turned onto his stomach and grabbed hold of a log floating by. He threw his arms over the wood and rested his head. He saw no way to get out of the gorge other than to let himself drift to wherever the river was taking him.

As the sun moved over the gorge, casting long shadows over the water, Lucas heard the echo of voices bouncing off the cliff walls. He had his eyes half-closed and was barely awake when he saw a sandy riverbank with three figures standing upon it—waving their arms at him. He lifted his head and thought he was dreaming when he recognized Dastan running into the water and swimming towards him. On the riverbank, he saw Nolan holding Davis back.

Dastan reached out and grabbed hold of the log to pull Lucas closer. He then wrapped his arm around Lucas's waist. Lucas let go of the driftwood and watched it disappear as it continued down the river and Dastan started swimming back, holding on to Lucas tightly. The current carried them a little further downriver as Dastan struggled to bring him back, but before long they found footing on the river floor. He had Lucas stand on his feet while still supporting him, and, in that way, Lucas left the water behind. Once on shore, he took the first deep breath he had taken in hours.

"I see you are wounded," said Dastan, gesturing to the cut on Lucas's hand.

"Yes," answered Lucas. "Byram's knife."

"You don't have to worry about him anymore," replied Dastan. He gestured to something near the water's edge some distance away.

Lucas followed his gaze and saw what looked like a heap of black cloth lying partially out of the water. A lock of fair hair blended in with the color of the sand.

"If it was not for Byram's body washing up here," continued Dastan, "we may have missed you. We found him only moments before you floated past."

Davis dropped on his knees beside Lucas when he reached the riverbank, and Dastan let go of him. "Are you alright?" he asked.

"Mostly bruised," answered Lucas. "I'll be fine. What about the chosen?"

"All accounted for," answered Davis.

"We'd best get back to them," said Nolan, mounting his horse. He had only given Lucas a brief look, but there was relief in his voice. "Can you ride?" he asked.

"I'll manage," answered Lucas, standing up and taking Nolan's hand when he reached down to him to pull Lucas up behind his saddle.

The ride back to the battlefield did not take as long as Lucas had expected. It turned out that whereas the gorge snaked its way through the mountains, there was a much more direct route to reach the section of the river where he was found.

Entering the valley where the fighting had taken place, Lucas could see Hakon's surviving soldiers on their knees. They were surrounded by warriors who were shielding them from a few angry workers, but most civilians were sitting down. The chosen and hunters were standing off to one side, watching a discussion in front of them. With his soldiers and Isaac by his side, Boran was in a debate with Albert. His arms were flailing with every word he spoke, while Albert appeared to be shaking his head in disagreement.

"Who is that?" asked Nolan when they approached the group.

"That's Albert," answered Lucas. "Byram's brother. But don't worry . . . he is nothing like him."

"Are you sure about that?" asked Nolan.

"Is your brother anything like you?" asked Lucas.

Nolan looked over his shoulder. "Dastan is more stubborn," he answered. Nearing Boran, he stopped his horse and helped Lucas down before he dismounted.

"Lucas!" said Albert when he saw him walk up.

"Albert," Lucas replied. "I see you have made it."

"Yes. And can you tell the king how I helped you with your plan to free everyone? That I am on your side?"

Boran had turned to acknowledge Lucas but now turned back to Albert. "You may have fought to get yourself free," he said, "but to claim you will remain loyal while insisting to have Hakon's soldiers released to you is an entirely different matter."

"On what grounds is he making this claim?" asked Nolan.

Boran frowned when Nolan spoke, and Lucas realized the two had never met, but now was not the time for introductions. It was clear Boran felt the same, since he continued without questioning Nolan's authority. "He says Hakon was his uncle, which makes him a contender to take leadership, and thus control the soldiers."

"A contender?" asked Nolan.

"I will have to fight Byram for it first," explained Albert. "That is, if he is still alive?"

"He's not," answered Lucas. He watched Albert's reaction and saw him nod as if he had already known the answer.

"Then there will be nothing standing in my way," said Albert. "I am the only direct kin left to Hakon."

"Hakon's soldiers are to be my prisoners," said Boran. "For me to do with as I please. They killed most of my army."

Lucas knew it was up to him to negotiate for the soldiers' lives. Otherwise, they stood no chance. "I understand, sire," he began, "where you're coming from. You have been defeated and humiliated. It would be natural for a king to seek revenge, but enough killing has occurred." Lucas paused, gauging the king's expression. "Soldiers follow orders," he said. "It is their commander who is responsible for their actions. Hakon is dead, so is Byram. The men surrendered as soon as their leader went down. They should, therefore, be allowed to return to their families, and I trust Albert will do what is right."

Having said his words and aware that the final decision wouldn't lay with him, Lucas decided to leave the discussion and rejoin Warrick, Zera, and the other chosen.

The chosen looked tired, and some were nursing wounds, but all stood up to greet him. Lucas was relieved to see them all alive and well.

"We found Hallam," said Zera after Lucas had greeted each chosen. "He didn't make it."

"I don't think he would have wanted to," said Lucas. He felt sad that Hallam would not experience better times but was grateful for his sacrifice and the chance to have gotten to know him.

It took until the late hours of the night to clear the valley and build pyres to burn the many dead bodies. Casualties had fallen on all sides, and pyres were constructed for each group. To honor him, Lucas had Hallam's body placed on the pyre dedicated to mountain warriors.

At first light, Lucas walked over to the bridge where Albert was taking his leave. Hakon's soldiers were at his side, relief spelled across their faces.

"I will not break my promise," said Albert, turning to him. "It's time for my people to let go of the past and their thirst for revenge. What happened between brothers so long ago should not dictate how we live our lives now. I will also find another use for the arena."

"I know you will become the leader your people deserve," said Lucas, "and I thank you for helping me." He knew Albert would do his best to change his people's ways, but it would take time, and there was a chance Albert would not achieve it in his lifetime. That was something Lucas felt he was going to have to keep an eye on.

Albert gave him a nod, then crossed the bridge—he was the last to do so. Behind Lucas, Nolan gave the order to see the bridge destroyed.

CHAPTER 28

Lucas was sitting on the edge of his bed and tying the laces on his boots. When he finished fastening them, he put his hands on his knees and stood up. He walked over to the desk and let his hand go over the stack of parchment that Grant had so carefully checked the last time he was in his room, to see if any correspondence had taken place. The memory of it seemed like a lifetime ago. The departure of Orson and the hunters also felt as though it took place much longer than a week ago. He picked up his sword and fastened the belt around his waist. He then looked around the room before opening the door and stepping out one last time. He made his way down the stairs and walked through the mostly empty halls. He only met a few servants scurrying along with rags and buckets to clean the marble floors. Most of the house staff had returned, but the lack of military personnel was noticeable.

Lucas stopped before the doors of Boran's private room. There were no guards, so he knocked and waited for a reply. When he heard the king's voice, he gripped the door handle and let himself in.

Boran was standing by the window with his back to him—looking out over the valley behind the castle. He was holding a chalice in his hand, from which he sipped as Lucas came to stand next to him.

Lucas could see what was holding Boran's attention. On the grass fields past the gates, Nolan and the warriors were training new recruits and soldiers called back from stations around the borders. The army was not nearly the size it was before, but would undoubtedly grow again over time.

"You have come to tell me you are leaving," said Boran without taking his eyes off the warriors. "I knew the day would come, and you would feel compelled to return to Itan."

Lucas didn't know what to say. He remained silent.

Boran took another sip from his wine, then after a moment of silence, he spoke again. "My father once told me that, as a young boy, he used to watch the mountain warriors practice. He said that they were a sight to see, and I know now that he didn't exaggerate. Their sword skills are likely what made him fear them after they betrayed his father and why he installed that fear into me."

"They are not to be feared," replied Lucas. "Mountain warriors have lived here and protected kings since the first king was named. This castle is where they belong. What you see outside now is what you should have always seen."

Boran gave Lucas a fleeting glance. "Then why do I not get the feeling that I am the true king? You saved my life three times, and yet, you are leaving me to be with Itan?"

"Itan requires my assistance," answered Lucas, "to stop the Hammonds. Just as you needed me to help fight Hakon."

"Then the time to decide the true king is yet to come?"

Lucas nodded. "It is."

ABOUT THE AUTHOR

Leonie Waithman lives in Texas with her husband and three children. When not writing, she is an avocational archaeologist and volunteers her time at a state historic site educating students about the Texas Revolution.